The Breath of Night

BY THE SAME AUTHOR

The Celibate

Pagan and her Parents

Easter

Unity

Good Clean Fun

A Sea Change

The Enemy of the Good

Jubilate

MICHAEL ARDITTI

The Breath of Night

ARCADIA BOOKS

Arcadia Books Ltd
139 Highlever Road
London W10 6PH

www.arcadiabooks.co.uk

First published by Arcadia Books 2013

A catalogue record for this book is available from the British Library.

ISBN 978-0-9573304-5-0

Typeset in Minion by MacGuru Ltd
Printed and bound by CPI Group (UK) Ltd., Croydon CR0 4YY

Arcadia Books supports English PEN *www.englishpen.org* and
The Book Trade Charity *http://booktradecharity.wordpress.com*

Arcadia Books distributors are as follows:

in the UK and elsewhere in Europe:
Macmillan Distribution Ltd
Brunel Road
Houndmills
Basingstoke
Hants RG21 6XS

in the USA and Canada:
Dufour Editions
PO Box 7
Chester Springs
PA 19425

in Australia/New Zealand:
NewSouth Books
University of New South Wales
Sydney NSW 2052

in South Africa:
Jacana Media (Pty) Ltd
PO Box 291784
Melville 2109
Johannesburg

For Rupert Christiansen

Do I contradict myself?
Very well then I contradict myself,
(I am large, I contain multitudes.)

Walt Whitman

But since you are neither hot nor cold, but only lukewarm,
I will spit you out of my mouth.

Revelation (New Jerusalem Bible)

The trouble with Christianity is not that it has failed, but that it hasn't been tried.

G. K. Chesterton

Preface

I first heard of Julian Tremayne during my all-too-brief engagement to his great-niece. Having been named for him, she felt a special affinity with him, not least given the circumstances of his murder. Julian was an English missionary who went out to the Philippines in the early 1970s. After more than a decade as a parish priest, he was implicated in the assassination of a local military commander and thrown into jail. The preposterousness of the charge, which even his enemies held to be a blatant attempt to intimidate him, provoked international outrage. The government, bowing to concerted diplomatic pressure, sent Julian home. Three years later, after the fall of President Marcos and against the wishes of his family, he returned to the Philippines where, travelling in a remote mountainous region, he was captured by a band of Communist guerrillas who brutally killed him. Even in death he was not silenced, since there have been reports of mysterious occurrences at his grave.

I treat such reports with a healthy scepticism. My own opinion, for what it is worth (and I am only a paid chronicler of Julian's story), is that the world would be a happier, more equitable and, indeed, more spiritual place without religion. I say 'without religion' but not 'without God'. By that I mean the God who can be found in the paintings of Raphael, Caravaggio and Roualt, the music of Tallis and Bach, the poetry of Donne and Herbert, as well as in countless individual acts of charity, right down to my own youthful sponsored walks on behalf of Christian Aid. I come from a long line of middle-of-the-road Anglicans. My father and grandfather, no doubt along with generations of Sewards before them, take the view that God, if not exactly an Englishman, is of an English disposition, deploring excessive religious zeal as much as any other intemperate display of passion. The Tremaynes, on the other hand, are an old Roman Catholic family, whose ability to survive the vicissitudes of post-Reformation, pre-Emancipation politics demonstrates the strength of their faith.

Julia and I met at Cambridge in the spring of 2003. She was reading modern languages and I history of art. Were I writing about her, I would fill paragraphs, chapters even, with tributes to her beauty, intelligence, generosity, glamour, wickedness and wit, along with the more intimate information that now seems obligatory in any account of a love affair. My concern, however, is with her uncle, and so I shall pass swiftly on to my first visit to their family seat, Whitlock in County Durham. The house was early Tudor with Dutch gables and russet brickwork. An east wing of Portland stone, added in the wake of the quarrying boom of the 1830s, gave it an asymmetrical charm. The current owner was Julia's grandfather, Gregory Tremayne, who had served as a junior minister under Mrs Thatcher. Since his wife's death the previous year, his daughter Isabel, Julia's mother, had acted as her father's hostess.

Julia issued me with such an extensive list of dos and don'ts regarding her grandfather that I was dreading my visit. In the event, Gregory (he was studiedly informal) could not have been more hospitable. I had scarcely taken off my coat when he offered to give me a guided tour. I was fascinated by the pictures, which were far superior to the usual country-house mishmash, but less enamoured of some of the other exhibits, notably in the trophy room. Bears, polar and grizzly, an elephant with yellowed tusks, a stag with arboreal antlers and many lesser specimens gazed glassily from the walls. Two skins, a lion and a tiger, were spread on the floor like crime-scene silhouettes. This gruesome menagerie had been gathered by Gregory's great-uncle Lennox, in his quest to eat every animal named in the Bible except, of course, for the griffons and unicorns. Julia, anxious that I should not be misled by family legend, dismissed Lennox as a fraud, claiming that the dishes of crocodile, jackal and wolf described in his diaries attested simply to the range of his travels and his reluctance to offend the culinary tastes of his hosts.

My second visit to Whitlock was in the summer of our graduation, when Julia and I went up to announce our engagement, only to find the news overshadowed by that of her grandfather's terminal cancer. His imminent demise cast doubt on the future of the estate. The slate quarries had been closed for years and the tenant farms no longer paid their way. Julia's father, Hugh, was willing to underwrite his wife's inheritance, but at the cost of sweeping changes, both administrative and aesthetic, which aroused as much opposition from the family as from the local residents. Within a year of his father-in-law's death, he leased several hundred acres of unprofitable pasture to a wind farm. 'Thirty turbines whirling away at an annual rent of £100,000 each. It's an ill wind,' he said, with a wry grin.

Meanwhile Julia and I moved to a flat in Battersea and took the first steps in our planned careers. Eighteen months later, both had been abandoned: mine by circumstance; hers by choice. Much to my chagrin, she was lured away from translation work by a friend who was setting up as a party organiser. Not even the ready supply of gourmet leftovers could reconcile me to the switch. My own dream lasted longer. Through a family friend, I was taken on by a Duke Street gallery dealing in Old Masters. After a year spent largely 'below stairs', cataloguing and researching, I sold a Cranach workshop painting of the Gadarene Swine to a Russian billionaire. Unfortunately, I had failed to do sufficient research into either the picture or the buyer. The former was not the simple gospel illustration it appeared, but a deeply unpleasant anti-Semitic satire, and the latter had recently rediscovered his Jewish roots. Fearing a scandal, my boss 'reluctantly' let me go. I did the round of London galleries but, whether their regrets were genuine or my reputation had preceded me, there were no jobs. Disillusioned, I reinvented myself as a critic, writing pieces for everything from scholarly journals and glossy magazines to sale catalogues and websites.

Then on 21 June 2007 everything changed. Not only the date but the time is for ever imprinted on my mind: 2.10 a.m., which, curiously, I see not on the elegant watch face I checked when the telephone woke me but in the clinical display of a digital clock. Julia and I had been invited to Kent to celebrate her Aunt Agnes's seventy-second birthday. I had to stay in town for an opening at the d'Offay gallery, so Julia drove down with her younger brother Greg. Of course I blame myself. Even if we had taken Greg's car, I might have offered to drive since, according to the autopsy, he was three times over the legal alcohol limit, or, at the very least, have insisted on his reducing his speed, which the skid marks showed to have been about eighty miles an hour. Had all else failed, I could have persuaded them to put up the roof and perhaps have saved their lives.

Ten days later I sat beside Isabel and Hugh at the funeral in the elevated family pew which, despite its whiff of feudalism, had the virtue of screening us from public view. Scores of friends came up from London, as did my parents along with my brothers and their wives, yet, for all their expressions of sympathy, I felt that my grief was marginalised. There was an unspoken assumption that I was young and would fall in love again but there would be no such grace for the Olliphants, who had lost both their children. In crude terms, it was as though their pain were not doubled but squared. Conscious of that and that Greg had been unattached, I promised to keep in touch. While I resisted returning to Whitlock, I spent several strained evenings in Chelsea, where we each tried to pretend that our memories made up for our loss. When, a year or so later, I met Belinda, a cellist with the LSO, Isabel and Hugh professed to be thrilled, inviting us to dinner where they quizzed her as if she were a prospective daughter-in-law. Their manner was so brittly polite that I resolved to refuse any further invitations even after I had broken with Belinda. For two years I restricted myself to Christmas card contact until, out of the blue, I received a letter from Isabel asking me to Whitlock to discuss a matter of mutual interest. Intrigued, and not a little nostalgic, I set a date.

My conviction that the past was behind me wavered as I drove through the main gates, whose heraldic crest, an owl and two halberds, had been freshly repainted. Juddering over the cattle grid, I gazed across the sunlit meadows where a cluster of wind turbines gleamed as bleakly as artificial Christmas trees. Much to my relief, the house remained true to my memory, and I climbed the uneven steps, savouring its fusty charm. I waited in the oak-panelled hall while an elderly maid went to inform her mistress of my arrival. She returned to lead me to the small drawing room where Isabel sat, as constant as the house, with only a hint of silver in her auburn hair to mark the passing years. Tears welled in my eyes as she called me Pip, a nursery diminutive which had lain dormant until I mentioned it to Julia who immediately adopted it, followed by her parents and brother. From anyone else, it would have sounded precious, as though it should be coupled with 'toodle'; from Isabel, it took me back me to a warmer, safer place.

She asked to hear all my news and I was embarrassed by how little I had to report. She listened appreciatively as I outlined my journalistic achievements, but the collection of reviews, interviews and articles, already modest in my mind, seemed even more so in the telling. Even my big break, a six minute spot on a radio arts programme, had led nowhere, after the producer, a Cambridge contemporary, had been seconded to Sport. The irony was that my greatest success had come from filing diary stories for another university contact, going to the very parties that I had once reproached Julia for organising. I had spent six months trying to write a novel but, despite the enthusiasm of a hand-picked set of readers, I was forced to admit that I had nothing unique, profound or even amusing to say. No 'late developer' tag could disguise the fact that I was a twenty-seven-year-old failure, barely eking out a living. It was then that she put forward her plan.

'Have you ever met a saint?' she asked, so abruptly that I took it for a trick question.

'Not to my knowledge,' I replied warily.

'You'd have known if you'd met my uncle.'

I assumed that she was using 'saint' in the broad sense of a good and selfless person but, to my discomfort, I realised she was using it in the strict sense laid down by her Church. She gave me a brief overview of Julian's life and work in the Philippines, along with details of his murder, which Julia had either found too painful to discuss or from which her parents had sought to protect her. Having returned to the Philippines and a new parish, he had gone on a spiritual retreat in an area which, unknown to him, was a stronghold of the NPA, a group of virulently anticlerical Marxists. They had ambushed and shot him, dumping his body in an open grave where it was not discovered for several months, by which time the bones had been picked clean, a fact which she confessed had first horrified her but which now seemed fitting: a literal surrender of the flesh, for which he had striven, symbolically, all his life. He had been identified provisionally by height (he was a foot taller than the average Filipino) and definitively by the family crest on his ring.

'I'm surprised that it wasn't stolen,' I said. 'Aren't the people abjectly poor?'

'They're also extremely devout. The two foresters who unearthed the body reported that it was bathed in a mysterious light and, on their approach, a bird appeared out of nowhere and hovered above it. They called the police, who confirmed their story, adding that, when they removed the bones, they smelt a honey-like sweetness and heard an ethereal music, which one of them compared to a children's choir and another to a harp.'

Isabel's face glowed with such conviction that I longed to share it, but the rationalist in me immediately looked for explanations in sunbeams deflected from mountain peaks, the sound of the wind whistling through leaves, and the sickly-sweet smell of putrefaction clinging to the bones. I even wondered about the language and how much might have been lost – or added – in translation, but I kept such doubts to myself, hoping that a blank expression would convey an open mind. I listened while

Isabel explained how her grandmother had wanted to bring Julian's remains back to Whitlock, but her father had convinced her to leave them in the country that he had made his home. So he had been buried in the cemetery of his former parish. Hugh had flown out to oversee arrangements and she herself had visited the grave some years later, when she accompanied him on a business trip to the Philippines. Over time, and despite being officially discouraged by the Church, a cult had grown up around Julian, whose intercession was said to have led to several miracles of healing. The sceptic in me, which had by now eclipsed the rationalist, suspected that it had been a wise move to leave the body in such a susceptible environment, but when I asked her why she thought that similar miracles did not take place at the graves of saintly men in England she replied that they occurred in countries where people prayed for them, which they no longer did in the West.

Just as her account was verging on the anecdotal, Isabel explained that three years ago a group of Julian's former parishioners had petitioned their bishop to have Julian declared a saint. Rightly assuming that I knew little about the process of canonisation, she summarised the key criteria: either martyrdom for the faith or the performance of two or more miracles. In the light of the cures, I asked whether Julian had not already met that second condition, but she replied that personal testimony was not enough; the miracles had to be authenticated by a team of experts. In addition, the candidate was required to have led an exemplary life: technically, 'a holy life of heroic virtue', exhibiting the qualities of zeal for the Church, consecrated virginity, poverty and obedience. While I was debating which of the four I would find it hardest to achieve, she declared that, in response to the petition, the Bishop had launched an investigation into Julian's virtues. His agents were gathering evidence which, together with copies of Julian's writings (of which there were precious few), would be presented in a document known as a *positio* to the Congregation for the Causes of Saints in Rome.

Although the impetus for the investigation came from the parish, Isabel gave it her wholehearted support. She kept a close eye on its progress, rapidly losing patience with both the agents' sluggishness and the Bishop's refusal to chivvy them. Hugh, more conversant with the local ways, mollified her by quoting an old joke: 'Is there a Filipino word for *mañana*?' 'Yes, but it doesn't possess the same sense of urgency.' Her unease as she repeated it underlined her exasperation. With Hugh's blessing, she decided to take a more active role, sending out someone to galvanise the investigation by compiling an independent report. To my amazement, I discovered that the someone she had in mind was me. Far from my usual gratitude for the smallest offer of work, I was seized by panic. Even as she tried to persuade me of my fitness, I listed my limitations: I had never been to the Philippines; I could not speak – could not even name – the language; and I was not a Catholic. She discounted each in turn, assuring me that I would be a fresh eye; that everyone spoke English; and that, as an Anglican, I would counter any charge of bias.

'But what if I let you down?'

'You won't. Both Hugh and I have complete confidence in you. He has any number of employees he could send. Or else we could hire a professional investigator. But it's far too important to trust to a stranger. Julian – St Julian – is all that's left of my family, apart from you, Pip. You see I think of you as family,' she said, making the one appeal to which she knew I would respond. 'I wanted nothing more than to see you married to Julia.'

She was so convinced of her argument that she expected me to agree on the spot. Staunchly resisting her blandishments during a tense lunch, I promised to mull it over and discuss any remaining concerns with Hugh when he came up from London that evening. My hopes of an afternoon walk were dashed when, claiming that no one could speak more eloquently for Julian than he had himself, she handed me a reliquary-like casket, which contained all his surviving letters home from the Philippines. My interest was roused as much by her allusion to 'pages of family gossip that you can skip' as by the prospect of a privileged account of Julian's mission but, sitting in the library where five years earlier Julia and I had pored over the gory entries in Lennox Tremayne's game book, I was gripped by the vivid descriptions of Filipino rural life. Even on a cursory reading, the letters made a compelling narrative which, perhaps perversely in view of the savage and shocking material it contained, whetted my appetite to go there.

I had no wish to rush to judgement – and besides, the crucial judgement would not be mine – but at first glance I could detect little obvious saintliness in the letters. There was courage and self-sacrifice, honesty and integrity, generosity and charity, and a host of other virtues; there were even hints that some miraculous phenomena had been manifest before his death. But there was also anger, resentment, obstinacy, self-righteousness and other shortcomings, which suggested that, if nothing else, Julian had been a deeply conflicted figure. Moreover, he lashed out not just at the landowners and officials who had exploited and abused his parishioners, but at those in his own family whom he believed to have failed him. Meanwhile, I was struck both by how rarely he returned home – twice in thirteen years was meagre even for a missionary – and by his parents' reluctance to visit him. Although I still found the concept of priesthood alien, I was intrigued by Julian's contradictions and inclined to accept the commission.

A snatched half-hour by the lake managed to clear my head if not to resolve my dilemma. When I returned to the house, a marked if elusive change of mood signalled Hugh's arrival. I found him in the drawing room, glass in hand, talking to his wife. Although he looked the same as ever: aquiline nose; full lips; wavy hair worn raffishly long at the nape; cheeks the pink of a child's paint pot; my picture of him had been transformed by Julian's. He apologised for not having been here to greet me, citing business meetings in the City. Even now I remained hazy as to what exactly his business was, taking my cue from Julia who had been far more forthcoming about her Tremayne than her Olliphant relatives. The letters had revealed a hitherto unknown Philippine connection, about which I questioned him. He explained that his great-great-grandfather had founded a trading company in the 1840s, when Spain first opened up the country to foreign commerce. Succeeding generations had diversified into textile manufacture, merchant shipping, quarrying and mining, and he was now part of a multinational conglomerate of Filipinos, Americans and Chinese.

Eager to know if he had read what Julian wrote about him, I gently broached the subject of their relationship. 'I had a lot of time for Uncle Julian,' he said, 'although I'm not sure that he would have repaid the compliment.' His sly grin left me none the wiser. 'He was something of a pinko, which you might think pardonable given the politics of the time, but in my humble opinion he took it a bit too far. Ended up going native – though he'd most likely have called it "going indigenous people".' He paused, seeming to recollect himself and the reason for which I had been summoned. 'But he was a first-rate chap. No doubt about it. Gandhi; Mother Teresa; you know the sort of thing. And, like me, he loved the Filipinos. He made it his mission to save their souls, just as I've made it mine to conserve their art.'

Declaring it a disgrace that Filipino culture was so underrepresented in the world's great collections, he offered to give me a preview – 'premature, I trust' – of the treasures he was bequeathing to the British Museum. Stifling my surprise at this improbable passion, I readily agreed and followed him into the billiard room, with its rows of monochrome pots, bowls and burial jars, for which I struggled to muster the requisite enthusiasm. I found more of interest in his study, notably a fifteenth-century crocodile made from carabao horn and conch shell, but my admiration for the intricately carved rice gods, which had once protected their adherents' huts and now adorned his walls, was tempered by the memory of Julian's disapproval. All that paled, however, beside my shock when he led me into the trophy room and showed off his latest acquisitions: six mummified heads 'salvaged' from a former headhunting tribe, many of whose descendents worked in his mines. To compound the horror, he had had them mounted and hung among the other exotic species. Even as I was working out whether this were a sick joke, a racist insult, or an existential howl of despair, I was struck by an image of Julia's skull smashed against the tree.

I fled upstairs, returning for dinner, which was served with due formality in the old hall. At the end of the meal, Isabel, more mindful of past than of present company, left us to ourselves. Wasting no time, Hugh urged me to accept his wife's proposal. With an affecting tenderness, he described how she had become increasingly withdrawn since the children's deaths, scarcely stirring from Whitlock. Honouring Julian's memory was the sole thing that gave her life meaning. Sounding strangely sheepish, he explained that she had an intense, almost mystical, belief that because Julia had been named for Julian and I had been engaged to her, I would be the one to revitalise the investigation. Knowing the Philippines as he did, he was under no such illusion, nevertheless he was convinced that my presence – and progress reports – would bring her hope. 'You've no idea how much she needs it right now.'

'I'd like to help. Truly.'

'So what's stopping you? I assure you I won't be ungenerous. Tell me honestly, is your life in London so wonderful?'

'You know it's not.'

'Well then, what do you have to lose?'

That was the moment at which I decided to take up their offer. The promise of unlimited time and limited responsibility, of extensive funds and expert assistance, was one incentive; the chance to travel to an unknown country and explore a unique, hybrid culture was another; the lack of alternative prospects and emotional ties was a third. Above all, however, it was Hugh's simple question, with its cruel but irrefutable logic, which persuaded me to book a flight to Manila for the early New Year.

One

My dear Mother and Father,

Greetings from the parish of San Isidro in the vicariate apostolic of Montagnosa, in the province of Luzon, in the archipelago of the Philippines. All I need add is 'the Earth, the Solar System, the Milky Way, the Universe' and you'll think me six years old again. Which is pretty much how I feel; everything is so vivid and exciting.

First of all, *mea culpa*. I meant to write weeks ago but, from the moment I stepped off the plane, I was caught up in a whirlwind. Besides, I wanted to wait until I knew where the Regional was sending me so that I could give you an address. The three months I've spent here have already made up for all the disappointment of Liverpool. I had to struggle so long to banish any tinge of envy for friends who were posted to Cameroon or Sudan or India. I should have trusted in the Lord. Not only has He called me to a country that is just as wondrous, but it's one that has escaped all taint of the British Empire.

Manila was magical. I trust Cora received my postcard. Some nights the sky really is that pink. There are those who attribute it to pollution, but I take a more romantic view. By day it's the people who provide the colour. Many of them are pitifully poor, yet they remain cheerful, even joyous. I'm thinking of a shoeless girl dancing a jig in the street, while an old man sat quietly repairing pavement cracks like a boy sifting sand on the beach. They've retained the gift, long lost in the more affluent West, of exulting in sheer existence.

Although I've been treated with nothing but kindness both here and in Manila, the Regional told me that the government regards foreign priests with mistrust, which is why the Society brought me in on a tourist visa. My first task was to exchange it for a work permit, which proved remarkably easy, but not without cost. I'll say no more except that the Mr Fixit, whom the Regional deputed to assist me, would be perfect casting for the corrupt official in *Casablanca* – you know, the French captain with the pencil moustache. Next, I was measured for a cassock (white), which was delivered the following day and which I am wearing as I write – though, in the insistent heat, I can't help envying the Filipino men who walk about bare-chested. I hear you gasp, Mother, across a distance of 7,000 miles. Don't worry, I gave you my word that I shouldn't go native, and I intend to keep it.

For three weeks I had the Society's house to myself, which I must admit I enjoyed (don't tell Greg, who'll think me even more of a recluse than ever), before I was joined by two fellow missionaries, first a rather crabby old man, another Julian, who'd been ministering to the plantation workers on the sugar island of Negros, and then, to my surprise and delight, by Hendrik van Leyden, who was at the seminary with me in Brabant. He spent a fortnight with us at Whitlock four years ago, do you remember? Chestnut hair; dimpled chin; eyebrows which, much to Cora's horror, met in the middle? Or maybe I should mention an eight-pound salmon: the one which, displaying an uncharacteristic – even unprecedented – indulgence, Father, you swore that you'd left for him? I'll say no more.

Hendrik and I were classmates once again, on a crash course in Tagalog run by the Dominicans (eight hours a day, six days a week for two months), after which the Regional considered us ready, with God's grace, to begin our mission. We've promised to meet up regularly, or as regularly as we can, given that Hendrik has been posted to a parish in Cabanatuan City in Nueva Ecija province. It may not be that far on the map, but distances in the Philippines have to be measured in more than miles. After a couple of hours on the North Diversion Road no one, not even Uncle Lawrence, would complain about the surface of the A1.

On my admittedly brief acquaintance, I'd say that the distance from San Isidro to Manila is greater than that between England and the Philippines. No, the sun hasn't addled my brain. Do you remember how horrified Cora – or was it Agnes? – was when the Misses Cuddleston told us that they'd never been to London and not even to Durham since the General Strike? There are old people here who've never visited Baguio City, which is barely an hour away and the closest thing to a metropolis. Manila is as remote from them as Moscow was from Chekhov's Three Sisters, except that, instead of yearning for it, they view it with suspicion. I shall miss the theatre, along with bookshops, newspapers, electricity (I'm writing this by a kerosene lamp), the morning post (we have a weekly delivery on market day), and I won't begin to mention the sanitary arrangements! But I do have a shortwave radio that picks up the BBC. And to live among such prayerful people makes up for it all.

The parish is huge, with 6,000 souls scattered across 400 square kilometres. It consists of the *poblacion*, the town centre both administratively and geographically, and twenty-four *barrios* (hamlets? neighbourhoods?), each of which is home to between one and two hundred families: some are within walking distance of the centre; others are out on the *haciendas* and can only be reached by car. I've inherited an old jalopy, but I'm told that one of the managers gave my predecessor, Father Teodoro, a brand-new Mercedes, so I live in hope! The most remote *barrios* are high in the Cordilleras, the vast mountain range that marks the eastern limit of the parish, and are only accessible on foot. While I remember, would you please send me a pair of hiking boots? 10½ if they do half-sizes, since my feet tend to swell in the heat.

So far I've barely strayed beyond the *poblacion*. Its heart is a large square, with the Church and *convento* (rectory) on the east side and the town hall on the west. Two rows of Spanish colonial houses, all cracked white stucco and fretwork shutters, half-hidden by thick-boughed frangipani and acacia trees, plus two small general stores, occupy the north and south. In the centre are a statue of the national hero, José Rizal, four weathered stone benches and a dried-up water trough.

It's no accident that the *convento* is the largest and best appointed residence in town. During the three centuries of Spanish rule, while the soldiers and bureaucrats were based in Manila, the country was effectively governed by a few hundred friars. There is of course an irony, which I'm sure you've not been slow to grasp, in my having become a missionary in order to take the gospel to places where it had never been heard, only to find myself in one where it can be heard more clearly than at home. I won't pretend that I'm not relieved to have escaped all the babble and clatter of England, along with its fashionable clarion calls – how anything can be described as 'liberation' that leads you away from the Church is beyond me! Moreover, although the people here have long had Christ, they're hungry for priests. I understand that, for perfectly valid reasons (age, ill health, pressure of work), Father Teodoro neglected to visit some parts of the parish from one year to the next. That's an omission I propose to rectify.

On second thoughts, please send me two pairs of boots.

The laminated fact sheet in the porch, complete with charming misspellings (the 'vaulted apes'!), describes the church as 'earthquake baroque' which, to my mind, fails to do it justice. It dates from the early 1600s when Philippine houses were flimsy wooden structures on stilts (many still are), the better to withstand wild animals and flooding. So it's easy to see how this lofty stone building would have filled the locals with awe. I doubt that it would find favour in your Holy Redeemer-trained eyes, but I'm already learning to love it. The heavy grey exterior, more buttresses than walls, has a touch of the penitentiary about it and the functional interior still bears the scars of the Japanese invasion in 1942. Several of the clerestory windows are missing, leaving the nave at times like an aviary (perhaps it will come into its own at Pentecost?). The chief decorative features are the *santos* – simple wooden figures dressed in garish robes that Agnes and Cora would have scorned to put on their least precious dolls – set in niches along the walls and above the altars. Yet, for all their roughness, they display the hallmarks of deep devotion. On the day I arrived, a young boy took my hand unprompted and led me to the high altar which, with its three tiers of glass-enclosed *santos*, resembled nothing so much as a toyshop window. He pointed to the central figure, a glazed-looking Christ, unremarkable except for long woven dreadlocks reaching down to his waist. 'Jesus Christ, He is so beautiful,' he said with tear-filled eyes, adding imperiously: 'Now you will kiss Jesus Christ.' Moved by his words, I put my lips to the squarely carved feet with as much reverence as I once had to the bronze toe of St Peter in Rome.

The boy, whom I have yet to meet again unless he were one of the horde of children who accompanied their parents to my first mass, is not alone in his piety. At odd moments throughout the day and at the end of every service, the faithful step up to one of the side altars and press their lips or their handkerchiefs to the *santos*. The mass, by the way, is in English which, I suspect, is as incomprehensible to much of the congregation as the Latin was in Gaverton a decade ago. Confessions, however, are in Tagalog. The Dominicans did their best to tailor their vocabulary to our needs (I doubt there are many language courses that teach elementary students the phrases for disrespecting one's elders, illegal foraging and lustful thoughts). Even so, I'm not always sure precisely what I'm absolving. Yesterday a young man left the church with a massive grin after a long and faltering confession during which, I must admit, I was utterly lost. Then again, there may be something opportune in my confusion. Since God's mercy is, as we know, infinite, it seems almost reductive to fashion the penance to the sin.

'Soft!' I hear your favourite epithet, Father, echoing across the drawing room. 'The boy's gone soft in the head!' Or maybe Mother is reading the letter aloud to you at breakfast, causing you to choke on your porridge, and your prediction that one of your children will be the death of you will finally be fulfilled.

Forgive me! I'd tear up the page and start again if I weren't so near the bottom. The fact is that I'm missing everyone so much. By trying to keep a clear picture of you in my mind, I've let myself be carried away. But please don't think that I'm depressed. If anything, I've been having too much pleasure, not least because I arrived on 13 May, two days before the feast of San Isidro, the most important date in the town's calendar.

'See the welcome we've laid on for you,' the Mayor said, when he greeted me outside the church. For a moment I mistook the twinkle for the truth. What arrogance! It was a saint they were celebrating, not a humble priest. The square and several of the side streets were festooned with bunting. It looked as if the whole town were wrapped in a cake frill. The church itself was crammed with fruit and flowers and vegetables, including a jackfruit the size of a beer barrel, which quite obscured the font. The *santos* had all been given their annual change of wardrobe at the hands of the *hermanas*, the daughters of the local land-owners. I may be wrong, but I detected a hint of genteel rivalry over the distribution; unsurprisingly, Our Lord, Our Lady and San Isidro are prized above the lesser saints. One young woman made up for being assigned the comparatively lowly Santa Barbara by decking her out like Marie Antoinette at Versailles. Next year, apparently, it will be my job to make the allocation – which is a treat in store.

This year my duties were confined to saying mass. That was nerve-racking enough since it was my first chance to meet the hundreds of parishioners who had streamed in from the outly-ing *barrios*. The church was packed, with several of the young men sitting on one another's shoulders. What's more, I'd had no time to write a sermon and simply adapted one on Loving Your Neighbour that I'd preached before last year's Liverpool-Ever-ton derby. But it seemed to go down well, with so many people shaking my hand at the end that I stopped worrying about the sweat. I even received a compliment – and a lunch invitation – from don Florante Pineda, our foremost local landowner. 'An excellent sermon, Father, I approve,' he said, as though the parish were his private domain.

After mass I had a chance to unwind, strolling through town and introducing myself to the people before the procession, which was due to start at three. Having adjusted my mind as well as my watch to Filipino time, I was expecting a half-hour delay, but not the ninety minutes in the hallucinogenic heat that it took for everyone to assemble. That said, I did as I was told and waited patiently (don't laugh, Father), until it finally set off, taking its pace from the lumbering water buffalo that pulled San Isidro's carosse, looking as incongruous in its sampaguita garland as Hector in Cora's Christmas Day crown. The carosse was covered with carrots, corn, cucumber and lettuce, the saint's early life as a farmer making him a particularly fitting patron for an agricultural parish. Our Lord, Our Lady, St Francis Xavier, St Charles Borromeo and a host of angels followed in slow succession, each attended by the family who'd taken charge of its care and adornment over the previous year. Then came a parade of *barrio* groups, among them a pack of *Gigantes*, ten-foot-high stilt-walkers with Humpty-Dumpty heads, and twenty youths performing a tribal dance, wearing loin cloths and flip-flops, and brandishing spears.

A band of ten girls, in floral crowns and white dresses (which had withstood the heat far better than my cassock), brought the procession to a close. Each represented a different facet of Our Lady: Divine Shepherdess; Immaculate Conception; Queen of Prophets; Mystical Rose and so forth. With one exception, each was escorted by a young man, looking at once proud and bashful. The exception was a remarkably pretty girl, whose radiant smile as she walked beside her mother made her the perfect representation of the Queen of Peace. The poise and excitement of the girls and the anxiety of the boys suggested that, for all the religious panoply, Mary wasn't the only virgin being venerated.

As they filed past, I wondered how many of the couples might be standing before me at the altar in the forthcoming months.

My hosts – no, I must call them my neighbours and soon, I hope, my friends – assured me that every Filipino loves a fiesta. At any given moment, somewhere across the country there'll be a festival to celebrate something, be it fruit, flowers or even fish, although the majority are in honour of saints. Some might see it as overkill, but I see it as the essence of incarnational theology: the communal expression of a world suffused with God.

Now I must go to bed. Their hot coconut toddy (think very rough gin) is lethal. And I've a busy day tomorrow: lunch with the civic auditor; followed by my first catechism class; then, in the evening, a film. The nearest cinema is in Baguio City where, from what I can gather, the presiding genius is Bruce Lee, but every once in a while a travelling company comes to town and sets up a makeshift (bed-sheet) screen in the square. Tomorrow night they're showing Yul Brynner and Gina Lollobrigida in *Solomon and Sheba* which, being a Hollywood epic from the fifties, contains the perfect mix of religiosity, romance, exoticism and violence for a Filipino audience today. They handed out publicity flyers at the fiesta. I enclose one just in case you think I'm making it up: 'They came from different worlds. He was a Catholic. She was a Protestant. Yet they dared to fall in love.'

I can see that I have my work cut out.

Your loving son,
Julian

Applause rippled through the plane as it glided on to the tarmac. Philip, sucking palliatively on a boiled sweet, wondered whether it sprang from relief at having survived the flight, happiness at being home, or common courtesy. The slick young business-man across the aisle, who had read both the *Economist* and the *Wall Street Journal* cover to cover, raised his eyes as if to excuse the foibles of his countrymen. Philip flashed him a wry smile, which he trusted conveyed the mixture of confidence and sen-sitivity that he intended to make the keynotes of his stay. He had misjudged the balance so far, his respect for the stewardess' headscarf having restricted his alcohol intake to two glasses of champagne, while the businessman had not only downed the best part of a bottle but met her for coffee during the six-hour stopover in Dubai. Feeling disgruntled, Philip gathered up his new grip, which looked cheap beside the businessman's brief-case, and stepped off the plane.

He followed the crowd down a series of corridors, past adverts for banks, hotel chains, computers and mobile phones, most of which were reassuringly familiar, before joining the long queue at Immigration. Its sluggishness was all the more frus-trating given that it was predominantly composed of Asians; he trusted that it was ignorance and not apathy that prevented his distinguishing between Filipino, Malay and Chinese. From his own experience of Heathrow, he would have expected them to be whisked through, but, gazing at the Wanted posters for New People's Army insurgents dotted about the concourse, he realised that domestic terrorism was the officers' prime concern. He was surprised by the posters since he had assumed that, like other such groups, the NPA had become a spent force in recent years. He peered hard, trying to read the small print without either drawing attention to himself or losing his place in line, finding

that the size of the suspects' photographs was in direct proportion to the bounty on their heads and, presumably, the danger
that they posed to the state. Although not yet accustomed to the
currency, he could see that 1 million pesos for each of the four
commanders would be a strong incentive for betrayal.

He reached the control booth, where the officer's suspicious
stare made him feel as though every joint he had ever smoked
were secreted about his person. He wondered if the suspicion
might arise from the fact that, for the first time in his life, he was
travelling not for pleasure but for 'research'. His passport finally
stamped, he made his way into the congested baggage hall where
he struggled to find the correct carousel. Having been given
advice, insect repellent and Travel Wash by his mother, who
was wary of hotel laundries; advice, mustard and foot powder
by his godmother, who had grown up in Ceylon; advice and a
dog-eared copy of *Dos and Don'ts in the Philippines* ('Do think
twice before you challenge a Filipino to a drinking match', 'Don't
assume all pretty girls are female') by his old school chum Brian,
who had spent the previous Easter surfing in Boracay; on top of
the books, computer, camera and clothes needed for an indefinite stay, he worried that he had packed too much, but his two
bulging cases paled in comparison with the precariously laden
trolleys of the Filipino passengers which, from the labels on the
boxes, contained plasma TVs, hi-fis, air-conditioning units and
at least one fridge.

Waved through customs with almost insulting indifference,
Philip walked across the lobby and out of the building. A blast
of heat hit him like the swirl of a sandstorm, and his light-
weight jacket hung as heavy on his shoulders as the cape he had
affected during his final year at school. With no public access
to the terminal, a horde of waiting relatives and friends packed
the forecourt and he scoured the few white faces for Max Bradshaw, Hugh Olliphant's agent in Manila, who was due to meet
him. He tried to recall Julian Tremayne's description of him
before reminding himself that it would be at least thirty years

out of date. Taking off his hat to any Englishman who could survive for so long in such an oppressive climate, he felt an urge to do so literally, lifting the panama that had been another of his godmother's gifts and mopping his brow. At that moment a tall, angular man in a whitish suit clambered over the barrier, to the consternation of a soldier, who looked far too young to be wielding a weapon on anything other than a games console. Holding up such a scrappy piece of card that Philip was only partially comforted to read his own name, the man moved confidently towards him. 'This is you, I presume?' Philip gazed at the spindly writing and nodded. 'Max Bradshaw. The pleasure's mine.' He held out a hand that was more slippery than sticky. 'Good flight?' He carried on without waiting for a reply. 'Whenever I travel long distance, I always start by looking around the plane to see which of the passengers I could eat if we happen to crash.' His broad grin revealed teeth as stained as his suit. 'I've texted Eddie – our driver – that you've arrived in one piece. Though when he'll get here is anyone's guess. Adjusting your watch is just the start of it. You have to adjust to a whole new way of doing things. It's called Filipino time.'

After twenty minutes, Eddie pulled up with a long list of excuses, which Max proceeded to rebut although, as they inched down the slip road and on to the freeway, there was no denying the heaviness of the traffic. A loud whir was the sole evidence of the air conditioning and, pressed against his neighbour who made no attempt to draw back, Philip realised that it was not only dentistry that Max treated with disdain. Feeling both nauseous and jet-lagged, he longed to shut his eyes but was kept alert by the running commentary, which took on a new urgency as they drove down Roxas Boulevard, which Max described as 'Manila's premier thoroughfare, also notable as the street where I live'. Bordered on one side by the sea and on the other by a long line of tower blocks and luxury hotels, interspersed with gaudy, single-storey nightclubs and sinister patches of wasteland, it appeared to embody all the city's contradictions. 'That's the

American Embassy,' Max said, pointing to a large white building on their left with the familiar flag flying high. 'Look at the crowds. Every morning you see hundreds of people queuing up for visas. Then, in the afternoon, you see them waving banners outside, protesting against US imperialism.'

'Not the same people surely?' Philip asked.

'I wouldn't put it past them.'

At the end of the boulevard they reached the hotel, where security guards stopped the car, opening the boot and the bonnet, and checking beneath the chassis with a periscope. They then continued down the forecourt, past more guards with sniffer dogs, to the main doors, where Eddie parked, a porter collected the luggage, and Philip and Max went through an airport-style scanner.

'Why all this security?' Philip asked Max, as he waited for his jacket and holdall to be X-rayed.

'You get used to it,' Max replied airily. 'Little men with big weapons, the same as everywhere. Only here we face two separate threats. One's the Moro Islamic Liberation Front. They're out to create a religious state on the island of Mindanao. I'm all in favour of covering up the competition, but mullahs and beards and floggings and stonings. No, thank you! The other's the NPA, a gang of diehard Marxists. And, in the Philippines, that means a mixture of Karl and Groucho.'

Max escorted Philip through the grandiose lobby, whose richly panelled ceiling, glittering chandeliers, thick carpet and plush sofas were a world away from the hurly-burly of the streets. As the six-piece orchestra played airs from operettas, Philip felt that he might have been back taking tea with his mother and godmother at the Savoy.

'Would you like to see the room?' Philip asked reluctantly, after collecting his key from the receptionist.

'My, you are forward! We've only just met. Don't worry,' Max said, as Philip struggled to conceal his dismay. 'I'll just sit here and wait. Waiting's what I do best.' He strolled to a table in front of the orchestra, while the porter led Philip to his room.

The blast of cold air when he opened the door was as fierce as the heat outside the airport. The room was large, square and impersonal, containing a ceiling-high four-poster bed with diaphanous curtains, a wall-length TV and cocktail cabinet, an L-shaped sofa and a smoked-glass coffee table on which sat a vase of waxy white flowers. The muted oatmeal and slate colour scheme was clearly designed to reassure the reluctant traveller that the external world would not intrude. The only indications that he was in Manila, rather than Rome, Sydney or Buenos Aires, were the vista from the window, a medley of greys and browns with a small patch of green in the foreground and a faint line of blue on the right, and the copy of the *Philippine Tatler*, which he idly flicked through while waiting for his luggage to arrive. The wallowing in wealth was even more obscene than in its English counterpart and, although he had abandoned activism after a student phase as predictable as puberty, he felt a tinge of sympathy for the NPA, which he expressed by overtipping the bellhop who brought up his bags.

Freshly showered, changed and powdered (and grateful for his godmother's prescience), he made his way downstairs to find Max still sitting at the table and drinking something green. Downing the glass in a single gulp, he jumped up. 'Lunch!' he declared, so vehemently that Philip half expected all those within earshot to drop whatever they were doing and join them. 'Should we try the Champagne Room?' Max asked, with a show of deliberation, guiding Philip through the lobby and into a room as intoxicating as its name. Sunlight streamed through the chinks in the heavy silk curtains, illuminating the wrought iron arches, mirrored walls, patterned glass and decorative grates, while leaving the body of the room in romantic shadow. Feeling as if he had trespassed on the transformation scene of a pantomime, Philip followed the maître d' round two large trees made entirely of crystal, which tinkled as they passed, to his table, where a waiter removed a mitre-shaped napkin from his plate and spread it decorously on his lap. 'Come on,' said Max, gazing at the menu as reverently as at a Book of Hours. 'Let's spend some of Hugh's lovely money.'

'Right you are,' Philip said, pondering what it was in this fey, feckless man that recommended itself to Hugh. Julian had cited his contacts in the Marcos regime, but that failed to explain why such a hard-bitten businessman had kept him on the payroll for a further thirty years. 'I gather you've worked with Hugh for a long time,' he said, probing the improbable relationship.

'Man and boy. But then I know where the bodies are buried,' Max replied, with a smile so arch that Philip suspected a double bluff.

The wine waiter came to take their order.

'Champagne,' Max said, as if anything else would have been unworthy of the room. 'Taittinger. We'll save the Dom Perignon for a special occasion.'

'Shouldn't we save all of it?' Philip asked. 'At least till I have some news about Julian.'

'Nonsense. It's not often I get the chance to live the high life any more. You've made an old man very happy – I use the word "old" loosely.' He laughed. 'What are the three most beautiful words in the English language?'

'I love you?'

'You're very young,' Max said, with a pitying look. '"Money's no object", of course.'

Philip might have been more convinced, had he felt more confident of achieving his mission. Worried that he would come up with nothing of value to the investigation, he would have preferred Max to have booked him into a more modest hotel. For all Hugh's expressions of marital concern, he would expect a return on his investment.

'I understand you knew Julian yourself,' he said, uncertain whether his slurred speech stemmed from jet-lag or champagne.

'I met him. I wouldn't say that I knew him; quite the reverse.

He came to Manila with Hugh and his wife before they were married. I got him an invitation to one of Imelda's most glittering soirées. There were people who'd have killed to be there – literally. But was he grateful? Anyone would have thought I'd taken him to a black mass.'

'You never saw him again.'

'Once, a couple of years later when I visited him in prison. Hugh asked me to take in some supplies and report back. He looked a good deal happier there than he had in Manila. In his element it seemed to me.'

'So, do you think he was a saint?'

'He certainly enjoyed playing the martyr. But I'm not the right person to ask. Our Saviour and I haven't seen eye to eye for years.'

'Do you have any religion at all?'

'Beauty,' Max replied with unexpected fervour. 'Beautiful art, beautiful music, beautiful people. They're my religion. And the Filipinos are the most beautiful people I know. How about you?'

'I don't know that many. Oh, you mean religion? Your typical wishy-washy Anglican, I suppose, of the hatch, match and dispatch persuasion. I'd put it better if I weren't so shattered. Or maybe not. I grew up in Berkshire, where the Sunday service was as much a part of the fabric of our lives as the church was part of the fabric of the village. Not that it went much deeper. It's a family joke that when the vicar said "my help comes from the hills", my mother took it that his charlady came from the Chilterns. What I envied about Catholics – at least the ones I met through Julia – was the seriousness of their faith. Julia was Hugh's daughter. We were engaged.'

'I know. I'm sorry.'

'It was three years ago.'

'I know.'

'Thank you. Between you and me, I've been in limbo for quite a while, since Julia's death in fact – though I don't like to make the connection, at least not out loud. In the end, I think that's why I agreed to come: a sense that whatever I did for Julian, I'd also be doing for Julia. And, when I'd done it, I might finally be able to move on.'

'I see.'

'Now I'm here, I long to get cracking. I had hoped to do a lot of the groundwork back home, but Google wasn't much help. The only mentions of Julian were linked to his older brother, Hugh's father-in-law: you remember, the Tory minister?'

'It rings a teensy bell.'

'So unless you've a better idea, I thought I'd start by sifting through the archive material in the National Library. Then I'd like to interview Julian's clerical colleagues, fellow missionaries, friends and former parishioners, along with anyone who claims to have been cured through his intervention. When I've collated all the material, I'll submit one report to Isabel and Hugh, and another to the Bishop. What happens after that is anyone's guess! The official investigators will be free to use anything I come up with or to carry on in their own sweet – and slow – way. Isabel still might not live long enough to see her dream fulfilled.'

'First things first,' Max said, as he gobbled up a melting sorbet, oblivious to the latest stains on his sleeve. 'You must take some time to explore the country, meet the people, see what Julian was up against or working with, depending on your point of view. If there's one thing I've learnt during my years in Manila, it's never to plan.'

Two

My dear Mother and Father,

Well, we've survived the rainy season. Benguet is a temperate province, so we've been spared the worst of the devastation; nonetheless, we've had our moments. I was travelling to Baguio by jeepney (the local bus, taxi service and delivery van rolled into one) when we were hit by a flash flood. The small stream ahead of us swelled into a raging torrent and the driver sent his two washees to wade through and find out where it was safe to pass. He himself sat idly smoking. Then, without a word, he revved up the engine and shot across. The passengers, who included one goat and several chickens, were flung about the aisle, narrowly escaping injury. Livestock apart, there wasn't a single bleat of protest. Not wishing to sound like a tourist, I took my cue from their silence. Later, however, I reproached the driver for his recklessness, which must have been even more alarming for the dozen or so people huddled on the roof. 'I'm sorry, Father,' he said shyly, 'I wanted to catch the spirits by surprise.'

The next day he came to nine o'clock mass.

Thank you so much for the parcel, which has finally arrived. The Regional told me that it took all morning to beat the customs officer down from 500 pesos handling charge to 20, but he chose to think of it as both a battle of wits and a test of forbearance. He brought it up here himself, which gives you some idea of its value. There isn't a single qualified doctor in town nor, it goes without saying, in any of the villages. Not that 99 per cent of the people could afford to pay for treatment. So they have to rely on folk remedies, which are, at best, useless and, at worst... well, I'll tell you my own experience. Three weeks ago I had a fever (nothing serious,

Mother, just a touch of flu). Consolacion, my housekeeper, called the district medicine man, who turned out to be quite literally a snake-oil salesman, since he prescribed a bottle of silt-coloured liquid with a small serpent coiled at the bottom. I never discovered if it was intended as an ingredient, a preservative or simply a garnish. Needless to say, I recovered without it, but then I have the constitution of an ox – or perhaps here I should say a carabao (water buffalo). For most of his patients it's kill or cure.

So you need have no qualms about sending me the antihistamines. I'm already dispensing them to the kids with scabies, which is pretty much the whole parish. I explained to their parents that, while they may not eradicate the infection, they will relieve the soreness. I'm less confident about the efficacy of the deworming tablets. Since I last wrote, I've discovered the scale of the problem. I took an eight-year-old girl, whose stomach had swollen up like a watermelon, to the hospital in Baguio. The doctor told me that, while it wasn't the tumour I'd feared, she was infested with a knot of about sixty intestinal worms, some as long as twenty centimetres and as thick as my thumb. They couldn't be removed without surgery.

I paid for the operation, which has been a double success since the resulting scar made her the envy of her friends. But I'm rapidly running out of cash and, with the best will in the world, no parish can rely on the largesse of its priest. So I'm keen to touch hearts – and wallets – back home. In your letter, Mother, you say nothing of my proposal for a monthly fast at the Holy Redeemer, with the money saved being sent out here. I'm sure Father Ambrose will approve. I'd write to him myself, but it'll carry more weight coming from you. It's such a small sacrifice for such a worthwhile cause. Please don't consign it to the box marked Julian's Hare-brained Schemes.

On a personal note, I'm especially grateful for the calamine lotion. It feels as if every mosquito within a fifty-mile radius has been using me for target practice. It's odd, but most of my parishioners are amused. Perhaps I flatter myself but, while I believe that they'd be genuinely distressed if I were to fall ill or have an accident, they enjoy the thought of my suffering a minor mishap. It's as though it gives me a taste of the constant hardship of their lives.

Meanwhile, rest assured that I'm being well looked after. She may not be Mrs Hawthorne, but Consolacion is an expert housekeeper. She too has had her share of sorrow. Does it go with the territory? Please supply three references, including one attesting to a deep personal tragedy that will guarantee your life-long devotion to the family you wish to serve. In place of Mrs Hawthorne's Adam and the Spanish Flu, she saw her husband murdered for resisting the Japanese invasion. By 'saw', I mean was made to watch while he was tied between two carabaos and torn apart. Widowed with four young children at the age of twenty-seven, she trekked from village to village selling vegetables. If you're favoured, she'll show you the dent in the crown of her head. In spite of it all, she remains cheerful and a permanent fixture at morning mass.

She's a creative cook in the loaves-and-fishes sense: what she can do with freshwater crabs and lichen is nobody's business, although our staple diet is of course rice. Central Luzon is the rice capital of the Philippines. While farmers elsewhere are restricted to a wet-season crop, here they've developed an irrigation system based on artesian wells, which allows them to plant a second crop in the dry season (you see, Father, I haven't totally turned my back on the land). Not that it seems to double – or anything like – their standard of living. People are truly dirt poor. Think Irish villagers during the Famine rather than the least skilled agricultural worker in Britain today. We have three *haciendas* (rice-growing estates) in the parish, each of which is home to around two hundred families, who live in the most primitive conditions: bamboo-matting walls; palm-frond roofs; earth floors; with no furniture other than sleeping mats and the odd chair. They have water pumps in the yard and share outdoor lavatories. The only shops are a handful of *sari sari* stores, which

(I can't have made it clear) are not dress shops. The people here can't afford silk; most of them can't afford cotton. They wear shorts, skirts and tops made from OLD RICE SACKS (I'm sorry but I feel like shouting). The *sari sari* stores are general stores selling a very limited range of canned food, cigarettes, soft drinks, cooking oils and household goods.

The only communal buildings on the estates are schools and chapels. The schools cater for all ages, although few pupils stay on beyond twelve. Books – and even chalk – are luxuries, but the children put up with such privations in their eagerness to learn. Every morning during term, they walk for miles across rice fields, many carrying the boxes that they use as seats. Maybe, as well as fasting, we could set up a scheme for local church schools to send out their old textbooks (unless someone – naming no names, Father – felt moved to pay for new ones himself)? History would be inappropriate and Geography need to be carefully vetted, but we'd be fine with Scripture, English and Arithmetic. They wouldn't have to be pristine; we're not proud.

Making do is the name of the game. Take the chapels. Only one of the three has walls and those are made of galvanised iron. It has no windows or, indeed, any decoration apart from a set of black-and-white photographs of the Holy Land, a gravure of San Isidro, and boards enumerating the Seven Sacraments and the Ten Commandments. Both the other two are open wooden structures that double as grain stores. Last week I arrived to celebrate mass at one to find the congregation busily removing sacks of rice. It puts sweeping the Holy Redeemer porch after a wedding in a very different light!

Goats, pigs and chickens wander around at will. Cocks crow raucously throughout the day. They're bred for fighting, which is the national sport – please don't say anything to Isabel or she'll write outraged letters to Mr Heath demanding that he send a gunboat. The big surprise, especially to one brought up on Father's Friesians, is the lack of cattle. The few white Brahman

you see around are so achingly thin that they look like an illustration of the Seven Lean Years.

The general poverty is thrown into stark relief by the wealth
of the *haciendos*. I'm not naïve. I grew up acutely sensitive to
the gulf between the grandeur of the Hall and the modesty of
the estate cottages. But you are closer to your most penurious
tenants than they are to the richest of theirs. I'll take the Pinedas
as an example – not altogether at random since I dined with
them last Sunday. The family lives in a large compound surrounded by ten-foot walls topped with brown shards of old San
Miguel bottles: a particularly cruel form of recycling. Guards
with automatic rifles man the gates. Why? I felt as though I were
paying a call on Ceauşescu. Their broad grins as they waved
me in made their weapons look even more incongruous. I followed the long gravel drive, lined by jasmine trees and bird-of-
paradise plants, to the big house which, with its flouncy façade
and chipped columns, put me in mind of a crumbling wedding
cake.

Don Florante is reputed to be one of the more enlightened
landlords. He takes a paternal interest in his tenants, advancing
them money for seeds and tools, selling them cheap rice during
droughts, and standing as godfather to their children (which,
here, involves far more than remembering them at Christmas
and birthdays). During lunch, a succession of men shuffled
in, heads bowed and holding out promissory notes, which he
scanned and endorsed without ever once interrupting our conversation. I don't know which I found more painful: the servile
postures that the men were forced to adopt; their effusive gratitude at his endorsement; or their seeing me, their priest, enjoying the lavish meal from which they were excluded, especially
after my sermon on Dives and Lazarus the week before.

Once the ladies had withdrawn, I challenged don Florante
about his treatment of his tenants, always conscious of how
you'd react, Father, should Father Ambrose question the way
you treated yours (I'm not comparing them, you understand,

merely showing the need for tact). On the assumption that the guards were armed against the threat of NPA guerrillas and not to deter a desperate farmer from filching a piece of machinery, I put it to him that the surest way to push decent Christians into the arms of the Communists was to make them feel exploited. Far from taking offence, he smiled and told me that he left all such matters to señor Herrera, his *encargado*. If I wished to discuss them further, I should address myself to him. Then he offered me a cigar.

Wasting no time, I made an appointment to see the *encargado* the next morning. I have rarely felt more compromised by my cassock. A heavily built man with pitted skin and an eye patch, Herrera steered me to a chair and, with a deference which we both knew was feigned, asked what he could do to help. I began by explaining that, as a priest, I was responsible for my parishioners' well-being. I expressed shock at the living conditions on the estate, adding that improving them was not simply basic justice but sound economics. People with full bellies worked harder (I'm not sure whether that's been proved, but it rang true and struck a suitably pragmatic note). I was dismayed by his response. Rather than acknowledging my argument and promising to take action, as I'd hoped, or agreeing with the premise but citing obstacles, as I'd feared, he launched a bitter attack on his tenants, who (I paraphrase) were 'lazy, shifty, sloppy, unmotivated, squandering money on drinking, gambling, cockfighting and' – this I recall verbatim – 'prone to other vices which, in your presence, Father, I hesitate to mention'. I'm a priest, I wanted to say, not your maiden aunt! He then claimed that the reason for their poverty was that they had such large families. Seizing my chance, I said that this was because they obeyed the teachings of the Church and asked whether he didn't find it odd that, while the tenants had eight, nine or ten children, he, don Florante and all the other bosses had only two or three. 'Not at all,' he replied. 'They live in smaller spaces so they touch each other more.'

Adopting a more conciliatory tone, he assured me that the Philippines was a wonderful country but it could be hard for a foreigner to understand its ways. I felt like a blundering English officer ordering his Hindu soldiers to use beef fat in their guns. 'Let's each stick to our own, shall we, Father? I won't tell you how to write your sermons and you won't tell me how to run my estate.' Then he called a security guard (armed of course) to take me back to my car which, to add to my humiliation, refused to start. My futile stabs at the ignition matched my bumbling efforts in the office and it required the intervention of the guard, stung by his friends' ribald comments, to make a quick and effective adjustment to the engine. Gazing back at the house, I saw the manager watching from the window and knew that I could kiss any prospect of a new Mercedes goodbye.

I returned to town feeling thoroughly wretched. I told myself that it was my first reversal and besides, the Church doesn't set the best example of sharing wealth. Drive around the province and even in the smaller towns you'll see *conventos* that look more like bishops' palaces. I honestly don't know how those priests can look their parishioners in the eye. But whoever may be at fault, it isn't the farmers, most of whom do back-breaking work in the gruelling heat and expect to be fairly rewarded. They feel entitled to one square meal a day (note, I said one) and not to be reliant on the snails, frogs and crabs that their children dredge from the irrigation canals or the few grains of rice that their wives glean from discarded stalks.

I'm sorry – was it Disraeli or Gladstone whom Queen Victoria accused of treating her like a public meeting? – but I needed to get that off my chest. I have to watch what I say here, even to my fellow priests. The political situation is far more volatile than you'd realise from reading the English papers. Until I arrived here, I had no idea that there were Communist revolts in several regions of the country. It's difficult to gauge the extent of their support. Sometimes the government plays them up in order to justify its reprisals and sometimes it plays them down in order to reassure foreign banks. The revolts are spearheaded by the NPA, the New People's Army, which began as a student protest movement, on the lines of our own Angry Brigade, only much more ruthless. The daughter of one of my parishioners is a member. Her mother looks after her four children while she trains with her unit in the hills. Meanwhile, her neighbour looks after the three children of a daughter who works as a hospitality girl (which barely qualifies as a euphemism) in Manila. Needless to say, the two grandmothers loathe one another. I, however, see them as two sides of the same coin or, more to the point, lack of coin.

They may be extreme cases, but families throughout the parish are regularly torn apart as one or other of the parents leaves for Manila to be the… I'd say rice-winner if it didn't sound flippant. Of course, the universal dream is to work abroad, as nannies, cooks, housemaids, bar boys or chauffeurs. It breaks my heart that this beautiful people's best hope is to turn themselves into the world's servants.

I'll leave it there. If you want to hear about the problems of tenant farmers, you need only take a stroll to the Gaverton Arms. Instead, I'll tell you of one of my more exotic adventures, among people you're unlikely to have come across even in the wilder reaches of County Durham. Last week, I drove sixty miles (see, I've taken on board your objections to the metric system) to the far perimeter of the parish and then hiked into the mountains to say mass for an Igorot tribe, whose ancestors have lived there since time immemorial. I felt as if I'd stepped into the pages of the *National Geographic*. They were practically naked: the men in black and red loincloths and the women in black, red and white skirts. The language barrier was firmly in place since, unlike the townspeople, none of them speaks English and very few speak or, at any rate, admit to speaking Tagalog. So I was dependent on Eddie, a local teacher, to act as interpreter. Custom dictated that, before anything else, we eat and drink together. They cooked a chicken in the age-old manner, first holding it upside down and bashing its head several times with a stick. NB, it's even more crucial that you don't breathe a word of this to Isabel or I'll lose what shred of moral authority I still possess.

After the meal, I held an open-air mass for 300 people. The crucifix on the altar bore a disconcerting resemblance to the rice gods carved on the door frames of their homes. They profess to be Catholics, but I suspect that their faith is only skin deep – and sometimes not even that: how many Catholics do you know who have their arms intricately tattooed with a mixture of plant juice, soot and hen's excrement, to protect them from evil spirits? I'm not setting out to destroy their ancient traditions and I'm well aware that the early Church adopted various pagan rites, but I will have no truck with worship in which Our Lord is merely one god among many, a native fetish rather than the Saviour of the world.

Then again, it's no wonder that the pagan influence lingers on when the Church has been so compromised. In recent years, there have been too few priests to tend their flocks. But all that will change, and I'm proud to be playing a small part in the transformation. I've saved the best until last. With Father Benito Bertubin from the neighbouring parish of the Holy Cross, I'm instituting a network of Basic Christian Communities. Father Benito, a truly splendid man, has just come back from a year in Brazil where he experienced such communities at first hand. They give people the opportunity to think for themselves, rather than always depending on their priests (which even Father must admit is in line with the new spirit emanating from the Vatican). Our most pressing task is to establish teams of lay leaders. We've sounded out the different *barrios* for suitable candidates, using the criteria that St Paul proposes for bishops and deacons in the First Letter to Timothy. We're planning to start selections in the new year, and then… watch this space!

Now I must leave you. I send you all my love and prayers for the Feast of the Nativity; I can't help feeling a pang that, for the first year since my burst appendix, I shan't be celebrating it with you. I'll have to make do with picturing everyone at the Christmas Eve carols, Boxing Day meet, New Year's Eve ball and, of course, Christmas Day mass. I shall be spending the day at the *convento*. I was invited for lunch at the Arriola mansion but I declined, much to Consolacion's delight. My place is here, to welcome any waifs and strays. Besides, I'm developing a taste for bat.

Your loving son,
Julian

Philip felt as if his whole body were covered in gum. He had
scarcely stepped out of the hotel, and he was already disorientated by the glaring sun and the swampy heat and the cacophony
of car horns. Leaving for his third and, he hoped, final day at the
library, he resolved to ignore the line of taxis in the forecourt and
walk the short distance across Rizal Park. First, however, he had
to brave the freeway on which the constant flow of vehicles bore
no visible relation to the working of the lights. As he wavered on
the kerb, a pedicab driver drew up in front of him, bombarded
him with questions and promised him 'the most cheapest and
most comfortable ride in Manila'. Treating the polite refusals as
a negotiating ploy, he repeatedly lowered his price, as though
the sight of a Westerner on foot were not just a wasted business
opportunity but an affront to his world view.

Trusting to the red light, Philip wove through the colour-blind
traffic and, by some miracle (although, given his mission, he was
wary of the word), reached the opposite pavement unscathed.
After pausing to gain both his breath and his bearings, he
entered the eerily empty park. A handful of joggers circled the
perimeter, oblivious to everything but the music in their ears; a
class of schoolgirls practised tai chi on the grass; a pair of lovers,
whom he romantically – or nostalgically – identified as students,
embraced beside a blaze of poinsettias; a vagrant lay sleeping on
a bench, his matted hair and tattered trainers telling as poignant
a story as any in the newspaper that covered him.

Philip strolled past the small crowd of tourists who were pho-
tographing the changing of the guard at the Rizal monument, a
majestic bronze statue, which neatly concealed its subject's lack
of stature, and made his way to the library. After handing his bag
to the security guard, who deflected his friendly 'good morning'
with the same stony expression that he had adopted all week,

he climbed the cheerless concrete stairs, dotted with wilting pot plants, to the Filipiniana Division, then up a further flight to the serial section. None of the three librarians, huddled behind the enquiry desk, showed him any sign of acknowledgement, despite his having been the only reader in the department for the past two days. After filling in a requisition slip, he took a seat in what, with its shelves of maroon ledgers, piles of cardboard boxes and stacks of loose papers, resembled the accounts department of an old-fashioned family firm. He waited impatiently for the papers to arrive and struggled to summon up enthusiasm for a task that had so far proved to be both tedious and futile.

Of the three main newspapers published during the Marcos era, none was available on computer and only two on microfiche. The months it would take to scrutinise each issue for any mention of Julian would exhaust Philip's patience as surely as it would Hugh's purse. He had therefore chosen to concentrate on three key events, all of which had attracted widespread press attention: Julian's alleged levitation during mass; his arraignment on the murder charge; and his violent death. Even so, there was a mass of material to wade through since, on the evidence of Julian's letters, it was impossible to put a more precise date on the levitation than June to August 1975 or on the court hearings than March to November 1984. And although his body was found on 10 November 1989, comment on the case continued sporadically for several months.

After two days of strained eyes over the microfiche and stained fingers from the newsprint, he had discovered little of significance for either 1984 or 1989. A report in the *Philippines Daily Express* filled in details of the murder charge that Julian had omitted, notably that his hip flask, easily identified by the owl-and-halberds crest, had been found (in other words, planted) on the ridge from which the fatal shots were fired. An article in the *Bulletin Today* featured the claims of various Baguio prisoners that they had heard Julian and his cell mate, Benito Bertubin, talking about their part in the shooting. Although their testimony was deeply compromised, it was clear that not all of his fellow inmates were as cheered by Julian's presence as he had led his mother to believe. Finding no reference to the miracle-working reputation which, according to Julian, had featured in several reports of the case, Philip concluded that the reports in question must have been foreign, which made sense, given the iron control that Marcos had exercised over the press.

He was further disappointed by the sketchy accounts of the discovery of Julian's remains in both the *Daily Express* and the *Times Journal* (the *Bulletin Today* by then having folded) and by the blandness of subsequent obituaries. Neither the Bishop of Montagnosa nor the Regional Representative of the Mill Hill Missionaries offered much beyond conventional tributes to his exemplary life, inspirational priesthood, and dedication to the poor and needy. The Regional alone praised his outspoken opposition to the abuses and atrocities committed under Martial Law, about which the Bishop was understandably reticent. But pastoral care and social protest, however admirable, did not make a man a saint, and he needed evidence of the heroic virtue and miracle cures that were crucial to the case.

A tiny librarian tottered from the stacks with six bound volumes of the *Times Journal*. The cloud of dust that arose as she deposited them on Philip's table suggested that the summer of 1975 was a neglected period of historical research. Philip prayed that he would light on something of substance; but, although the words 'miraculous healing' and even 'joyous phenomenon in Mountain Provinces village' caught his eye, they had no connection with Julian. Moreover, given that the 'joyous phe-nomenon' was a middle-aged woman who, after thirty years of childless marriage, had fallen pregnant with triplets when Christ appeared to her during mass, and the 'miraculous healing' was that of a sixteen-year-old boy who had grown a new eye after being touched by the emissary of the king of the dwarves, it was no surprise that a priest's levitation, which would have caused a sensation in Berkshire, was small beer in Benguet.

After a morning in which he eliminated further lines of enquiry rather than uncovering anything of note, Philip went down to the lobby to meet Max. He had texted at breakfast that he had urgent matters to discuss, although, on past form and given the reference to 'one of my favourite eateries nearby', Philip assumed that his primary motive was to lunch at Hugh's expense. Anxious not to waste time, he was relieved to find that Max had already arrived but embarrassed by the sweeping bow with which he greeted him in front of the security guard. They made their way out into the street where a knot of men was poring over the boards and booths of a makeshift maritime recruitment agency. Clutching his money belt like a truss – and hating himself for it – he watched, both fascinated and appalled, as engineers and fitters and stewards and mates signed away their lives like the victims of an eighteenth-century press gang.

'Is it legal?' he asked.

'It's Manila,' Max replied. 'That's a question you learn not to ask.'

Dragging him away, Max hailed a pedicab, even though Philip, his confidence bolstered by the earlier excursion, suggested that they walked. 'We're doing our bit for the local economy,' Max said, belying the claim by haggling over the fare. 'It makes them look at you with more respect,' he added, as the driver looked at them with undisguised loathing.

The price agreed, Philip stepped over the gaping gutter and into the rickety sidecar, where he sat squashed against Max who appeared to relish both their intimacy and his discomfort. To his horror, the driver pulled straight out into the road, executing a U-turn in the face of the steady stream of traffic. Max patted his thigh in mischievous reassurance as they braved the tumult of honking, before waiting at the lights, where an intrepid pedlar threaded through the stationary vehicles selling cigarettes by the stick and gum by the piece. Turning down a side street, they proceeded for a couple of blocks before stopping outside the restaurant, whose frontage was adorned with crude plastic versions of the rice gods in Hugh's study. The pavement was almost as tricky to negotiate as the road. Ahead of them a man, wearing nothing but shorts, soaped himself as nonchalantly as if he were in his own bathroom. To his left, three men played cards on an oil drum surrounded by a jeering and gesticulating crowd; to his right, three women sat stirring brightly coloured stews and bubbling pots of rice while their children frolicked at their feet, perilously close to the wobbly stoves. All around them were stalls selling food, drink, scarves, T-shirts, sunglasses, lighters and pirated DVDs.

They entered the restaurant, where the maître d' greeted them with a mixture of familiarity and obsequiousness. Feeling guardedly adventurous, Philip opted for the local cuisine and, attracted as much by the name as by the ingredients, which the waiter listed as 'beef, anchovies, eggplant, bok choy, garlic and beans', ordered *kare-kare*. Max, meanwhile, ordered cuttlefish.

'Do you never eat Filipino?' Philip asked.

'With *my* stomach?' Max replied, with a theatrical shudder. Having dispatched what he described as 'the serious business of the day', he questioned Philip about his researches, showing neither surprise nor concern at the lack of results.

'I still have one hope,' Philip said, as perturbed by Max's indifference as he would have been by an open rebuke, 'or rather two: the *Philippines Daily Express* and *Bulletin Today* for June to August 1975. They may make some mention of the levitation. I've booked a slot on the microfiche machine for 2.30.'

'You're a glutton for punishment,' Max said, devouring a fistful of fried peanuts.

'There was nothing in the *Times Journal*, which surprised me since Julian definitely mentioned reporters coming up from Manila. Either their accounts must have been censored or else the newspapers can't have been preserved.'

'What were you expecting? A photo of him hovering two foot above the nave?'

'It was worth a try. Besides, I'd just have been kicking my heels till we went up to San Isidro. Any news on that front by the way?'

'Don't worry. It's all in hand.'

'Great,' he replied, trying not to sound sceptical. 'I thought that might be what you wanted to discuss. I'm sure it's the most fertile field of enquiry. I have a list of all the people I'd like to interview: his former housekeeper, that is if she's still alive; parishioners, several of whom are named in the letters; fellow priests and missionaries; the lay leaders with whom he set up the Basic Christian Communities; and, of course, anyone who's been touched by one of his miracles. Before then, I should call on the Bishop. It's only polite, not to say prudent, since I need him to fill me in on the progress so far and let me have copies of all their documents. That way I won't waste time going over old ground.'

'For one so young, you have a morbid obsession with time. Haven't I told you that time here is flexible?'

'I'm sorry,' Philip said, afraid that his impatience was itself a sign of inflexibility, 'it must be how I'm made. Isabel Olliphant gave me a letter of introduction to the Bishop. Do you think I should send it straight to him or ring to introduce myself first – or simply turn up at the door?'

'None of the above,' Max said. 'I've made an appointment with the Vicar General – he's like the Bishop's support act – who's coming to Manila on Tuesday.'

'To see me?' Philip said, keen not to betray his excitement.

'To see the Cardinal. You're just an extra.'

'Of course,' Philip said, feeling crushed.

The food arrived. Max tore into his cuttlefish while Philip picked tentatively at the *kare-kare* and its accompaniment. Honour demanded a show of enthusiasm, but he was relieved to find that the rich, salty stew, with the thick tang of peanut butter and the tart green mango salad, merited it of its own accord. The fermented shrimp paste, however, was an acquired taste.

'Have you made plans for this evening?' Max asked.

'Dinner in the hotel followed by another session of Pay for View, I expect,' Philip said. 'I'm catching up with all the films I missed on the plane.'

'Not tempted by the fleshpots of Manila?' Max asked, his yellow grin accentuated by sweetcorn.

'Not remotely,' Philip replied, unnerved by a question that took him back to the early hours when, alone and restless, he had abandoned *Moneyball* and turned to the adult channel, tantalising himself with the trailers. He trusted that it was disapproval of the commercialisation of sex and the exploitation of women that had prevented his pressing Enter, and not just revulsion at joining the ranks of middle-aged businessmen, too cheap or too flaccid to make their demands in person, let alone the fear that either Max or Hugh would decipher the entries on his bill.

'I have a couple of friends coming to dinner whom I'd like you to meet.'

'Men friends?' Philip asked, a little too fast.

'Let me think. Yes, as it happens. Is that a problem?'

'No, of course not. Not at all.'

'Good. Ray Lim works at the National Museum. He's been invaluable in obtaining export licences for Hugh's collection. Red tape!' Max made a snipping gesture with his fingers.

'We'll have that in common. I read art history.'

'Dennis Santos is something else. I can't play Mary Poppins throughout your trip. You need an interpreter, a driver and a bodyguard.'

'Come on! I don't scare that easily.'

'I'm serious. Nothing in this country is the way it looks. You think because the Filipinos have Spanish names and speak English that you understand them. Big mistake! Dennis is bright, streetwise and fearless; he'll keep you out of trouble. True, at first sight, he might seem like trouble himself, but that's just an act. I've told him all about you and the canonisation process, and he's very keen. In his own way he's quite devout. And I make no bones about it; you'll be doing me a favour. He's scratched my back in the past. Now I try to scratch his.'

'Well, I'm happy to help out. So long as it's understood that I reserve the right to say "no".'

Max crossed his heart with a flourish that did not inspire confidence and pressed Philip to join him in a glass of brandy. He declined, insisting on the need to go back to the library, while avoiding any compromising reference to time. He finally reached the microfiche room only twenty minutes late and set up the machine. After three hours of staring at newsprint by turns faded, smeared and out of focus, his head was as groggy and his notepad as blank as if he had accepted Max's drink. He handed the spools back to the assistant, his frustration at having exhausted all his leads tempered by relief at having no further call to return, and took a pedicab to the hotel, where he had a quick shower to refresh himself, followed by a long bath to relax. Cocooned in a bathrobe, he stretched out on his bed, switched on the TV and flicked between BBC World and CNN, comparing the relative value of news stories with a trainspotter's rigour. He put on the designated dinner wear of T-shirt and jeans, which gave the Home Counties boy in him an illicit thrill, and took a taxi to Max's flat in Legaspi Towers, a destination that met with his driver's approval: 'Very favourite building. Much people go there.'

They drove down Roxas Boulevard and drew up outside a shabby tower block with a rust-coloured – and coated – frame, and chipped white balconies. An apathetic security guard waved Philip through the low concrete porch into a huge atrium, bordered by shops, offices and a hair salon, with a torrential water feature at the centre. He took the lift to the fifteenth floor and walked along a cheerless, uncarpeted corridor lined with steel doors as heavily padlocked as bank vaults. Spotting the one open grille, he pressed the doorbell, which Max answered, wearing a silky pink pinafore apron. Philip fixed his gaze on his face.

'Welcome to Casa Bradshaw,' Max said, stepping aside to reveal a room as cluttered as a museum repository.

'Wow!' Philip said, staring at the two life-size ebony gods guarding the window who took virility to extreme lengths; the large brass cockerel inlaid with beads and mother-of-pearl; the rattan tub chairs and sofa, with clashing zebra- and tiger-print cushions; all cast in a variegated glow by a string of fairy lights hung with brightly patterned paper lanterns. Meanwhile, every wall, ledge and table was crammed with photographs of women in tutus and men in tights, several posed with Max and all inscribed to him.

'Wow's the word,' Max said, taking his astonishment at face value. 'Sit yourself down. Asia or Africa?' He pointed to the respective cushions. Philip opted for the tiger print, which was closer. 'Quite right. When in Rome…. Would you like a drink? I've made some pink gin, in keeping with the theme of the evening.'

'Is there a theme? I didn't realise.'

'Friendship. Speaking of which. Ray!' He called through the open door. 'We're waiting!' He turned back to Philip. 'He'll spend all night powdering his nose.'

Philip smiled at a euphemism he associated with his grand-mother, only to discover, when Ray appeared, that it was to be taken literally. He was reluctant to judge another culture, let alone another subculture, but the light dusting of make-up on Ray's elderly face, together with the frilly diaphanous shirt which exposed every hollow in his scrawny torso, were deeply unappealing.

'Ray Lim, curator, entrepreneur and life-long reprobate, meet Philip Seward, saint-catcher and innocent abroad.'

'Not that innocent,' Philip said, shaking a hand as pliant as a puppet's.

'Oh, what a firm grip!' Ray said. 'Let me look.' He studied Philip's palm. 'Such bold lines! I shall tell your fortune later.'

'What?' Max intervened. 'That he'll meet a small, grey, raddled Chinoy? Hands off!' He wrenched Philip away. 'Come and sit down and let Mother pour you some of her Ruin.'

Max walked over to a drum-shaped drinks cabinet and pulled several ice cubes from the belly of a plastic Buddha. Philip moved to the sofa, discreetly shifting continents to avoid Ray. He accepted a full tumbler from Max, hoping that he had not stinted on the soda. 'Cheers!' he said expansively.

'To your very good health,' Ray said, fluttering a large butter-fly-covered fan.

'Bottoms up!' Max said, smacking his hand once again.

'How long have you lived here?' Philip asked, sounding unnervingly like his mother.

'Since before you were born,' he replied. 'Oh my God, it really is!'

'My friend Max came to this country with Dame Margot Fonteyn,' Ray said reverently, pronouncing her Christian name with a hard 't', which Max made no attempt to correct.

'Were you a dancer?' Philip asked, reassessing the photographs.

'In my dreams,' Max replied fervently. 'No, I met Margot through a mutual admirer. We hit it off and she took me on as a sort of general factotum, an aide-de-camp.' Ray tittered at a pun he had clearly heard many times before. 'We first came to Manila in 1976 with the Australian Ballet.'

'And you stayed on?'

'Not immediately. Margot danced in Manila several times. Imelda liked nothing more than to sit and chat in her dressing room and, when Margot was busy, she made do with me. She told me about her plans for a Philippine National Ballet and, out of the blue, asked if I'd like to run it. At first I thought it was a joke – not that she was known for her sense of humour – but she was perfectly serious. The next day she summoned me to her office and repeated her offer. I pleaded inexperience, but she laughed it off, claiming that she always followed her instincts and she'd never met anyone – except herself, of course – who felt so passionately about ballet. So what could I say but yes? Yes, yes, yes!'

'I take it you've cut your ties with the company?'

'There is no company; there never was. Poor Imelda. She was a genuine visionary. Just think of the nerve it took to put a foreigner – and an unknown one at that – at the helm of such a high-profile project. She poured millions – and I mean millions – into the country's cultural life. And for what? She was vilified, attacked and betrayed on all sides.'

'Is it any wonder? While she was pouring millions into dance or whatever, half the population was starving.'

'Who was it said that Man cannot live by bread alone? Don't answer! I grant that Imelda had her faults. She could be petty and erratic and self-deluding. She was so desperate to be seen as sophisticated that she started a rumour that she was a lesbian. And yet... and yet she had courage and style and imagination. She put the Philippines on the map. The one thing no one can deny is that Manila's a far less exciting place to live than it was in her day.'

'So have you never thought of coming home?' Philip asked.

'To Mr and Mrs Bradshaw, RIP? No, thank you. This is my home. Besides I don't have the proverbial pot to piss in.' Ray laughed. 'Imelda gave me this flat for life. If I went back to England, I couldn't afford the rent on a bedsit in Bexhill-on-Sea. Ray, I'll leave you to do the honours while I twiddle some knobs in the kitchen.'

He curtsied and went out. Philip lingered beside the sofa until, sensing that Ray was poised to pounce, he moved to the wall, taking a sudden interest in the dancers' photographs. He speculated on what Max must have said for Ray to subject him to this absurd and, frankly, offensive charade. Did he try it on with every young man he met or had he singled him out for special treatment? And if so, why? Did sandy hair, green eyes and broad shoulders send a specific message to Filipinos, or did Ray take the arcane view that every ex-public schoolboy was gay?

'Are you all right?' Ray asked, as Philip inadvertently growled.

'Fine, thank you. The drink was a little strong.'

'Max is too generous. He wants us to have fun. He forgets that we are not all such lusciouses as him. You must come to have your meals at my house. My wife and my sons will be delighted to welcome you.'

'You're married?' Philip asked, stifling his surprise.

'Thirty-six years. We have three sons and one girl. One of my sons went to Princeton University and now he is making law in America. The other two are in Manila and have big business. I am a very proud father.'

The doorbell rang, cutting through Ray's chatter and Philip's confusion.

'I'll go,' Max called from the kitchen.

'It will be Dennis,' Ray said. 'Such a naughty boy to keep us waiting.'

'What does Dennis do?' Philip asked quickly. 'Max was a little cagey.'

'He is number one dancer. Max says that, the first time he saw him, he was swept off his knees.'

Philip smiled at the mangled idiom as Max entered with a tall, muscular young man in a baseball cap, blue jeans and classic red Coca-Cola T-shirt of the kind that Philip and his university friends had ironised into Cocaine. 'Philip, this is Dennis.'

'Philip Seward, good to meet you,' Philip said, holding out his right hand, which hung lamely in the air.

'Your face!' Ray shrieked. 'Dennis, what have you done to your face?' He fanned himself in horror.

'I am robbed; I am cheated; I am betrayed!' Dennis exclaimed, with an extravagance to match Ray's fanning. 'Angel Placenta cream. It promises top-notch results in twenty-eight days, or else full money is coming back. And look, this is Dennis after less than one whole week!'

Philip gazed at his blotchy red forehead and peeling cheeks. 'Angel Placenta?' he asked Max.

'Skin whitening,' he replied. 'It makes you weep. All those beautiful bronze boys whose greatest desire is to look as washed-out and pasty as us.'

'I go back to Quiapo. I tell this man – this thief – I will be cutting off his dick – if he has one – and feed it to my dog.'

'If you had one,' Max muttered.

'He shows me box and says "Here is written: *Do not go out in sun for one week.* Have you done this?" I tell him I do not go out to beach, right? I do not lie by swimming pool with sexy girls. But is February; is sun. Will I walk in street with bag on top of my head? And he tells me "yes". Just like this. "Yes." And I spit. I spit on floor and inside heart.'

'Don't panic,' Max said. 'It's not permanent. A couple of weeks and you'll be right as rain.'

'How am I to do work? How am I to do show? How am I to pay for bed?'

'Well, as to that, I told you about Philip.'

'This afternoon I give massage to rich *kano*. He is telling me I have sickness. Me, Dennis! Feel!' He flexed his biceps, at which Ray shot out his hand. 'No, you!' He turned to Philip, who tentatively patted the muscle. 'Are you wishing for boy?'

'No!' Philip replied, taken aback. 'Strictly a ladies' man.'

'I am best masseur in Manila. I have testaments from many world-famous persons. Ask them,' Dennis said, pointing to Ray.

'But I thought you were a dancer.'

'Of course I am dancer. First am I dancing and then I am giving massage.'

'Dennis is a big star at the Mr Universe club,' Ray said.

'You're a go-go dancer?' Philip asked incredulously.

'I am macho dancer,' Dennis said, as though refuting a slur.

'Dennis is also running messages sometimes for my sons,' Ray said, giving his arm an approving squeeze, which Dennis shrugged off, albeit mildly enough to keep his options open.

'Grub's up!' Max said, wheeling in a trolley. 'Sausage and mash, to remind Philip of home.'

The school-dinner menu made the meal even more incongruous. In-between mouthfuls, Philip recounted his mission to Ray and Dennis, the former reflecting on the contrast between the multitude of Christian saints and the handful of Immortals in his own tradition of Taoism, while the latter reserved his interest for Julian's murder charge.

Conversation was interrupted by a robotic announcement: 'Will the owner of the black BMW please proceed to the lobby.' Philip started as Dennis pulled out his mobile phone.

'You see, I am best driver in Manila.' He glanced at the number. 'Business!' He turned to Max. 'I take this in bedroom.'

His familiarity with the flat confirmed Philip's suspicions about his relationship with its owner. Ray's account of their first encounter now sounded all too precise.

'So what do you think of him?' Max asked, as Dennis went out.

'You didn't mention that he was a gay go-go dancer.'

'He's not.'

'All right, a dancer who go-goes with gays.'

'Of course, if you feel threatened.'

'I don't! As long as he's up to the job, the rest of his life's no concern of mine.'

'You won't regret it, and the moment you do, he's out on his ear.'

Dennis returned, greeting the news of his engagement with a shrug, as if the slightest expression of gratitude might be seen as weakness.

'Now I am leaving,' he said. 'I have business.'

'What business?' Max asked.

'Just business. You will text me soon, yes?' he asked Philip.

'I'll get your number from Max.'

'I will show you to my sister.'

'I'm sorry? Why?'

'You are saying you do not like boys.'

'I know but – '

'Then you will be liking her. She is much like me, but more good and not so smart.'

'I'm here to work,' Philip said, scenting danger.

'Of course you have work. All people who come to Manila have work, but I also bring them to have good time. I am best guide in Manila; I am best driver; I am best bodyguard. All famous persons, they come to Manila and ask for Dennis.'

'Really?'

'I can see you are famous person too.'

'Thank you.'

'And how am I seeing this? Because you ask for Dennis.'

Grinning triumphantly, Dennis went out, leaving Philip in two minds about having hired him. It was true that he would profit from Dennis's native cunning and gain a greater insight into Filipino life than he would from Max; nevertheless, he would need to remain constantly wary of a man who would not scruple to take advantage of him and anyone else with whom he came into contact. It was clear that, no matter how much at odds they might be elsewhere, Max and Dennis were as one in their belief that they could manipulate the callow Englishman. It would be both a duty and a pleasure to prove them wrong.

Three

17 November 1972

My dear Mother and Father,

As you see, I'm writing this myself, so you can stop worrying. Three weeks of bed rest in Baguio and I'm as right as rain. I was under sisters' orders which, believe me, are far stricter than doctor's. I now have an inkling of what Agnes and Cora went through at school. No books meant no books. Not even the Bible slipped under their radar, although they took it in turns to read psalms to me in the afternoon. I wasn't allowed visitors, cigarettes or a radio, and Lights Out was at seven. I've warned them that I'll have my revenge when I come back to hear their confessions; they'll be working off the Hail Marys for the next twenty years. 'It'll be worth it, Father,' the Mother Superior said, 'to know that you're fully recovered.' They're wonderful women and I'm for ever in their debt.

It takes a serious illness to make a priest stop and pause. I spend so much time ministering to the sick and the dying that it's easy to suppose myself indestructible. Then one insect bite and wham, my head's cracking, my chest's crimson and my joints feel as if they've been set alight. On the positive side, I was deeply touched by the parish's concern. From now on, whenever I feel daunted by my own inadequacy or by the casual cruelty of everyday life, I'll look back on the constant stream of well-wishers, some of whom walked thirty miles or more to see me, bringing food that they could ill spare but which it would have been the gravest insult to refuse. Even the *baylan* came – she's the local wise woman (think a Philippine Miss Thurrock in a white wrap and armlets). Staying safely outside the gate, she handed Consolacion a green paste made of powdered larvae and palm oil which she swore, if rubbed on my chest, would cure me at once. Dismissing Consolacion's protests, I insisted that she threw it out, although I suspect that she's kept it for her own use.

I begged the Regional not to bother you, but he said that he had no choice. He told me that Greg had offered to fly out at a moment's notice. That was decent of him. I know we've had our differences but, to me, he's still the twelve-year-old boy whom Nanny sent to bed in onion-filled socks when he had flu and who's not eaten an onion since, rather than the junior Home Office minister. As soon as I'm feeling 100 percent – and not just the current 97.5 – I'll write to thank him. With my convalescent scrawl even harder to decipher than usual, it's unfair to inflict it on anyone but you (I mean that as a compliment). On which note and in belated answer to your query, Mother: yes, it is BAT I've been eating. Please don't think that I'm piling on the agony, let alone trying to outdo John the Baptist with his locusts – which, incidentally, are regarded as a delicacy in some parts of Luzon – but bat is a much undervalued source of protein. Besides, after Great-Uncle Lennox, it ill behoves a member of the Tremayne family to cast aspersions on anyone else's diet.

I'm back in harness, although not in cassock. I've made use of my enforced break to bring in a change that I'd long been contemplating. In a bid to remove the barriers between priest and people, I've resolved that, except in church, I shall wear the same clothes that they do… well maybe not nylon shorts and flip-flops, but something casual. The move hasn't been universally welcomed. Some of the *haciendos* prefer their priests in skirts (not least symbolically), but they're in a minority. I suspect it may be one that includes you (I remember how Father harrumphed when nuns first exposed their shins), nevertheless I'd be most grateful if you'd send me half a dozen shirts (white, short-sleeved, 15½ collar) and grey or beige cotton shorts (32 waist – don't worry, I've only lost a couple of inches). It may comfort you to know that, even with Consolacion's dedicated ministrations, the cassock was getting very stained – and not just from sweat. One of their more arcane superstitions is that, if a baby urinates on someone who's holding him, they'll bond for life. I've lost count of the number of mothers who've handed me their leaky children. I'm thinking of putting up a sign, along with 'Please don't play ball games in the churchyard', 'Please don't pee on the priest'.

As if infant incontinence weren't enough, we now have a dog. I've no idea what breed he is. There's a hint of Golden Retriever and another of German Shepherd, but the rest is anyone's guess. I bought him in Baguio where he was one of sixty puppies cooped up like battery chickens and destined, I fear, for a similar fate. And no, I wasn't being the dewy-eyed Englishman; I can't spare the time for animal rights when there's so much to do for humans. I'd just been given the all clear by the doc and was taking my first steps outside the convent when I heard a furious barking. I wouldn't be my sister's brother if I'd passed by on the other side. Moreover, I wanted to celebrate my good news. I'd have liked to buy the whole pack, but I'm running a parish not a kennel. So I chose one at random. Not that Grump has shown his appreciation. Two chewed sandals, one upturned rice jar and countless soiled floors later, and I suspect that Consolacion would be happy to casserole him herself. We had the 'either he goes or I go' conversation the day I brought him home, although neither of us took it seriously. I promised that I'd be the one to clear up his mess but, the moment I pick up a cloth, she prises it from my hands (I'm not sure whether she considers it beneath my dignity or enjoys the sense of martyrdom). She vehemently refuses to buy dog food, which is understandable from someone who had to feed her children on scraps. Instead she gives him leftovers, including bat bones, which splinter just as easily as chicken's, but when I pointed out the danger she laughed. Either dogs here have developed cast-iron stomachs, or else canine life, like its human counterpart, is cheap.

In other news, the big story is that President Marcos has imposed Martial Law which, although it sounds frightening, is much like Mr Heath's State of Emergency, only with guns. Of course there are dangers in awarding the government additional powers, but the overwhelming consensus among people of all sorts is that it's a crucial step towards healing the nation's ills. Indeed, I'm told that behind the scenes it was a prerequisite for obtaining further foreign aid. City dwellers will benefit from the crackdown on weapons, drugs and pornography (my visit to Hendrik in Cabanatuan was an eye-opener), while in the country we've been promised radical land reform. As you'll have gathered from my previous letters, farmers here have a raw deal. They do all the work and then the landlords take half the profits – more if you count the high interest they charge on loans for hospital fees, building repairs and even emergency grain. If the proposed changes go ahead, and it's a big if since legislation here is often shelved, tenants will enjoy a far greater measure of independence, paying a fair rent and reaping the rewards of their labour.

It's an irony you may or may not relish, Father, but I've become as intimately involved in land management as if I'd stayed on the estate. I suspect, however, that conditions here are more like those in the time of your great-great grandfather than anything to be found at Whitlock today. The farmers have a sense of indebtedness that goes way beyond indenture. They feel an almost mystical bond to the *haciendos* who, more often than not, are either their or their children's godfathers. I wince every time that I see don Florante Pineda or don Bernardo Arriola standing at the font. The relationship is far too Sicilian for my liking. The godfathers pay the expenses of the baptisms just as they later do of the funerals of children (so many of the funerals I conduct are of children) who die as a direct result of policies that they themselves have put in place.

Their loyal tenants, however, see it differently. All their criticisms and complaints are levelled at the managers, for whom I've gained increasing sympathy. They're the ones on the spot, while the *haciendos* are carousing in Manila and their wives are on shopping sprees in Hong Kong. Take the Romualdez family, the third of our large landowners and the ones with whom I'm least acquainted, since they're so seldom here. I can't tell you how often I've heard people say: 'If only don Enrico knew how the *encargado* treats us.' Well, last week he had a chance to find out, when he paid a rare visit to the estate. Although I was still recuperating, I drove out to watch his semi-regal progress in a carriage drawn by two carabaos and garlanded with sampaguitas, the sweet-scented national flower. He sat next to his wife, doña Teresa, a plain woman wearing her trademark black, and opposite his children, Regina, as brightly dressed as her mother was sombre, and Joey, who exuded an air of scornful indolence, which he had no doubt practised at Harvard. The entire *hacienda* had turned out to line the route. Joey winced at every jolt of the carriage; Regina simpered beneath her sunshade; doña Teresa waved modestly; and don Enrico threw sweets to the children, who darted dangerously close to the wheels. At the compound gate he announced, to tumultuous applause, that there would be free beer for everyone. Four of his lackeys carried out a dozen crates and the crowd toasted their beneficent landlord. Within an hour, all their grievances had been forgotten. No wonder cynics claim that San Miguel should be the country's patron saint.

Two days later I received a visit from doña Teresa who, having heard of my fever, gave me a statuette of Our Lady she'd bought on a recent pilgrimage to Medjugorje. While Consolacion, whose esteem for doña Teresa's piety seems to stem entirely from her wardrobe, served iced tea and caramelised plantain, I took the opportunity to ask a favour for one of my parishioners, Leonora Veloso. Leonora is a seamstress, a spinster in her forties, much like Mrs Henshaw's niece – was it Jean or Joan? – anyway, the one whom Cora accused of sewing secret codes into her skirts. Her brother was killed on a building site in Baguio and his wife died shortly afterwards of a haemorrhage (I've heard rumours of a botched abortion, but Father Teodoro must have discounted them since he buried her in hallowed ground). The couple's four children were orphaned and Leonora took them in, even though she can barely support herself. On the one hand, she embodies the practical compassion that the Church enjoins on us all; on the other, as she freely admits, she's acting out of duty rather than love. The children are fed and clothed, but they're also berated and beaten. Consolacion, who is my eyes and ears in the parish, told me that, while I was ill, the neighbours regularly heard their screams. I'm afraid that one day Leonora will snap and then... you can fill in the rest. So I asked doña Teresa if she might be able to find a job for Girlie (my predecessor was inclined to be lax at the font), the eldest niece, who's twelve years old.

Doña Teresa offered to take her on as a maid, 'out of respect for you, Father', which isn't quite the motivation that I'd have wished. Nor do I feel altogether happy about finding jobs for children, especially as servants, but I have to be practical. This is a world without safety nets. Maybe Greg's right and Britain renounced its sense of personal responsibility when we brought in the Welfare State; but we gained far more than we lost. The next time he jumps on his soap box to denounce nannyism (not that I recall him objecting when Nanny P pandered to his every need), you might care to tell him about Leonora or, better yet, Ariel and Grace Quebral, whose four-year-old son, Joel, was suddenly stricken with diarrhoea. Diarrhoea here isn't the mild irritation it is at home and, as Joel began to shrink – no, shrivel – before my eyes, I had to prepare his parents for the worst. Which was when Ariel told me that Joel hadn't been baptised. They'd never had sufficient cash to pay for the christening robe and celebration lunch, which are mandatory in *hacienda* culture. So I performed a hurried ceremony in a fetid room a few hours before he died.

Sometimes it's hard not to despair.

Consolacion took Joel's death especially hard but, when I questioned her, all she would say was '*Kagustuhan ng Diyos*' ('It's God's will'). '*Kagustuhan ng Diyos!*' Is it the Church that's bred this fatalism? I'm starting to think that we could learn from the

Protestants with their history of revolt. Maybe the Basic Christian Communities (BCCs) will be a spur for action? They've come on by leaps and bounds, and we now have more than eighty across the two parishes. Our aim is for about twice that number. We finished training the lay leaders in August and, although we had eleven dropouts, which upset me more than it did Benito, our remaining choices have been vindicated. We couldn't have wished for a more dedicated team. The sessions were intense. We held twelve residential weekends when, with the help of three priests from the diocese plus the Sisters of the Holy Face of Jesus, we encouraged the men to examine both their own communities in the light of the gospel and the gospel in the light of their own communities. It was a revelation to me too. Through all my years of study, I'd never realised that the Bible was so politically charged.

No doubt you'll echo Benito's view of my naïveté. He even called me Father Oxford until I explained that, however kindly meant, it stung. I presume that he pictured an ink-stained scholar in mortar board and gown, mulling over the minutiae of Greek and Latin translations. Little does he know! For the first time in my life I'm beginning to understand the Bible, and it's precisely because I'm not agonising over the historiography and exegesis but rather looking at it through the lens of the lay leaders' lives. It may sound glib, but they teach me far more than I do them. Every Friday evening, a hundred or so men pour into the *poblacion* from the outlying *barrios*. We study and debate the weekly readings – sometimes quite heatedly. Then, fully primed and taking their share of the Host, they return home to lead their Sunday services. Thus people, who were long deprived of the Word of God and the Body of Christ, now have regular access to both. What's more, we've shown them that they needn't be passive recipients of everything the authorities – that includes priests as well as landowners and politicians – dole out, but they can take decisions for themselves. I'm proud of us – yes, I say that without boasting; I can think of no other group who'd so readily relinquish their own power.

But you needn't take my word for it; I'm hoping you'll soon have a chance to see for yourselves. Have you given any more thought to a visit? The flight's long, I admit, but you could stop over for a day or two in Singapore – or would that bring back too many memories for Father? Please don't let all my horror stories scare you off. There's some spectacular scenery, such as the 2,000-year-old rice terraces, which are only a few hours' drive away. Accommodation in the parish may be basic (although I'm sure that the Pinedas or the Arriolas would be happy to put you up), but the hotels in Manila are excellent. As for food, I guarantee that the bats and locusts will be confined to the cellars. Joke! The moment I know that you're coming, I'll shave off my beard so you won't need to disown me. Truth to tell, I was a little hurt when Greg wrote that you were spending New Year with Alice's parents. I can promise you that our seas are just as blue and our beaches as golden as any in St Bart's. Plus, the people are a lot less pompous than the Leveringtons, but I won't go into that. I treasure your letters, both Mother's chatty and Father's concise ones (that's a hint that you're allowed to write on both sides of the page), but they're no substitute for seeing you face to face.

On the subject of letters, I should warn you to avoid anything intimate. I've been reluctant to say so before because I'd hate to inhibit you, let alone deter you from writing at all, but letters here are opened – not clandestinely steamed but blatantly slit. At first I blamed it on the censors, but I soon learnt that news is regarded as communal and, when the mail is delivered every Wednesday (to the town hall, not to the door), it's almost a case of first come first served. They're inveterate gossips with as detailed a knowledge of bloodlines as the most ardent devotee of *Debrett's*. Having exhausted their own family's news, they turn to their neighbours'. It's quite harmless but there are things, about Cora for instance, which you mightn't wish to share with the world. It'll sound far-fetched, but it's possible that some titbit will be passed to another priest and then to Manila, where it'll reach the ears of the Regional who'll report it back to his aunt in Cheltenham and, hey presto, it's all over Catholic England.

One last request if I may: I know you're proud of our ancestry, Father, and rightly so, but I'd rather you didn't put 'the Hon' on the envelope. People here, who know no better, assume that I must be related to the Royal Family or, at the very least, heir to an ancient dukedom. Which is exactly the sort of nonsense I'm trying to escape. Plain Father is enough.

Your loving son,
Julian

No twenty-first-century tourist entering Intramuros could be in any doubt as to the enduring legacy of colonial power. The grey stone walls that had once marked the confines within which only Europeans were permitted to live might now be crumbling and dotted with Buddha belly bamboo; the conquistadores and courtiers might long since have returned to Spain; but the wooden relief of St James trampling four Moors underfoot, which adorned the main gateway, attested to the abiding influence of the Catholic Church. In its heyday, Intramuros, the city within walls, which the Spanish with supreme arrogance defined as the city itself, had been home to one cathedral, twelve churches, several monasteries, convents and church schools. It now housed the Catholic Bishops Conference of the Philippines building, where Philip was due to meet the Vicar General of Baguio at three o'clock, an appointment for which, as usual, he had arrived early.

Afraid that his undue punctuality betrayed a deep lack of confidence or, worse, a desperate desire to please, he envied those who could turn – no, roll – up for meetings at the last minute, but whenever he tried, even for meals with his mother or godmother, it reduced him to panic. So, finding himself with an hour to spare, he asked the taxi driver to drop him in front of San Agustin, the oldest surviving church in the city, which he had been planning to visit. It presented an unusual picture: the lopsided pink façade flaunting its truncated tower like a beggar's stump, as if the building itself were soliciting alms. Four Chinese fu dogs guarded the entrance, which he welcomed as a corrective to the triumphalist tableau of St James, until a glance at his guidebook revealed that they had been placed there in memory of the Chinese workmen who had died during the church's construction. He made his way inside where, once his eyes had adjusted to the shadows, he was enchanted by the *trompe l'oeil* frescoes. He stood in the transept, gazing up at the intricate pattern of columns and vaults, and wondered how far the painterly deception on the dome reflected a priestly deception about what lay beyond.

He continued to explore, losing track of the time, until the hourly carillon brought him up short. He hurried down the nave, past a group of elderly tourists who were blithely ignoring the No Flash notice, pulled open the door and ran across the square to the CBCP building, its initials reassuringly emblazoned on the front, although its entrance turned out to be 200 yards down a side street. His horror at the unsightly air-conditioning units protruding from every window changed to gratitude when he stepped into the foyer and the sweat trickling down his arms began to freeze. As he took a seat and waited for the Vicar General, he peered at the security guard who had waved him through with culpable laxity. Did he go further than Dennis in seeing a white skin as a mark, not just of attraction but of virtue, or did he assume, more cynically, that it would stick to white-collar crime?

Lost in contemplation, Philip was caught unawares when the Vicar General, a small, balding man, whose rimless glasses matched his thin lips, walked over to introduce himself. After enthusiastically shaking hands (and then discreetly wiping his own on his cassock), the Vicar General led him upstairs to a meeting room where he sealed his welcome with a cup of English Breakfast tea. Philip, loath to be thought insular, was relieved to find that it was his host who was the Anglophile, his vowels growing ever more refined as he reminisced euphorically about his six-month-long placement in a seminary outside Guildford. Philip, not to be outdone, voiced his admiration for the Philippines, while admitting that he had yet to venture beyond the centre of Manila.

'We are a poor country, Mr Seward,' the Vicar General replied, 'you must take us as you find us.' He handed him a plate of crackers. 'They are not like your English squashed fly biscuits,' he said sadly. Then he sat down, added three spoonfuls of sugar to his cup and fastidiously smoothed his cassock over his knees. Philip was startled to see that his socks were the same deep purple as his sash.

'How are my good friends, Hugh and the Honourable Isabel Olliphant?' the Vicar General asked.

'I didn't know you knew them,' Philip replied, feeling strangely threatened by the connection.

'I have met Hugh many times when he has visited his mines in the Cordilleras. I have met the Honourable Isabel only once, when I was staying in Guildford. Hugh is a great champion of our people – and of our art. But for all that, I'm afraid that he doesn't trust us. Why else has he sent you?'

'I'm sure it's not a lack of trust.' Philip squirmed as though the charge had been levelled at him. 'More like a lack of patience. Hugh is an "I want it done yesterday" sort of guy – man, whereas people here are much more laid back.'

'What does he expect from us? The Bishop, as you are aware, has authorised an investigation into Father Julian's sanctity. This will not be reporting overnight.'

'No, of course not. But, knowing how hard pressed you are, Hugh (not that I can speak for him) felt that you'd welcome another pair of hands. And here they are.' He held them up self-consciously.

'I assure you that we too are eager for the canonisation to take place. We have 75 million Catholics in the Philippines and only one saint. San Lorenzo Ruiz.'

'Yes. Julian wrote of attending his beatification ceremony when Pope John Paul II came to Manila.'

'It would be a great blessing for us to have another saint. Not a Filipino by birth of course, but the next best thing. An honorary one, if I may make the claim.'

'He certainly felt more at home here than anywhere else. He identified deeply with the Filipino people, especially the peasants. He led his parishioners in their struggle against oppression.'

'Like any other candidate for sainthood, Father Julian has to exhibit four virtues of a holy life. Poverty, chastity, obedience – '

'And zeal for the Church. Yes, Isabel explained. I bear them constantly in mind.'

'Then you'll be aware that nowhere among them is there any mention of political action, no matter how righteous the cause.'

'Surely that depends how you define zeal for the Church?' Philip replied, pleasantly surprised by how much he had to contribute. 'Is that zeal for the institution, whether in Rome, London or Manila, or for the message of Christ as delivered in the gospel? Look at Joan of Arc. She had precious little respect for institutions of any sort; she took up arms in a political, not a spiritual, cause; yet she was canonised.'

'True, but she had to wait for almost five hundred years. From what you've said about our friend Hugh's impatience, I'm not sure that she's the best example.' He gave him a thin smile.

'Did you know Julian yourself?' Philip asked, changing tack.

'Unfortunately not. I don't come from these parts. I was born in a fishing village on the island of Palawan and moved to Manila to study. I became a priest in 1988, the year before Father Julian's death. Much has changed since then. We now have many more priests and, of those, many more are native-born Filipinos. We're not so dependent on foreign missionaries as we were in Father Julian's day.'

'There's a Filipino priest whom Julian refers to repeatedly in his letters. Benito… wait, I have it here.' Philip leafed through his notebook. 'Benito Bertubin. He clearly had a profound influence on Julian's thinking, as well as working alongside him and, later, sharing his imprisonment. Unless you have any better ideas, I'd like to start by interviewing him.'

'I wish I could help. We've tried very hard to contact him over the years, but with no success.'

'According to Julian, he went to live on Negros after his

release. So last week I contacted all four dioceses, and the Chancellor of Bacoloid – '

'Bacolod.'

'I'm sorry – told me that he'd returned to Luzon in 1995.'

'Father Benito was a man with many enemies. I fear the worst.'

'If he were dead, surely you'd know? There must be some record.'

'Not necessarily,' the Vicar General stated firmly. 'The Philippines isn't England. A million people leave the provinces each year and move to Manila. Do they all register with their *barangay* captain, let alone the local mayor? No. Thousands simply vanish from sight.'

'But not a priest? Are there no Church archives?'

'If he were there, we would have found him. What you must understand is that the population grew by 25 million during the Marcos years. An unparalleled increase, and at a time when the government machinery was already overstretched. Nevertheless, that 25 million constitutes an extraordinary expression of hope.'

'In what way?' Philip asked, suspicious of the clerical tendency to cast even the most unpalatable facts in a positive light.

'That in their darkest hour, people still felt confident enough to bring new life into the world. They had faith in their future, indeed, faith in their Faith.'

'Some might see it rather as an expression of despair. Mightn't they have wanted – consciously or not – to replace the children whom they were expecting to die of disease, malnutrition and ill-treatment?'

The Vicar General looked at him with narrowed eyes. 'Are you a Catholic, Mr Seward?'

'No. I thought you knew,' Philip replied, flustered. 'I sent the Bishop a letter of introduction from Isabel.'

'She said that you had a family connection. We assumed – '

'I was engaged to her daughter, Julia, who died.'

'Yes of course. A great tragedy. *Kagustuhan ng Diyos.*'

'Thank you,' Philip said tersely.

'But you are an Anglican?'

'Yes, in a high-days-and-holidays sort of way. The last time I attended church regularly was at school. No, I tell a lie; it was in the few months after Julia's death.' His throat suddenly felt dry. 'I've always had a sense of something other – something beyond – although I worry that this may be no more than a refusal to face up to reality. I'm sorry; you must hear this sort of thing all the time.'

'I'm not a Protestant, Mr Seward.' The Vicar General eyed him carefully. 'Why do you think the Olliphants chose you for this job?'

'Apart from the family connection? I suppose they thought I'd bring a useful objectivity.'

'Objectivity is an illusion and never more so than in matters of faith. May I ask you a personal question?'

'Please do,' Philip said apprehensively.

'Did you love your fiancée?'

'Yes. With all my heart.'

'But did you examine that love from every angle? Did you subject it to rigorous analysis? Did you require empirical proof?'

'Put like that, the answer's no. It was far too precious. I'd have been afraid to jinx it.'

'Exactly. You felt it in your innermost being, which was enough. You knew that, as an educated man, you could always find arguments against it and it was far too valuable to put at risk. If that's true of your love for a woman, why shouldn't it be true of your love for God?'

'Impartiality might have been a better word,' Philip replied, deferring to the Vicar General's logic. 'I'm neither an apologist nor a detractor. I've always valued freedom of conscience more than dogma, not least because, if God did make us in His own image, moral discrimination must be one of His greatest gifts. Julian followed his conscience even when it brought him into conflict with the civil and economic and, yes, the religious authorities. That's another thing about him I respect.'

'Which is very admirable and, if I may so, very British but, to speak plainly, our big fear is that, not understanding the way things work here, you may do more harm than good.'

'Believe me, I'm not as green as I look. I really want this investigation to succeed, partly of course for Isabel but also for Julia. Even though she was four when Julian returned here for the final time and had only the haziest memories of him, she always insisted that they enjoyed a special bond. One of her proudest possessions was a photo of herself as a toddler on his knee.'

To his surprise, the Vicar General responded by passing him the plate of crackers. Sampling the eggy taste and floury texture, Philip couldn't help thinking that Isabel and Hugh had missed a trick by failing to send him out with a case of Garibaldis.

'So how have things gone these first ten days?' the Vicar General asked between nibbles. 'What have you discovered that the rest of us have missed?'

'Not much. Not anything, to be honest. The story's as full of holes as if it'd taken place three hundred years ago, not thirty. Julian referred to newspaper reports in two of his letters. Either I've been looking in the wrong place or else they're lost.'

'Many of the papers of the time were no more than cyclo-styled sheets. They lasted a few issues before they were shut down. It would have been dangerous for people to keep copies.'

'Even a library?'

'Most especially a library.'

'I went to the National Census Office in Quezon City and called up his death certificate. Oh, I see! Is that what you mean by not understanding the way things work? Have they made a complaint? I'm sorry. It's just that I'm not used to being given the third degree when I ask for a public document.'

'No, no one has said anything.' The Vicar General looked anxious. 'Unless they went straight to the Archbishop.'

'Not that the certificate was much help. It gave his name and place of death, and put the cause of death as two bullet wounds through the ribcage, adding that the state of the remains prevented more detailed analysis. It was signed by Dr Somebody, the Chief Medical Legal of the National Bureau of Investigation, and Inspector Somebody Else, the Scene of Crime Officer, but there was no mention of the foresters or the policemen and their mysterious experiences.'

'Please, do not worry. Such signs, however gratifying, would carry no weight in the *Positio*. It's the claims of Father Julian's miracles that we must investigate thoroughly,' the Vicar General said, drinking his tea with his little finger cocked, as no doubt mastered in Guildford.

'How many have there been?'

'Four or five, I think, although the number may have grown. There are always those ready to jump on the bandwagon. They may be perfectly innocent, like the farmer who declared that, after two failed harvests, he sprinkled earth from Father Julian's grave on his rice field to produce a bumper crop. Simple people have long confused the caprice of Nature with the hand of God. More often, however, the claimant's motives are base: a bid to court publicity or to extract cash. In that category I am certain that we can place the Ibaloi man who declared that he woke one night to find Father Julian standing over him in combat uniform, holding up two rifles in the shape of a cross.'

'Perhaps he was dreaming?'

'Or drunk,' the Vicar General replied bluntly. 'We have questioned him several times, but he refuses to retract. On the other hand there are two claims worthy of serious attention. One is from a woman with cancer to whom Father Julian appeared in her sleep, telling her to go at once to church and pray through the night to the Holy Mother. Her family tried to dissuade her since she could barely stand, but she defied them and, within three days, her tumour had vanished. The other is from a peasant boy with a withered leg, whose parents took him to pray at Father Julian's grave and, by the next morning, his leg had straightened and he was able to walk.'

'That's amazing. Is there any – forgive the word – *objective* evidence?'

'Both families have made sworn statements, as have several friends, the parish priest, the woman's former employer and various officials. We have before-and-after medical photographs of the neck but none of the leg. The boy's family couldn't afford doctors.'

'But the personal testimony is valid?'

'Most certainly, although it has yet to be confirmed. Some of the boy's neighbours dispute the story.'

'On what grounds?'

'Ignorance and superstition! It pains me to admit it, but some of our more remote villages are rife with pagan practices. At their heart is a wretched creature: an infamous sorceress known as the *baylan*.'

'Yes, Julian mentions her in some of his letters.'

'I would be very interested to see them if you have them here.'

'Of course,' Philip replied, even as a voice in his head counselled caution.

'These credulous people maintain that it wasn't a miracle at all but that the boy's family had offended the *baylan* who, in revenge, put a curse on his leg. Once they'd paid a forfeit, she lifted it.'

'Fascinating!'

'Really?' The Vicar General frowned.

'I mean as a piece of folklore.'

'Now perhaps you understand why the process cannot be rushed. Each of these claims has to be scrupulously investigated and then, if the evidence seems sufficiently strong to us, it will be sent to Rome where it will be further examined by a panel of seven doctors, nine theologians and fifteen cardinals and bishops.'

'Impressive,' Philip said, although he would have preferred a medical majority.

'While we will do everything we can to gain recognition of our new saint, our first concern as always must be to prevent the Church from falling into disrepute. We have already seen signs of a cult growing around Father Julian, something that is expressly forbidden before he is declared *Blessed*. Various domestic items preserved by his housekeeper have been removed and venerated as relics. The current priest at San Isidro has had to give up the traditional Lenten and Easter vestments after someone cut threads from the chasubles. Most troubling of all is the furore surrounding Jejomar Agbuya, who claims to have known Father Julian in prison, although we have no records of their meeting.'

'Unsurprisingly,' Philip said, tempering his interjection with a smile.

'In the twenty-five years since then, he has been convicted of several more crimes although, considering their seriousness, not to mention frequency, the ease with which he has obtained release should give cause for concern. He was awaiting trial on a charge of violent robbery when he had a vision – or at least succeeded in convincing both the prison governor and the judge that he had had a vision – of Father Julian, who told him that, if he had himself crucified in Pampanga on Good Friday, then God would forgive him his sins and the court would show him clemency.'

'I've heard about those crucifixions. Aren't they the ones that use actual nails?'

'Unfortunately, yes.' The Vicar General reddened, as if acknowledging a family failing.

'I should like to see them.'

'No doubt. They now market them as a tourist attraction.'

'I meant that it might be useful for our purposes,' Philip replied, blushing in his turn.

'Why? Such sideshows bring shame on our faith and our country. The flagellants who parade through the streets, blood streaming down their backs, are the dregs of society: drunks, drug addicts and petty criminals who suppose that if they share Our Lord's suffering one day a year they are free to add to it during the remaining three hundred and sixty-four. It is through abstinence and prayer, remembrance and alms-giving, that we honour His sacrifice, not through vain display.'

'I quite agree, but given that I'm here and that Good Friday's only a month away, it would be a missed opportunity – even a dereliction of duty – not to witness it for myself. If Julian does effect a change in this man, surely it'll be just as great a miracle as any of the physical healings?'

'But not, I am afraid, one that will carry such weight in Rome. Nevertheless, you must do as you think fit, provided you do nothing to hinder – let alone jeopardise – the official investigation. For my part, I shall ask my secretary to send you a list of people you might wish to meet in the parish. But remember, please, that the Church is all that many of them have. It was Europeans who brought the faith to these islands. It would be doubly cruel if you should now be the ones to take it away.'

After a few strained pleasantries, the Vicar General showed Philip out. With time to spare before meeting Dennis, he strolled through the cathedral square until, overcome by the heat, he accepted a ride from the pedicab driver who was trailing him, pinging his bell as much to ward off competition as to announce his services. He squeezed into the cab, hugging his knees, as they headed out of the walled city and towards the Pasig river.

The sunlit sheen of the shanty-town roofs was reflected in the turbid waters, as they crossed the Quezon suspension bridge and entered Quiapo. The occasional glimpse of a carved wooden doorway, wrought-iron balcony, baroque cupola or art deco façade among the rows of post-war apartment blocks, was a reminder of the city's eclectic past. With traffic stalled at a crossroads, the intrepid pedicab driver took to the gutter, skirting – sometimes scraping – the kerb, leaving Philip clinging to the roof at an angle of forty-five degrees. After ten days in Manila, he had grown accustomed to the incessant hooting, which was used, not to signal intent or even frustration, but as a basic means of self-expression: an 'X marks the spot' in a gridlocked world. Street children, standing on a weed-ridden verge, clambered down at the sight of a stationary Coca-Cola van and, in full view of the waiting motorists, tried to snap off its padlock with a stone. No one stirred and even the driver barely roused himself, waving them away as languorously as a hippopotamus wafting tick birds with its tail. The children scampered off, turning their attention to the pedicab, whose driver, determined to protect his fare, picked up a stick and, deaf to Philip's protests, lashed out at them before gathering speed, leaving several bruised, impassive faces in his wake.

Philip's spirits rose as they entered Chinatown. Images of dragons abounded: some on arches; some on shop fronts; some on balloons and soft toys; and one, disconcertingly, on the side of a parked fire engine, spewing an ornate gust of yellow flames across the purple paintwork. A rich assortment of smells assailed him: pungent spices; roasting flesh; sweetly soporific incense, even before he had identified the stalls, restaurants and shrines from which they emanated. A succession of jewellers' windows was filled with glittering chains, brooches and pendants. He longed to explore, abandoning the bumping, jolting pedicab for one of the horse-drawn carriages favoured by his fellow tourists, but he had arranged to meet Dennis on Recto Avenue at five and, as ever, he was eager not to be late.

Dennis's instructions had not inspired confidence. Explaining that the properties were unnumbered, he had told Philip to meet him outside the pizza parlour next to the pawn shop between Legarda and Loyola Streets. Even so, when the pedicab driver deposited him on the kerb in front of a row of seedy-looking shops where all the merchandise, whether books, DVD players, computer monitors or jeans, was piled higgledy-piggledy in windows smeared with dust as thick as frost, Philip was convinced that he must have made a mistake.

'Is no mistake. Is address. Is 250 pesos,' the driver said. Philip, still dubious, held out a 500-pesos note.

'No change.'

'You had change when we set out. I told you that I only had a few coins and a 500-pesos note.'

'Change then. No change now.'

'But we didn't stop anywhere en route!'

'No understand. No change. 250 pesos.'

Philip, aware that they were attracting an audience, and one more likely to side with the obdurate driver than the cheated tourist, handed over the cash. Feeling ever more vulnerable, he walked up and down the block, observing the electronics shop boasting *Not-To-Be-Missed Bargains* in lurid lettering that was either askew or incomplete, the bodybuilding gym, whose members flaunted themselves in the window as blatantly as the mannequins in the lingerie shop next door, the *One-Stop Pawn Shop and Lending Investor*, and the run-down hotel offering *Rooms for rent: three hours minimum*. He was astounded by the stationers openly advertising school identity cards, diplomas, ATM cards, social security cards and a whole range of numbered forms that presumably related to different aspects of government bureaucracy. It was as if everything in Manila were fake, from these certificates through the Prada belts, Ralph Lauren T-shirts and Armani perfumes hawked for a few pesos in the malls, to the pretty girls he had been warned against in Brian's guidebook. Would the same hold true of its miracles and even its saints?

He dismissed the question and turned back to the windows, trying to make sense of the *Bed Space (Aircon and Non-aircon available)*, that was ubiquitously on offer, when a tap on his shoulder made him first jump and then scowl.

'What on earth have you been doing? Do you have any idea of the time?' he asked Dennis.

'Business,' Dennis replied, as enigmatically as ever. 'I have many pans on fire.'

'We had an appointment for five. What's the time now?' Philip pressed his wrist in Dennis's face.

'I cannot read watch. Time too small.'

'No, time too late. Five thirty-seven. Is there any reason?'

'Business,' Dennis repeated sullenly.

'Well, now that you've finally arrived, do you mean to hang about in the street or are we going back to your flat?'

'I have no flat. I have no room. I have bed. I take you there; others kill you. Maybe I do.'

'So why bring me all the way out here?' Philip asked, chastened less by the threat of violence than by the wretchedness of Dennis's life.

'This is where we must meet. We go now to sister. We take jeep.'

He led the way to the jeepney stop which, in the absence of any sign, was reassuringly busy. Each jeepney had not only its designated route but also its unique name and decoration. On current form, these were evenly divided between the sacred and profane. Philip was disappointed to find that *God is Almighty*, *Amazing Grace*, *Jesus Christ the Lord* and *Christian Joy* were not heading in their direction. *Playgirl*, which was, was full to bursting. They finally found room in *Rambo*, which shot off at lightning speed. Clutching at the overhead rail as he lurched on the hard metal seat, Philip looked fondly at *Guardian Angel* in the adjacent lane.

'Put down your hand from window!' Dennis said. 'When we are stopping, kids will climb up and break wrist to steal watch.'

'Come on! I wasn't born yesterday.'

'Is true! Last week, this friend of me, she has earrings. They are grabbing back her head to pull them off. She is nearly breaking neck.'

Despite his scepticism, Philip removed his hand and kept it firmly in his lap for the remainder of the ride. They alighted as abruptly as they had boarded, the driver dropping them off at a corner, where Philip was almost run over by a motorcyclist whose tiny son sat behind him, clinging to his back like a koala cub.

'From now on we'll stick to taxis,' Philip said, wiping his face with a handkerchief, which rapidly turned black. Dennis led him down a side street that was full of restaurants. They stopped at a large blue-and-white sign inscribed *Kamayan*.

'Is here we must meet sister.'

'Sure. But don't forget that we must also plan our trip to Benguet. I spent the morning with the Vicar General, who's sending me a list of people to interview.'

'Sister is working very hard. Today she has afternoon off. You must not be boring to her.'

'I'll do my best, but you're not the only one with business.'

'You are sad English. I am sorry for you.'

'Why?'

Disdaining to reply, Dennis marched into the restaurant. Philip followed in exasperation. For days he had wanted to discuss arrangements, but Dennis had plied him with excuses that would have tried the patience of a saint, and Philip was not Julian. Now he was fobbing him off with his sister – that is, if she really were his sister and not some bar girl he was seeking to pimp. As soon as Philip saw her, however, his suspicions vanished. He knew better than to pin his faith on looks, but no one with such a candid smile and modest demeanour could be an imposter. Dennis introduced her simply as 'my sister', which she elaborated to 'Maribel May Santos'.

'That's a lovely name,' Philip replied, trusting that the compliment was sufficiently anodyne. Blushing, she lowered her gaze. He hovered awkwardly while Dennis grabbed the empty chair next to her, leaving him to sit at the opposite side of the table, a perfect vantage point from which to study her. Her *café crème* complexion was enhanced by a hint of make-up on her eyelids and cheeks, giving her the delicate charm of a hand-tinted postcard. She wore a purple peony in her chignon, and he wondered whether it was for his benefit or the usual accoutrement of an afternoon off. He glanced from Maribel to Dennis in search of a family likeness but acknowledged, to his shame, that he still could not see beyond skin tone. Such resemblance as he detected was largely vocal. She had the same light timbre and lilting vowels as Dennis, although they suited her better. For the first time in Manila, Philip found himself talking to someone without feeling either compromised or sullied. He pulled out his handkerchief to wipe his forehead and promptly put it away.

'Now we must eat food,' Dennis said, picking up a menu. Philip was distracted by the sight of his fingernails, their spectacularly full moons eclipsing his own faint crescents. 'I am so hungry, I can eat a whore.' Maribel screwed up her nose. 'Why must you look at me like this? Is good English words. Ask him.'

'The standard phrase is "eat a horse".'

'I am killing Max. He is telling me this to make everyone laughing at me.'

"With you, not at you. It's our English way of teasing. Have you met Max?' Philip asked Maribel.

'I have had that honour,' she replied. 'He does many kind things for Dennis. You do many kind things for Dennis.'

'But not the same ones,' Philip said, determined to dispel any confusion.

'Do you like being in Manila, Mr Philip, sir?' she asked.

'Oh yes, very much. Right now I can think of nowhere I'd rather be,' he replied, with a sincerity that thrilled him. 'But it's a city that can be hard work for strangers.'

'I know,' she replied.

'Really?' Philip glanced at Dennis, his head buried in the menu. 'I presumed – I've no idea why – that you were both born here.'

'You are very kind,' she said, a smile illuminating her face. 'Our home is in Cauayan, a third-class city in Isabela province. Our mother runs a small medium enterprise, selling snacks. We have our own house with a fridge.' Dennis snapped shut the menu and spoke to her in Tagalog. 'And we have other modern conveniences. In the garden we grow many indigenous plants and vegetables. We have our own palm tree. Every year when we were smalls, Dennis would climb to the top to bring down the coconuts.'

'Why must you say this? You are making him think I am like monkey!'

Dennis's tone made his sister look so crestfallen that Philip wanted to thump him. Maribel, however, responded more temperately. 'You are a monkey,' she said. 'You are a naughty monkey.' Dennis grinned, giving Philip a glimpse of the carefree boy that life in Manila had all but obliterated. The waiter came to take their orders.

'I can eat a horse,' Dennis said pointedly.

'I'll check with the chef, but I think we've run out,' the waiter replied, joining in the joke. Philip, unable to read the menu and refusing Maribel's offer to translate, asked for exactly the same as she did, *rellenong bangus* and *laing sa gata* which, to his relief, turned out to be nothing more exotic than stuffed milk-fish and yam leaves in coconut sauce.

'Don't they bring us any cutlery?' he asked in a bid to distract Dennis, who was looking at him smugly.

'Are you not seeing sign? This is *kamayan* restaurant. Is Tagalog word for Using Hands.'

'Really?' Philip asked, thinking of the coconut sauce.

'My brother is right,' Maribel said, 'but he is also wrong. Of course you will have a spoon and a fork if you wish.'

With a sniff that left no doubt as to his disapproval of such affectations, Dennis took out his phone and began to text, leaving Philip and Maribel to talk. She filled in the family background that Dennis had left blank, with a description of her younger brother and sister, and their father who had left home, breaking off after a reprimand from Dennis.

'So when did you come to Manila?' Philip asked, suddenly conscious of her youth.

'The 17 July 2010,' she replied.

'I am sending her bus money,' Dennis said, while his fingers worked as nimbly as a tailor's.

'Do you live together?' Philip asked, recalling Dennis's shared room.

'Good heavens not!' Maribel replied. 'I live with my aunt. She is very strict.'

'She is not liking me,' Dennis said.

'Naturally she likes you. You are her nephew.'

'She is not letting me come through her door.'

The conversation was interrupted by the arrival of the meal. Dennis tore into his *lechon de leche* but, in spite of the greasy pork crackling and the sticky rice, his fingers remained surprisingly clean. Philip felt infantilised by his spoon.

'This is delicious,' he said, savouring the tender flakes of fish, chopped ham, carrots, peas and raisins, seasoned with lime and pepper and what tasted, improbably, like Worcester sauce.

'It makes me very happy that you like our food,' Maribel said, smiling.

'I like it very much indeed,' Philip replied, an assessment that he was forced to qualify when the waiter brought Dennis his side dish, a plate of barbecued chicken intestines, which looked as if they had been salvaged from a pathology lab.

'Are you a student here?' he asked Maribel.

'Oh no,' she replied, shielding her mouth as she ate. 'I am a fulltime operative of 24:7 *Solutions Incorporated Manila*. Is it familiar to you?'

'How must it be?' Dennis interjected. 'He is Englishman.'

'We are the third largest call centre in Manila, serving all the major cities of the United States of America,' she said proudly. 'There are four hundred seats in our workplace and one hundred applicants for jobs each day.'

'Wow! You must have really impressed them.'

'Is me who is getting this for her,' Dennis said, his mouth full of entrails. 'Is usual you must have three years in college, but I have a friend and we are doing business. So.'

'Dennis is the kindest brother,' Maribel said, giving him a look which in other circumstances Philip would have found touching. 'It was hard for me, but I went on a course and now I have a certificate. I am proficient in English. Would you say I am proficient in English, Mr Philip, sir?'

'I'd say you were very proficient. Proficiency plus.'

'You are making a joke at me.'

'No, I promise.'

'At this moment I work for a bank – US American bank not Filipino bank – but every night I study from books. I learn medicine.'

'Do you want to be a nurse?' Philip asked. 'I mean a doctor?'

'Oh no, I want to be a medical transcriptionist. It is the most desirable job in Manila.'

A request for the owner of the black BMW to proceed to the lobby drew less respectful looks from his fellow diners than its recipient had intended. Dennis muttered a few angry words into his phone before pushing back his chair.

'Don't tell me,' Philip said. 'Business?' Dennis looked at him coldly. 'We've still not made any arrangements for our trip!'

'I am calling you tomorrow. I leave you to be sure sister is going to work for nine o'clock. No monkey business. See, I know my English.' He grinned. 'Is not just Filipinos who are monkeys.' He scraped the remaining offal into his napkin and sauntered out.

'I am worrying very much for Dennis,' Maribel said. 'Sometimes he is angry with the world, but the world is not always being kind to him. When our father left home, he has given up school to help our mother. He read in the paper about many jobs building a palace in Kuwait. My mother did not want him to go, but he would be making very much money, some to send to her and some to put to one side to buy a bakery.'

'As in baking bread?'

'Yes, this is always his dream. You will not know this, but my big hard brother is as soft inside as the dough. He came to Manila with 3,000 pesos he was borrowing from my mother, my uncle, our teacher and our priest, to pay for his passport and his aeroplane. He gave the money to the agent, but when he returned to the office two days afterwards the agent was disappeared and so was the desk and the chairs and the files and the calendar and even the name sign.'

'Didn't he call the police?'

'What would be the use? Everything disappears in Manila: money; rooms; people.'

'So what did he do?'

'He had not even the money to pay for his ticket home, but still he went to the bus station. It was where he was sleeping since he came to the city. And there he met a man who has found him work in a bar.'

'Is it that easy?'

'It is in this kind of bar,' she said, with a new note of bitterness.

'So you know about the Mr Universe?'

'Yes, but I am the only one. My mother thinks that he is working in a restaurant. And he will not go home until he can pay back this money. Sometimes I am fearing that he will not go home at all.'

Maribel started to weep. Philip leant across the table to take her hand, which felt both natural and right. The moment vanished with the return of the waiter, who rattled off the dessert menu with a curtness bordering on contempt. Philip, suspecting that he had broken a taboo by taking her hand in public, released it abruptly, which surprised Maribel but failed to placate the waiter, who grew visibly impatient as she dithered over her choice.

'I have a sweet tooth,' she explained to Philip.

'And a sweet mouth to go with it,' he replied.

They both blushed. The waiter's lower lip curled over his pencil and Philip realised with dismay that his change of attitude was caused by Dennis's departure and by the assumption, all the more painful for echoing his own, that Dennis was pimping Maribel to him. Furious, he longed to break something, if not the man's nose then at least his bright yellow pencil, but he was anxious not to distress Maribel, who seemed oblivious to everything but the food. She finally opted for some preserved jackfruit.

'Make that two,' Philip said.

'Are you sure you do not wish to have some cassava cakes or coconut rice?' Maribel asked in alarm. 'The jackfruit is, how do you say, a bought taste?'

'An acquired taste?'

'Do not bought and acquired mean the same?'

'Often, but not always.'

The waiter hurried away.

'Your English is so hard. I try to make every day improvements and still I make many mistakes. Whenever I am having an afternoon off, I must read an English novel.'

'Do you have any favourites?'

'What I like most of all are sad stories with happy endings.'

'In England we call them romances.'

'I think that I would like an English romance,' she said, so artlessly that Philip was smitten.

The waiter brought the jackfruit and, as he chewed the flesh, which was as tough as a jackboot, Philip realised that he should have heeded Maribel's advice. Nevertheless, an aching jaw was a small discomfort in such captivating company. Listening to her description of her favourite soap opera, in which a mermaid princess was washed ashore where she fell in love with a handsome fisherman, Philip felt himself succumb to a similar enchantment. He was quick to deride his own foolishness. There was no denying her beauty, charm and what he could only describe as natural dignity, but the warmth he felt for her was the same that he felt for the simple innocence of his nieces. He could no more take advantage of her than he could of them – even though Gemma, Catherine and Cristobel were eight, nine and twelve, and Maribel, as he had found to his relief, was nineteen.

On the other hand, unless her artlessness were an act – and one way beyond the skill of any nineteen-year-old he had ever known – she was not wholly indifferent to him. Apart from Dennis's scorn and his own embarrassment, what did he risk by putting it to the test? He had shied away from intimacy for

too long. His few affairs since Julia's death had been so unfulfill-
ing that he had come to believe that his only chance of lasting
happiness had died with her. Friends, for whom bereavement
followed as precise a recovery pattern as flu, accused him of
clinging to his grief in order to avoid dealing with life. Belinda,
who had come closest of anyone to taking Julia's place, claimed
that he had created an image of his perfect fiancée to which no
other woman could measure up. In which case Maribel might
be just what he needed: a holiday romance so far removed from
his everyday world that there could be no comparison with Julia
nor any suggestion of betraying her memory.

All that mattered now was to be sure she felt the same.

'Oh my goodness,' she said, breaking off her story to consult
the fake Rolex dangling from her wrist. 'It is 8.40 p.m. I must be
at my desk at 10 p.m., which is 9 a.m. in New York and Wash-
ington, DC.'

'Shall I order a taxi?'

'Oh no, I will take the bus.'

'Are you sure?' He tried to find a neutral way of offering to pay.

'Very sure. But I would like it if you want to walk with me to
the stop.'

Heartened, Philip paid the bill, even giving the disparaging
waiter the benefit of the doubt. He followed Maribel out and
through the warren of backstreets in which scores of homeless
families were bedding down for the night. Some were laid out on
the roofs and bonnets of cars like unidentified corpses; others,
wrapped in threadbare blankets, were stretched out on the pavement in front of open stores and cafés. Philip, keen to respect
their privacy, suggested crossing the road, but neither Maribel
nor any of the people neatly sidestepping the recumbent bodies
appeared to share his qualms. Some even stopped for a chat as
though with sunbathers on a beach.

They joined a crowd at what Philip took to be the bus stop,
even though the only sign was *Please Don't Piss Here* scrawled on
the wall. Judging by the stench, it had been repeatedly ignored.

'I hope I'll see you again,' Philip said hesitantly.

'I too would like that very much. Please to text me.'

'I don't have your number.'

'Dennis will tell it to you.'

'No,' Philip said, anxious to cut out the middleman. 'You give it to me please.'

'If you wish. Do you have something to write it on?'

Philip reached for his notepad, as a flurry of anticipation ran through the crowd. 'Quick! Is this your bus?'

'It will wait. Do not worry.'

She wrote down her name and number with exquisite care, blowing on the biro as if it were ink. She passed him back the open pad, and he noted that the 'i' in Maribel had been dotted with a tiny circle. As the bus opened its doors, he put his hands on her shoulders and kissed her. The kiss was as easy and unforced as the rest of their encounter. She returned it with a gentle warmth, letting her tongue linger for a moment; which might have been accidental. The hint of garlic on her breath made him grateful that they had chosen the same dish.

She broke off the kiss and climbed into the bus, turning back to him at the door. 'Have a good day, sir,' she said, as though she were already at her desk.

Four

My dear Mother and Father,

I trust you've recovered from the funeral. No doubt you're swamped with paperwork. There are advantages to death among people whose only effects are a rice jar and some scraps of bedding. I've been living in my memory all week. By a strange coincidence I caught the tail end of a play on the World Service. A boy (I couldn't work out whether he were at boarding school or borstal) was describing his family. 'Everyone loves his grandmother,' he said. I wept. Whatever our differences, Greg, Agnes, Cora and I were as one in our devotion to Granny. I'm sure that the same goes for Nancy, Ann, Portland and all the cousins. She never made us feel small – even as children – but always supported us in everything we did. For me, of course, that was following my vocation.

Whether she truly believed that my vow had been an integral factor in Father's return from Burma, she encouraged me to do so. Long gone were the days when the Tremaynes aimed to produce a priest every generation, but while the rest of you were insisting that God wouldn't hold me to a vow made as a five-year-old, she realised that it was what I wanted. Had I simply wished to convince Him of my sincerity, I could have promised to sweep the paths or share my sweet ration or run more errands for the convalescent soldiers; I would never have pledged myself to the priesthood if the idea hadn't already been in my mind.

There's nothing I'd have liked more than to have been with you for the service but, even if the Regional had given me permission, I couldn't have left the parish. Tensions are running high right now. I'm one of the few links between the military and the people. If I'd gone, who's to say what horrors would have awaited me on my return?

Running high is an understatement. After three years of Martial Law, it's plainly not the temporary remedy we were promised. Our hopes of President Marcos have faded as fast as his pledges. Far from tackling corruption, the government has institutionalised it. In Britain, party leaders identify the national interest with that of their class; here they narrow it down to their clan. We supposed that our distance from the capital would protect us from sustained scrutiny, but the *poblacion* is as closely monitored as Manila. There's nothing subtle about it. Armed men swagger through the streets, intimidating, arresting, raping and torturing. Some are from the army, some the police and some the constabulary (forget any notion of PC Simon Freeman, it's a particularly ruthless special unit). They attack each other almost as often as they do us, so that our only hope of redress lies in their increasingly brutal turf wars.

It's the young men who, inevitably, feel their oppression most keenly and, in a bid to avoid friction, I've reverted to my Ampleforth training, seeking to settle their differences on the field – or, in this case, the court. I fear that, given your respective aversion to balls that are neither bowled at a wicket nor knitted into socks, you'll already have lost patience with my basketball stories. But I trust you'll permit me my increasingly rare moments of triumph. Having hit my head on so many door frames that it's now as dented as Consolacion's, I deserve some recompense for being 6'4" in a country where the average male is 5'3". Indeed, I suspect that my unlikely athletic prowess – I write as the free throw champion of the region – has been a more effective recruiting tool for the Church among a certain sort of disaffected teenager than the most colourful fiesta. By deploying all my negotiating skill, I managed to set up a game between the constabulary and the parish. I thought it wise to confine my presence to the sidelines and to call on don Bernardo Arriola to act as referee. In spite of his blatant bias towards the constabulary, we trounced them 88 – 57. That's when my public-school code let me down. Instead of sportsmanlike handshakes as they left the court, the losers stormed through the crowd and into their jeeps. A few days later, two of our star players went missing. One was found castrated by the roadside and the other strangled in a ditch.

I should have played. At least they'd have had no need to geld me. I'm sorry; that was a remark in execrable taste. Horses are gelded; men are impotent; priests are set apart. But you'll understand my bitterness when I tell you that I was the one left to console their parents and preach forgiveness; I was the one left to consign their corpses to the earth.

The conflict, as ever, centres on land: who owns it; who works it; and who covets it. It affects the whole parish, from the farmers to the Ibaloi. Don't bother racking your brains; I haven't mentioned them before, at any rate not by name. For four years I've been calling them the Igorot, a blanket term coined by the Spanish for all the Mountain People, and they've been too polite to correct me. Can you imagine Alasdair McLeod or Ewan Dalgliesh showing similar forbearance if a blundering Filipino had described them as English? It was only when I was studying some legal documents that I realised my mistake. The Ibaloi have lived in the Cordilleras since antiquity. Unlike more recent settlers, they have no property deeds since they hold that land comes from God – a view that you'd think would find favour in an ostensibly Christian country. You'd be wrong. The President has earmarked the Ibaloi territory to recompense his cronies. So first, he passed a law designating all land with a slope of more than 18 degrees – which pretty much covers the entire area – as a forestry reserve on which no one is permitted to live, farm or hunt. Then, he gave the logging concession to Miguel Arriola, don Bernardo's cousin.

Arriola, who's been felling trees so fast that he's already caused several landslides, needs a reliable road to transport the wood. Don Bernardo has offered to build one through his estate.

I've no wish to impugn what may be genuine family feeling, but I can't help thinking that the huge government subsidies for the future national highway have played a part. What do you suppose the IMF and the other international agencies who are funding the project would say if they knew that it would result in hundreds of people being thrown off the land? Would they display the same chilling indifference as when they demanded the institution of Martial Law in the first place, or would they start to question the nature of their aid? The only good to have emerged from this sorry story is that it has prompted the Ibaloi and the lowlanders to set aside their long-standing antagonism and make common cause.

So, when don Bernardo brought in bulldozers to raze the crops and demolish houses, the Ibaloi came down from the mountains to join the farmers in forming a human barricade as, for that matter, did I, Father Benito, the Daughters of St Paul, and hundreds of members of BCCs from across the province. Not that it made any difference. The following day he called in the constabulary, who more than repaid his favours on the bas- ketball court as they dispersed the protesters at gunpoint. For a moment I feared that there might be a massacre, especially when some of our more hot-headed youths started to stone the soldiers in a bid to avenge their friends and teammates, but Benito and I succeeded in calming them. At the end of the day, the physical wounds were light but, as people contemplated the devastation of their homes and livelihoods, the emotional scars ran deep. Don Bernardo has offered compensation but, so far, it's amounted to nothing more than a few sacks of rice.

Benito and I drove to Baguio to solicit help from the Bishop who, while assuring us of his concern and promising to speak to don Bernardo, was at pains to emphasise the danger of his taking too public a stance. He played his usual trick of hinting that he was constantly grappling with forces beyond our ken and that it was only by the most adroit balancing act that he kept the entire diocese from plunging into chaos. Benito, who despises the Bishop's fawning on his political masters, maintained that his real fear is of losing the friendship of the *haciendos*, with their invitations to lunch, golf and weekends on their private yachts. I prefer to think that his motives are pure, as was borne out when he authorised us to brief church lawyers on behalf of the dispossessed farmers and tribesmen. They've lodged papers with the judge, but it may yet be months before the preliminary hearing and years before the case is resolved. This doesn't stem from any Jarndyce v Jarndyce-like tangle but from the relentless pressures on the courts.

Don Bernardo resents our involvement, which he regards as particularly unjust since he's one of the few landowners to have embraced the spirit of reform and turned his shared tenancies into leaseholds. The trouble, as he well knows, is that this doesn't necessarily work to the farmers' advantage. Indeed, it's a moot point as to which system is the more inequitous (don't reach for your dictionary; I realise as I write that I've hit on a handy amalgam of inequitable and iniquitous). The share tenant is vulnerable to the proportion of his harvest due to the landlord, and the leasehold tenant to a fixed rent that takes no account of the all too frequent crop failures. Meanwhile, American agronomists have been pressing for the introduction of high-yield rice hybrids, which make far more sense on paper than on the ground. The additional expenditure on pesticides and fertilisers leaves the small farmers in even greater debt.

Whatever their lasting benefits, the pesticides and fertilisers have had a devastating short-term impact. Not only have they killed off many of the rodents and crustaceans that families forage to supplement their diet, but they've led to the deaths of several babies. I don't know if it's a practice unique to Luzon or if it even occurs in darkest Durham, but for centuries mothers here have weaned their children by rubbing soil on their nipples and well, you can fill in the rest. The BCCs are struggling to educate women about the dangers of herbicides, but the lesson has come too late for Maricel Solito and Joel Quizon.

How does one honour the death of a child in the midst of such high infant mortality? I feel like a chaplain on the Somme, feebly reiterating that the value of a life bears no relation to its length. Was Granny Tremayne a worthier person than Granny Courtenay because she outlived her by two decades? Of course not. Just as some of us are tall and some short, some fat and some thin, some black and some white (I've omitted 'some rich and some poor', which I no longer regard as part of the natural order), so some die young and others live to a ripe old age. And the grieving parents listen respectfully while I spout my platitudes. Do you think that may be why priests are required to be celibate, not because of compromised loyalties, let alone the need to safeguard church property, but to shield us from everyday emotion? It takes a measure of inhumanity to interpret the will of God.

I don't want to give you the impression that I'm lonely. These people aren't just my parishioners but my friends. Nevertheless, there are moments when I long to be with someone who shares my background as well as my beliefs. So I welcomed the chance to spend a few days last month with Hendrik. After his success in Cabanatuan, he has been rewarded – if that's the right word – with a new parish in Angeles City, which he was eager for me to visit. I can only suppose that he was trying to test my resilience. In which case, I failed dismally. You've heard of wool towns and mining villages? Well, this is a sex city. That's its entire *raison d'être*. We walked through streets that resembled the corridors of a giant brothel. Every depravity – that's no exaggeration – was on offer, the one variable being the price. After fifteen minutes I began to think more kindly of the *haciendos*. They at least only steal their tenants' livelihoods; they allow them to keep their souls.

Hendrik remains undaunted. He brushes off the regular death threats he receives from pimps and bar owners as if he were one of the Ibaloi trusting in talismans. He's befriended several of the prostitutes, helping them to obtain medical checks and treatment, and even, in a few cases, to rebuild their lives, but he concedes that it's a Sisyphean task. For every woman who leaves the streets, two more arrive to take her place. His main concern is to provide a refuge for the children, some no older than five or six: children who should be playing in the fields, not flaunting themselves in doorways. What kind of men take pleasure in such perversion? What force of collective amnesia allows them to bury their own innocence? As I watched little girls hitch up their skirts at the first glimpse of trouser, I understood what led revolutionaries to take up arms.

Righteous indignation is all too easy at one remove, so I'll stick to asking questions. Is it any accident that Angeles City with its 80,000 prostitutes (no, I haven't added a nought for effect) sprang up on the perimeter of one of the two largest US bases in the country? What do you suppose Uncle Sam would say if he knew how his favourite nephews were spending their well-earned Rest and Relaxation? Would that fierce-looking white-haired man raise one of his bushy eyebrows at the nightly rape of women and children by his servicemen, or would he turn a blind eye to the regrettable fallout from saving the free world?

The Philippines has, of course, borne the brunt of US imperialism throughout the twentieth century. I'm aware that I'm treading on delicate ground here and that you, Father, have every reason to be grateful for the American presence in the Pacific in 1945. But we've moved on, at least on the face of it. Please bear in mind that I never adopted the blanket anti-Americanism of my contemporaries. I was in Roosendaal at the time of Grosvenor Square but, even had I been in London, I wouldn't have marched. Shameful as it is to admit, I supported the war in Vietnam. Now, after three years in the Philippines, I see Communism less as a universal threat than as a secular version of the gospel. What's more, I've discovered the true story of the American invasion of the Philippines: how they freed the country from the Spanish only to annex it for themselves, reneging on their promises and killing 600,000 Filipinos along the way. Is it any wonder that

Benito refers to it as the first Vietnam and berates his country-men for celebrating independence from Spain every 12 June and then following it with Filipino-American Friendship Day every 4 July?

I suspect that by now you'll be reading this alone, Mother, after Father has retreated to the smoking room, wondering, as so often, what he did to deserve such a son. Cora's quirks, whether sabotaging the hunt or disrupting the harvest supper, could always be excused by her condition. I have nothing but my faith to excuse mine. If, on the other hand, you've stuck it out this far, you might want to give up here. Things don't get any jollier.

Sexual violence isn't confined to Angeles City; I'm dealing with it in my own parish. I can't remember if I mentioned it, but a couple of years ago I found a job as a maid in the Romualdez household for Girlie, a twelve-year-old orphan. Everything seemed to be going well. Doña Teresa expressed satisfaction with her; Girlie enjoyed her work and helped to support her sisters and brother. Last spring, however, I noticed a change in her: she became sullen and strained, which I put down to a combination of growing pains and the fact that doña Teresa's public displays of charity aren't always matched in private. Then, during confession, she told me that the Romualdez son, Joey, had raped her. Don't worry, I'm not breaking any rule since I persuaded her to speak to her aunt Leonora who, much to my surprise, marched straight up to the house to confront Joey, who made no attempt to deny the charge. You may think that the admission does him credit, but having talked to him myself, I see it less as a sign of contrition than of contempt: for the girl, for her family and, indeed, for the law.

I offered to drive Girlie and her aunt to the police station, but Leonora preferred to handle the matter alone. I welcomed her newfound confidence until I discovered that, far from pressing charges, she'd brokered a backstairs deal with don Enrico, which not only denied Girlie restitution – except in the crudest financial sense – but left her vulnerable to fresh assaults. All my arguments were in vain. I assumed she was afraid the publicity of a trial would damage Girlie's reputation, but Benito, with a candour bordering on cynicism, explained that, in the right circumstances, rape could be the making of a poor girl in the Philippines.

I'm learning what a loaded word justice is. While doña Teresa primly assured me that she would bear Girlie no grudges ('It's our cross to be the object of envy and spite'), don Enrico was defiant. He summoned me to see him and, having kept me waiting for an hour, received me on the lavatory. I noted with alarm that there were two adjacent seats and wondered whether he expected me to join him. To my relief, he left me hovering by the door while he explained, with unconcealed disdain, that after four years I had failed to understand the way things were done here. 'We're all equal before the law,' I said. 'Which law?' he asked. 'Man's law? Martial Law? Marcos's law?' 'God's law,' I replied, 'which transcends all the rest.' 'But who pays for it?' he asked. 'Who maintains the altar on which you celebrate mass, the pulpit from which you preach?' To my horror, I realised it was a serious question. He believed that, by dint of making the greatest contribution, he had the right to the greatest respect. So much for the widow's mite!

Before signing off, I must mention an extraordinary event that took place at the requiem for Gener, one of the young men murdered after the basketball match, which has brought me a lot of unwelcome attention. I was halfway through the Dies Irae when I felt a mysterious lightness come over me. It's impossible to describe and I'd have attributed it to the heat in the packed church and the emotion of the service if several people hadn't seen – I'm loath to put it into words even without picturing your response – me levitate. Like you, I'm inclined to scepticism. These are people who regularly report seeing Christ's face materialise on doorknobs or watching Him dance in the paddy fields. Perhaps it was a trick of the light: a sunbeam hitting my feet that made me appear to rise? On the other hand, I know what I felt in myself and the loud gasp from the nave was entirely spontaneous. One of the altar boys brought me down to earth (not literally!) when, with that distinctive blend of the sacred and secular, he whispered that he hoped I'd use my magic leap in our next match.

I thought you'd rather hear the story from me than at second hand. It's amazing how quickly rumours spread. We've already had to fend off reporters from Manila. I don't expect you to credit it but you might try to keep open minds. That said, I can picture you looking concerned, Greg roaring with laughter and Agnes pursing her lips. Cora, however, will understand.

Your loving son,
Julian

The owner of the black BMW summoned so regularly to the lobby took control of the rented silver Honda. He made such minute adjustments to the driving seat, mirrors and air conditioning – the latter without consulting his passenger – that Philip half expected him to remove a DENNIS sticker from his bag and attach it to the windscreen. His frustration was understandable. Having finally found himself behind the wheel, he was stuck in a massive bottleneck in Caloocan City. Philip refrained from pointing out that, had he picked him up at seven o'clock as planned, and not ninety minutes later with the risible excuse that his rooming house had burnt down, they would have avoided the worst of the traffic. Instead, he turned to the back of his newspaper, catching up with the daily antics of long defunct British cartoon characters, and tried to ignore the insistent tattoo being drummed on the dashboard, the fitful flapping of half-broken wipers that redistributed dirt across the glass and the violent curses, thankfully in Tagalog, that greeted anyone who attempted to overtake.

After further delays and prolonged blasts on the car horn, they finally arrived at the North Luzon Expressway. The urban sprawl gradually gave way to open country, in which a vibrant patchwork of rice, maize and melon fields extended back to a spectacular range of blue-tinged, cloud-capped mountains. Dennis increased his speed, at the same time turning up the radio. Deafened by the screech of Filipino hip hop, Philip searched in vain for a way to ask him to switch it down that would not sound peremptory. So, making no comment, he gazed out of the window, where his attention was caught by a series of billboards featuring a craggily handsome middle-aged senator with a grin so broad that he at first appeared to be advertising toothpaste but, on closer inspection, was claiming credit for the *Asphalt Overlay on*

Two New Traffic Lanes. Intrigued, he questioned Dennis, who was singing along with a lyric decrying 'four hundred years of tears for the brown man'.

'No surprise he has big smile,' Dennis replied testily. 'Is known he is buying 8,000 hectares of land after reforms and now he is needing way to reach it. You look at all new road in this country and is ending at some rich man's gate.'

They turned off the expressway and down a side road, whose pitted surface made Philip think more kindly of the senator's construction project, however venal. Even Dennis was compelled to reduce speed in order to negotiate the bumps, potholes and, at one point, a large pile of boulders. Nevertheless, Philip feared for the chickens strolling nonchalantly across the road, as though for no other reason than to lend substance to the hoary riddle. After driving for miles without spotting a single car, house or person, they arrived at a small group of shacks where Dennis stopped, saying: 'Now we must make piss, yes?' Philip followed him warily into the scrub, choosing a spot where he stood alone but not aloof. As he zipped up his trousers, he was grateful to find that the locals, alerted to their arrival, were watching them with an air of benign apathy, which rapidly changed to expectation when Dennis called out 'Now we must eat something, yes?'

Avoiding the shack which offered *Live Goat Meat for Sale*, Philip joined Dennis at a food stall. 'What is it?' he asked, gesturing to the tureen.

'*Pagkaon,*' the stallholder replied, leaving him none the wiser. Pangs of hunger overwhelming his qualms, Philip nodded his acceptance. She served him a paper plate of rice mixed with brown bits, which he preferred to chew than to identify. After eating his fill, he followed Dennis to a stall stacked with hundreds of lychee-like fruits.

'Is *lanzones*. Is very good, yes?'

'Then let's buy some,' Philip said, anxious to expunge the memory of the *pagkaon*, only to change his mind when the stallholder made straight for a pile infested with ants. 'Is it Poison A Foreigner week?'

'Is best. Is because they know is sweetest,' Dennis replied, brushing off Philip's objections as casually as the woman brushed off the ants. 'Insects more clever than English.'

Philip watched Dennis gorge himself on the *lanzones*. No amount of water could satisfy his craving for the succulent, if putrid, flesh. Back in the car, he contemplated the remaining journey with increasing irritation and after Dennis extolled the fruit for the fourth time ('Is sweet like my *burat*') he snapped off the radio.

'I'm sorry, but I can't hear myself think.'

'Is not for thinking; is for listening,' Dennis replied, with an offended air, which made Philip feel even more mean-spirited. To his relief they came to a crossroads, where a sign reading forty kilometres to Baguio showed that they were finally approaching their destination. As if on cue, the traffic grew heavier, with lines of cars, lorries and even a local jeepney, so packed that six of its passengers were sitting on the roof. The sight of them clinging on precariously as they rattled down the unmade road felt like a symbol for the balancing act that was their daily life: a symbol reinforced when Dennis drove past at excessive speed, covering them in dust.

At 4.30 they arrived in the centre of La Trinidad, the small town between Baguio and San Isidro where Philip had elected to stay. They found their hotel, a white concrete building with a row of posts jutting from the roof as if supporting a phantom storey, and pulled up beside a sign reading *No Stopping At Any Time, Parking Only*. Its three stars would have inspired greater confidence if more than one had been lit.

Even a single star struck Philip as generous once his eyes had adjusted to the gloom of the lobby. He dared not envisage the domestic arrangements of the guidebook writer who had described it as 'the sort of place where you instantly feel at home'. On one side two bamboo banquettes with blue foam rubber cushions constituted the lounge area and on the other three dark wooden tables, with chequered vinyl cloths and a motley assortment of chairs, comprised the restaurant. In the centre a plywood partition, plastered with tourist-board posters, doubled as the reception desk and bar. The golden beaches, azure seas, verdant rice terraces and picturesque fishing villages might have been expressly designed to tantalise the unwary visitor with the delights to be found elsewhere.

Philip walked up to the desk and thumped the bell, which emitted a derisory ping. An attractive woman in her mid-thirties with a cast in her left eye emerged from a back room to greet him, answering all questions about his reservations with the single phrase 'It is correct'. Philip would have felt happier had she been able to dispel his reservations about the hotel. After handing him a registration form which, to his bemusement, requested details of his weight and distinguishing characteristics ('the only 6'1" sandy-haired Caucasian in town'?), the woman, who introduced herself as Lerma, spoke a few words of Tagalog to Dennis; Philip trusted that it was the language that made the welcome sound warmer. She gave Dennis a different form, which he deliberately withheld from Philip's view. With both forms completed, Lerma summoned Armin, a slight, rubbery man, who was watching them from across the lobby. Handing him Philip's key, she pointed to his case – a small grip that Armin picked up as cautiously as a trunk – and asked him to show their guest to his room.

Philip followed the plodding porter up the rickety stairs, down a drab corridor and into an airless room, which filled him with dismay. The bed frame stood six inches from the floor as if in an awkward compromise between Western and Eastern practice. The single pillow sagged like an empty mailbag. The lighting was as dim as in the lobby and there was no reading lamp. Armin switched on the electric fan, proving that the guidebook description of *fan-cooled rooms* contained a modicum of truth, although its loud whir would make it impossible to use at night.

He then proceeded to demonstrate the room's other amenities, opening drawers and drawing curtains, only to be caught out when the wardrobe's sliding door slid out of its groove. Urging Philip 'No use to worry; I fix', he propped it against the wall, where it served to conceal a large damp patch, and led the way into the bathroom, whose cracked tiles and frayed matting finally gave Philip a reason to welcome the gloom. When Armin picked up a red plastic bucket and mimed flushing the loo, Philip was doubly grateful to have forgone the *lanzones*. He felt an urgent need to wash his hands and, with the hot water tap running dry, looked expectantly at Armin.

'Sometimes no hot water,' Armin said, turning the cold water on fully as if to compensate.

'How often?'

'Sometimes.'

'How long does it last?'

'Sometimes six weeks,' Armin replied, smiling so broadly that Philip felt certain he must have misunderstood.

He dismissed Armin and unpacked his case. He then took a freezing cold shower and, bracing himself with the thought of all the backpacking privations he had missed by spending his gap year in Rome, lowered himself on to the bed, where he fell fast asleep. He woke shortly before eight with a crick in his neck and a fierce, if unverifiable, conviction that someone had been spying on him while he slept. He dressed and went downstairs, to find that one of the tables had been laid with spoons, forks, paper napkins and four bottles of sauce: barbecue; soy; sweet chilli; and banana ketchup. It was hard to believe that the previous evening he had dined in the filigree elegance of the Manila Hotel Champagne Room. The gulf between the capital and the provinces, which Julian had observed forty years ago, did not appear to have narrowed. True, there was now electric light, but it was barely strong enough for him to read the menu; which turned out to be no great loss since it was as notional as the hot water. At Lerma's prompting, he opted for the chicken adobo.

'Is that the only dish available?' he asked suspiciously.

'It is correct.'

Dennis swaggered down the stairs ten minutes later, and Lerma ordered Armin to bring the food. She addressed the old man so abruptly that Philip was shocked to learn that he was her father.

'Is true!' Dennis said, taking Philip's scepticism as a personal slight. 'She tells me is family business like bakery shop. This hotel is belonging to her husband who is away in conference in Cebu.'

'Let's hope it's on hotel management,' Philip said, at which Dennis looked up from his plate with a scowl. As soon as he finished dessert (a bright purple ice cream which tasted of sweet potato), Philip returned to his room where, reluctant to strain his eyes, he listened to his favourite Doors tracks on his iPod, falling asleep to the sound of Jim Morrison urging him to 'Ride the Snake to the Lake', a lyric that sneaked disturbingly into his dreams. After another cold shower he went downstairs, where Dennis was already eating breakfast.

'This is a first! Did you sleep well?'

'I do not sleep. I am with woman,' he announced in the smug tones of the first boy in the class to sprout pubic hair.

'What woman?' Philip asked, just as Lerma's arrival rendered the question superfluous. Their air of sexual complicity left him feeling even more excluded than their conversation. He was gripped by such irrational jealousy that he was grateful the regulation cutlery did not include knives. His frustration peaked when Lerma, offering them a dish of *daing na bangus*, translated it as 'grilled milky fish', taking him back to the first meal he had shared with Maribel. Wretched, he pushed his plate away.

'This fish is cold.'

'Is supposed to be cold.'

'Then it's too tough,' Philip replied, knowing that the bitter taste in his mouth had nothing to do with the food. 'Besides, we must leave for San Isidro at once. We're not here to amuse ourselves.'

'No, you not funny at all.'

Dennis cleared his plate as slowly as he could without openly rebelling and, after an affectionate exchange with Lerma, followed Philip to the door.

'Now we must go. I am ready.'

They drove the few miles to San Isidro which, to Philip's delight, he recognised from the descriptions in Julian's letters. As they circled the main square, he pointed out the town hall and the row of crumbling colonial houses to Dennis as confidently as he had pointed out the Ferry Hotel and Bellrope Meadow to Julia on their first ever visit to Cookham. They stopped outside the church, as much the centre of Julian's world as it had been of Stanley Spencer's and therefore an essential port of call.

'Do you want to see inside?' he asked Dennis.

'I am feeling very tired,' he replied resentfully, as if it were work that had kept him awake all night. Pulling down his baseball cap, he curled up in his seat.

Philip walked down the path, lifted the rusty latch on the creaking door and entered the church. As he surveyed the simply furnished interior, breathing the stale fumes of incense and watching the motes of dust dancing in the light from the clerestory windows, he felt a strong sense of mystery. The crudely painted stone-block walls, the clumsily foreshortened figures on the dome and the tinselly altar offended all his artistic instincts, while reviving religious instincts he had supposed dormant. Satisfied that he was alone, he edged along a row of chairs and fell to his knees.

Discomfort had never struck him as an aid to prayer but, for once, he was willing to endure it since he was not addressing God but trying to reach closer to Julian. Although he had been no more than a temporary custodian, the church was somehow infused with his presence – or at least his priesthood. Philip closed his eyes and tried to picture himself among the awestruck mourners at the murdered basketball player's requiem. Alerted by a cough, he gazed up and, for one heart-stopping moment, he wondered if he too might be witnessing a miracle, but the priest looming over him was a fresh-faced Filipino. He jumped to his feet and introduced himself, at which the priest, flushed with excitement, invited him into the sacristy, offering him a cup of tea with such doleful disparagement of the facilities that Philip felt obliged to refuse. Looking relieved, Father Honesto expatiated on the parish, to which he had recently been posted after studying in Rome. 'God is testing me,' he said, as though he were St Anthony hounded in the desert, rather than the overtaxed priest of a provincial parish. 'The people here are good people – very good people – but they are so small. They have no imaginations in their heads. They take mass like if it was medicine.'

Philip was disturbed to hear someone who could have been no more than two or three years his senior sound so jaded. He compared him with Julian who, in the face of calumny and persecution, never lost his faith in the ability of ordinary people to effect change. Was Honesto's disillusion that of an ambitious priest mouldering in a backwater, or a shrewd judge of human nature?

'I will show you something very special,' he said, unlocking a wardrobe and taking out a purple chasuble trimmed with gold brocade. 'A gift for Advent from the family of Father Julian,' he explained, holding it up like an auction house porter. 'His mother and sister made this pattern with their own two hands.'

'Really? His mother?'

'This is what his housekeeper has told me. She is very old, but her memory for this is strong. My predecessor could no longer keep wearing it when… look!' He pointed to a frayed edge. 'The good people have too much enthusiasm for their new saint. But I will share with you a secret – see, you will hear a priest's confession. Sometimes when the church is locked and I am alone, I put it on to pray and I feel that Father Julian is here beside me. That is why I am so happy to find you have come. The Bishop is a very busy man. He does not always see the whole of the picture; he does not always see people for everything that they are worth. You are here from England; you will quicken things up. The Holy Father will give us our saint. Clever people – cultural people – from all over the world will come on visits to San Isidro and I will write its history.'

'Great! I didn't realise that so much had happened here. Apart from Julian, of course.'

'It will be a history of the spirit which, with much humbleness, I will mix together with my own. It will show how a very ordinary man, so very ordinary that his Excellency the Bishop does not remember my name, can also think big thoughts.' For a moment he appeared to be lost in them. 'But I am holding you back. You have many people to meet: many ancient friends of Father Julian. And I must visit a farmer in a long-way-off *barangay*. By now he may already be dead.'

'I'm so sorry; I had no idea. I'll go at once. But if I may beg one last favour? Would you point me in the direction of the cemetery, that is if it's within walking distance? I'd like to pay my respects.'

'Of course. It is on the back side of this wall. We will need to go out through the church.'

Father Honesto led the way through the sanctuary, genuflecting casually to the altar. They emerged in a shady courtyard where four young boys were playing football. Catching sight of the priest, they rushed up to kiss his hand. Barely slackening his pace, he made the sign of the cross over each in turn, as he conducted Philip into the street and up to the cemetery gate.

'Here I must leave you,' he said, 'but I am hopeful that we will meet again during your stay in San Isidro.'

'I look forward to it,' Philip replied. Too shy to shake a hand that had received such reverence, he gently bowed his head.

As he walked through the buckled gate and down the overgrown path, he felt an immediate sense of peace. A passion for brass-rubbing in his teens had put paid to the fear of graveyards that had haunted his childhood, but ever since Julia's death they had held a new appeal. Although he shrank from returning to the Gaverton churchyard where she lay in a nursery coupling with Greg, he regularly visited them elsewhere. While others lit candles in memory of their loved ones, he sat on a bench or a tomb, if it were sufficiently old and nondescript, and communed with his. It was as though all the graves in the world were connected and, like a medium summoning a spirit guide, he could reach through them to Julia.

The connection here was particularly strong, since the grave he sought was that of her uncle. The densely packed rows of snaggled stones were hard to negotiate so, without any map or guide, he made for the largest monument, which stood against the church wall. Long before reaching it, he realised his mistake. Even Hugh, who had overseen the arrangements, would have baulked at burying so unassuming a priest in so grandiose a tomb. Moreover, a cursory glance at the inscription revealed that it was not in fact a tomb but a memorial, erected ten years after Julian's death by the Knights of Columbus, *In Loving Memory of all the Unborn Children, Victims of Abortion, May God Have Mercy on Us*. A marble tablet by its side was engraved with a letter from *An Unborn Son to his Shameless Mother*. After reading the first three lines, he turned briskly away.

One of his rare quarrels with Julia had been over her readiness to defy the Vatican line on birth control while supporting it on abortion. Even so, he was sure that, were she with him today, she would back down. Nowhere was the gap between the sanctity of life and the dignity of living wider than in the Philippines where, by the Church's own reckoning, hundreds of thousands of unwanted children roamed the streets of the major cities. Their short, violent, abused and abusive lives showed that the mercy which the Unborn Children sought for themselves was more urgently needed elsewhere.

He wandered at random through the graves, finding several familiar names among the epitaphs. Bernardo Arriola, one of Julian's prime antagonists, lay alongside his wife beneath a huge slab of black granite, inscribed only with their dates of birth and death: the latter revealing that doña Yolanda had survived her husband by a mere nine days. A stark white cross in the next row bore the name of Augustin Herrera, manager of the neighbouring Pineda estate, with the phrase *Born 12-4-37 Last Seen 2-8-93*, leaving Philip wondering if it were the local equivalent of *Not Dead, Only Sleeping*, or the pointer to an unsolved crime. Across the path, closer to them in death than he had ever been in life, Gener Jimenez, victim of the fateful basketball match, was buried beneath a small pile of stones.

Mindful of his imminent meeting with Felicitas Clemente, the widow of Julian's cell mate, Juan, Philip walked back to the gate where he was hit by a powerful fragrance. He swung round, unnerved by the memory of the policemen who had retrieved Julian's corpse, but saw, to his relief, that it came from a huge stack of freshly cut sampaguitas. Beside it was a simple plaque *Fr Julian Tremayne MHM 11 September 1940 to June 1989. Requiescat in Pace.* As he gazed at the grave, Philip felt strangely empty. Willing himself to feel something profound, he fell to his knees, but all that resulted was a slight stitch and considerable frustration that the writing on the various petitions and prayers dotted among the flowers was either smudged or faded. Standing up, he took four quick photographs and walked back to the car, where he was amused and touched to see Dennis giving mock driving lessons to three boys whose hands barely reached the wheel.

The boys scampered away so fast on his approach that he dreaded to think how Dennis had described him, but when questioned Dennis simply replied: 'Peasants! They are having fears of everything.' He evinced a similar contempt when Philip insisted on changing his T-shirt in preparation for his visits. 'Why you bother for these sweaty people?' he asked, as if a few squirts of deodorant were all it took to obliterate any trace of his own rustic past. Philip, conscious that in Dennis's world respect was confined to those higher up the social scale, said nothing as he took out Felicitas's letter, with directions that seemed to have come straight from a *Boy's Own* story: 'Turn right at the house with the green shutters, carry on down the road until you reach the shrine to Santa Barbara, turn right again and drive on until you pass the broken-down jeepney. Don't worry, it has been there for years. Follow the path past a row of houses, and mine is the last but one with the two mango trees in the front.'

Despite his own lack of botanical expertise and Dennis's belief that to admit to ever having seen a mango tree would damage his metropolitan image, they found the house without difficulty. Felicitas, a raw-boned septuagenarian with a long neck, closely cropped white hair and sparkling eyes, was waiting for them in the garden where, after a brief exchange of greetings, Dennis chose to remain, listening to his Walkman, stretched out against one of the mango trees. Philip, meanwhile, followed Felicitas indoors. He had never knowingly met anyone who had been tortured and, although he found it hard to view Felicitas's ordeal in the same light as those of her fellow victims, he had a sickening suspicion that her bow legs were not solely the result of old age. Despite his protests, she insisted on offering him the one armchair, so he perched on the edge of the tattered cushion, while she hobbled around the room fetching the obligatory snack.

The absence of a fridge at least spared him any further concerns about ice, but as he sipped a warm, oversweet Coke alone, they were replaced by concerns about her poverty. The small, dark room was pitifully austere. The walls were made of unplastered breeze blocks and woven bamboo, on which were pinned a series of magazine illustrations of orchids and a recycled 2007 calendar cover of the Mount of Olives. The floor was bare concrete with two coconut mats, which looked as though they were also used for sleeping. The single window lacked both glass and shutters, and was boarded at the bottom, presumably to deter intruders since there was nothing to interest thieves. The only furniture was a folding table and four mismatched chairs, a non-functioning fan, and a scratched and stained dresser, on which sat a framed photograph of an unsmiling middle-aged man, whom Philip took to be Felicitas's late husband, alongside a plaster statue of Christ, His right hand raised in benediction and His left clutching a bible.

Philip regretted his lack of experience, as he struggled to phrase his questions. He knew that she had worked in the BCC school and spoke near-perfect English, so that there should be no problem of comprehension. What worried him was the effect of asking her to recall – even to relive – the traumas of her past. Accustomed to old ladies whose greatest losses were their looks, he felt humbled in the face of one who had endured so much. He hid behind his Coke and cassava cake, whose stickiness was a further obstacle to conversation, while Felicitas pulled out a plain wooden chair and sat, poker-backed, hands clasped and ankles crossed, as if on a dais.

She stared at him with a mixture of expectancy and alarm that overrode his doubts. 'You must miss your husband dreadfully,' he said.

'Juan died bearing witness for what he believed,' she replied, the faint lilt adding pathos to her words. 'No one can ask for more than that.'

'Really?' Philip asked. 'I don't want to sound facile, but shouldn't we be able to bear witness to our beliefs in safety?'

'Maybe in the West,' she replied, without irony.

'I understand that he was killed by the son of the murdered policeman?'

'Yes, you are right. A twelve-years-old boy. Not even a man!'

'If he'd been older, would it have made it easier?'

'No, but it would have made it fairer. He would have less of his life still to live: less of the life that he stole from Juan and he stole from me.'

'Do you still attend church regularly?'

'Yes, of course.'

'And have you been able to forgive him – the killer?'

'I pray that, before I die, I will have the heart to forgive him. Sometimes prayers can be harder than pain.'

'Even after all these years?'

'I believe that God gives each one of us a task in life. Mine must be to learn how to forgive.'

'In the last letter that he wrote – or at least the last one that we have – Julian spoke of paying you a visit on his return to the Philippines. I can't remember his exact words, but it sounded as though you blamed him in some way for Juan's death.'

'He has said this?' She looked at him in horror.

'I may have misread it,' Philip added quickly.

'If I made him think this, I am truly sorry. Please, you must understand that it has never been my meaning. When he came back, everything was very hard. Juan had been taken from us when so many other men – so many wicked men – were still living. But not Father! He was the best – the finest – man I have ever met. Oh my, I feel... I must have a little water.'

'Let me,' Philip said, standing. 'Should I fetch some from the kitchen?'

'My friend, the kitchen is in the yard.' She pointed to a cloth-covered jug. 'There!' He filled the glass standing beside it and handed it to her. She drained it in a single gulp.

'More?'

'No, thank you. I am well now. I am sorry; it was just hearing what you said. Would Father really think that I am blaming him?'

'No, I'm the one who's sorry. Come to think of it, I'm not at all sure that he was referring to you. I'm pretty certain that it was one of the other widows, other wives. I got confused because he mentions Juan so often and always in such glowing terms.'

'Juan loved Father so much. He would have given his life for him – not that he did, of course. He used to say that it was Father who made him a man. Please, you must not misunderstand me! He was forty years old with a grown-up son and a schoolgirl daughter when Father came to San Isidro, but it was Father who opened his mind.' She moved to the dresser and took out a photograph of Julian and Juan, looking as ill matched as a comedy duo, leaning on axes beside a half-built bamboo hut. 'Together, they have built our first chapel.'

'It's a wonderful photo. They both look so determined. It's clear that Juan was Julian's right-hand man in the BCC.'

'And Father was always true to him. When they were sent into prison – Father Julian and Father Benito, Juan, Rey, Rodel and Julius – some of them (I will not say their names because they were all good men, such good men) believed that Father was going to abandon them. It would have been very easy for him. Every day there were visitors giving him a chance to be free if only he would put a distance between himself and the rest. He was making an embarrassment for Marcos, for the Church, for his Society, for his family. He would not even have to say that Juan and the others were guilty, just that he could not know that they were innocent. Perhaps I do not make the difference clear? My English is not so good.'

'Trust me, it's excellent.'

'But Father would never desert his friends. He knew that they would be in great danger without him. He was their shield, just like he used to say that the Lord was his. He stayed in the prison with them for more than one year. Six men in a little room, three times as little as this.' Philip looked around, trying to gauge the area, but faltered at the sight of the two coconut mats, which took up a third of the floor. 'It was hard for all of them, but so much harder for Father. He had been growing up in a house like the Malacañang Palace.'

'He told you about it?' Philip asked in surprise.

'Oh no, not at all. He would not like us to know. But Consolacion, his housekeeper – we were great friends together then – found some pictures from a letter he had thrown into the basket. She pulled them out and showed them to me. She made me be sure to be secret.'

'I understand.'

'And, after all that, he thought that I blamed him for the death of Juan?'

'No, not at all. As I tried to explain, it was my mistake. I muddled you with one of the other wives.'

'Does this make it better? How could anyone blame such a good, kind man?'

'After all, he did go back to England. Even though he knew it would leave his fellow prisoners exposed.'

'He had been sent many letters. His mother was dying! He had no choice and it broke his heart.'

'Yes, of course. I'm not suggesting that he sneaked off to save his skin. But the fact remains that his mother recovered, while Juan and his friend, Julius Morales, died.'

'Who knows? If Father had not gone back to her, she might never have recovered. Perhaps it was seeing him that made her well? She loved him very much. I have a son who I have not seen now for many years – perhaps almost as many years as you have been living – a son who some nights I think of with so much pain that, when I look down at my mat, I expect that it will be covered with blood. I could not even ask this son to come back to me to bury his father.'

'Would that be Rommel?'

'How do you know this is his name?' Felicitas asked, cupping her cheeks in panic.

'Julian mentions him in his letters to his parents.'

'Father wrote to them about Rommel?' A note of pride displaced the panic.

'Certainly.'

'Did he write about him to anyone else?'

'Not as far as I know. The letters to his family are the only ones we have.'

'I am sorry. Now I am the one of little faith. I know that Father would never betray anyone. He was a good man, the best man that I have ever known.'

'So do you think that he was... that he should be made a saint?'

'It is not for me to decide this. It is for the Bishop and the Cardinal and even the Holy Father himself.'

'Ultimately, of course, but I'm here to canvass opinion on the ground.'

'Father was a very humble man. He believed with his whole heart that every one of us was equal. He would never take praises for himself, instead he would always say: "It was a team effort." I can hear him in my head speaking now. "It was a team effort." These were his favourite words.' She put her hand over her mouth, as if she had no right to appropriate them. 'Would he have wished to be set apart?'

'Perhaps if it were for the good of the Church and the people?'

'Yes, you are right. You have never met him and you know what was important to him better than me.'

'Not at all, I'm thinking aloud.'

'You are quite right. Of course he should be made a saint.'

'If it were up to me, virtue alone would be sufficient qualification, but Rome requires hard evidence. So I'm also seeking out witnesses to his miracles. Were you yourself in church to see him levitate or present at any of his cures?'

'Yes, I was at the mass for Gener. He is a boy that I have known from the day when he was born. I can say what I have seen but I cannot swear it on the Bible since, at the same moment when Father rose in the air, a ray of light fell from the window like a golden curtain. I could see and I was blind, both at the same time.'

'A ray of light that might have had mystic significance?'

'I do not understand. Please to explain.'

'Do you think that ray of light came from God?'

'All rays of light come from God.'

'So you don't think this one was miraculous?'

'I think, but I cannot be sure of my thoughts. What I can be sure is that I saw Benigna Vaollota with her neck like a bullfrog and the next day it was thin again like a swan. But was it Father who appeared to her in her dream or was it Our Lord himself? Look!' She held the photograph next to the statue, forcing Philip to acknowledge the rudimentary resemblance between the two gaunt faces, blond heads and short beards. 'I ask this because it can be so hard to tell, especially in a dream. And even if it was Father who called her, was it him or was it Our Lord who cured her? I am happy that it is not me who has to decide this. For myself – just for myself – I would say to wait. Look at San Lorenzo Ruiz. He had to wait more than three hundred years, until the Holy Father came to Manila. But then who knows where this world will be in three hundred years? Perhaps it is best to take this chance now while there is still time.'

Philip sensed that she had told him as much as she knew, but the moment he stood to leave she pressed him to stay to lunch. Dismissing his offers of help so forcefully that he feared he might have breached one of the most sensitive Philippine 'Don'ts', she limped in and out of the room with a series of dishes, some in wooden bowls, some in polished coconut shells and some on what looked like banana leaves. With the food laid out, she summoned Dennis, who sat with uncharacteristic restraint, waiting for permission to start. It was only when she made the sign of the cross that Philip realised, just in time, that she had been saying a silent grace.

No sooner had they finished eating than Philip was distracted by a bespectacled head peering round the door. Felicitas warmly welcomed the elderly woman, along with her three companions, explaining that they were friends and neighbours whom she had invited to come and share their memories of Julian. As they wavered at the edge of the room, Philip sprang up to give one of them his seat, motioning to Dennis to do the same. While his offer was repeatedly refused, Dennis's was immediately accepted, prompting him to retreat to the yard. With the two older women occupying the spare chairs and the two younger ones claiming to be happy on the mats, Philip leant forward and picked up his pad, taking copious notes as if to justify his privileged position.

One by one, and with a hint of rivalry, the women testified to Julian's good works. The first spoke of his funding the building of a primary school in the *poblacion* and the second, stouter than the rest, whose every other sentence began 'Modesty aside', spoke of his sponsoring her son's dental studies in Manila, which had enabled him to work in America. Even as he congratulated the proud mother, Philip recalled Julian's deep disapproval of such migration and felt torn. The two younger women both told hospital stories: the first described Julian's arranging for her to have her intestinal worms removed, with such rapture that Philip half expected her to produce the parasites pickled in a jar; the second described his arranging for an operation on her mother's cataracts. Philip wondered whether the success of these procedures, miraculous to those unfamiliar with modern medicine, might have fostered a folk memory of his healing power.

Three of the women had attended Gener's requiem, which had clearly been an expression of communal defiance as much as of private grief, while the fourth, a birdlike woman with soft eyes, sunken cheeks and wisps of hair escaping from an ash-grey bun, complained bitterly that her employer, doña Arcilla Pineda, had refused to let her off work. None of the other witnesses shared Felicitas's scruples about swearing to the levitation, although each echoed her emphasis on the sunbeam that had fallen on Julian to dazzling effect. Far from scenting collusion, Philip saw the consistency of their accounts, so long after the event, as proof of its extraordinary impact on them. Even so, the rationalist in him (which was under daily attack in the Philippines), having first ascribed the phenomenon to an outbreak of mass hysteria, now speculated that it might have been a simple trick of the light.

'Thank you all so much for your testimony, your deeply moving testimony,' Philip said, conscious of the irony that he, who had been hired to substantiate Julian's virtue, should now be playing Devil's Advocate, the role traditionally taken by the Promoter of the Faith when the prospective saint's case came under scrutiny in Rome. 'It'll be of great value to the investigation. I hate to impose on you further, but I wonder if one of you might introduce me to Consolacion, Father Julian's housekeeper.' The uneasy silence that greeted her name left him feeling as if he had farted in church. Felicitas, acting as spokeswoman, warned that she would refuse to see him, just as she had everyone else who had come to talk about Julian in recent years.

'Modesty aside,' came the inevitable interjection, 'I think I can speak for us all in saying how hurt we have been to see her turning away from us.'

'And from Father Julian.'

'She will not go any more to the church.'

'Has she lost her faith?' Philip asked.

'She goes to the Independent Church.'

'Into Baguio, in her grandson's car,' Felicitas said, as if this compounded the treachery.

Philip mused on what might have occurred to alienate Consolacion from the Church and sully her memory of Julian. Why was the former keeper of the flame now prepared to see it extinguished? Given the women's intransigence, it was clear that he would have to solve the mystery alone. Meanwhile, after accepting an invitation from Jocelyn Alvarez, the dentist's mother, to meet Benigna Vaollota the following afternoon, he said his goodbyes and went to fetch Dennis who, having run down the battery on his Walkman, sat staring blankly into space. He was doubly reluctant to ask directions from a woman, but Philip, refusing to take any chances, dispatched him inside to consult Felicitas. His foresight was vindicated when they found themselves in a web of unnamed streets, as they drove to visit Rodel Jimenez and Rey Sison, Julian's two surviving cell mates.

After passing a makeshift sports pitch, on which six young men, three a side, were playing a strange hybrid of football and volleyball, featuring high leaps, swooping kicks and the occasional flying somersault, they turned down a dirt track, lined with small wooden shacks, one of which, with its open hatch, *San Miguel* sign and three small tables, proved to be their destination. The only customers were two elderly men, who stood up as they approached. Introductions were effected, with Dennis showing a morbid interest in the bulbous, tongueless Rodel. At Philip's request, he fetched four bottles of beer and handed them around the group, before taking his cue from Philip's 'Now we must get down to business', one of the few directives that he was guaranteed to respect, and moving to the adjoining table where he sat vacantly.

While addressing his questions to Rey, Philip made sure to include Rodel who, although speechless, was not silent. As Rey described how Julian had opened their eyes to the truths of the Bible, Rodel scribbled on his slate, holding it up to read *You must not exploit a poor and needy wage-earner.* Philip thanked him heartily and made great play of copying it in his notebook. Rey, clearly more accustomed to his friend's practice, ignored it and continued with an impassioned account of the founding of the BCCs, the battles with the *haciendos*, Quesada's death, their own imprisonment, and the murder of their two friends and colleagues, all of which chimed with Julian's letters. Throughout their conversation Rodel chalked biblical quotations on his slate, which Philip duly took down.

Rey broke off as a man walked past, his demeanour at once swaggering and shifty. He stopped to stare at them before spitting, sufficiently close to his own feet to forestall retaliation, and continuing down the road.

'Who was that?' Philip asked.

'Albert Alias,' Rey replied. 'He used to be the hit man for the Mayor. He killed many, many good people. Now the Mayor is in prison, he is on his own.'

'Isn't it dangerous for him? Aren't there relatives of the victims out to exact revenge?'

'They too have to take care. Everyone knows that the Mayor will not be locked up for long. Already he has been let out several times. In the autumn it was for the marriage of his daughter. There were pictures in the papers. So many smiles.'

'And the authorities didn't intervene?'

'He is too useful for them. At the last election he delivered to the government a thousand votes in a *barangay* where there were five hundred people. We should be very proud of our long-lived town. It is said that half the people on the electoral roll are more than a hundred years old.'

Rodel scribbled *Methuselah lived for nine hundred and sixty-nine years* on his slate, only to rub it off in fury.

'So you would endorse what I've heard elsewhere,' Philip asked, unnerved by the one's tone and the other's gesture, 'that nothing much has changed since Father Julian's day?'

'We have changed,' Rey said, banging his bottle on the table. 'We have changed. That must change something.'

Dennis looked up on hearing the noise, at which Philip caught his eye and waved his own bottle meaningfully. Scowling, Dennis stood and fetched them a second round. Rey took a long swig and resumed on a new note.

'This beer was first brewed by the friars. The Augustinians in Manila. Did you know that?'

'If I did, I'd forgotten.'

'I suppose this is one good thing we can thank them for.'

Rodel scribbled *Let him drink and forget his misfortune, and remember his misery no more* on his slate.

'Did you also know that when the friars first came here they held long debates to decide if the Filipinos – "these uncivilised natives" – could be considered fully human?'

'That's monstrous!'

'Is it?' Rey asked. 'What are we? No more than slaves. Look at him!' He pointed to Rodel. 'No, not at his face.' He thrust his hand at Rodel's crotch. 'There is nothing there.' Philip stared at the ground. 'At least he has an excuse. What can you say for the rest of us?' He began to weep. Rodel gently clasped his shoulder. Dennis watched, transfixed.

'Only that Julian had faith in you. His life, not to mention his death, was governed by his love and respect for the Filipino people. If Rome endorses his miracles, St Julian of Benguet may be an inspiration to generations to come.'

'Is that what this country needs? Another saint? More processions and music and ribbons and *lechon*? I know one man who would not agree. Father Julian said that what we needed was knowledge and action. No more saints, unless they are leading armies like St George!' He took another long swig of his beer. 'No, of course he should be a saint. He was a good man, a great man, a miracle worker. Give the people what they want. If he can make them happy, is that not a miracle? You should go now. We have told you all we can.'

Philip stood up, knocking the table and spilling one of the bottles. 'Oh, I'm so sorry.'

'It is of no importance. It is beer, not blood.'

Rodel scratched something on his slate but, before he could hold it up, Rey grabbed it and flung it to the ground. Rodel stared at it impassively.

'You should go!'

Returning to the hotel, Philip went straight up to his room, switched on his laptop and began to transcribe the testimonies. He was midway through Felicitas's account of the requiem when the light went out and the fan whirred to a halt. After waiting a minute for his eyes to adjust, he edged gingerly round the sharp-angled bed and into the corridor, following the contours of the walls to the stairs and down to the lobby which, to his consternation, was pitch-black, without a glimmer of illumination from the street. His hollow 'hello' was greeted by an unruffled 'We are here, Mr Seward' from Lerma and a loud guffaw from Dennis.

'I am coming to help,' Dennis said. 'I am man; I am fearing nothing in dark.'

'Neither, you'll be pleased to hear, am I. But I am afraid of breaking my leg. What's happened? Has the hotel's fuse box blown?'

'No, it is not here,' Lerma replied. 'It is all the town, maybe all the province.' She lit a candle and placed it on the hatch.

'Has there been a massive power cut?'

'No,' she said, with a laugh. 'It is the Governor. He tells his men to switch off the light.'

'The Governor's ordered the black-out of his own province?'

'It is correct,' she replied placidly. 'He is a director of companies who ask for a big grant to build a new plant with coal. So one or two times in each month he makes sure there is no energy, to show the people the need for more supply. Even when we all know there is enough from the hydro-energet… how do you say it?'

'Hydroelectric power.'

'It is correct.'

With no functioning stove, Lerma proposed a dinner of dried cuttlefish, which Philip politely declined. He did, however, accept the candle, which seemed to be the only one in the hotel, and, clutching it tightly, picked his way back to his room. Sparing both his eyes and his iPod, he opted for an early night, waking after an uninterrupted ten hours feeling fully refreshed. Which was more than could be said for Dennis, who stumbled down to breakfast with hooded eyes and haystack hair, looking as if he had barely slept. Giving him time for only a single bowl of rice, Philip insisted that they leave for San Isidro and his appointment with Regina Romualdez.

Regina, alone of the town's ruling families, had agreed to see him. Although Julian had barely mentioned her in his letters, the hostility he had shown towards her father and the opprobrium he had heaped on her brother made Philip anxious about his reception. In the event, he was pleasantly surprised. Dennis drove through the open gates of the *hacienda*, past a now unmanned sentry box, and down a long avenue of typhoon-twisted trees to the cracked portico of the big house. An elderly maid met him at the door and led him into a large salon, whose mildewed walls and faded grey-green curtains mirrored the gentle dilapidation of the façade. While she went to fetch her mistress, he tried out an eccentrically shaped chair with vastly elongated arms, leaning forward until his bottom was suspended in the air, at which moment he was simultaneously seized by cramp and greeted by Regina.

'Wouldn't you be more comfortable here?' she asked, pointing to a battered leather sofa.

'Thank you,' he replied, dislodging himself with difficulty. Despite his embarrassment, his mishap seemed to have eased her, and her voice was far friendlier than it had been on the phone. She spoke perfect English with a mid-Atlantic twang and, after the usual small talk while the maid served iced green tea and savouries, he took out his notepad and asked for her impressions of Julian.

'What sort of impressions?'

'Whatever springs to mind.'

'Deceit,' she said emphatically. 'I'm sorry, is that not what you were expecting?'

'Can you elaborate?'

'At first all the families were happy to see him. We knew that he was one of us. We thought that he would be an ally, but we were wrong. It felt as if he wanted to attack the world he had been born into, but he could not do that in England, so he came here, where the people are easily led, where they listen to the promises of a kind man with an educated voice and, of course, a white face. Do I make myself clear?'

'Perfectly. Please go on.'

'A priest should make promises, of course, but they should be about the next world not this one. He should not interfere in politics. According to him, whenever my father wasn't exploiting his tenants, he was busy trying to buy their loyalty. But didn't he do the same? The people loved him not because of the sermons he preached, which they were too ignorant to understand, but because of the money he gave for their medical fees and classroom equipment, and even some farming projects. And where did it come from? His family, who were no different from us, only thousands of miles out of sight. And for this they want to make him a saint? Shouldn't a saint look in the mirror? Or would that be vain?'

'I'm sorry. I've no wish to reopen old wounds.'

'They have never closed; they will never close. Your saint did not understand how we live here. He failed to appreciate the links between my family and my tenants' families, which have been forged over many generations. You met Tanya, my maid, now the only maid for this whole house. Her sister was a maid for my mother but she had to leave. It was very sad. Perhaps there was wrong on both sides. But we have put it behind us. Tanya has been with me for more than twenty-five years. That is our way.'

'I think that's what Julian objected to. He didn't want a world that was split into masters and servants.'

'No, he and his friends wanted revolution. They were terrorists, even if they had no guns – and, believe me, there are many who swear that they did. Suppose they'd succeeded, what then? They get rid of Marcos and end up with Mao or Pol Pot. Do you think that the people would have been happier with that?'

'With respect, you ended up with Cory Aquino.'

'Ah yes, the plain, simple lady, beloved in the West, who smiled and spoke softly and didn't spend money on shoes. What precisely did she do for the peasants? She brought in land reform, which hit small estates like ours while great ones like hers were exempted. Our tenants – our former tenants – can't afford to run their own farms and we can't afford to help them. So now we are all worse off.'

'It may surprise you to learn that Julian was equally disillusioned by the Aquino government.'

'Forgive me, but I am not interested. What happened to the *hacienda* broke my father's heart. I say this as a fact. He felt a pain in his shoulder during lunch and two hours later he was dead. I have been left to take over, to run things as best I can, never knowing if we will still be here from one harvest to the next.'

'Don't you have a brother?'

'He is no longer in the country,' she replied curtly. 'I am sorry; I cannot help you. For me, Father Julian is no saint – not at all. There is injustice in the world, along with cruelty and suffering, but they count for nothing in the face of eternity. It is the priest's job to keep our minds on the justice and peace to come. You remember Jesus's words when Judas condemned Mary for pouring the precious oil on His feet: "You will always have the poor among you." I like to think that they have a particular significance in the Philippines.'

'Elsewhere He spoke very differently. "Blessed are the poor", for a start.'

'*Blessed*, exactly! He did not say *rich* or *happy* or even *well-fed*. There is an order on earth and there is an order in heaven, and it is our job to respect the first and to prepare for the second. I love and honour all the saints. Father Teodoro, our priest before Father Julian, called them the rungs on the ladder to God. I treasure that phrase. As a girl, I used to dress the *santos* for the feasts, until Father Julian forbade it.' She screwed up her eyes as if in pain. 'Whatever the Bishop decides – whatever the Congregation in Rome decides – I refuse to believe that in ten or twenty or even one hundred years' time – another little girl will be dressing the statue of St Julian.'

Seeing that there was nothing to be gained from further questioning, Philip took his leave of her and went outside to find Dennis, who was sitting on his haunches, puffing contentedly on a thin cigarette.

'Now we go back to the hotel?'

'No, the *poblacion*,' Philip replied, priding himself that he was now able to pronounce the word with native sibilance. Dennis looked at him like a child who suspected his parents of reading his diary, but said nothing. They headed back into town, where Philip proposed to pay a call on Consolacion. Although she had replied to neither his nor the Vicar General's letters, he was pinning his hopes on a direct approach. Page after page of Julian's correspondence attested to their closeness and, despite her bewildering loss of faith, she of all people must wish to see his virtues recognised by the Church. She might not even have read their letters but, like many old people daunted by unfamiliar writing and postmarks, have buried them at the bottom of a drawer. Casting his mind back, he wondered whether Julian had ever mentioned that she was literate, before dismissing such conjecture as both desperate and distasteful.

With supreme self-confidence, Dennis led them down several dead ends before finally chancing on the right road and drawing up outside a small house, with breeze-block walls and a corrugated-iron roof. As he walked through the well-tended garden, past a sparse vegetable patch and a half-dozen banana trees, Philip felt like a devious antique dealer out to cheat an old lady of her treasures, which was doubly absurd when he would be helping to preserve the thing that she treasured most: Julian's memory. He reached the door, where his knock was anticipated by a cheerful man in his mid-thirties, as crisp and spruce as his shirt.

'Hello! I hope I'm not disturbing you. My name is Philip Seward. I'm here to – '

'Yes, I know. This is a small town. News travels fast.'

'In which case you have me at a disadvantage.'

'I'm Mark Villena,' he said with a broad smile. 'The local schoolteacher, for my sins, as you English say.'

'We English generally have good reason.'

'And Consolacion's grandson. She came to live with Jennifer – my wife – and me ten years ago. Next month she will be ninety-four.'

'That's a great age,' Philip replied, wondering whether she might prove to be one of the few genuine centenarians on the electoral roll. 'I trust she's in good health.'

'She has various aches and pains, and some difficulty walking, but her mind is as sharp as ever. Her biggest problem is that she's blind, so she can no longer read the Bible every day.'

'That's sad,' Philip said, feeling more ashamed than ever of his recent surmise.

'I should tell you now that she won't talk to you about Father Julian. She won't talk about him to anyone, not even Jennifer and me. I'm sorry if this means that you've had a wasted trip.'

Undeterred, Philip emphasised the importance of the meeting, not just for Julian's sake but for Consolacion's, to help her gain 'closure' (a term appropriated from his grief counsellor) after a loss so harrowing that she could no longer bear to speak Julian's name. Mark, visibly impressed, agreed to plead his case and, while promising nothing, asked him to return the following day.

After eating a hot dog and noodles at a stand in the *poblacion* square, Philip left Dennis stretched out on a crumbling stone bench and walked through the near-deserted streets to keep his appointment with Jocelyn Alvarez. He had been nonplussed on asking her for her address to be told to 'take the left road from the east side of the plaza and look for the pink building; you will not miss it'. In the event, the bright salmon walls, which seemed to blush at their own audacity, bore out her words. It was a huge house by neighbourhood standards, with two floors and an attic, a wide verandah at the front and a small flight of steps leading to a second door at the side. As he strolled up the gravel path, Philip was curious to know how Jocelyn could afford it, but no sooner had she come out to greet him than the mystery was solved. It belonged to her son who, she declared unrepentantly, 'was making much more money as a nurse in Los Angeles than a dentist does in Manila'.

Modesty was once again set aside, as she led him indoors and claimed credit for much of the design and decor, including 'two comfort rooms on every floor'. That her son shared her taste was evident from the faux Gainsborough portrait of him in a powdered wig and frock coat, painted by a Beverly Hills artist who, according to Jocelyn, was a 'personal friend of First Lady Reagan', and which hung in a place of honour on the sitting-room wall.

'You will be hungry,' she said, reaching for a bell, even though a maid was hovering within earshot. The switch from the emollient English she adopted for Philip and the tart Tagalog with which she chivvied the maid verged on the grotesque. Philip watched as the girl wheeled in a trolley that would not have been out of place in the Berkshire drawing rooms of his youth, trembling for her as its wheels caught on the fringe of the rug which, fittingly, was a giant reproduction of a 100-dollar bill. Disaster averted, she handed him a glass of iced tea, with a mint and lemon garnish, and a far more varied selection of sticky cakes than he had been offered by Felicitas the day before.

Jocelyn, meanwhile, regaled him with a series of anecdotes about Julian, who had baptised one of her children, married another, and buried two more within the space of eight years. 'He was a good man; he came from such a good family,' she said, as if virtue had been in his blood: first 'honourable', then 'venerable', then 'blessed'. 'I was fortunate to meet his niece and her intended when they came to stay. Please to say to doña Isabella good morning from the woman in the churchyard. She will know.'

'Of course,' Philip said, cloyed by both the chatter and the cakes. 'Do you think it is time to send for señora Vaollota.'

'She is in here already.'

'Really?' Philip looked around.

'Of course. She is in the kitchen. I keep her there with the other woman while you have your tea, so that you will not become disturbed. Modesty aside, I think that you enjoy your conversation more with me. I have spoken English in Hollywood.'

Resigned to the need to share her visitor, she rang for the women who entered with a diffidence that Philip suspected owed more to their presence in Jocelyn's sitting room than to meeting him. Jocelyn introduced him as Philip *Seaweed*, evoking painful memories of prep school, while not seeing fit to introduce them at all, so that when the older of the two launched into a fervent account of how praying with Father Julian had destroyed the tumour on her breast, he assumed that she was Benigna and had forgotten the English 'neck'. It was only when she added that her cure was not considered a miracle because she had previously been treated by the *baylan* – at whose name Jocelyn looked as if she might spit, were it not straight into Benjamin Franklin's eye – that Philip realised she was someone else entirely, who found the lack of official recognition for her recovery as distressing as the original disease.

'I know this is him. I felt his hand like a blade on my breast, cutting out all that is rotting and wicked but also making me whole. It is me – I am the one – who is the first to tell the world that he is a saint. Is this not true?' She appealed to Jocelyn, who nodded sagely, and to Benigna, who hung her head. 'So you must tell my story. Victoria Lopez. You know how to write this name?'

'L – O – P – E – Z,' Philip replied.

'Yes,' she said and then, as if taking no chances, walked over to check his notebook.

'Honestly!' Jocelyn said, affronted on Philip's behalf. 'Mr Seaweed is a famous person. I think that he can know how to write a simple – a very simple – name like yours.'

'Not that famous,' Philip interjected. 'But perhaps Benigna will tell us her story?' he asked, turning a page deliberately.

In contrast to Victoria, Benigna had to be coaxed at every step, although it was this very hesitation and humility in the face of what had happened to her that Philip found most compelling. Echoing the Vicar General, she described how, after her neck had swollen 'like a puffer fish', Julian appeared to her at night and told her to go straight to the church. She insisted, however, that she had been wide awake. 'I was not sleeping for three days.'

'How can you be sure that it was Father Julian? Did you know him when he was the parish priest? You must have been very young.'

'Yes, this is true, and I do not remember his face at all. But I have seen many pictures. And when he spoke to me – like so many people, you will say to me that I am dreaming – but I hear his voice from when he is giving me my names at my christening. I feel his arms round me like when he is holding me in the water. This is the first miracle, no?'

'It's certainly remarkable.'

'And the second miracle is when I come to the church – after my husband and his mother and his father and all of the people are telling me "no" – I am finding that the door, it is open. At night it is always locked. Father Marlon, he swears that he has locked it also after mass, but it is open for me to go inside. And I kneel on the steps. It is hard for me to sit up in the bed, but when I am there it is easy to kneel. And when I look up, I see Father Julian with the Blessed Virgin. And she is smiling at me. But it is not just a smile on her lips; it is like the whole air is smiling. And I am there through all of the night, but it does not feel like a night; it does not feel like time at all. Then my husband, he carries me back to my bed and for three days they are afraid I am dying. But on this third day I have no lump on my neck. I have no wound and no mark. You must look!' She twisted her neck to reveal the unblemished skin. 'After this everyone is happy for me and I am happy, but I am also sad. I hear a voice – although it is not the same voice of Father Julian – telling me to give up this life and go inside a convent. But my husband, he speaks to Father Marlon, and the priest, he tells me that God will be wanting me to stay with my family, so this is what I am doing. But all the time I am thinking that this can be another message from the saint.'

Philip thanked her for her moving testimony. After another glass of iced tea and a respectful flick through Jocelyn's Los Angeles album he escaped and returned to the hotel. As he sat in his room typing up his notes, trying to capture the women's views and voices, he had a strong sense – almost a revelation – that they might be a springboard to something more. For the first time since abandoning his novel, he saw a way to revive his literary ambitions. A dread of personal revelation had led him to defy the conventional wisdom to write about what he knew; but now, either by chance or providence, he found himself in a world so different from his own that he would be able to make the unknown his theme. Fired with enthusiasm, he sketched out a series of plots about foreigners grappling with Philippine culture: first, an adventure story about a gang of rogue marines who stayed on after the US withdrawal and mounted a military coup (he could hear Hollywood tills rattling); next, a mystery about an aid worker in Manila who uncovered an organ-farming racket run by the Vatican (less cash but more kudos); finally, a romantic comedy about a troupe of ballet dancers, headed by a thinly disguised Margot Fonteyn (Max's memories would be invaluable), who toured the country, losing their hearts to the locals.

He dismissed each idea as fast as he jotted it down, taking his notepad with him to dinner where Dennis, seizing his advantage, pulled out his mobile to text. Even so, Philip felt too euphoric to stop and, after wolfing down his food, he returned to his room, where he continued to map out characters and scenarios before ripping up his notes, a destruction which for once felt creative, and settling down for an early night in a bid to bring his subconscious into play. Any dreams were lost, however, when he was shaken awake by Lerma.

'Please, mister, please. You must hurry and leave this hotel!'

'What?'

'Please, mister, please!' She continued to shake him, even though he was wide awake.

'What's the time?' he asked, shrugging off her hand and looking at his watch. 'Quarter to two!'

'Please, mister, my husband has come back a day too soon to surprise me.'

'It's a hotel! Aren't you supposed to have guests?'

'He surprises me in the bed with Dennis.'

'Dennis?'

'It is correct. He has run away into the car.'

'My car?'

'It is parked in the street, in the other side of town. I take you there.'

'Tomorrow,' Philip said implacably. 'He's made his own bed – or whatever – let him lie in it.'

He turned on his side, emphasising his resolve, at which she began to shake him harder. 'My husband will search for him. I am fearful; you must leave.'

'Oh, for heaven's sake!'

'You must pack up your case. I will make your bill.'

'What?'

'For your visit.'

'Of course! Don't forget to charge for sundry services,' he added with a bitterness that seemed to stem from his groin.

Angry and frustrated, he threw on his clothes and gathered up his few belongings. Feeling like an actor in a second-rate farce, he hurried into the corridor, where he was met by Armin, who took his grip and, steering him away from the main staircase, led him down an even more dingy and decrepit staircase at the back. As they sneaked through a bare concrete hallway, past sacks that might have been filled with rice, vegetables, or the body parts of adulterous guests, Philip studied Armin in the hope of finding out what he felt about such goings-on, but his face gave nothing away. Lerma met them at the door and wordlessly thrust the bill into Philip's hand. A cursory glance showed that, whatever the hotel's failings, he had not been overcharged.

'I don't suppose you take American Express?' he asked, dragging out her misery.

'Only cash,' she said anxiously.

'Master card? Visa?'

'Only cash.'

He peeled the notes from his wad and, as an afterthought, peeled off two more for Armin, who mutely bowed his head.

'Armin will take you to find your car,' she said, as she disappeared into the hotel.

'No "We hope to welcome you back here soon"?' Philip called after her, before following Armin down a shadowy alley, past rows of closed shops, unlit houses and a jeepney depot, to his car, which stood alone in an otherwise empty street. Armin handed him his grip, bowed his head again and walked briskly away. Seeing no more sign of the fleeing lover than of the vengeful husband, Philip began to wonder whether 12 March were the Filipino equivalent of 1 April. He punched the door in exasperation and, hearing a rustle, peered through the window to find Dennis cowering beneath the driver's seat.

'Open the door, you idiot!' Philip shouted.

'Why you wait so long? Quick, quick!' Dennis replied, turning on the ignition before Philip had even sat down.

'Take it easy!' Philip said. 'I've already had my sleep broken. I'd prefer to keep my neck in one piece.'

'We go to Manila, yes?'

'No, we go to San Isidro. I have a very important appointment at eleven o'clock tomorrow – today.'

'Then we go there now,' Dennis said, taking no chances.

'Unless you have a better idea. Perhaps another hotel where you can bed the proprietor's wife?'

'She good, yes? I see you are liking her. But, no, she is only liking me.'

'Who wouldn't like you? A gutless little cheat, scared stiff of being beaten up. You're irresistible.'

'What you mean? She is begging me to go away. She is afraid I am killing him.'

'Oh, shut up!' Philip said and, much to his surprise, Dennis did.

They parked on the outskirts of San Isidro, where they opened the windows, pushed back the seats and curled up for what remained of the night. Dennis's bubbly snores, following closely on his brazen 'Goodnight', were the final indignity for Philip who, torn between fatigue and fury, steeled himself for a lonely vigil. He awoke several hours later to a gust of foul breath, which he instinctively blamed on Dennis, until he turned to find a goat staring through the window. His startled yelp scared off the animal and roused Dennis, whose unkempt, unshaven, bleary-eyed confusion would have been amusing had it not been such a mortifying reflection of his own. He felt grubby and parched, and for the first time wished that he had come here during the rainy season, when he would have been able both to take a shower and slake his thirst. He tried to shift position, but his body rebelled at the slightest movement and so, easing himself out of the door, he leant back against the roof and cautiously stretched.

He did what he could to freshen up, using face wipes on his face, neck and chest, along with liberal dabs of aftershave. He brushed his teeth with bottled water in full view of a gang of schoolchildren who, he trusted, were impervious to Western eccentricity. He put on a clean pair of socks and T-shirt but refused to risk a change of underpants, even in the semi-concealment of the car. Dismissing Dennis's pleas of hunger with an iciness he was determined to maintain until they returned to Manila, he asked him to drive to the *poblacion* square. With more than two hours to spare before he had arranged to call on Consolacion, he was planning to go back to the cemetery, but seeing a steady stream of people entering church he decided to follow, staying for what turned out to be nine o'clock mass. Despite his deep-rooted ecumenism, he thought it both polite and politic to remain in his seat when the communicants went up to the rail. At the end of the service he lingered behind to greet Father Honesto, who thanked him profusely for coming, adding that, had he known, he would have preached in English.

'But would everyone else have understood?'

'I speak to them every day.'

Ensconced in the musty sacristy, while the priest made tea on what looked like a Bunsen burner, Philip reported on his progress in the parish, expressing disappointment at having failed to track down the family of the boy with the withered leg.

'They left San Isidro last year. There had been some trouble. The father was a very greedy man, who tried to make money from the miracle. Many of his neighbours took offence. It was better that they left, although perhaps not better that they went to Manila. I do not know where such a family will live when they are there. It is like looking for a mullet in the sea.'

Philip returned to the car, where a newly compliant Dennis drove him straight to Consolacion's house to be greeted again by Mark.

'I'm afraid that I may be a little early,' Philip said.

'No, it is good. I have stayed away from the school. I am happy for you that she will speak to you. Come inside with me, please.'

Feeling both elated and apprehensive, Philip followed Mark through a dark hall into an uncluttered living room, where a grizzled woman with filmy eyes, sunken cheeks and skin like a dried-up riverbed, sat in a low armchair, her legs wide apart, listening to a madrigal on the radio.

'You must go close up to her,' Mark said to Philip. 'She is blind.'

'I can see,' Consolacion said in a surprisingly clear voice. 'Only not with my eyes.'

Confused by both Mark's injunction and Consolacion's response, Philip walked up to her and, praying that it was not presumptuous, lifted her hand from her lap to shake. She pulled him gently towards her, running her fingers across his chest and face. 'Yes, I can see the resemblance,' she said.

Philip wondered if she had mistaken his relationship with Julian or were referring to something beyond the physical. Mark switched off the radio and told him to sit next to his grand-mother, who was also rather deaf.

'I hear enough,' Consolacion said uncompromisingly. Philip hoped that she could not hear the nervousness in his voice, as he told her how thrilled he was to meet someone about whom he had read so much.

'Really?' she replied, with an indifference that might simply have been her natural tone.

'Father Julian mentioned you in every one of his letters home.'

'I was his housekeeper for thirteen years. I lived with him for longer than I lived with my husband.' Her eyes misted at the memory of one or both. 'We had a dog. I forget his name.'

'Grump.'

'What is it you say?'

'Grump! The name of the dog.'

'No, that was not it. I should know the name of my own dog,' she said, with a conviction that threw doubt on the rest of her testimony. Philip looked at Mark, who put a finger to his lips, at which Consolacion, as if sensing the movement in the air, spoke to him briefly in Tagalog.

'Please to excuse me,' he said. 'I will bring some snacks.'

As he left the room, Philip asked Consolacion for her memories of Julian. She repeated the familiar stories of his kindness, although with none of the warmth that he would have expected from one who had lived with him at such close quarters. Mark brought in the snacks, plain pastries filled with coconut and peanuts, which contrasted sharply with the sticky confections he had been offered elsewhere. They chatted generally about Julian, with Mark, who turned out to be older than he looked, adding his own impressions of the man who had funded his education.

'He was good to all the people in my family,' Consolacion said. 'He was good to all the people in the parish. To some of the people he was too good.'

'I suppose that it goes with the territory,' Philip said.

'I am not understanding.'

'I'm sorry. Part of being a priest.'

'Not all priests are so good,' Consolacion said. 'Not one especially: Father Benito. He had been living in Brazil. He brought back many ideas. Bad ideas. It was not for me to say, but Father knew that I did not believe in them.'

'*Lola*,' Mark said in a voice full of warning.

'Am I not to speak? Mark does not wish me to say any words against Father Julian. He paid for him to study at the university.'

'Yes, *Lola*, we have already told him this.'

'Have we?' She sighed. 'Well some things are good to be told again. They are good in the middle of much that is bad.'

'I think you must go now,' Mark said to Philip. 'It is wrong to be reminding her. I am sorry.'

'You think I forget? I remember these things every day. No, he has come to ask me questions. I shall give him answers.'

'No, *Lola*, I do not wish it.'

'You do not wish it, perhaps,' Consolacion said, addressing the air to one side of him. 'But you are not the one who is going to Hell.'

'No one here is going to Hell.'

Philip listened enthralled, unsure how much their Hell was a figure of speech and how much the full eschatological works.

'I am. I am the one who has lied. When they asked me where he was on the night when they arrested him, I swore that he was at home, sleeping. I swore this on the Holy Bible.'

'But you knew that he wasn't?' Philip asked, while Mark stared at his feet.

'I have heard him go out.'

'Were you trying to protect him?'

'I thought that he had a woman. I had not seen any sign of it for myself, it is true, but he had been stopped by the soldiers with a pregnant woman on the road to the hospital. There was much talking in the parish. Like many of the people, I expected that the baby was his.'

'And you weren't shocked?' Philip asked incredulously.

'When I was a girl, we had a priest here from Spain. When he called us his "children" in the church, we all used to laugh because we knew that, for the cases of Anna and Joshua Padero, this was not just a way of speaking. It is strange, I can remember their names but I am forgetting his. Do you remember, Mark?'

'*Lola*,' he said mildly, 'that was eighty years ago.'

'Was it? Yes, you are right. When people said how it was strange that they were having European faces, the priest said that it was because this woman – his woman – had prayed before the *santos* of the Blessed Mother. A beautiful *santos* that he had brought to San Isidro from Spain.'

'And you believed him?'

'He was the priest and I was a small girl; naturally, I believed him. And my mother believed him. All of the people believed him.'

'But Father Julian didn't have a woman?'

'No, he had a different secret. And I was the only one person who knew.'

'Won't you tell us what it was?' Philip asked eagerly.

Consolacion pressed on as if she had not heard. 'When he went back to England, he asked me to put into boxes all of his things: all of his papers and his books and his records and his clothes. And in one of his pockets I found a small map of the place where he had been spending that night.'

'Do you still have it?'

'I burnt it. I burnt it and I have tried to forget it. But I see it in front of my eyes now. They say I am blind, but I see it.'

'*Lola!*'

'What was it of? Please tell me.'

'That's enough now,' Mark said. 'She is exhausted. You really have to go.'

'Just one more minute, please!' Philip said, his gratitude to Mark rapidly waning. 'Surely, if it was anything significant, the police would have found it? They must have searched the house.'

'The police came to the *convento* only twice, once to arrest the Father and once to question me.'

'And you never showed this map to anyone?'

'I burnt it.'

'Why? What were you afraid of people seeing?'

'I burnt it, and ever since then I have never been once inside the church. Not even for the deaths of my friends. Mark drives me to Baguio to our own church – '

'The Philippine Independent Church,' Mark interjected.

'But I have never been once inside his church. He has healed others, but he has taken away my faith. And now you wish to make him a saint!'

'Not me, the people of San Isidro – your neighbours. They are the ones who petitioned the Bishop.'

'Yes, I know this. A saint!'

'And the map? Was it really so incriminating? What did it prove? That he knew where the killers were hiding? That he took them the last rites?'

'I forget. I am an old woman. I have been living for too long and I am frightened to die.'

'I know nothing about the Independent Church, but does it have no place for confession? Can't you be absolved of the lie, the sin, whatever you choose to call it?'

'But you wish to make him a saint and my sin will grow bigger. My sin will grow bigger every time that some person prays to him.'

'Why? Even if you disapprove of the rebels, surely you accept that, as a priest, Father Julian had a duty to bring them the sacraments?'

'Mark!' She held out her arm, which he moved to take. 'I am tired now. Thank you for coming here, but it is time that you must leave.' She shuffled towards the door, every punishing step echoing her anguish. 'You are right; it is not good for us to worry about these things which we cannot change. *Bahala na ang Diyos.*'

Five

My dear Mother and Father,

I hope this finds you safely back in Whitlock and not pining for the tropical sun. Both your cards have arrived, along with Mother's letter. Many thanks. For some reason the post is far more efficient from Mexico than from England. Maybe Greg should ask a question in the House?

Chichen Itza has amazed everyone who visits the *convento*. I'm not surprised that you didn't attempt the climb. Your story of the retired accountant wooing the South African millionairess made me laugh out loud, Mother. I'm delighted you found some kindred spirits among the passengers – not least the all-important bridge partner. Though how you managed to persuade Father to leave home in the first place is a mystery. But now you have, what about that long promised trip to the Philippines? There's no excuse to put it off, especially when you got on so well with the cabin staff. As you've seen for yourselves, they're an exceptionally kind and accommodating people.

When – I refuse to say *if* – you come out here, you must be sure that it's in February or March, avoiding both the extremes of temperature and the worst of the storms. In your letter, Mother, you mentioned rough seas in the Atlantic. I don't wish to sound like Mrs Healey trumping everyone's misfortunes with tales of her ill-fated family, but against your blustery winds I raise you an F3 tornado. Consolacion, never the cheeriest of souls, had been predicting calamity ever since the downpours started and the breeze remained scorchingly hot, but the first hint of danger came when Grump tore through the house like a thing possessed. All at once we were plunged into darkness.

I rushed outside to see dense black clouds sweeping across the sky around a silvery vortex, shaped first like a cigar and then a spike. The palm trees bordering the square were bent double, their trunks swinging to and fro like women shaking their hips to a furious drumbeat. Coconuts tumbled on to corrugated roofs like volleys of gunfire. Then the roofs themselves broke loose and wheeled through the air. I was transfixed by the eerie spectacle until Consolacion grasped my shoulder and pulled me indoors. We squeezed under the kitchen table with only Grump between us. This must be what started the rumours about Father Teodoro, I thought, easing Consolacion's hand away from my thigh and on to my rosary. Then, after five or ten minutes, which seemed to stretch into eternity, the winds died down as quickly as they'd blown up and we stepped out into Armageddon.

Roofs, doors, shutters, windows and furniture had been flung about the square. The old colonial houses had had their balconies and verandas torn off, and stucco façades shattered by the uprooted trees. At the centre, the Rizal statue had been turned into a modernist war memorial. For the first time I gave thanks for the parish's poverty: that the windows were made of capiz shell not glass; that there were no fallen power cables underfoot; and that my car, which had been dragged fifty yards down the road, was an old jalopy. The *convento* had escaped fairly lightly, with only the fretwork smashed and the outhouse flattened, but, as ever, the most resilient building was the church. Except for a few windowpanes and a bench dedicated to don Florante's mother (which had been universally shunned on account of her collaboration with the Japanese during the war), it remained intact. The people, needless to say, hail it as a miracle. I, however, am racked with shame to think that generations of friars should have devoted so much time and money to strengthening God's house, while leaving His people exposed.

The devastation in the countryside was even greater than in the town, although the blocked roads meant that it was two days before I could set out to investigate. Women sat stupefied on dirt floors, guarding the boundaries of their former homes, with no walls but scattered palm fronds and no ceilings but the sky. Their few sticks of furniture were now simply sticks. Dogs, goats and hens straggled through the wreckage, while a disorientated sow circled round and round her former pen, her seven piglets trotting aimlessly at her heels. Men on all three estates lined up outside the manager's office to claim their emergency rice rations and to negotiate loans to rebuild their homes. The work has already begun although, naturally, there are priorities: on the Pineda estate it's the repair of the private generator without which the food in their two refrigerators will rot; on the Arriola estate it's the reconstruction of the hutches for don Bernardo's prize-winning cocks. 'Hutches before houses?' I hear you ask. Quite.

The *haciendos* aren't the only ones to have failed in their duty. The soldiers who paraded daily through the streets have been notable by their absence. You might think that they'd want to build bridges – literally, given that two have collapsed on the Agno – but according to their commander, who could barely conceal his indifference, his forces have been called away to deal with a disturbance near Bokod. As for the civil authorities, the Mayor is on one of his regular furloughs in Manila and, rather than hurrying home, he's stayed on to solicit aid.

Meanwhile, I've put the church at the disposal of the homeless. When I visited the Romualdez to beg for bedding, doña Teresa offered to 'cut up all my petticoats if it will help any of those poor wretches'. I assured her that blankets would be more use. In the event she sent a gardener with a basket of old rice sacks. Consolacion monitors the evacuees with a rigour which, in another life, would have made her the perfect Ampleforth matron. Woe betide any boy who turns the font into a make-shift goal or girl who sneaks up the sanctuary steps to brush the *santos's* hair.

Like everyone else, the children help with the repairs. It's quite common to see toddlers scurrying behind their older brothers and sisters, dragging scraps of wood and metal twice their size. Even so, the work would be taking far longer had we not received support from an unexpected source. Returning one afternoon from the ravaged Pineda *hacienda,* I sensed a new mood in the town. I was putting it down to delayed shock and a gradual awareness of the back-breaking task ahead when I came across a knot of young men and women erecting a shack. Among the unfamiliar faces I recognised Alma Balitaan, a former parishioner who, shortly after my arrival, had quit her family to join the NPA. She looked equally startled to see me; the last time we met I was at least three skin tones lighter, clean-shaven and in full clerical fig. I hesitated to greet a member of a terrorist group which, even allowing for government distortion, had committed numerous atrocities. Then the sight of her four children working alongside her, the youngest clinging tightly to her skirts, alerted me both to the price she'd paid in leaving them and the risk she was taking in coming back.

Despite the official propaganda, which brands them as psychopaths and outcasts, most of the group remain in regular contact with their families. Hearing from her mother about the typhoon, Alma had brought her comrades down to help with the reconstruction effort, although in accordance with their code her mother's house has had to wait its turn. From its inception – and this certainly hasn't been broadcast by the government machine – the NPA has given practical support to the farmers. They're not Robin Hoods (at least not in a BBC teatime version); they carry guns and make no secret of their readiness to use them. Nevertheless, they're far from the cold-hearted killers we've been led to suppose. Their commitment to building a just society is much the same as mine; except that I look to Christ and they look to Mao. Indeed, on first principles, it would be true to say that I'm closer to them than to you. Forgive me – and correct me! – if I'm wrong but it strikes me that in your different ways you're both dyed-in-the-wool pessimists: Mother, with your belief that we're slaves to our sinful nature; Father, with your belief that we're doomed to repeat the mistakes of the past. Whereas Alma and her friends, with their conviction that life is perfectible, fill me with hope.

They stayed with us for a week before being tipped off by a sympathetic policeman that their presence had grown too conspicuous, whereupon they vanished into the mountains as swiftly as they'd come. The next day we buried Ronald Veloso, the typhoon's one fatality. So far I've refrained from describing a Filipino funeral, partly because I've no wish to fuel Father's view that my faith is morbid (I must have been one of the few teen-agers with a martyrology hidden under his mattress) and partly because I'd hate either of you to write off their practices as prim-itive. Nevertheless, given your account of Richard Goddard's requiem, Mother, you'll be relieved to know that things might have been worse. If Cora was disturbed by Richard's open casket – and, for all Greg's horror at her attempts to wipe off Richard's 'make-up', he clearly overreacted – she'd have been traumatised by Ronald's corpse. Having been sewn up and embalmed, it was placed on a chair in the centre of the room to preside over the nine-day wake. Each evening his brothers slaughtered and roasted a pig (I couldn't help wondering if one were the diso-rientated sow from the *hacienda*). On the ninth day the corpse was placed in a coffin, which according to custom was a snug fit, to prevent the spirits of his loved ones from joining him. It was then closed and carried to the church. Although the service itself stuck close to the missal, you might be surprised to learn that even I no longer went straight home from the cemetery but took a roundabout route – just in case!

The overwhelming response to the typhoon was resignation, as seen in Consolacion's favourite phrase '*Bahala na ang Diyos*' ('Leave it to God'). Coming from a very different world where we pray 'Your will be done', with the tacit proviso of 'except to someone as loving, faithful and honourable as me', I'm apt to fall into the trap of regarding the Filipinos as innately more devout. But faith is not fatalism. It's too easy for people living in abject poverty to invest their power in authority figures. So prevalent is their tendency to infantilise themselves that I've given up referring to them as 'children of God', preferring even the loaded word 'servants'.

I see it as my job to help them reclaim their power, acting, if you like, as an honest *encargado* between them and the landlord. Like any good *encargado*, I have my pet projects, the first of which is the introduction of worm casings. I doubt that's a phrase you ever expected to hear from me, someone who, to quote you, Father, 'can't tell a compost heap from a haystack', but five years with the BCCs have taught me more than thirty at Whitlock. On the one hand the only way to make the land pay is to plant high-yield rice, which requires pesticides and fertilisers the farmers can't afford. On the other, the overuse of those pesticides and fertilisers by greedy *haciendos* is drawing the goodness from the soil. So the farmers lose out both ways. What are they to do? Pay more for their rice and end up in worse debt? Sit back and pray for a miracle? Or sign up to Father Julian's vermiculture programme? Our goal is to build a factory, but for now we're based in the church crypt, where we have fifty large clay pots filled with worms producing several tons of manure each week. It's cheap, full of nutrients and, much to my relief, it doesn't even smell.

After initial qualms, the farmers have embraced the scheme. I've been at pains to point out that the worms come from the earth (their province) and not from the sky (mine). The *haciendos* and *encargados*, while forced to acknowledge the benefits, are less enthusiastic. A hungry tenant is a subservient tenant. I've been rebuked more than once for 'politicising the gospel', a charge I utterly deny. Any halfway diligent reader of the Bible knows that Our Lord's words can be interpreted in different – even contradictory – ways, but there's no disputing the message of His life: His challenge to the rich and powerful; His identification with the poor, the marginalised, and the oppressed. Señor Herrera, don Florante's man, led the attack on me. Citing my contacts with both Alma and Rommel Clemente, the son of one of our lay leaders, he accused me of having secretly joined the NPA. Risible, I know, but I have to take such things seriously. With opposition parties silenced, the only challenge to the government comes from the Church. Most of the bishops are in cahoots with the regime, but a few brave priests have spoken out. As a foreigner, I'm well protected, but I must keep on my guard. Rumours spread; mud sticks.

What Herrera didn't know was that the day before our meeting I'd received a request from the NPA to lend them my car for use in a mission. Assuring me that there would be no bloodshed, they explained that they were desperately short of vehicles to ferry operatives from one base to another. After a night of soul-searching I refused.

Was I wrong? Having witnessed their courage and idealism, I would like to have helped, but such practical assistance felt like a step too far. Is that the defence of time-servers everywhere? As an ex-officer, Father, you must have a view on this. If you've any advice for one whose gospel of nonviolence is wearing thin, please don't hesitate to write.

Meanwhile, remember me to everyone at Whitlock.

Your loving son,
Julian

Philip stood beside Max at the entrance to the Chinese cemetery, waiting for Ray to escort them to his family tomb. Having dressed in suitably muted colours, he had been disconcerted to find Max wearing a Hawaiian shirt and Bermuda shorts, as gaudy as the gateway above them, and prayed that his manner would be more subdued than his clothes. He was already feeling anxious about the invitation to meet the relatives and honour the ancestors of such an unlikely family man.

'Relax,' Max said, 'or as you people say, "Chill!"'

'I've never said "Chill!" in my life.'

'That's half the problem. You're not here to meet your bank manager but to enjoy a slap-up lunch.'

'It's not the food that spooks me but the setting.'

'Take it from your Uncle Max, it's a compliment. I must have known Ray six or seven years before he invited me to join them on Qingming, and here you are, scarcely five minutes off the plane!'

'That's one of the things that spooks me. What if his wife and kids get the wrong idea? Is the Lady Precious Stream act reserved for selected company? Does he butch it up at home?'

'At the risk of repeating myself: 'Chill!' They're not naïve; they're well aware of Ray's catholic – sorry – tastes. And here's Amel now.' Max waved to the man heading towards them. 'Amel,' he said, giving his cheek a pat, 'this is your father's new friend, Philip.'

Amel's broad grin at the ambiguous phrase bore out Max's claim of his ease with his father's proclivities. Everything about him spelt sophistication, from the slicked-back hair and monogrammed white shirt to the grey silk trousers and snakeskin loafers. Which made it all the more incongruous that he should call him 'Mr Philip', like an ancient retainer addressing the son of the house.

'A thousand apologies! I had no idea you were waiting.' He glanced at his watch, as if to absolve himself.

'Don't worry. We've only just arrived,' Max said with a smile.

'Are you ready?' Amel asked. 'I'm afraid it's a bit of a hike.'

'I'll be fine,' Philip said, gazing at the gradual slope and trusting that he was being treated as a typically effete European and not as his relatively fit self.

Max and Amel strolled ahead, chatting with an intimacy Philip would not have expected and leaving him to marvel at the mausolea, many as big as houses, all of them bigger than the houses he had seen in San Isidro. Christians, Buddhists and Taoists lay side by side in sepulchral splendour, united by both the refusal of the colonial authorities to admit foreigners into existing cemeteries and the wealth that had enabled them to circumvent the ban. With tombs dating from every decade since the 1850s, the architectural diversity rivalled the religious. Ornate pagodas and multi-tiered temples flanked neo-baroque chapels and squat, open structures, reminiscent of Mies van der Rohe. As with so many other vistas in Manila, the effect was marred by the occasional ruin which, nonetheless, provided a welcome corrective to the prevailing pomp.

The alien ethos and grandiose setting contrived to deny Philip his usual sense of graveyard peace. He felt no closer to his dead than when he had visited the Great Pyramid: a thought which was eerily underlined as he confronted that monument in miniature. Guarded by a youthful sphinx, several generations of an extended family sat round a dining table in its courtyard. Their conspicuous display emboldened Philip to scrutinise them when Amel stopped for a brief chat.

'Friends of yours?' Philip asked, as they moved on.

'Only on Qingming,' Amel replied, with a smile Philip refused to think of as inscrutable.

'So, is this the most important day in the Chinese calendar?'

'It's the most important day for our dead – the equivalent of your All Souls' Day. Although, if I'm not mistaken, that expresses

– or at least grew out of – a belief that praying and making offerings to God would lessen the sufferings of the dead. Whereas we don't believe that the dead suffer – at least no more than the living. For us, the afterlife is not separate from life but a part of it. Our ancestors are here with us. They take care of us, just as we do them. So we come here to venerate them and to bring them what they need for this new phase of their existence.'

'Christians aren't that different,' Philip said. 'We also believe that some dead people – saints – will look after us. Although of course they don't have to be our ancestors. By definition, very few of them have descendants.'

'You have saints on the brain,' Max said tetchily.

'Why else have I come to Manila?'

Moments later they reached the top of the incline, standing in front of a flamboyant building with a blood-red façade, upturned eaves and a pair of undulating dragons on the roof.

'Is this it?' Philip asked, awestruck.

'I wish!' Amel replied, laughing. 'This is the Chong Hock Tong temple. Our family tomb is on the other side.' He led them down a side avenue to an elegant grey mausoleum with a pink doorway, framed by tall, narrow windows made of engraved glass. They walked into a shaded courtyard, dominated by a life-size griffin, and up to fretwork doors, which Amel slid open. All at once, Philip was hit by a blast of cold air as strong as that in the hotel lobby. Despite the traditional painted lanterns, the light was dim, but as his eyes gradually adjusted he made out two large black sarcophagi to his left, with garlanded bas-reliefs of a man and woman above them, a row of wall graves on either side and an incense burner in front. Several lacquer chairs and a formal dining table stood at the back of the room and, as Amel pointed out to him in the nick of time, a small carp pond was set into the inlaid marble floor.

Ray welcomed them with a shrill 'Cooee', which paid little regard to either the solemnity of the tomb or the presence of his wife. With his hand proprietarily poised in the small – and sweat

– of Philip's back, he ushered him over to meet his 'good lady', a pale woman whose hair and dress – a glittering ruby butterfly in a braided chignon and a turquoise silk cheongsam with a line of beaded fans along her left leg – made up for the impassivity of her face. Philip took her hand and thanked her effusively for inviting him. 'My husband has told me so much about you,' she said, her voice trailing off as if in boredom. 'We are honoured that you could join us.' Philip thanked her again and ceded his place to Max who, bowing slightly, raised her fingers to his lips with the old-world courtesy that must once have endeared him to Imelda.

'This is my daughter, Janice,' Ray said, indicating a young woman in a black silk brocade jacket and skin-tight blue jeans, buried in the *Philippine Tatler*. She lowered the magazine languidly. 'Ciao!' she said, with a pout of her purple lips.

'Janice, you look more delectable every time I see you. Would that I were thirty years younger,' Max said, as though age were the only check on his ardour. He contented himself with kissing her on both cheeks. Philip, meanwhile, gazed at the open magazine, trying vainly to identify the featured gala, until Ray steered him towards the final member of the party, his elder son, Brent, who sat with his laptop at an ebony writing desk. He held up his left hand to forestall his father while he sent an email, before turning with a broad smile to Philip, echoing both his mother's words about the honour of his visit and his brother's mode of addressing him by title as well as by name.

'Please excuse me; I'm just finishing off some work,' Brent said.

'Of course,' Philip said, turning back to Amel. 'Is it my imagination, or do you have Wi-Fi in here?'

'Yes, you're right. Our ancestors want us to thrive, so we must have the chance to do business when we come here. And they want us to relax and eat well and enjoy the time we spend in their company, so we have the kitchen and the shower and the comfort room and the TV.'

'It's extraordinary,' Philip said guardedly. Even by Manila standards, the contrast between the high-tech cemetery and the squalid shanty town propped against its walls struck him as extreme. His unease was deflected by the arrival of Ray's brother Daio, his wife Faye, their daughters, sons-in-law and grand-children. Even Janice roused herself to greet them. Philip was transfixed by the sight of the whole family, led by Daio, kneel-ing in front of the sarcophagi and bowing their foreheads to the ground as if kowtowing to the Dowager Empress. They then went out to the courtyard, where everyone, young and old, rolled up pieces of printed paper and cardboard and threw them into an elegant stone burner with a ceramic dragon's head on the lid.

'This is *kim*,' Amel whispered to Philip, 'the offerings we make to assist our loved ones in the afterlife.'

The ritual concluded, Ray led the way to the dining table, where the maids served a sweet-and-sour chicken and melon soup, although a list of ingredients failed to do justice to the wealth of its flavours. Philip longed for more but was too shy to ask, watching helplessly as the maids cleared away the bowls, includ-ing the two for the ancestors, which had remained untouched at either end of the table. The ancestors – welcome spectres at the feast – were equally generously served with the main course. While the rest of the diners chose between shredded beef, crispy duck, sausage and sticky rice, sea bass in black bean sauce and suckling pig, their plates were heaped high with a portion of each. Philip could not help reflecting on the half-starved resi-dents of the shanty town. Had Julian been of the company, he would no doubt have upbraided the Lims as roundly as he had once done the Arriolas and Pinedas – although, as Taoists, they would, of course, have been outside his authority: an exemption that gave Philip some comfort as he reached for a deep-fried clam.

Sitting next to his hostess, he tried repeatedly to engage her in conversation, only to be thwarted at each attempt when, after the briefest of replies, she turned to speak to one of the maids.

Feeling snubbed, he focused on his food until Daio, who had been talking business with Brent, turned to him abruptly. 'I understand that you are here to bring the country another saint.'

'Nothing so grand,' Philip said, blushing. 'I'm compiling a report for his family, which may lend weight to the official submission. So far I've come up with little apart from some local colour.'

'So must you be going back to England?' Mikee asked coolly.

'Yes, soon I expect,' Philip replied. 'I've spoken to my employer, who wants me to stay until after Easter, when one of Julian's fellow missionaries, Hendrik van Leyden – a friend since student days – returns from Holland. But before that I've a less orthodox assignment. I'm sure you've all read about Jejomar Agbuya, the prisoner who claims that Julian came to him in a vision, promising that his crimes would be pardoned if he had himself crucified on Good Friday.'

'In Manila?' Faye asked with a shudder.

'No, *Nanay*,' one of her daughters said, 'at the *Kalbaryo* in Pampanga.'

'In my view he's an utter fraud,' Philip said. 'But it'd be irresponsible not to follow it up.'

At the end of the meal, Amel accompanied Philip and Max to the cemetery gates, where Dennis was waiting. They drove off, jolting and lurching through the clogged streets before grinding to a halt on Rizal Avenue.

'Does he know what's wrong? Has there been an accident?' Philip asked, as Dennis wound down his window and shouted to the driver of the adjacent car.

'No, is rally in park. Many crowding people.'

'Politics,' Max interjected. 'It's the curse of this country.'

'No,' Dennis said. 'Is not politics; is Church. Is *Couples for Christ*.'

'I rest my case,' Max said.

They lapsed into silence, broken only by Dennis's high-pitched humming, as they crept forward, gathering speed as soon as they passed the park. Halfway down Roxas Boulevard, Dennis turned sharp left, negotiating a warren of narrow side streets until brought to a standstill by a row of traffic cones. 'Now we will walk,' he said to Philip, who trusted that *Diamond Rent a Car*'s insurance contained provision for parking in such desolate spots. They made their way past lean-to shacks, some built of corrugated iron, others of planks and plastic sheeting, with upper floors as flimsy as a house of cards. A cat's cradle of wires and cables festooned the roofs. Remnants of obsolete posters turned every available wall into a collage. Three scraggy boys in shorts and flip-flops played skittles with empty San Miguel bottles. Two young girls sat on their heels, braiding each other's hair. An older girl kept watch over a line of washing, scowling at every passer-by as at a potential thief.

Philip's misgivings, prompted by Max's refusal to reveal their destination, dwindled when they emerged from the fetid threat of the slum into a large square dominated by a white church with two wedding-cake towers, which made it the perfect setting for the ceremony currently taking place. Huge posters of a bride and groom, framed like the stars of a Bollywood movie, hung over the porch, which was draped in purple and white bunting.

'Is this my surprise? An authentic Filipino wedding?'

'Do I look like Patience Strong?'

His anxieties returned, Philip surveyed the forecourt where a small group of guests had gathered. 'I feel sorry for the women, all dolled up in this sweltering heat. It's easier for the guys. They just have to wear those *Tagalog* thingies. Hell! What to do you call the traditional Filipino shirts?'

'*Barong Tagalogs*,' Max said.

'Is not Filipino; is Spanish,' Dennis said. 'They are making it lawful we must wear these because they are frightened of us. They are wanting to see we are not hiding our swords.'

'Really? I read it was because the pineapple and banana fibres were cool in the heat.'

'You read this in books; I know this in heart!'

'Yes, of course. I don't mean to belittle – '

'You think we must say thank you to the Spanish?' Dennis said, widening the scope of his grievances. 'Thank you! Is so very kind of you for coming to this place and stealing our lives and our money and our names.'

'Your names?'

'Just like they are taking away our clothes so we cannot fight them, so they are taking away our names so we cannot know who we are. They are giving us all foreign names, like I am Dennis.' His anguish made Philip ashamed that he had let himself be influenced by the name's comic-book associations. 'Then they are giving us family names from where we live. So I am Santos because my ancestors are living near to graveyard and dead people are supposed to be like saints. But, if you are living near to church, your name must be Iglesias. If you are living near to governor's palace, your name must be Reyes. If you are living near to gardens, your name must be Flores.'

'It's lucky your ancestors didn't live near to the sewers,' Max said, 'or you might have been Cloacas.'

'You are bad man,' Dennis said, looking at him with loathing. 'You are wishing to make all things into joke! But soon you will be laughing with your tears.' Philip felt a rush of sympathy for Dennis, caught in the chasm between cultures, with nothing to cling to but the faint hope of revenge. Here was someone who sought to whiten his skin, while singing about the oppression of the brown man: who cherished his village faith while compromising it nightly in the capital. Whatever the contradictions of his own life, they paled in comparison to Dennis's.

'Oh, don't be such a drama queen!' Max said. 'Let's go and see some cocks.'

'What?' Philip asked, more suspicious than ever of Max's surprise. Before he had a chance to protest, the air was filled with a raucous crowing. He swung round to face a circular concrete building, like a cross between a small sports stadium and a sixties church. A red flag fluttered on the roof and mawkish music blasted out of tinny loudspeakers. An old man on crutches scuttled crablike towards the gate.

'This is the surprise?' he asked Max.

'The same.'

'Cocks as in cock fight?'

'You look disappointed. Why? Did you think I meant "country matters"?' Max sniggered.

'Do you plan on going inside?'

'Of course. We haven't come all this way to admire the architecture.'

'What's the point?' Philip asked.

'Is good. Is *sabong*. Is Filipino national sport,' Dennis interposed.

'You see,' Max said. 'If we turn back, we'll be insulting the entire Filipino nation. Besides, if you're squeamish now, what will you be like on Friday when we go to Pampanga for the crucifixions?'

'That's quite different.'

'Why? Or do you have lower standards for men than cocks?'

'I shan't rise to that.'

'An interesting turn of phrase.'

'If we're going, let's go.'

They walked towards the gate, past street traders hawking fish balls and noodles, peanuts, cigarettes, water and slices of pineapple, from improvised stalls on tricycles. Dennis bought some grilled chicken feet, or *Adidas*, which Philip found doubly distasteful given their surroundings, and followed them into the arena. They took their seats, breathing in the heavy scent of sweat, tobacco and pork, while the packed crowd shouted and signalled its reactions to the ongoing fight. A cacophony of cheers and catcalls marked its climax. A jubilant man, presumably the owner, leapt into the ring and raised the victorious bird to his lips, kissing its beak, while a contemptuous attendant dragged its defeated rival through the dirt.

'As a rule, the winning owner gets to eat the loser,' Max said.

'Is not good,' Dennis said. 'Chicken is too tough. You must cook it for many hours, until no more fire.'

Excitement gripped the arena as, after a garbled announcement, a fresh bout began. Two owners carried their roosters into the ring. One was brown with white chest feathers; the other grey with a black tail. The men strutted around the ring as if they themselves were the contestants, before unsheathing the blades on the birds' ankles and withdrawing to opposite corners. The referee thrust the two birds together, goading them to peck at one another's throats and tails, tasting the blood that would incite them further. Feathers flew, as they fell to the ground and lunged at each other in fury. All around them the crowd was similarly inflamed, jumping up and down in its seats, applauding and jeering.

'I don't see anyone taking bets.'

'Over there!' Max said, pointing to a group of white-shirted men with their arms outstretched. 'They're called *kristos*.'

Taking no chances, Philip sat on his hands, since a quick scrutiny of the *kristos* suggested that they would look less charitably on any accidental gesture than the gentlemanly auctioneers he knew at home. The roosters, meanwhile, appeared reluctant to give the crowd the blood for which it was baying. As the stupefied brown bird retreated to a tumult of invective, its frenzied owner rushed forward, yelling at it to fight, until he was held back by an attendant. Philip watched in horror as the referee picked up the two exhausted birds, pressing their beaks together, until the grey one, striking out in panic, fatally stabbed its opponent's chest. The brown bird collapsed, the referee counting it out like a floored boxer, before the attendant dragged it from the ring, leaving its owner to slink away, a chorus of derision in his ears, as though the lifeless cock were, literally, a slur on his virility.

During the break, women patrolled the stands with trays of refreshments. Philip bought a tub of noodles for Dennis and cans of Sprite for himself and Max. For once the synthetic sweetness was a welcome antidote to the sharp, ammonic tang in the air. The relief was transitory, since further bouts followed in swift and sickening succession. Striving to understand their appeal, he could only suppose that the short, squalid struggle was in some way cathartic for people with equally brief, brutal lives. There was certainly none of the grace and skill on display in the national sport of their former colonial masters. Whatever literary inspiration the country might yield him, it would not result in another *Death in the Afternoon*.

The start of a new bout put paid to his hopes of making a discreet exit. Two more birds were brought into the ring, the differences more pronounced than ever: one almost wholly white; the other, nearly twice its size, black with red markings on its tail.

'You must put money, much money, on this white chicken,' Dennis said, either showing his customary faith in pale colouring or else instinctively identifying with the underdog. 'This man who brings him is a friend of me. He is telling me this is stolen.'

'Is that good?' Philip asked, but Dennis was busy semaphoring his bet, leaving Max to reply.

'Apparently, it's lucky. The entire culture's based on these superstitions.'

'It's beyond me.'

'Don't knock it! If it weren't for superstition, you'd be out of a job.'

Grimacing, Philip turned back to the ring where the white bird was being trounced. '*Putang Ina!*' Dennis exclaimed. 'This is bad chicken. His owner, he is giving him drugs like junkie. He is sewing hot chillies up his *puwit* to make him fight.'

'A principle which might be usefully applied elsewhere,' Max said.

Philip had no need to ask for the meaning of *puwit*, since Dennis's hiss made it all too clear. He focused his attention on the ring where the black cock, his hackles up, swaggered round his dazed rival, lashing out in all directions and slicing his chest with his blade. A thunderous cheer rose up from the crowd, followed by a low moan from Dennis, looking as broken and bruised as the dead cock.

He was roused by one of the *kristos* who, with a prodigious memory for the quick-fire transactions, came to collect his debts. 'Poor Dennis,' Philip said to Max, as they watched him extract the banknotes from inside his shorts with the painful precision of someone removing a splinter.

'Is not fair. This match is fixed,' Dennis said. 'This owner, he is bringing man to train chickens. From Texas!' he added, as if it were the ultimate treachery.

With Dennis bewailing the injustice of life in general and America in particular, they left the arena. Suspecting that Dennis would seek to cut his losses by reaching an accommodation with Max, Philip strode ahead. Entering the street, he was hailed by a trio of sweaty, stocky young men.

'Hey mate!' shouted one, with the image of a muscle-bound torso straining across his barrel chest. 'Good to see another white face!'

'Hello,' Philip replied warily.

'You English? Put it there!' Philip, relaxing now that the connection was merely national, shook hands with all three of them.

'Been watching the fights, then?' asked another, with a cork hat, peeling nose and Union Jack tattoo on a pasty leg.

'Unfortunately, yes. If you're thinking of buying a ticket, don't bother! You'd have as much fun at a factory farm.'

'It's the experience, innit?' said the third, whose high forehead and clip-on sunglasses gave him a bookish air that was belied by his open beer can and *I'm a Lesbian* T-shirt. 'It's their culture. Gorra respect their culture, donchya?' He held out the can, which Philip politely refused.

'Well, don't say I didn't warn you,' Philip said, moving away as Max and Dennis approached.

'Aren't you going to introduce us to your friends, Philip?' Max asked in his most pointedly epicene tones. Reluctantly, Philip presented Max and Dennis, after which the three tourists supplied their own names: Warren, Jez and Trevor.

'And what are you doing in this den of vice and iniquity?' Max asked with a jaunty smile. 'That's to say Manila.'

'We're on holiday, aren't we?'

'Are you? That's what I'm trying to find out.'

Trevor looked at him with suspicion. 'Yeah. We're on an adventure tour. We've been all over. Angeles City. Olongapo. Subic Bay. The company guarantee your money back if you spend more than one night in the two weeks on your tod. You can't say fairer than that now, can you?'

'You most definitely can't,' Max replied.

'I help you,' Dennis said. 'I know all bars. Hot girls, sexy girls.'

'Thanks for the offer mate,' Jez said, 'but it's all laid on. Different girl every night. Two or three if you're up for it.'

'Are we up for it?' Warren asked. 'Does a squirrel love his nuts?'

'Some of them are so young it shouldn't be legal!' Jez said.

'But it is, mate,' Trevor said quickly. 'Everything above board.'

'And a regular supply of Viagra for young Jez here,' Warren added.

'Hey, speak for yourself. Balls of steel, me!' Jez said, with a pelvic thrust that spilt his beer.

'What about you, mate?' Warren asked. 'What brings you out here?'

'I'm with the World Health Organisation,' Philip said with a glare that dared Max or Dennis to contradict him. 'We're investigating a lethal new drug-resistant strain of syphilis.'

'You're having a laugh!' Warren said.

'I wish I were. It's spreading like wildfire through the bars and massage parlours of Thailand and the Philippines.'

'You're kidding me!' Trevor said.

'We're trying to keep it under wraps to prevent panic and reprisals. I'm only telling you because it sounds as though you and your friends may be at risk.'

'Not me, mate,' Jez said. 'Cover my stump before I hump!'

'If only it were that easy, but this new strain is a hundred times more contagious than HIV. Skin-to-skin contact is all it takes. But we're holding you up. Besides, we have to get back to the field – that is, the bars, the field of study. Enjoy the *sabong*!'

Leaving the three men stupefied, Philip led Max and Dennis towards the car.

'Well, young Philip,' Max said, 'you've quite taken my breath away. Where did all that come from?'

'They deserved it,' Philip said defensively.

'They certainly did. Men that ugly shouldn't be allowed to have sex, even with women.'

Back at the hotel, Philip found a message from Maribel, cancelling their date for the evening. Frustration welled up in him as he punched her number into his phone, to be replaced by guilt when she explained that her supervisor had rearranged her shift to punish her for arriving late on Thursday; which had been entirely due to his keeping her back for a flurry of last-minute kisses. He had taken her protests for the ploy that they would have been in England; he should have known that, however flexible time might be elsewhere in Manila, at the call centre it followed the clock. The supervisor had warned her that with the scores of applicants for every seat, no one was indispensible. Philip, trusting that a casual reference to the Bishop would resolve the problem, had promised to contact the supervisor himself, which drew such an effusion of gratitude from Maribel that he felt ashamed.

Just to think of Maribel – to picture her face, her smile, her skin at once porcelain and pliant, her small but sufficient breasts with their nipples like afterthoughts – brought on a surge of emotion so strong that he feared he might drown in it. She was the one fixed point in an ever-shifting city. He delighted in her bashful glance, her tinkling laugh, her over-precise turn of phrase. He felt himself shine in the glow of her admiration. Yet how much did he know of what went on inside her head? She gave every sign of enjoying their embraces. But how much was it passion and how much compliance? Was she as eager as he was to take their relationship a stage further? In which case, might she have misread his hesitation as indifference? He was still unclear if she were a virgin. The fact that they had never spoken of it – that he could not envisage their speaking of it – was evidence of the gulf between them. He was older than she was, richer than she was, and white. He was the one with power, which meant that, as an honourable man, he had no right to force the issue.

On the other hand, just how honourable was he? Did he truly care about Maribel or was his prime concern to make a good impression – on himself as much as everyone else? Was he afraid of leading her on or of feeling ashamed when he left her stranded? If the former, why had he insisted that she meet him after the Palm Sunday service, instead of going for a clean break? His stay in Manila was temporary and, unless she expected nothing more from him than a few decent meals and the opportunity to practise her English, he was bound to hurt her. He had no wish to play Pinkerton to her Madame Butterfly.

His loneliness grew unbearable. It was Saturday night, and he was stuck in a hotel room with only the TV for company. Conscious that he was crossing a line, he picked up the remote control and switched on the adult channel. For weeks, he had tempted himself with the trailers. Now, despite a firm belief that pornography was nothing but prostitution by proxy, he set about ordering a film. The only way to dissociate himself from Warren, Jez and Trevor was to ensure that the title he chose was American rather than Asian. So, in the vain hope that humour might mitigate the offence, he settled on *Hannah Does Her Sisters*.

Six

My dear Mother and Father,

First, a word in my defence. I didn't ignore your phlebitis, Mother; I wrote to you as soon as I heard the news from Agnes. It's not the only one of my letters to have gone astray, although that implies that it's accidental. I've done some sleuthing and found that postmen steam off the stamps to sell in Manila. It's hard to blame them when they're so badly paid, but I wish they'd stick to government circulars. So I hope that you'll withdraw the charge that I care more for strangers than I do for my own family (I prefer not to use the word 'natives' except in the strict ethnographic sense). How can it be 'Out of sight out of mind' when your silver wedding photograph stands in pride of place next to the crucifix by my bed?

As for your second charge, however much you may disapprove, please, please avoid any further allusion to my political activities. You've no idea of the trouble it might cause. Faced with an increasingly restive population, the authorities are cracking down on the least hint of dissent. Having silenced the official opposition, it's now focusing its efforts on the Church. The radical message of the gospel turns even the most reactionary priest into a symbol of resistance. Whereas once my cloth would have granted me immunity, it now puts me in the firing line. Last month I was arrested and questioned about my links with the insurgents. It's easy to make light of it now, but it's remarkable how quickly your confidence dissolves when you're blindfolded, bundled in the back of a scorching hot van, and driven at breakneck speed to an unknown destination.

I steeled myself by pretending that I was the hero of a

thriller who, for the purposes of the plot, would have to escape unscathed, but as I sat alone and handcuffed in a stale-smelling room, straining to pick up the voices in the corridors (several with distinct American accents) I felt more and more like an innocent bystander whose wanton murder spurs the hero to revenge. Finally, two officers cross-examined me. Refusing to remove the blindfold, they asked me about my association with the NPA and the CNL (Christians for National Liberation). It was clear from both their scattershot questioning and indifference to my replies that their intention was to intimidate rather than to convict me. They released me after a few hours, unharmed apart from some bruises on the neck and wrists, which fade into insignificance beside the horrific injuries sustained by thousands of innocent Filipinos. As you'd expect, the result has been to strengthen my resolve. Nevertheless, I'm anxious not to give them fresh ammunition. Next time they might not show such restraint.

Fortunately, I'd fully recovered by the time of Isabel's arrival. She had enough to take in after seven years, without seeing me hurt. In other respects, of course, she was the one who'd changed. When I left England, she was a gawky teenager; now she's a confident young woman. No, she's a kind, intelligent, beautiful, vivacious and confident young woman, a credit to Greg and Alice, and above all to herself. To my relief, I found that some things about her had stayed the same. She still has the hearty laugh with the glissando that puts me in mind of sliding down banisters and the mellow tones that bring back memories not just of her younger self but of her aunts. When I closed my eyes, I might have been listening to Agnes or Cora. Whatever the Leverington influence elsewhere, her voice is pure Tremayne.

Nowhere was her confidence more marked than when we went to Manila. I was amazed by the ease with which she negotiated a city that is a labyrinth even to the locals. She does, however, have an unfortunate tendency, acquired no doubt from her boyfriend, to suppose that anyone with a brown skin is out to cheat her. For all her elegance and charm, I can't help missing the wide-eyed enthusiasm that led her to dedicate her life first to animals, then to children and finally to the planet. After three years of reading art history, it's inevitable that both her perspective and her priorities have changed. When I asked about her plans, now that she'd finished at St Andrews, she became uncharacteristically coy, mumbling something about museum work and Alice having a friend who was head of ceramics at the V&A. I realised that I'd put my foot in it and that her answer – indeed her entire future – depended on Hugh.

I may be reading too much into it, Mother, but when you wrote how fond Greg and Alice were of him you said nothing of what you thought of him yourself. Should I be similarly circumspect? Surely not to you? He's a highly personable man, polite to a fault (addressing me with the deference due to an ancient cardinal), but at the same time suspiciously detached. Instead of expressing his feelings, he seems to file them away for future reference. Whereas Isabel is utterly besotted with him, he treats her with wry detachment. Indeed, his one sign of passion during their whole trip came when his agent in Manila brought him a late Neolithic burial jar dug up – and, as far as I could tell, removed illegally – from a cave in Palawan. Is it just me or does either of you find it odd that a thirty-two-year-old should be an obsessive collector of antiquities? I took great care not to voice my reservations; you'd have been proud of me – no, really you would. I was determined not to cast a single shadow on Isabel's happiness. 'You do like him, Uncle, you promise?' she asked me several times a day. Perhaps it was that 'Uncle', so much more intimate than the familiar 'Father'; perhaps it was the joy of seeing her again after so long; or perhaps it was simply joy in her joy; but I couldn't help but answer 'yes'.

Isabel filled me in on the family news. I was relieved to hear that for all his disappointment at not being given a Cabinet post, Greg was happy with the Employment portfolio. Besides, as I reminded her, it wasn't so long ago he was certain that he'd be passed over on account of his support for Mr Heath. I knew that he was worrying unduly. Mrs Thatcher doesn't seem the sort to bear grudges. Since moving here, my politics have veered to the left, but I'm still excited by the prospect of our first woman prime minister. I was immensely heartened by her quoting St Francis outside Number Ten. Can you imagine any of her predecessors having done the same?

I hope that Isabel and Hugh appreciated how hard Consolacion worked to make their stay a success. In the week before their arrival, no parishioner was allowed to cross the threshold and at times I wondered if I too might be banished to the yard. Grump's scavenging trips were severely curtailed, which I'm sure was what lay behind his hostility to Hugh, since he's usually such an excellent judge of character. I tried to reassure Consolacion by showing her the letter in which Isabel wrote that they were looking forward to 'roughing it', but she wasn't convinced. Her greatest fear was that Isabel would return to Whitlock and report that she wasn't taking good enough care of me. In the event, Isabel insisted that she'd never seen me look so well. One bonus of her trip is that she'll be able to relieve any nagging doubts you may have about my health.

I'm not sure that Hugh was quite as keen to rough it as Isabel. Despite – or perhaps because of – his previous forays into the country, he brought along a suitcase full of water purification tablets, pills of every description, Lipton's tea and loo paper. With no spare bedrooms, Isabel slept – 'like a log' – on the sitting-room sofa, while Hugh cricked his neck on a camp bed in the study. Had they come as recently as last year, the *haciendos* would have fallen over themselves to put them up, but our relations have so soured (I won't go into details, which I'm sure by now you can supply for yourselves) that they didn't even make the offer. Protocol compelled them to acknowledge the presence of two such well-connected foreigners, so the Pinedas invited us to lunch (which, to everyone's relief, a service in an outlying *barrio* kept me from attending) and the Arriolas to an evening barbecue where I spent much of the time talking to don Bernardo's mother, who's stone-deaf.

A less lavish but far more congenial affair was the birthday party thrown for me by some of the BCCs. Thirty-nine! I've warned them that I'm booking myself into a monastery next year. It was such a treat to have Isabel here, especially since it was the one occasion on which she defied Hugh, who went off to inspect his mines alone. She was particularly excited to meet the four Ibaloi tribesmen who'd trekked down from the mountains. Has she told you about the magnificent crucifix they carved for me? It was intended for the *convento* but I've put it in the church. It seems right that the people should kneel before a rough-hewn Christ in their own image rather than a polished one with an imported face. Meanwhile, I worked my way through the huge pile of parcels Isabel had brought from home. Thank you so much for the record player. I'm thrilled to bits by it, not to mention the inspired selection of LPs. It may be a while before I have a chance to play them since there's still no electricity in the *poblacion*, but we've been promised that it's on its way. The wait will only whet my appetite.

The rest of the family did me proud, even Uncle Lawrence with his crested hip flask, although I suspect that he's been reading too much Graham Greene. To my surprise, since he's never been a natural present giver, Greg excelled himself with the briefcase. Agnes's shirts are just what I wanted, or rather they will be once Consolacion has taken them in.

At five days, Isabel and Hugh's visit was all too short. I took them to Baguio and Mount Pulag, and north to the rice terraces of Banaue, but the mists were too thick to see them in their full glory, and Hugh complained loudly about the dirt-track/death-trap roads. As planned, I drove back with them to Manila where Hugh kindly offered to put me up in their hotel but, despite the lure of fine linen and air conditioning, I preferred to remain independent at the Society's house. That's when I rang you, Father. I'm sorry that the crackling lines and time lag made the conversation sound so stilted. Which is why I didn't try again. Although, of course, I'd have loved to talk to Mother.

Hugh introduced me to one of his associates, Max, an Englishman of about my age, a strange mixture of scruffiness and sophistication, with a widow's peak and a goatee, wearing a heavily stained linen suit and doused in a sugary scent that put me in mind of Granny Courtenay's parma violets. He's fanatical about ballet, having come here in some unspecified capacity with Margot Fonteyn and stayed on at the behest of Imelda Marcos to run a home-grown company. He won't hear a word against his patron, whom he reveres for 'being herself' – whatever that means! His conversation veers between the vapid and the offensive. He appeared to think that I'd respect the candour with which he attacked the Church (being himself?). Mindful that I was Hugh's guest, I challenged him only once, when he referred to the Holy Father in the feminine. I'm astonished that Hugh, who strikes me as a man's man to the core, can stomach him. Isabel found him amusing, but then she studied art.

Max evidently opens doors for Hugh, the grandest of which are those to the Malacañang Palace. The Marcoses were holding a reception during our stay. Having already secured invitations for Hugh and Isabel, Max offered to obtain one for me. I can't think why, unless he wanted to impress me with his influence. My first instinct was to refuse, but then I remembered your story of being taken to tea with Hitler in Munich in the thirties, Mother. As a boy, I used to rewrite history, devising a scenario in which you pulled out a knife and stabbed him, preventing war from breaking out, Father being sent to Singapore and – last, but not I fear, least – sweets being rationed. It was a thrilling fantasy and one which reverberated thirty-odd years later, as I put on a cassock (I'd decided to wear full canonicals) and wondered how easy it would be to conceal a knife.

The Hitler analogy is not as far-fetched as it sounds, since the Marcoses are known, at least in BCC circles, as the Molochs of the Malacañang. No one would deny, however, that they're able to put on a show. We entered the palace grounds through vast cast-iron gates embellished with imperial eagles (which, to be fair, date from the American governorship). Footmen, sweat streaming from their powdered wigs and seeping through their white cotton gloves, flanked the path leading to a low white building. Max, anxious that I should esteem the honour, whispered that this was one of the very first receptions since Imelda had had the palace remodelled. We entered the vestibule and were conducted into a small wood-panelled room, where we waited along with what seemed like half the diplomatic corps and the cream of Manila society. A major domo escorted us up a wide staircase lined with portraits of great European explorers, more suited to the former colonial administration than to the current effusion of national pride. From there we entered the main hall.

Despite the glittering chandeliers, the low ceiling and the capiz windowpanes gave the room a sombre feel. My eyes were drawn to two gilded thrones, which looked as though they were on loan from Versailles. 'Are they part of the remodelling?' I asked Max. 'Don't worry, Father,' he said unctuously, 'they're purely symbolic.' While nervous flunkeys served overfull glasses of champagne, I wandered through the room, finding the artworks more appealing than the guests. A flurry of activity heralded the arrival of our hosts, who made their way to the dais where the President welcomed us, while his wife gazed at him as though posing for a bas-relief on his tomb. Even as he was speaking, all eyes were fixed on her. That was hardly surprising, given the shimmering green and blue of her dress, which turned out to be made of actual peacock feathers. After the official toasts to the guest of honour, a Hong Kong banker who, according to the well-informed Max, is financing many of the Marcoses' projects, the President left. Imelda then circulated among her guests with what, even I am compelled to admit, was effortless charm. As you know, I'm not a natural society portraitist and I'm sure that Isabel will already have painted you a vivid picture, but for what it's worth here's mine.

Imelda appeared genuinely pleased to see Max, who kissed her on both cheeks, which had the sheen of fine china. He introduced each of us in turn and she took my hand so delicately that it felt as if she were brushing my fingers with a feather. I'm far too low down the clerical hierarchy to interest her, but she gave me a smile of what I can only describe as vivacious blankness. If that makes no sense, think of a sea with a rippling surface above leagues of eerie calm. She emits such a powerful aura that although she can have stayed with us for no more than ninety seconds, she left us all revitalised. After she'd moved on, the party seemed devoid of purpose, so I slipped away. The next morning I said goodbye to Isabel and Hugh, who were leaving for Boracay, and returned to San Isidro. I won't dwell on the horrors that greeted me. I suspect that you've had as many rapes, tortures and murders in these letters as you can bear. But just because I don't mention them, don't imagine that they've come to an end. Like everyone else here, I lead a double life. Half the time I'm going about my day-to-day activities; the other half ferrying the injured to hospitals and the dead to their graves.

Please don't be alarmed, but since returning from Manila I've suffered something of a crisis of confidence – or is it identity? More than ever before, I've been forced to question the nature of my role. On the one hand the brutal repression while I was away shows that, if nothing else, my presence offers some protection against the excesses of the regime. On the other it's become increasingly clear – at least to me – that the words I speak and the Church I represent erect a barrier between the people and God. By telling them that they are the living embodiment of His love when they endure such unceasing oppression I'm denying the truth – the validity – of that love. For too long the Church has comforted – some would say anaesthetised – the poor with the claim that they'll receive their reward in Heaven. But Christ also said that the kingdom of Heaven was at hand. Was He referring to an imminent apocalypse? In which case how come we're still here 2,000 years later? Or did He mean that by following

Him we could establish His kingdom on earth? I know which I choose. Even the mass, the fulcrum of our faith, is as much a symbol of His liberating us from tyranny as of His redeeming us from sin. After all, He instituted it at a Passover supper, the meal that celebrated the deliverance of the Jews from bondage in Egypt.

In a bleak world, my one hope lies in the BCCs. Whether setting up credit unions to make loans to destitute farmers or offering food and shelter to the dispossessed, they're at the forefront of the struggle to empower the community. By teaching people that they have a right to a reasonable standard of living, by encouraging them to band together to resist the soldiers and landlords who intimidate them, they are giving them back their self-respect. By putting victims in touch with lawyers who plead their cases in the courts they show them that justice isn't the preserve of the rich and powerful. Repression breeds violence breeds repression. The BCCs are working tirelessly to break that cycle. By channelling our faith into the fight for justice, I'm convinced that we're a step closer to building the kingdom of Heaven on earth.

Not everyone who shares our objectives shares our beliefs. There are many who've turned away from Christ along with the Church. Their weapons aren't words but M-16 rifles. I may not – I cannot – endorse their tactics, but I have to respect their integrity and commitment. For too long I fell for all the official disinformation about the NPA. They may be godless (although I have my doubts about that), but they're certainly not shameless or savage. Moreover, I have conclusive proof that the army commits crimes, which it blames on the NPA as justification for increasing its own powers. I know of soldiers shooting farmers who've refused to pay them protection money, claiming that, if they don't need protection from them, they must be getting it from the rebels. I've lodged so many complaints with the local Constabulary Commander that he no longer even goes through the motions of filing reports.

As a foreigner and one whose faith is his lifeblood, it's easy for me to urge restraint. But you'd have to have the patience of Job – or St Job, as Consolacion insists on calling him – to wait for the don Enricos and don Florantes of this world, let alone the Marcoses, to change their ways. Ever since I saw how unsparingly Alma, Rommel and their friends threw themselves into the rebuilding work here, I've kept in indirect contact with them, passing on intelligence that might be useful. It's remarkable how much a priest can pick up. Whether it's because the police chiefs, army commanders and *haciendos* believe that priests, like God, must be on their side or else because, despite the lip service they pay to the Church, they regard its clergy as of little consequence, they discuss raids and manoeuvres openly in front of me. I know of at least one occasion on which my information saved an NPA unit from ambush. Yet the military think me so incompetent that even when they interrogated me they failed to make the link.

I must end now since Consolacion has called me twice already for dinner and antagonising her is a far more daunting prospect than antagonising the *haciendos* (I'm only half-joking). Isabel and Hugh are driving up tomorrow to say their goodbyes before they return to London. Knowing that there's no danger of this letter being intercepted has permitted me to write far more freely than would otherwise have been the case. After all, if Hugh can smuggle out crates of ancient treasures without alerting the authorities, Isabel should be able to take a few sheets of paper. I shall be miserable to see her go. Even though she's spent much of her time in Borocay and the Visayas, just to know that she was a few hundred miles away has made me feel so much closer to home. I realise that the chances of your coming out here are growing ever slimmer. Even if you both feel strong enough, my disputes with the *haciendos* make it harder for me to put you up in comfort. There again, you may see me sooner than you think. Isabel is convinced that Hugh is about to propose and I've promised her that I'll come back to marry them.

Meanwhile, I hope that you'll remember the Philippines in your prayers, Mother, and that you, Father, will use any influence you have with Greg and the Foreign Office to put pressure on Marcos to respect human rights. However bad things may be here, I'm far from desperate. The Holy Spirit isn't static; it evolves and deepens over time.

Your loving son,
Julian

Dennis threw up his hands at the slow-moving traffic, wafting a raw, animal scent towards the passenger seat. Philip, reckoning that for once Max's aura of mildew and talcum powder might have been preferable, tried to account for the lapse in one who was usually so fastidious.

'How reliable is the water supply in Manila?' he asked casually.

'Rains come in May,' Dennis replied. 'Till then is dry.'

'No, not the rains. The mains supply to bathrooms and showers. Is it ever cut off like the electricity in San Trinidad?'

'That is bad town. Small people,' Dennis said, frowning at the memory of his humiliation. 'Manila is great modern city.' He hooted angrily at a ragged cigarette seller weaving between cars.

'I suspect that what young Philip is asking, in his usual mealy-mouthed way, is why – not to put too fine a point on it – you reek,' piped a voice from the back.

'Is not Dennis who reeks, is traffic! How can I move more fast? Look!' He waved expansively, spreading the stench.

'No, reek! Pong a little. Not your usual fragrant self.'

'I am dancing all through night. Is holiday. Many baklas in club.'

'Did you have no time to shower?' Philip asked, now more concerned about Dennis's competence than his smell.

'No shower on Good Friday. Is sin.'

Philip, amazed to find evidence in present-day Manila of a folk belief Julian had encountered in San Isidro thirty years before, shrugged off his qualms and turned his attention to the traffic. On current progress they would arrive in Pampanga too late for the crucifixions. For once the delay was due not to Dennis's timekeeping but to the hordes of people heading north for the Easter break. Refusing to panic, Philip gazed across the empty pavements at shop signs, which might have been devised to divert the flustered foreigner. First came a grocer selling *Fresh Frozen Chicken*, then a carpenter making *Modern and Antique Furniture* and finally a large billboard advertising secretarial vacancies for which *Experience is needed but not required*.

A small boy stepped up to the car and tapped on the windscreen, holding his hand out for change. As Philip searched in his pocket, Dennis, with eyes more bloodshot and a manner more febrile than usual, opened the glove compartment, pulled out a gun and aimed it at the boy, who sprang back in terror, almost falling beneath the wheels of a passing jeepney.

'Are you mad?' Philip asked, his heart leaping. 'Put it down!'

'Is good. Is gone.'

'Where the hell did you get it?' Philip swivelled round to face Max. 'Did you know that he had a gun?'

'Boys and their toys,' Max replied nonchalantly.

'Is my job,' Dennis said. 'I am bodyguard so I must be ready to kill for you.' He curled his lip and Philip pictured him repeating the phrase without the preposition.

'We're talking about a kid of five or six!'

'So? He grows.'

'Yes, but not in the few weeks I'll be in the Philippines.'

'Manila is most dangerous city. I know some most dangerous people.'

'Is that meant to be reassuring?'

'Boys, boys,' Max interposed, 'there's no need to bicker. And Dennis, if you must wave your weapon about, put away the symbol and stick to the real thing.'

'I am never understanding English,' Dennis said. 'You are saying "Do this, Dennis," and then "but you must never let other persons see". I put gun in box, like you ask.' He replaced it in the glove compartment. 'But I leave lid open,' he added, truculent as ever.

'I think somebody's overdone the *shabu*,' Max said.

'What's that?'

'A drug the bar boys take to keep themselves going.'

'Like Viagra?'

'Not that sort of going!' Max said, laughing.

'Is you who are needing Viagra,' Dennis interjected, turning so sharply to face Max that Philip was grateful for the gridlock.

Dennis yawned and pulled into the kerb, signalling to a teenage girl who was cooking *Adidas* on a rickety stove. She kicked a younger girl dozing at her side, who stood up without complaint, trotted to the window and handed him a bag. Philip stifled the urge to retch as the cloying, greasy smell pervaded the car. 'Feeling better now?' he asked.

Dennis looked at him with contempt, chewed on a claw and wiped his hands on his shorts. He took out his mobile and, with an eloquent stare at the stalled traffic, began to text. His repeated chuckles at his own wit strained Philip's patience. 'You're sure we'll be in Pampanga by eleven?' he asked, struggling to remain calm.

'Yes.'

'That's "yes, we will" or "yes, I'll do my best"? Because it's vital that we catch the whole ceremony.'

'Yes,' Dennis replied.

Philip leant back, trying to be fatalistic about Filipino fatalism. An unpunctuated sign reading *Slow Men at Work* was almost too good to be true and he laughed out loud, drawing a scowl from Dennis, who seemed to be jealous of anyone else's high spirits.

'Whatever it is that you two are on, would you pass a bit of it back here?' Max asked.

'Suppressed hysteria,' Philip said.

'Oh, I've been on that for years.'

Philip felt that any amount of delay would have been bearable had Maribel come with them. He would have ceded the passenger seat to Max and snuggled up to her in the back, gently tracing the creases on her palm. The mere thought sent tingles through his flesh. It was outrageous that an American bank, of all places, should keep its call centre open on Good Friday.

What was more important: that its customers had access to their accounts 24/7 or that its staff had the right to practise their faith? To make matters worse, she had sent her excuses via Dennis, underlining a relationship that he was trying to ignore.

To Philip's surprise, Dennis's forecast proved to be accurate and they arrived in the centre of Pampanga shortly after eleven. While somewhat unnerved to find himself stuck behind a rickshaw with a large wooden cross strapped to its seat, Philip was grateful that for once, Dennis's tenuous sense of direction was not put to the test. Every car, bus and jeepney was heading towards the *Kalbaryo*, and they followed the flow. 'We have come,' Dennis proudly announced, as they drove beneath a banner welcoming them to San Pedro Cutud. 'Now we find space.' After negotiating a fee – part parking ticket, part protection money – with a trio of teenage boys who were determined to make the most of their annual bonanza, they joined the crowd streaming down the street. Sensation-seeking tourists and camera crews from across the globe mingled with smiling locals, some in T-shirts, jeans and flip-flops, and others in homespun versions of Roman uniforms and Jewish robes. Tagalog texts echoed over loudspeakers, the lilting voices muffled and occasionally drowned by the tooting of tricycles and the strident cries of street vendors. Only the ubiquitous cocks supplied an authentic – if overemphatic – biblical note.

A line of ten or twelve barefoot flagellants shuffled past, their faces swathed like terrorists, their trousers caked with blood from their butchered backs. Their bamboo scourges rent the air, as they thrashed themselves in rhythm. Two men walked between them, pressing small paddles studded with glass into their flesh.

'That's barbaric!' Philip said.

'It's to keep their wounds open,' Max said. 'In this heat, the blood congeals fast.'

'Isn't that a good thing?'

'Not if you're an exhibitionist. See!' Max indicated two of the flagellants who were offering their scourges to passers-by. Most recoiled, hurrying on to the more camera-worthy cruelty at the end of the road, but a few took up the challenge, with one middle-aged Westerner lashing out like a prep-school master on the eve of a caning ban. His wife screamed when her yellow sundress was splattered with blood.

'You're sure you don't want to have a go?' Max asked Philip, as they were swept forward.

'Please!'

'Everyone's a winner. They suffer for their sins and you get to act out a fantasy that would cost you good money anywhere else.'

'Is there nothing you hold sacred?'

'Come on! You can't pretend that this is a profound spiritual experience for you.'

'Not for me, no, but it is for them.'

'Really? Take off your rose-tinted glasses and look around,' Max said, grabbing Philip's arm, causing him to bump into a passing legionnaire, buckling his sword. After apologising profusely, Philip examined his surroundings. On every side were stalls, some selling drinks and snacks, others inflatable horses, dolphins and Spidermen. One, either making a connection that would have warmed Julian's heart or simply offloading surplus stock, displayed a stack of Che Guevara T-shirts. Tourists chatted on their phones and Filipinos texted. In large banners, Pepsi and Jollibee prided themselves on sponsoring this year's *Kalbaryo*. 'So which is it? The Via Dolorosa or another marketing opportunity?'

'Why did you agree to come since you despise it all so much?' Philip asked, deflecting the question.

'Revenge.'

'On me?'

'You flatter yourself!' Max said with a laugh. 'No, on all the high-minded Christians who made my life hell for so many years. And there's another reason, but you won't want to hear it.'

'If you say so,' Philip replied.

'Pain is one of the few things that still excites me. Oh, don't give me that look! It's always consensual and usually my own. Where's Dennis?' he asked, in a train of thought Philip preferred not to follow. 'Well, I did say it was a marketing opportunity.' He gestured towards Dennis, who was talking to an expensively dressed woman with Titian hair and freckled skin. 'Like a moth to a flame – or should that be a hustler to a flame-haired hussy?'

They walked down a street as nondescript as a parking lot to the start of the Passion procession. The only sign of life in the boarded-up shacks came from the T-shirts and shorts hanging out to dry. The only blast of colour in their junk-shop gardens came from the boughs of purple bougainvillea, as deep-rooted as the residents. Somehow the destitution and squalor felt even more desperate here than it had in Manila. When a gaunt teenager ran past with an intricate tattoo of the Man of Sorrows across his back, Philip was left to reflect once again on the relationship between the violence of the people's lives and the brutality of their culture.

Although seven sets of Christs and thieves were due to be crucified, only one man was to personify Christ on the way to Calvary. He stumbled forward, blood streaming down his cheeks from the crown of thorns and crippled by the cross, followed by a motley crew of soldiers, some wearing Roman helmets and tunics, and others orange T-shirts and sunglasses, who punched and kicked him as he fell down the mandatory three times. They, in turn, were followed by a group of wailing women, two of whom held up a large cloth stamped with multiple images of Christ: a Veronica's handkerchief that resembled a Warhol silkscreen.

They arrived at a patch of wasteland on the edge of the *barangay*. Three crosses stood on a mound in an otherwise desolate landscape. The Christ, bent double, staggered up the path, collapsing at the foot of the mound, where he was again whipped by the centurion and kicked by the soldiers. Stripped of his robe to reveal a blood-and-grime-streaked torso, he was led up to the central cross, which had been lowered in readiness for the cruci-fixion. The crowd, true to its biblical role, surged forward, eager not to miss a single gory detail. Philip, his throat choked with dust and his stomach churning from the crush of hot, damp bodies, trailed behind Dennis who, with characteristic temerity, marched up to the press compound and, despite their lack of accreditation, secured entry. Proximity proved to be a mixed blessing as they watched the first three men being nailed to the wood. With the fake Rolex on the centurion's wrist providing a momentary dis-traction, Philip thought of Isabel Olliphant at Whitlock, elegantly sipping tea beneath the El Greco, and wondered whether this were the religion she so ardently espoused that she would not rest until her uncle became one of its saints. He thought of Ferdinand Magellan, five hundred years earlier, facing appalling hardships as he crossed the globe in the name of the Universal Church and wondered whether this were the religion for which he had sacri-ficed himself, along with so many of his company. Was he alone in seeing the irony in the West, having exported its faith and then lost it, now claiming it back as a tourist spectacle?

True to their code, none of the victims uttered a sound when their hands and feet were nailed and their crosses raised. Silence descended on the crowd, broken only by the amplified keening of Mary and the rhythmic scourging of the flagellants at the base of the mound. Watching what was as much a display of machismo as of devotion, Philip recalled the Vicar General's attack on the participants' sincerity and was fired with indigna-tion on their behalf. So what if their motives were mixed? Were his own, or the Pope's, or even Julian Tremayne's, 100 per cent pure? These were not men with the means to donate to charities or subscribe to galas or even take part in sponsored walks. What else did they have to contribute but their flesh?

He could not conceive of submitting to such a trial. Was it just that his pain threshold was too low or did he lack the neces-sary faith? How he envied people who were able to affirm their belief in such a direct – albeit extreme – way, while his own was riven with questions and qualifications! Nevertheless, even the most unsophisticated Christian knew that Christ had suffered on behalf of humanity. Were they not disparaging – indeed, deriding – that, by seeking to sacrifice themselves?

After five minutes of searing exposure, the men were lowered, first the penitent thief, then the impenitent, and finally Christ, and the nails prised out with surprisingly little blood. Meanwhile, the next three participants were led up the mound and laid on the crosses. Philip wondered if one of them might be Jejomar whom, despite repeated requests to the prison authorities, he had yet to meet. Neither Max nor Dennis nor a crotchety Korean journalist was able to help, and he was left with no means to identify him but a grainy snapshot in the *Manila Times*. Abandoning the attempt, he turned to the crowd, whose markedly different response to the various participants set him thinking about how they were chosen. Jejomar's involvement showed that they did not have to be local. Was there a rigorous selection process, or was it open to anyone who volunteered? And, given that the two thieves shared all the pain and none of the glory, was there a natural progression from this year's thief to next year's Christ?

He turned back to the mound just as the centurion drove a nail deep into the penitent thief's foot. An Australian cameraman pushed forward, anxious for a shot that was as crucial to the crucifixion coverage as the vows to a wedding video. Philip, following his gaze, caught a look of anguish on the thief's face, which was more chastening than any grimace. The crosses were again raised, and the men underwent their pseudo execution before being lowered on to stretchers and rushed to the recovery tent. Through the open flap, Philip saw the previous trio, propped up on pallets, clasping cups in lightly bandaged hands, looking no more depleted than blood donors.

An air of expectancy gripped the crowd as the next three participants stepped on to the mound. The taut, elaborately tattooed torso of the man in the middle, a striking contrast to his two oddly flaccid companions, convinced Philip that this was Jejomar. His identity was confirmed when, with overblown humility, he held up a crucifix, supposedly given to him by Julian in jail, which he now revered as a talisman. Taunts and jeers broke out when, rejecting both of the obvious roles, he stationed himself by the central cross, but they were silenced by the dignified fortitude with which he embraced his fate.

While refusing to accept that names held any mystic significance, least of all in the Philippines where Bambi, Bogie, Joker and the like were bestowed, not in the playground but at the font, Philip had no doubt that, by trumping all the Jesuses, Josephs and Marys of their acquaintance and calling their son after the entire Holy Family, his parents had destined him for higher things than a life of crime. Yet, ironically, that crime had led him to this intense identification with Christ. The Julian connection, however bogus, made Philip particularly sensitive to Jejomar's ordeal. The few minutes that he spent on the cross were agonising, even for a spectator. Finally, the signal was given to let down each of the crosses in turn. The two thieves were carried off to the recovery tent but, with what seemed like lunatic bravado, Jejomar waved the stretcher bearers away. Tottering only slightly, he stood beside his cross and, to the amazement of the crowd, stretched out his totally unscarred palms.

'Is miracle,' Dennis cried, falling to his knees. Shouts of joy, praise and wonder erupted all around them. Some of the onlookers jumped up and down; others joined Dennis in kneeling. Parents lifted their children in the air. People at the back, whose view was obscured, fired questions at those further forward, who stood dumbstruck. One man clambered on to the mound, as eager to touch Jejomar's palms as Thomas had been to touch Jesus's wounds, only to be beaten away by the centurion.

Philip remained stock-still, his eyes fixed on Jejomar, certain that the temporary loss of blood to his hands and feet must soon be restored. What other explanation could there be? Even if Jejomar had been prepared to resort to fraud, obtaining a supply of rubber nails and training himself to balance on the narrow footrest, the centurion and his assistants would have been sure to denounce him. The crucifixion ceremony was far too sacred for them to subvert. As the seconds slipped by without so much as a speck of blood to be seen on Jejomar's skin, Philip was forced to acknowledge that he might have witnessed a genuine miracle, and one for which the photographic evidence would be of inestimable value to Julian's cause.

Pandemonium broke out as the crowd surged forward to reach Jejomar, who swaggered back and forth, holding up his hands like a Baptist preacher. The prison guards, who had been chatting to their Roman counterparts, rushed up the mound to surround him. Patently less impressed by his feat than their fellow spectators, they snapped on his handcuffs and, for the first time, he seemed in danger of collapse. To a storm of protest, they dragged him through a gap next to the press compound. Seizing his chance, Philip rushed out and blocked their way.

Wasting no time on preliminaries, he addressed Jejomar: 'Did you feel Father Julian?'

'No, Jesus Christ. Jesus Christ, he is with me.' He struggled to raise his wrists to his crucifix. 'Jesus Christ, he makes me light like a bird.'

'But did you pray to Father Julian?' Philip persisted, as a guard elbowed him aside.

'Yes. To Father Julian. To Father God. He say for me to go out of prison and preach the gospel to all the sinners, so that they end up like him, not like me. You say this. You show them this.' Once again he held out his manacled hands and, although even at close range Philip could see no scars, he smelt the coppery tang of blood.

As he tried to make sense of the conflicting sensations, the guards threw Jejomar into an unmarked black van, which was immediately circled by camera crews and tourists. They jumped back in a cloud of dust when the driver, oblivious to anyone in his path, sped out of the enclosure. Philip walked back to the mound where, in a bizarre return to normality, three more crosses were being raised.

'Satisfied?' Max asked.

'I'd say *perplexed*.'

'Then can you be perplexed in the car? I need to find a loo. At my time of life, I excrete when I'm excited.'

'Of course,' Philip said, feeling deflated. He turned to Dennis who, to his surprise, was still on his knees. 'Are you all right?'

'Is miracle.'

'Well, perhaps. That's why I'm here. To look for proof.'

'Is miracle.'

'It's no use trying to reason with him, not where Our Saviour is concerned. Upsy-daisy!' Max grabbed Dennis's arm. Philip waited for a show of anger or at least resistance, but Dennis complied without demur.

'Is miracle.'

'Yes, and I'm the Archangel Gabriel,' Max replied.

'Surely you must allow that it was extraordinary?' Philip asked Max, as they trekked back to the car.

'Is miracle,' Dennis repeated distractedly.

'If it was, then it wasn't one of Jessica's. Look at the yogis and swamis who pierce their bodies without bleeding – remind you of anyone? – or walk through fire without a single burn. They simply have to psych themselves up. If you're looking for a miracle, try Margot dancing the Rose Adagio when she was pushing fifty. Now that was truly divine.'

They returned to the car to find the bonnet sprayed with blood which, either from squeamishness, superstition or the hope of gaining kudos with his friends in Manila, Dennis flatly refused to wipe.

'I vote we give Pampanga a miss and go straight to Angeles City,' Max said, his delicate bladder notwithstanding. 'It's only ten minutes down the road, so you'll appreciate the contrast.'

'I know this place. Is very bad place,' Dennis said with a grin. 'Is very good.'

'I know it too. At least by repute,' Philip said. 'If I'm not mistaken, it's where Julian came in search of one of his parishioners. Isn't it full of brothels?'

'Don't get your hopes up too high. The stews have lost their savour.'

'What?'

'Oh, never mind! The town grew up to service the US airbase. And when the Yanks pulled out, so did the girls. But there are still enough veterans reliving their glory days on military pensions to keep the place afloat. They rent rooms in former whorehouses and every afternoon they head down to the bars.'

'How depressing!'

'What do you know about it?' Max asked, so violently that Dennis swerved. 'You come here still wet behind the ears and turn up your nose at the rest of us.'

'What? I never.'

'You have no idea the things these men have seen out here. How easy do you suppose it is for them to go back to Swindon and sit around making small talk?'

'Swindon?'

'What?'

'How many American airmen came from Swindon?'

'Did I say Swindon? I meant Ohio; Kentucky; Illinois. Oh Sigmunda!' Max giggled. 'See what happens when you make me lose my cool.'

They arrived in Angeles where, as if to crown the day's incongruities, no sooner had they parked the car than they spotted an autonomous flagellant whipping himself while a trio of bar girls watched idly from a doorway. They lunched at the oddly named Beach Café, before making their way down the main street, whose garish signs and brash billboards smacked more of an amusement arcade than a red-light district. After passing *Rauncho Notorious*, *Paradise Island*, *Bottoms Up* and *Miss Lucy's*, Philip paused outside *The Birdcage*, staring through the smoked-glass windows at the sole occupied table, where two thickset elderly men sat beside two sloppily dressed young women, none of them looking at each other or, from what he could see, exchanging a single word.

'I pictured something glitzier,' he said.

'You find more of that in Manila.'

'Manila is best. I know all bars. Hot girls, sexy girls.' Dennis repeated his patter.

'They cater to a different clientele,' Max said, ignoring him. 'Japs and Koreans who want a little glamour. Feathers before fannies. The Yanks are more upfront. A couple of drinks and they get straight down to business. And business it is. The one thing you can say for these girls is that they're cheap.'

'Is there anywhere we can have a quiet beer without being hit on?' Philip asked.

'Fear not, I promise we'll protect you from temptation. How about here?' Max stopped outside an American-style saloon with a log-cabin façade called, for reasons of either copyright or confusion, *My Little Chickadey*. 'Sacrilege!' he said, pushing open the batwing door and leading the way into the colourless barroom. The Western theme was confined to the exterior. In place of the brasses, barrels and bridles of Philip's imagination were a jukebox, plastic tablecloths and a smell of alpine air freshener. The one idiosyncratic touch came from three rocking horses on a minuscule stage, which wobbled ominously as they crossed the floor.

The only other customers were four grey-haired men in Hawaiian shirts sitting with a young girl in what Philip prayed was a purely social arrangement. Two of her colleagues, more buxom than the average Filipinas, leant wearily on the bar.

'Plastic tits. Is no good,' Dennis said, giving them a disdainful look.

'Says the man who's never stuffed a sock in his jockstrap,' Max said.

Dennis hissed and planted himself at a table where, after deferring to Max, Philip drew up a chair. A well-preserved

American in his mid-sixties, with a dimpled chin, piercing blue eyes and hair the colour and consistency of lichen, came up to take their order. Watching him walk back to the bar, Philip wondered aloud whether he might be an ex-serviceman.

'There's an easy way to find out,' Max said.

'He might take offence.'

'So?'

'English is big wussy,' Dennis said.

Keen both to prove him wrong and satisfy his own curiosity, Philip questioned the barman – who turned out to be the owner – on his return. 'I hope you don't mind my asking, but were you stationed here yourself?'

'I sure was. I did three tours of duty between 1982 and 1991, when our president, in his wisdom, decided to get the hell out.'

'Did you move in here when the base was closed down?'

'No sir. I went home along with the rest of the guys, but I got antsy. It's hard for the Flips – no disrespect – ' he said to Dennis – 'to understand when they queue up all day outside the Embassy for visas, but some of us kinda like it here. I guess you know what I'm speaking of, sir,' he said, taking the measure of Max at first meeting.

'I do indeed.'

'So when a buddy tipped me off that Ramos needed help training men to wipe out the insurgents, I was on the next plane back, lickety-split.'

'You mean as a mercenary?'

'What are you? Some kind of bleeding-heart liberal?'

'Not at all. I'm just interested.'

'It's no big deal. I was attached to the Alsa Masa group in Davao City. In public the government was dead against everything they did, but in private...' He laughed. 'Those guys were crazy mothers. Whenever they captured one of the gooks, first thing, they cut off his ears and drank his blood.' He smiled and shook his head, as at the foibles of a favourite uncle.

'Why this?' Dennis asked.

'Well, my friend,' he replied, leaning towards him so closely that their foreheads brushed. 'You people do have some awful weird customs.'

'Did you see them yourself?' Philip asked.

'See them? I got the video! I'll even show it to you if you twist my arm.' Philip stared at his huge biceps. 'But not today. That would be disrespectful.'

'Of course,' Philip said, suspecting the man's sanity. 'Are you still involved with the group?'

'Hell no! I'm too old for all that malarkey. Found me this top-notch establishment that was shutting its doors. I wanted to give some other young fellows the chance to enjoy the same facilities I did.' Philip glanced pointedly at the four old men circling their prey, but the owner ignored him. 'And it's paid off. It may be quiet now, but in a few hours it'll be heaving. *The World Sex Travel Guide* and *Filipina Escort Guide* have both named us the best bar in Angeles.'

'What about the girls?' Philip asked.

'What about them?"

'Do they have any say in things, or are they just "facilities"?'

'Is he for real?' the owner asked Max. 'These girls know that I'm on the level. They come to Steve, they get looked after.' He winked at the two bar girls, one of whom blew him back a kiss. 'I give them rooms and food and penicillin. I never try to screw them on the bar fine.'

'I can see you're all heart.'

'I think you should take your friend away. My customers don't hold with this kind of Commie talk.'

'I wouldn't worry. They're too busy drooling over that poor girl to take any notice.'

'Typical tight-assed Brit! What's your problem? It's a law of nature: supply and demand. Besides, the Flips are different. You can't judge them by our standards.'

'I'm not; I'm judging us by our standards.'

'Just get the hell out of here! Before I start to forget my manners.'

'With pleasure!'

Philip walked to the door, flinging it open with a defiance that dissipated in the ten minutes he waited for Max and Dennis to follow.

'What took you so long?'

'I had to pay,' Max replied placidly. 'Besides, I wanted a few words with our brave GI.'

'Now you're trying to provoke me.'

'Judging by your recent display, I wouldn't have to try too hard.'

Their exchange was interrupted by a request – the first in a fortnight – for the owner of the black BMW to proceed to the lobby. Philip, who had made a change of ringtone a condition of his continuing employment, looked sharply at Dennis.

'Is not my fault. Is Maribel. She is calling you, but you have only messages.'

'Yes, I'm sorry. I forgot to switch my phone back on after Pampanga.'

'She says she is finishing her shift and she will meet you whenever we are coming home.'

Philip gazed at the girls selling themselves in the *Heatwave* doorway and felt ashamed. Dennis's words sounded uncomfortably close to the 'Hey, mister, want to meet my sister' heard in every backstreet from Cairo to Bangkok, except that in this case the relationship was real.

'Thanks. Will you tell her that I'm very sorry, but I have to work tonight. I'll ring her over the weekend.'

Seven

My dear Mother and Father,

So Easter is over for another year. I trust that all went well at
Whitlock. Do you still get up at dawn on Sunday to watch the
sun dance on Beedles lake, Mother, or do you prefer to wait
for High Mass? Our Holy Week traditions here are very different. There are some I'd happily dispense with: not taking a
bath on Good Friday for a start! On the other hand, I'm still
charmed to see Consolacion's granddaughters standing beneath
our banana tree, waiting for one of the heart-shaped bunches to
fall. And, in church, I can scarcely make myself heard over the
noise of the children jumping up and down on the seats. At first
I was amazed to see mothers, who normally stifle the slightest
murmur, encouraging such unruliness, but when I challenged
one she replied without a hint of self-consciousness that it was
'so they can grow up as tall as you, Father'. Enough said!

Elsewhere, the week was less of an opportunity to reflect on
Christ's Passion than a focus for the mounting tensions in the
parish. It began on Palm Sunday when the *hermanas* refused
to lay their cloaks down at my feet as I approached the church.
On one level I was relieved, since I'd long been embarrassed by
a display that smacked more of Sir Walter Raleigh and Elizabeth
I than Our Lord's entry into Jerusalem. On another I was aware
that the girls, bitter rivals among themselves but ever quick to
close ranks against outsiders, were acting on their fathers' orders
to protest against my agenda. But they'd misjudged both the
man and the moment. The gospel reading was Christ's throwing
the money changers out of the temple and I'd prepared a sermon
on the danger of placing the profit motive at the heart of society,

but in response to the provocation I scrapped it and launched a blistering attack on usury in all its forms, particularly that of landlords who drove their tenants into debt and then charged them extortionate rates of interest.

The following Monday I received an invitation (for which read summons) to the Arriola *hacienda*. As if to emphasise its urgency, don Bernardo sent his car. 'Will no one rid me of this turbulent priest?' might well be his watchword, since he holds me personally responsible for the radicalism sweeping through the estate. I suspect that he hankers for the bad old days of the Tridentine Mass, when the gospel was concealed in a fog of incense and incomprehensibility. He looks on the Church as an agent of social control, its wafers and fiestas a modern equivalent of bread and circuses. From the start, he bitterly objected to the BCCs and responded by raising the rents of any tenant who joined. On one occasion he sent his security guards to break up a meeting, which was being held in a school on his estate. That they used excessive force (you might regard the use of any force as excessive) was only to be expected from what is, in effect, a private army made up of ex-prisoners, many of whom are not even officially 'ex', but having been released from the provincial jail on his orders owe both their liberty and their loyalty to him.

Beyond that his hands are tied, first by his nominal allegiance to the Church, then by my 'powerful connections' and last, but by no means least, by my standing among the people. This has been enhanced by another extraordinary and, to some, miraculous event. You may recall that a few years ago a large congregation professed to have seen me levitate during a requiem. I've tried to put it out of my mind; I've read about mass hysteria and, given the nature of the service, emotions were running high (although I'll never forget the intense and ecstatic sense of weightlessness). Last month there was a second such incident. One of my parishioners had developed a tumour on her breast the size of a grapefruit. The *baylan* gave her various herbs, to no effect. It goes without saying that she lacked the wherewithal to pay for a doctor and, when I offered to help, she flatly refused since she was terrified of the surgeon's knife. I went each morning to pray with her and on the last occasion, when she was too weak even to raise her head, she clasped my hand and pressed it to her breast. Anxious not to offend a dying woman, I left it there although it felt as if it were on fire. The next day the tumour started to shrink and within two weeks, it had vanished without trace. The woman hailed it as a miracle, crawling to church on her knees and making all sorts of preposterous claims on my behalf.

I've no doubt that there's a perfectly rational explanation. It may be that the *baylan*'s herbs had a delayed impact or that the growth itself was temporary: some kind of giant cyst. There may even have been no growth at all. I'm sure I don't need to cite Cora's 'pregnancy' to tell you that the mind can play strange tricks on the body. On the other hand she's unlikely to have had the same desperate yearning for a tumour as Cora had for a child and when I touched it, it certainly felt real. Either way, there's no question among people here that they've witnessed a miracle and once again I've become the subject of unwanted publicity. I'm not claiming any special powers – quite the reverse – but I have to be alive to the possibility that God may be working through me. After all, if He uses me every day to celebrate the mystery of the mass, why shouldn't He use me to perform a more mundane miracle?

The *haciendos* are faced with a dilemma. There's nothing they'd like more than to trade on people's credulity, yet I'm too much of a maverick to be trusted with greater influence. So they have to tread cautiously. A few days after don Bernardo's summons, don Florante Pineda invited me to lunch, which promised to be a more relaxed occasion until I met my fellow guests: the Bishop; the Mayor; the Senator; the Police Chief; the Constabulary Commander. We gathered in don Florante's 'den' and after several generous glasses of whisky, which in my case were shared with a nearby hibiscus, we proceeded to the dining room. I felt sorry for the Bishop, forever walking a tightrope between social obligation and pastoral care, since it soon became clear that despite the best efforts of doña Arcilla's cook, the main dish on the menu was me.

I was attacked from all sides with, of course, a veneer of courtesy proper to the occasion, although like all veneers in this climate it quickly cracked. To my surprise, my most formidable adversary was Melchior Quesada, the Constabulary Commander, whom I'd previously dismissed as a uniformed thug, not least because of the four gold teeth he bares at every opportunity. It turns out that as a boy he felt called to be a priest and was sent to a minor seminary, but his father died and his mother was forced to withdraw him. He joined the army and claims that he is now serving God with a gun. I was shocked to see myself through his eyes, not as a man who has left behind family and friends to save souls in a far-off country, but as a foreign agitator who regards the semi-literate peasantry as more fertile soil for revolution than the educated workers in the West.

I'll jot down the gist of our discussion as best I can; it helps me to clarify my thoughts and may help you to understand my position. I suspect you'll find many of my ideas as unpalatable as they do. After all, one of the charges against me – voiced by the *haciendos*, left unspoken by the others – is that I'm a traitor to my class as well as my cloth. Their objections all boil down to my involvement in politics or, as the Senator put it less contentiously, 'public affairs'. Quesada challenged me outright: 'Didn't Jesus Christ tell us to "pay Caesar what belongs to Caesar and God what belongs to God"? Shouldn't priests leave the rest of us to deal with worldly affairs and fix their own minds on Heaven?' 'Not at all,' I replied, with a confidence that confirmed their prejudices. 'Our Lord was seeking to extricate Himself from a dilemma. He found a formula to appease the authorities, not a principle for compartmentalising our lives. Besides, He knew better than anyone that everything belongs to God.'

With a show of deference that fooled no one, Quesada appealed to the Bishop to arbitrate. The Bishop, whose increasing befuddlement had, I suspect, been part of a prearranged plan between don Florante and his butler, stuttered that in his view the only purpose of life was to save one's soul. I intervened, both to state my case and to protect the Bishop, whose slurred speech was arousing the open derision of our fellow guests. 'Yes, but poverty and oppression endanger the soul along with the body. A woman whose children are starving may break the seventh commandment, just as a man driven mad by tyranny and injustice may break the fifth. So as a priest, I'm obliged to concern myself with the here and now as much as the hereafter; indeed, the two are inextricably linked. If a priest is to stand in the person of Christ, he can't avoid being political – ' I should point out that, as well as paraphrasing, I'm eliding several remarks. 'Our Lord was killed not because He preached the kingdom of Heaven but because He was accused of fomenting rebellion. He posed a threat to the civil and religious hierarchies. Remember, too, that however inclusive His message He directed it entirely to outsiders. Even the Holy See, which is hardly a hive of sedition, enjoined all Christians, clergy and laity alike, to devote themselves to eradicating poverty in the *Populorum Progresso* encyclical.'

In case you – that's you in Whitlock, not you at the lunch – dismiss this as the pious fancy of a privileged Westerner, let me remind you that the Philippines isn't Africa. We have typhoons and floods, to be sure, but we're not devastated by droughts and famines. The country abounds in mineral deposits and natural resources. If people are starving here, it's not from the harshness of Nature, let alone the indifference of God, but as the direct result of the rapacity of those at the top, several of whom were seated round the table. So I took the offensive. 'When I said that poverty endangers souls, I wasn't referring to the souls of the poor, who are driven to sin out of desperation. The rich who condemn them to such hardship live in far greater danger. I'm more and more convinced that the distinction between sheep and goats is that between rich and poor.'

'If that's true,' Quesada said, his fixed smile leaving me in no doubt on which side of the divide he stood, 'shouldn't you show more concern for the rich who face the prospect of eternal damnation?' Don Bernardo weighed in with the charge that I had near enough demanded that he be thrown out of church on Palm Sunday. I was about to reply when the Bishop slumped across the table in a stupor.

The look of scorn on Quesada's face still haunts me. Was its intensity the product of his own frustrated vocation? Does envy lie at the heart of his fanaticism: the sheer contempt for the suffering of others, which leads to the routine 'Not under my command, not under my command', whenever I file a complaint against an individual officer? I've no way of knowing. What I do know is that nothing I said at lunch, any more than from the pulpit, will have the least effect on his or his men's behaviour. Since when did celibacy become emasculation? Or is that a question you prefer not to contemplate, let alone answer?

Forgive my bluntness, but the situation here demands it. Unrest is rife on every estate, most violently on the Arriola. I told you how President Marcos awarded don Bernardo's cousin the logging concession to a chunk of the Cordilleras, displacing hundreds of Ibaloi families in the process. Don Bernardo then proposed to build a road for the transportation of the wood, displacing hundreds of his own tenants. His attempts to bludgeon them into submission have proved less effective now that they have the backing of the BCCs. Indeed, there can be no clearer proof of the adage that 'keeping the poor in ignorance keeps the rich in power' than the depths to which he and his fellow *haciendos* will stoop to have the BCCs suppressed. Having failed dismally, he has kept up the pressure by bringing in casual labourers to operate machinery, assist with the planting and harvest, and do essential repair work on the dykes and ditches, thus depriving the *hacienda* families of vital income.

The newcomers live in ramshackle bunkhouses, in conditions that hark back to the days of Thomas Hardy. They have no beds, blankets or mosquito nets but sleep on the bare floorboards. They have no sinks or lavatories but share a pump and relieve themselves in the bushes, wrapping their excrement in scraps of paper and flinging it on to the midden. Walking past an abandoned bunkhouse, I feared that it must have been the scene of a gruesome murder, but it was simply the stench of unwashed bodies that lingered from months before. Should they protest about their conditions, the men risk instant dismissal and the loss of their meagre savings to pay for the ticket home. Friction is inevitable between the men who've been robbed of their jobs and those whom they blame for stealing them. Don Bernardo employs his security guards to keep the peace and in the process inflict a few sharp blows on his opponents. Matters came to a head last week when a hired hand was killed, after allegedly raping the daughter of one of the tenants. The guards retaliated by breaking the father's legs and setting fire to several of his neighbours' farms.

So I'm sure you'll understand, Father, why I couldn't come home for your seventy-fifth. Agnes wrote me a detailed account and Greg dictated a brief one to his secretary. He's promised to send me the photographs, which I'm longing to see. I gather that the morning room was piled high with presents. On which note, I trust that you've received a letter from Ryan Alvarez, the young dental student whom I'm sponsoring in your name. I only hope that he keeps his word not to head for the big bucks overseas but to stay and serve the community. It would have been wonderful if Isabel and Hugh could have planned their celebration to coincide with yours but, Hugh's work commitments aside, I doubt that Whitlock would have withstood the strain. Still, there's less than a year to go until the return of the prodigal. Will we recognise each other or must I carry a red rose and a rolled-up copy of *The Times*?

I miss you both and remember you always in my prayers.

Your loving son,
Julian

No matter how hard he fought against it, a part of Philip rebelled at being rowed across the lake by three slightly built women. Maribel, however, was in her element. Her supervisor at work, a cousin of one of the founders, had told her of the feminist collective who took visitors out on rafts, serving them meals of freshly caught carp and fern salad, while they sat back and enjoyed the view. He could not escape the suspicion that the wealth of photographs she had taken were as much to curry favour at the call centre as to capture the moment, but with the mid-afternoon sun gently toasting his skin, the buttery taste of the fish and piquancy of the leaves lingering in his mouth, the soft plash of the oars rustling in his ears and, not least, Maribel's sweet-scented hair tickling his chin, it was a minor cavil in an otherwise perfect day.

Alerted to a stirring in the trees, he looked up to see a monkey hanging from a branch. 'There!' he said, pointing it out to Maribel with the excitement of one more accustomed to squirrels. Suddenly the stillness was shattered, as one of the women screeched an instruction to the others and they paddled furiously into the middle of the lake.

'No!' Maribel said, pressing down his hand. 'It is not permitted to point.'

'At a monkey?' Philip asked, perplexed.

'No, it is not the monkey. It is the *kapre*; you will make him angry.'

'What's a *kapre*? Some kind of wild woodland animal?'

'Yes, he is most wild. He is full of hairs; he lives in the *balete* trees and he smokes a big cigar.'

'Wait a minute! You don't mean... Julian – Father Julian – wrote of his parishioners believing in such mythical creatures. You're not telling me you do too?'

'I most absolutely do,' she replied, as affronted as if he had questioned her faith in St Paul. 'If you anger him, he will throw coconuts from the trees, which will hit you on the head and maybe sink this boat.'

'You're sure of this, are you?' Philip asked, both delighted and dismayed by her credulity.

'I am, and so are all these people.' She addressed the women, who laid down their oars as soon as they were safely out of range. While they chatted among themselves and cast the odd reproachful glance his way, Philip felt a growing sense of isolation as the only male European rationalist on the raft. Allowing his imagination to run riot, he fantasised that the woods had once been the site of sacrifice to a Philippine mother goddess and that the collective was a front for the revival of the cult, to which Maribel was seeking induction by bringing them their latest victim. He weighed up whether to make a grab for the nearest oar before they immobilised him, or to jump overboard and strike out for the shore. He was a strong swimmer and the water looked calm, but as with everything else in this country, there was no knowing what might be lurking beneath the surface, let alone slithering through the undergrowth when he reached land.

'You must eat this,' one of the women said, as she chopped open a coconut and handed it to him, along with a wooden spoon to scoop out the meat. He held it to his mouth, gulping the juice so greedily that it ran down his chin.

'You wish for something to wipe it clean?' Maribel asked.

'Yes, please.'

'Here.' She handed him a tissue.

'Can't you do better than that?'

'I do not understand.' Philip mimed a kiss. 'Oh, you are the most wicked man,' Maribel said, casting a hurried look at the women, two of whom were sitting on the edge of the raft, dangling their feet in the water, while the third was slicing a pineapple.

Philip worried that he might have offended Maribel's modesty, which had already been strained by their proximity on the raft, but her broad smile reassured him that she was blushing with pleasure not embarrassment. To his joy and relief, she was at ease with their newfound intimacy. It was a week since they had first slept together, an event which, for all his agonising, had been as relaxed as it was blissful. While part of him had been grateful to discover that she was not, after all, a virgin, thereby freeing him from both pressure and responsibility, the other part felt let down since, humiliating as it was to admit, he had been attracted as much by her innocence as by her naïveté. Moreover, he was tormented by thoughts of her previous lover – for his own peace of mind he stuck to the singular. Was he a boy from the village, her consort in the Santa Cruz procession whom she had left behind when she moved to Manila, or a student in the city, perhaps a trainee doctor who had sparked her desire to work as a medical transcriptionist and whom she had selflessly renounced when he won a scholarship to train abroad? The one candidate that he refused to contemplate was a fellow Westerner, still less one introduced to her by her brother (the backstreet solicitation rang mockingly in his ears). He had delicately broached the subject, only to retreat when she turned as pale as if he had drawn attention to a scar or a missing toe. His one consolation was her insistence on keeping their new arrangements secret from Dennis. 'Am I likely to discuss my private life with him?' he had wanted to ask, before realising how insulting that would sound. Instead, he had promised to say nothing to anyone and been rewarded with a flurry of kisses.

'Thank God we didn't ask Dennis to bring us!' he said, roused from his reverie.

'You are not angry with him? He is no longer making texts when he is driving? You will not send him away?'

'Don't worry,' Philip replied, touched by her sisterly concern. 'He's safe with me.'

'He is a good boy, but sometimes he has to be bad to be strong. And now he has many worries.'

'Well, if he must get involved in all those shady deals.'

'No, it is our father.'

'Has he been back in touch? Or have you found out where he's living?'

Maribel's face crumpled like a crushed flower. 'I have always known this, but I have not been telling it to you.'

'I don't understand.'

'But you must! You must understand how I am doing this, so you have no shame for our family: so you do not think Maribel comes from such bad people that I do not wish to see her again.'

'I would never think that. You know I would never think that! What does it matter where we come from?' Philip asked, as the gulf between them widened.

'My father has come from prison,' Maribel said, pressing her hand against her mouth as if trying to force the words back inside.

'He's been released?'

'No, he is still in there. He is in there for all the rest of his life. He has been raping my sister.' At the sound of the word, two of the women looked up with haunted eyes.

'And you? Did he touch you too?' Philip asked, afraid that he might be sick.

'No, but he has never been touching Analyn either.'

'Then how could he? Are you sure you mean *rape*?'

'You will be sad that you have ever met me. You will think that all Filipinos are wicked people and liars. You will never believe one more thing that I say.' Maribel began to sob, prompting the women to look accusingly at Philip. Undaunted, he asked them to resume rowing, trusting that the gentle motion would calm her. 'My father is a bad man. He has been hitting us all with sticks. Even Angel Boy.'

'Angel Boy?'

'He is my second brother. He has a leg like the root of a tree. He has been born like this after my father forced my mother to lie with him during the day.'

'I'm so sorry.'

'But most of all, he hits my mother. He hits her and he rapes her and she takes herbs so that she stops the babies, and he hits her harder than before when he finds out. And Dennis says that he will kill him. My mother is fearful that these words are true, and so she says that he must go away. He does not wish to go. He is worrying about what my father will do to us. But my mother says that he will help us more by sending money. So he finds a job in Kuwait. But I have been telling you this already.'

'Yes.'

'When Dennis has left home, my father has become more cruel. He is jealous because Dennis has a dream and he has not. He has nothing in his head but drink and… ' She is unable or unwilling to put it into words. 'He hits my mother so hard, until she cannot walk out of the house because her face is as purple as a *ube*.'

'Was there nowhere you could go for protection?' Philip was no longer so ingenuous as to suggest the police. 'What about your priest?'

'Father Elmo is praying with us. He is telling my mother that she is married to my father and that her sufferings will be short.'

'You mean it won't be long until he beats her to death?' Philip asked in disgust.

'No, you must not be saying this!' Maribel grabbed his hand between both of hers and squeezed it tight. 'He means that my mother will be in Heaven for ever while my father is being burnt by the Devil in Hell.' Her quiet conviction was more chilling than any cry for vengeance. 'But my mother will no longer wait. She is frightened for her own body and she is frightened for ours. So she is telling Analyn what she must be saying so we can escape. There is a law in the Philippines against anyone who is raping a child. At first they have been sentenced to death. But this is a gentle country and our last president has ended this sentence. Now they must be put into prison for life. This is what has happened to my father.'

'So he was found guilty?' Philip asked, uneasy in spite of himself.

'Oh no,' she replied blithely. 'He has only been in prison for three years, so there will be many more years until there will be a trial. With God's grace, he will be dead long before this time.'

'Then what's Dennis's problem?'

'It is my uncle – the brother of my father – he has made a visit to see my mother, and he has said to her that Analyn must be telling the truth to the judge, or he and the cousins of my father will kill her.'

'Is he serious?'

'I am sure of it. You will think that he is right, because my mother and my sister have been making false charges. But we are poor people. I am swearing to you that there has been no other way.'

'Please don't upset yourself! I understand.'

'To save us all, Analyn must be giving up her own chance to marry. No man will take a wife who has been disgraced.'

Maribel's voice was so anguished that for a moment Philip considered stealing Dennis's gun and heading north to take the law into his own hands: a thought that felt not only absurd but shameful, when he compared his image of a lone avenger, born of black-and-white films on wet winter afternoons, with Maribel's, born of brutal experience. Despite the baking sun, he began to shiver and asked the women to row them back to the shore. He countered Maribel's apologies for ruining the after-noon with gratitude that she had confided in him. Neverthe-less, he was aware that his sympathy was constrained not just by circumstance but by time. In less than a fortnight he would be on a plane back to London and this extraordinary adventure be reduced to a series of dinner-party anecdotes ('did I tell you how my drug-addicted driver pulled a gun on a kid in the street?') or, if he pursued his literary ambitions, an exotic setting for a novel. In either case, Maribel would become a shadow of her true self, as broken as her English.

What was the alternative? There was no way that he could invite her to live with him. He could barely support himself, let alone a girlfriend. Besides, how would she survive in an alien culture thousands of miles from home, where her motives for being there would be viewed with mistrust?

That was always assuming she agreed to come.

Plunged into gloom, he was relieved when, after a long and clammy coach ride, they found themselves back in Manila. He led Maribel through the crowded hotel lobby with an assurance tempered by the awareness that he too was an interloper. Familiarity had not dulled her enchantment with his room, which she wandered up and down, as if to absorb its opulence. She then wrapped herself in one of the bed-curtains, which he caught in a surreptitious photograph, only to delete it in response to her rising panic. She escaped into the bathroom where she ran a perfumed bath, putting up merely token resistance when he slipped in with her. Half an hour later, they lay in matching bathrobes on the bed and, after ringing her aunt to say that she was staying at a friend's, she amused herself by scrolling through the television channels. Her instant retreat from the Adult Films filled him with shame and, as a penance, he agreed to watch a local soap opera in which the actors shouted so loudly that he feared for his reputation with his neighbours. He toyed with taking her to eat in the Champagne Room, but the thought of the waiters' supercilious smiles persuaded him to order room service and for the rest of the evening the boundaries between food, sleep and sex were deliciously blurred.

He awoke shortly after two to find a jaunty Filipina on the still running TV wishing him a 'Happy Period'. The girl, who was advertising tampons, was followed by a plump matron, who promised that by drinking her brand of powdered milk his baby would grow up to be taller, cleverer, more attractive and, from what he could make out (the problem was no longer one of intelligibility but of logic), a more talented chess and cello player than by drinking any other. The shock, first of the adverts themselves and then of their juxtaposition, was compounded by the memory that at one point during their fervent lovemaking, his condom had split. Grabbing the remote control, he slammed the off switch, but it was harder to silence his anxieties. Breaking out in a sweat, he edged away from Maribel, who was breathing deeply beside him, her skin a burnished copper in the dim light, a sweep of hair veiling her left cheek, even as the rest of her lay exposed. Wiping his hand on the sheet, he ran his fingers down her side, gaining confidence with every inch. It was impossible for anything more substantial than a dream to be trapped inside that tranquil body.

He fell asleep, to be roused by an alarm call at eight, with only the standby light on the TV to remind him of his earlier unease. Maribel was appalled by the mess, smoothing sheets, plumping pillows and arranging dirty dishes on the trolley. It was all he could do to keep her from running them under the tap, as if to remove any compromising residues from the eyes of the chambermaids. They breakfasted in the room, with Maribel saving four miniature pots of jam to take home, which Philip supplemented with a diverse collection of shampoos, conditioners, shower gels, soaps and moisturisers, which he had set aside for her over the previous week. His delight that such a trifling gift could give her such pleasure faded when, on the brink of leaving, she dashed into the bathroom and brought out two spare lavatory rolls which, with a wordless entreaty, she slipped into her bag.

Maribel's gentle presence was replaced by Dennis's abrasive one when, half an hour after she had left the hotel, he arrived to drive Philip to San Juan for his meeting with Hendrik van Leyden. Reaching the Society's headquarters, a grey clapboard house that might have been transported from a plantation in Virginia, Philip pressed the doorbell which, to his surprise, was answered by Hendrik himself. He was a tall, broad-shouldered man, with grizzled hair in a de facto tonsure and a single bushy eyebrow that stretched across his face. His skin was startlingly white, as if he had not caught the sun in forty years, which must have impressed the Filipinos. Unlike Julian, who had been eager to break down the barriers between priest and parishioners, he wore a cassock, albeit one that was frayed, stained and so shiny at the elbows and knees that the black cloth looked silver. He clasped Philip's hand in his spatulate fingers and led him through the sombre hallway to a study, which was in total disarray. Even the books on the shelves were arranged at odd angles, while those on the floor were piled with flea-market abandon. Papers, letters, bills and journals were scattered on the desk, sofa and chairs. A Dutch passport, its cover scorched by a coffee cup, lay next to a pair of broken spectacles and a heap of coins.

'Please, sit down,' Hendrik said in a guttural accent. Philip looked helplessly at the cat curled on his allotted chair. 'Nancy, bugger off!' The cat did not stir. Hendrik moved towards her. 'This is what I get for taking you off the streets.' He turned to Philip. 'I rescued her from a pimp who'd been maltreating her. I named her Nancy after *Oliver Twist.*' The cat pre-empted her eviction by jumping to the floor and limping away on her three legs. Philip sat facing a large framed sampler with the delicately stitched motto: *Whosoever touches pitch will be defiled.*

'I see you're admiring my sampler.'

'Very much. I'm trying to place the quotation. Is it St Paul?'

'Ecclesiasticus. I commissioned it from one of the girls in the Angeles refuge. Can I give you something to eat or drink? Tea? Juice? Water? I know I have biscuits somewhere.' He shifted a stack of papers on his desk.

'That's very kind, but no, thank you. I had an enormous breakfast at the hotel.'

'Very wise! What I'd give to have my meals cooked again! Ever since the Regional brought me back here on my seventieth birthday, I've had to fend for myself.' Philip wondered whether the rest of the house were in similar chaos. 'But enough chit-chat! Tell me about your great enterprise. Are these islands any closer to having a new saint?'

'If they are, it'll be no thanks to me. I've been here two months and I'm not sure that I know much more about Julian than when I arrived. If my being here has accomplished anything, it's been to focus the minds of the Bishop and his team. I feel like my mother visiting my great-aunt in her nursing home. There was nothing she could do for her – my aunt didn't even recognise her – but she showed the staff that there was someone looking out for her interests. That's the most I can hope for now, unless you come up with some leads.'

'I wish I could, but I'm not that familiar with Julian's life here. We weren't close.'

'Are you talking physically or emotionally?'

'A bit of both. I suspect he would have been confused and embarrassed and maybe even – yes – angered by the investigation. He used to say – tongue-in-cheek, of course – that I was the saint. There's no need to write this down,' Hendrik said, as Philip opened his notebook. 'He called me Nick – after St Nicholas – in his letters.'

'Have you kept them? I'd love to take a look.'

'I'm afraid they were lost years ago. I find it so hard to keep track of things.' He gestured abstractedly at the clutter. 'Besides, they were largely about private matters, of no relevance to the *Positio*. Nick! Yes, I had forgotten that. Although, by the end, we were back to Hendrik. I suppose he found Nick dangerously equivocal.'

'In what way?'

'Nick – Old Nick. From our Dutch word, *nikken*.'

'Would that be after your estrangement?'

'Our what?'

'I'm sorry, maybe I've misunderstood, but in one of his prison letters he wrote that your friendship had run its course.'

'*Run its course*?' Hendrik ruminated. 'How very Julian! I'm not sure how long its course was to begin with. Ours was a friendship more of circumstance than choice. If you want someone close to him, the "beloved disciple" as it were, you need Father Benito Bertubin.'

'That's all very well, but he appears to have vanished off the face of the earth.'

Hendrik looked at him in bemusement. 'The refuse dumps of Manila may be hell on earth, but they're still on it.'

'Excuse me?'

'Father, no, plain Benito – I may be mistaken but I think he left the priesthood – is working just a few miles from here with the people who live on refuse: that is *on* it and *off* it.'

'Even if he's no longer a priest, surely the Church authorities would know that? The Vicar General of Baguio told me categorically that they had no idea where he was.'

'They may not.'

'Do you think that's likely?' Hendrik shrugged. 'Then why should he lie to me? Benito knew Julian better than anyone. They were locked up together for a year. Are they afraid that his politics will be a black mark against Julian with a conservative Curia?'

'Maybe Benito himself will give you the answer?'

'Do you have his address?' Philip struggled to keep the excitement out of his voice.

'No, but you don't need it. Just ask any taxi driver to take you to the Payatas refuse dump.'

'Is it that big?'

'Estimates vary, but some say 60,000 people live on it.'

'You mean *off* it?'

'No.'

'I'm finding it hard to get my head around this. A high-ranking priest deliberately misled me. I suppose, given all the clerical cover-ups of recent years, I shouldn't be surprised. I'm sorry; I don't mean to offend you.'

'You haven't.'

'And I mustn't abuse your hospitality, that is your time. I'll go to Payatas of course, but meanwhile, if there's anything you can think of to tell me, anything at all... Julian wrote that he met you in Brabant, which seems a strange place for an Englishman to study.'

'There's always been a strong Dutch flavour to the Society. Our founder, Henry Vaughan, sent one of his closest associates to establish the seminary at Roosendaal in 1890, which was where I met Julian some seventy years later. We liked and, I trust, respected each other. But that was as far as it went. Intimacy was frowned upon. We were cloistered young men. Well, I don't need to spell it out for you with your English public schools.'

'Most of them now admit girls.'

'Progress or merely change? Not that the Church is particularly keen on either. Discipline at the seminary was very strict. We were required to gather in groups of three or more. "*Numquam duo, semper tres.*" The Master of Novices even chose our companions for walks. In any case, Julian was something of a loner. Though maybe that was forced upon him. People were wary of him because he'd been to Oxford.'

'But I thought he read theology.'

'Quite. Oxford was regarded as a hotbed of heresy. Everyone – staff and students alike – were afraid that his spiritual values had been put at risk by his course.'

'Nonetheless, you must have formed a special bond since he invited you to Whitlock.'

'I can't have been the only one.'

'You're the only one he mentions. But then you're the only one he met again out here.'

'I was so nervous. It was my first time – and my only time – to visit one of your old English houses. Julian told me not to worry if I broke the rules. His parents would make allowances for me as a foreigner. You may imagine how much that put me at my ease!'

'Did you meet the whole family?'

'Just his parents and his sisters. His brother was working – in London, I think.'

'And what was your overall impression?'

'That they were the oddest people I'd ever met. Not his mother – she was a very gracious lady – but as for the rest of them, I think that the polite word – the English word – is eccentric. At our first meal, the maid brought round a tray of chops. We ate a lot of chops. Julian's older sister – I forget her name…'

'Agnes.'

'Agnes, that's right.' Hendrik smiled. 'She refused it and I asked if she was a vegetarian. She looked as horrified as if I'd asked if she was a virgin. "Certainly not," she replied, "but I only eat meat that I've killed myself." And the maid brought her a slice of game pie.'

'I thought it was his younger sister, Cora, who was the eccentric one.'

'That's putting it mildly! She was obsessed with a television newsreader. She used to copy down passages from his bulletins and decipher his secret messages to her. Later that summer Julian was called home because she had fallen pregnant. She swore that the newsreader was the father and stirred up a lot of trouble, writing letters to him, to the papers and to the BBC. To make matters worse, she swelled up – Julian said it looked as if she was carrying twins – and her father blamed one of the men working on the estate. Then the newsreader was taken off the air – I'm quite sure there was no connection – and, overnight, Cora's stomach shrank. It was as though she had had the baby, except that there was no baby. For the rest of his life Julian felt guilty that he had not done enough to help her, that he had spent so much time away from home. On the other hand he was convinced that if he'd stayed, he would have ended up like her.'

'Mad?'

'Disturbed,' Hendrik replied with a frown. 'To my mind, most of the problems stemmed from their father. He had the coldest smile I've ever seen. I kept out of his way as much as I could. Though there was no escape when he invited me fishing. To everyone's surprise, I caught a large salmon. "You're not feeding the five thousand, you know," he said icily, before remembering to shake my hand.'

'A curious remark to address to a trainee priest!'

'He had no love for the Church, much to Julian's regret. I'm sure you know the story of his vocation?'

'Only the barest outline. If you can fill in any details...'

'Not many, I'm afraid. His father had been captured by the Japanese in Singapore. He spent years in a prison camp, long after the fighting in Europe had ended and other boys' fathers had come home. All the children prayed every night for his safe return, but Julian went one further and vowed that if his father survived, he'd become a priest. The irony – no, the tragedy – was that, by pledging himself to God, he'd done the thing most calculated to alienate his father, who had lost his faith in the war – at least Julian claimed it was in the war, although I suspect that he was trying to justify it.'

'Do you think he'd still have become a priest if his father hadn't returned from Burma?'

'Most definitely, but then I believe that a priest is called by God.'

'That must be a comfort.'

'It was once.'

Hendrik's face clouded and Philip preferred not to probe.

'It must have been a shock – it was for Julian – when you met up again in Manila.'

'Absolutely. He was the last person I was expecting. I thought he was still in Liverpool.'

'Yes, what was that about? It seems an unlikely place to send a missionary.'

'Especially Julian! He was our star student and we assumed that he'd be given one of the more challenging postings. I remember when I first heard about it. The Rector of the House was hosting his traditional post-ordination party for family and friends. Halfway through, he announced that the Superior General was ready to see us in his study. One by one we went in, then came back and shouted out where we were going, to be greeted by a burst of applause. I was off to Pakistan – a remote part of Sindh province. Then Julian came back and called out "Liverpool!". There was a deathly silence, until at last someone started to clap and everyone else followed suit. The Rector explained that because of his exceptional qualities, Julian had been chosen to stay at home and nurture the next generation of missionaries, and Julian insisted that he was happy to fulfil whatever task God had assigned to him, but there was no denying that it was a blow.'

The cat limped back into the room.

'So how long did you spend in Pakistan?'

'Four years: the four happiest years of my life. I lived there among the Kutchi Kohli, a Hindu tribe who worked as sharecroppers for feudal landlords.'

'Much like the tenant farmers in San Isidro.'

'Except that they were already Christians, whereas I had the inestimable blessing of saving souls for the Lord.'

'Yet you moved here?'

'Not from choice, believe me! I was deeply reluctant to come to a place where the Church was so well established.'

'It does seem strange to send missionaries to such a fanatically Catholic country.'

'The Philippines have always been an anomaly in the Society's operation, but after the expulsion of the friars the Pope called on Western missionaries to come to the aid of the Church here and we've stayed on ever since. Like Julian, I soon found my niche. Despite working in such different worlds, we felt the same need to join the struggle for justice.'

'Maybe in years to come (not too soon, I trust!), another bishop not a million miles from here will be putting together another *Positio*?'

'I wouldn't bank on it,' Hendrik said, pointing to the sampler. 'You've read the writing on the wall.' Philip glanced at it again, as the cat leapt on to his lap. Startled, he attempted to stroke her head while balancing his notepad on her knobbly back. 'I invited Julian to stay with me in Angeles. He had boasted – no, that's not fair, *enthused* – about all the progress he was making in the parish: the Bible study groups and agricultural projects and health education classes he'd set up. His life was as straightforward as mine had been in Pakistan. I wanted him to appreciate what it was like for those of us who were fighting a more insidious enemy, not economic oppression but human desire.'

'Surely the danger occurs when the two come together? Sex-starved soldiers with dollars to spare. Julian was appalled by what he saw in Angeles and in a letter home (no doubt censored) he laid the blame squarely on the shoulders – and the pockets – of the US military.'

'He was right. The Filipinos tell a joke to make light of their long history of Spanish and American occupation: "We spent three hundred years in a convent and fifty in Hollywood." But they've picked the wrong myth. It wasn't Hollywood so much as the Wild West. And the sheriffs were just as corrupt as the gunmen. They polluted the whole environment. There were even monkeys around the airbase who became addicted to American Wonder Bread.'

'Is that a metaphor?'

'No, it's a fact. They soon learnt that a few simple tricks would earn them their daily crusts. The girls – or LBFMs as they were known – weren't so lucky.'

'LBFMs?'

'Little Brown Fucking Machines.'

'Oh, I see.'

'They had to perform more and more sophisticated tricks, as the men's appetites grew more and more jaded. After all, when you've had a different eighteen-year-old every night for a week, you're happy to pay a dollar or two extra for a sixteen-year-old and then a fourteen-year-old and then a twelve-year-old. Need I go on?'

'I get the picture.'

'But they did go on. On and on right down to children of five or six. Baby Brown Fucking Machines.'

'Julian was full of praise for your efforts to rescue them, despite all the threats from the pimps and bar owners.'

'And the Mayor who claimed that I was jeopardising commerce and the military chiefs who claimed that I was jeopardising morale. And the mothers – don't forget the mothers, since they were usually the ones who sold the girls.'

'But not at five or six?'

'How does a prostitute live when she's too old or sick to attract custom? Either she earns a few pesos doing laundry for her younger colleagues, or else she prostitutes her own children. Some combine the two, sprinkling soap powder in the girls' drinking water to keep them from infection.'

'It's unbearable, even at a distance, yet you worked there for – how long?'

'Thirty-four years.'

'How did you ward off despair?'

'I'm a priest, Mr Seward,' Hendrik said.

'Of course,' Philip replied, uncertain if he had been given an answer or a rebuke.

'At the end of the day – at the end of a life – the most any of us can hope for is that our actions result in more good than bad.'

'Isn't that rather pessimistic for a priest?'

'I'd prefer to think of it as realistic. I'm not a monk praying in a cloister; I'm out in the world. And this – this you can write in your pad – ' Philip realised with a jolt that he had been so engrossed in the conversation that he had stopped taking notes. 'I'm convinced that even in his far-flung parish Julian felt the same.'

'I've always understood that to a Christian, motives mattered as much as – if not more than – results.'

'Which is why I need to redress the balance,' Hendrik said, staring at him hollow-eyed.

'I don't follow.'

'And I hope that you never will. I have fought many enemies over the years, but the most powerful, the most persistent has been myself.' Philip's stomach clenched as Hendrik's words presaged a confession. 'In a world where priests are held to be guilty of every sin that they condemn, let me make one thing absolutely clear: I never laid a finger on any of those girls, never touched them with more than a handkerchief to dry their tears or a flannel to wipe off the dirt. But I had thoughts. And in thirty-four years the thoughts built up until they became the secret story of my life.'

'Was there no one you could talk to?'

'Yes, Julian. I went to visit him in San Isidro and I talked to him more candidly than I have talked to anyone before or since. I told him of the toll that the work was having on me, body and soul: how I saw the wraithlike children, not yet come into the fullness of their sin, and I was overwhelmed with love for them. But it was not the love that Our Lord instructed us to feel for "these little ones"; it was longing. I told him that I saw the bruised and broken girls in the refuge and, even as I bathed their wounds, I was stifling the urge to inflict more. I was sure that it was only my horror at the effects of other men's lusts that saved me from succumbing to my own. I told him that I had resolved to write to the Regional and ask to be sent somewhere there were fewer temptations – somewhere like San Isidro,' he said sourly.

'But the Regional didn't listen?'

'I didn't write. Julian talked me out of it. Not having known him, you can have no idea of his powers of persuasion. He charged me to remember that God had sent me here for a purpose. He was testing me, and I had no right to run away. He – Julian, not God' – Hendrik laughed – 'told me that I must turn my weakness into strength, my vice into virtue, and that, having recognised the offence in myself, I would be better able to fight it in others and that, by fighting it in others, I would defeat it in myself.'

'But you didn't?'

'No, it grew ever more consuming: awake, asleep and, most painfully of all, at prayer, until I stared at my crucifix and saw not salvation but sin.'

'Did you speak of it again to Julian?'

'He spoke of it to me; he wrote to me; he even sent me a cheque for the refuge, a mark of faith that felt more like a mockery. He returned to Angeles some years later in search of a missing parishioner. And that was the last time I saw him. I realise that he was shocked, not just by the depravity of the bars but by my detachment. No matter that I needed to mix with the owners for the sake of the girls; I had failed his test, which I sometimes think was more exacting than God's. There was certainly more of Moses in him than of Christ.'

'So I take it that you don't regard him as a saint?'

'Did I say that? It depends how you define "saint". For me, a saint has to be full of humanity and not just of God. He has to have blood as well as chrism in his veins. He has to understand the corruption that we lesser mortals find in ourselves and so enable us to rise above it. Whereas Julian had none of that. He was somebody who never touched pitch – who never even caught a whiff of its fumes – his entire life.'

Eight

My dear Mother and Father,

Forgive me if this is shorter than usual, but what with catching up in the parish and the visit of the Holy Father I've been run ragged since my return. It struck me halfway through yesterday's mass (that's how bad it's been) that I'd promised to let you know I was back. I apologise for the delay, although I trust that Father's typically frank reminder that you'd hear soon enough if there were a problem reassured you, Mother.

Apart from bringing me back in one piece, the flight had little to recommend it. I was sitting beside a well-groomed man in his thirties with the attention span of a gnat (although, given the tenacity of gnats in the *convento*, I'm maligning them). On hearing that I was a priest, he lectured me – at length – on the iniquities of organised religion. Thankfully, he fell asleep somewhere above the Alps, giving me the chance to reflect on the trip. It's a truism to note how the month sped by. After the initial adjustments (sorry about the beard; I thought I'd warned you), we'd barely resumed our old rhythm when we were plunged into the excitement of the wedding. Then, a week later I was preparing to fly back. In spite – or, indeed, because – of all the letters we'd exchanged, there was so much ground for us to cover. Do you suppose that anybody has the luxury of picking up where they left off? Perhaps Cora? But then I suspect that she has a fairy-tale sense of time.

I was delighted to find you both looking so well: a few creaks perhaps, but then that's only to be expected. The diet's working wonders, Mother, and while I admit that Agnes might have exempted the wedding cake, please try to stick to it. Agnes hasn't changed a bit, I'm happy to say, nor for that matter has Greg, except around the middle. Success evidently agrees with him. Alice was the one who looked drawn. It may have been the strain of the wedding, but I do hope that Greg isn't taking her for granted. Forty-eight is a difficult age for a woman. With Isabel married, Sophie working for Greg and Vicky at college, she must feel lonely. She told me that she's spending more and more time in Suffolk. It's a lovely garden, but it isn't Eden.

On a brighter note, you and Alice and the orchestra and the florists and the caterers and everyone concerned should congratulate yourselves on a splendid occasion. Isabel looked radiant (I know I'm prejudiced) and Hugh looked suave (ditto). It's not for me to criticise the guest list, but I fail to see why Greg felt the need to invite quite so many government colleagues. He might as well have hung blue rosettes on the marquee. And who were all those braying young men? Exile may have skewed my perspective, but it strikes me that in the ten years I've been away the country has grown heartless. Even in sleepy Gaverton people are more self-serving – the Jenny Henshaw I left behind would never have put her mother in a home so that she could work part-time at the co-op or the Simon Freeman have left the police because he could earn more dealing in second-hand cars.

I promise that it won't be another ten years before I return, although not for the reason you suggest, Father. At this rate you'll live to be a hundred! Nonetheless, the longer I stayed in England, the more I realised that the Philippines is now my home. When I stepped on to the tarmac in Manila I was filled with a warmth that went far beyond the weather. I wish you'd taken the chance to visit when I first came out here. The landscape may be beautiful, but it's the people who make it special. Perhaps I can best explain by quoting one of their creation myths (they have A LOT), which Mark, Consolacion's youngest grandson, told me only the other day. His grandmother scolded him, but I was enchanted. In the beginning, God created human beings from clay – so far so Genesis! But here's the twist; He put them in a kiln to bake. He left the first batch in for too long; they came out burnt and were the ancestors of the black race. He tried a second batch, which He removed too soon. They were only half-baked and were the ancestors of the white race. So He took particular care over the third batch. They came out a perfect shade of brown and were the ancestors of the Filipinos.

Boastful and naïve it may be, but there's a grain of truth in it as I found when, the week after I returned, I conducted a very different wedding. I'd love to have seen the Leveringtons' faces, let alone those of Greg's high-powered friends, if, instead of a tastefully embossed card, they'd received a slice of pork wrapped in a bamboo leaf. That's the traditional Ibaloi invitation, which was delivered to me at the *convento* by the bridegroom's youngest brother. The next day I drove up to the mountains, where I was greeted by the whole village, in their best beads and feathers. I didn't officiate alone but shared the honours with the *mambunong*, their tribal priest. After years of agonising over their dual loyalties, I've grown reconciled to their worship of two supreme beings: their own *Kavuniyan* and the Christian *Shivus* whom, unsurprisingly given their history, they see as the more powerful. So, at ceremonies where both gods are invoked, ours takes precedence.

I found the hybrid service deeply affecting. At the end, the bride and groom were escorted through the village to the new hut that the community had built for them (no parental deposits and twenty-five-year mortgages here). The thick smell of barbecued boar, at once intimate and ominous, filled the air, as the couple presided at the wedding feast. I drank so much *tafey*, a lethally potent rice wine, that the details of the celebration elude me, but I do recall being dragged out to join in a dance, which couldn't have been further removed from my sedate foxtrot with cousin Nancy at Whitlock. I was given a strip of cloth to hold in the air and induced to take a few steps around the floor while one of the older girls, also holding a cloth, twirled in front of me. A trio of women played on bamboo pipes and their male counterparts beat gongs in what seemed like ever-increasing delirium, although that may well have been the effect of the wine. I staggered back to my seat, where one of the elders explained to general amusement that it was a courtship dance. My partner was mercilessly teased.

Even as I've been contemplating the richness of the indigenous religion, the country has been revelling in the full panoply of papal power. In February, the Philippines welcomed the most important visitor to its shores since Magellan. For months the entire population has been in a state of frenzy, which reached its height when President Marcos, who has been counting on the Holy Father's visit both to prop up his popularity at home and enhance his prestige overseas, was persuaded to lift Martial Law. For the first time in more than eight years, workers are free to associate and even to strike, the military is subject (at least on paper) to the courts and opposition supporters can no longer be imprisoned without trial. Those of us who cling to the possibility of peaceful reform feel new hope. Others (no names, no pack drill but, if you've followed me this far, you'll know whom I mean), maintain that it's too late for such cosmetic gestures and that only through bloodletting will the country be cleansed.

Time alone will tell which of us is right, but what can't be denied is that the visit has given a tremendous boost to the nation's morale. I took part in two open-air masses, in Manila and Baguio, and I was overwhelmed by the euphoria and reverence of the vast crowds, many of whom had been camping in the sweltering heat for days. To see the forest of outstretched hands passing the sanctified wafers from one to another was truly to feel in the presence of Christ. The most moving service of all was the Pope's beatification of Lorenzo Ruiz, a seventeenth-century clerk who travelled with three Dominicans to Japan, where he chose to be tortured to death rather than renounce his faith (I don't need to tell you, Father, about Japanese cruelty, but this was particularly barbaric). In a country so devoted to the saints that you stumble on ornate shrines in the most obscure places, this first domestic canonisation is long overdue.

At the same time the visit was a definite coup for the President, not least in the propaganda opportunities of the Manila mass, where he sat on a dais directly beneath the Pope and insisted that he and his family should be the first to receive communion. Imelda, too, basked in reflected glory, criss-crossing the country in her private jet, so that wherever the Holy Father touched down, be it in Cebu, Mindanao or here in Baguio, she was waiting to greet him, always in a different outfit but with the same broad smile. On the other hand the Pope failed to give the regime the unequivocal backing it wanted. In Manila he elected to stay with the papal nuncio rather than in the lavish palace Imelda had built for him – entirely out of coconut: the wood, that is, not the shells. And, while a huge clean-up operation ensured that he was spared the sight of the usual rubbish on the city's streets, the government was unable to keep him away from the slums when he came up to Baguio. Above all, in a sermon on the island of Negros, he roundly attacked the oppression of the poor and appealed for universal brotherhood.

On the other hand – is that too many hands? Perhaps not for such an adroit pope – his visit was less reassuring for those of us who wish that as well as assuming his immediate predecessors' names, he shared their radical zeal. At a mass for 5,000 clergy in Manila he informed us that our role was purely spiritual and that we must on no account involve ourselves in politics. Yet isn't that what we've always done, especially in the Philippines? Señores Arriola, Pineda and Romualdez would undoubtedly endorse a viewpoint that turns us into little more than government stooges, stalwarts of the status quo. But are we to leave others to fight for justice, while we stay safely behind the lines like army padres? Is the Blessed Sacrament to be nothing more than a placebo?

As I sit in the gathering dusk on the veranda, drawing this letter to a close before my lamp attracts an army of moths, I'm conscious of a deep stillness hanging over the *poblacion*. Will it last the night or will I be woken by the sound of gunshots or distant screams? For a moment I find it hard not to envy Father Ambrose with his gentle round of daily offices and pastoral visits, his spotless church and spacious presbytery, his intellectual conundrums and doctrinal dilemmas. But then I think of those hands, lovingly passing our Saviour through the crowd, and I know that the path I've chosen, however rocky and tortuous, however dimly lit, is the right one.

Your loving son,
Julian

The news of Analyn's death put all Philip's plans on hold. She had been shot by a masked gunman on her way home from mass and the identity of the perpetrator was not in doubt. With his demands rejected, her uncle had carried out his threat. Philip, who was used to resolving disputes by negotiation, struggled to comprehend the crime. Did the man despair of his brother receiving justice in a case that might drag on for decades? Did he regard domestic violence as a minor offence compared to perjury? Was he defending family honour or merely male prerogative? On the other hand, was there some scrap of humanity, some shred of compassion, in his choosing a moment when, to Catholic eyes, Analyn was at her closest to God?

Cultural differences aside, Philip was bewildered by Maribel's and Dennis's responses. After an initial bout of weeping, Maribel acted as if she had been bereaved of a distant cousin, shunning the emotional displays of her soap opera heroines in favour of a fatalism akin to Consolacion's '*Bahala na ang Diyos*', while Dennis swore vengeance on his uncle with a passion worthy of Orestes. Rather than heading home to comfort their mother, as Philip had expected, they returned to work. Maribel could at least hide behind her script. Dennis was more exposed, dancing into the early hours at the club and then driving to the hotel the next morning with a bleariness that owed as much to *shabu* as to grief. He refused to take time off, as though it were only through relentless exertion that he was able both to endure his loss and punish himself for his inadequacy.

While anxious not to intrude, Philip offered to accompany them to Cauayan: an offer which was accepted gratefully by Maribel and grudgingly by Dennis, who made it clear that his sole inducement was the car. On the day of departure he arrived at the hotel, sporting the same bright red T-shirt he had done at their first meeting, reassuring Philip, who had feared that Max's claim that a T-shirt and jeans were acceptable funeral attire betrayed both his own slovenliness and a disregard for Filipino sensibilities. Maribel, too, showed no sign of mourning, wearing a pink smock and leopard-print leggings and, as ever, carrying her lotus blossom parasol. The only person sombrely dressed was their aunt, whose olive-green blouse and charcoal-grey skirt seemed to reflect her temperament as much as the occasion. Dennis greeted her with the traditional *mano po*, lifting her right hand to his bowed head, a gesture of respect which, judging by her frown, had little effect. After a nudge from Maribel, he introduced Philip.

'I am Hapynez,' she announced. 'With one "p" and a "z". It is a most original spelling.'

'For a most original lady, I'm sure. We meet at last! I've heard so much about you. From Dennis, that is.'

'It is an honour for me to meet such a distinguished gentleman.'

'If I may say so, your English is excellent.'

'I have a certificate in conversational fluency, critical thinking and confidence building from the American Institute for English Proficiency.'

To his consternation, Philip discovered that Hapynez was not waving them off but travelling with them, a fact of which neither her nephew nor her niece had seen fit to inform him. His heart sank still further as she headed for the back seat, depriving him of the proximity to Maribel, which alone would make the ten-hour journey bearable.

'Are you sure you wouldn't be more comfortable in the front?'

'I wouldn't dream of it. Look at your legs!'

Resigned to the separation, Philip steeled himself for the long drive along the North Luzon Expressway. In sudden panic, he opened the glove compartment and rummaged inside.

'What do you look for?' Dennis asked.

'A map,' Philip replied, relieved to find nothing metallic.

'We do not need map. I am knowing this way like bird.'

'Great,' Philip said, trusting that Dennis's homing instinct was still alive after four years. If not, there was his hawk-eyed aunt, currently denouncing the pouting lips on a giant toothpaste poster, to keep him on track.

Two hours and several denunciations later, they left the expressway to find themselves the only car rattling along a rutted side road through a vast sweep of rice fields. The road stretched beyond the horizon, broken at intervals by unmanned checkpoints with signs reading: *Please bear with us. Your safety is our prime concern.* Philip wondered whether the lack of guards meant that the danger had passed or the concern had waned. The landscape was uncannily empty, with even the occasional farmer looking like a scarecrow, his face muffled to protect him from the heat and dust.

At one o'clock, they stopped for lunch in a town which, for all Hendrik's caveats, might well have been twinned with Holly-wood. The *poblacion* square itself housed the *Bread Pitt* bakery, which Philip thought it wiser not to draw to Dennis's atten-tion; the *Way We Wear* dress shop, boasting a wide range of 'preloved clothes'; and the *Petal Attraction* florist's, where his offer to buy Maribel a bouquet of roses was vetoed by her aunt. He began to tire of her constant carping at Dennis and was relieved when they settled in a small café opposite a church, whose narrow spires, green-tiled roof and whitewashed façade instantly identified it as Iglesia ni Christo, enabling her to direct her scorn at a sect whose Disneyland architecture belied its apocalyptic views.

'They believe that Jesus Christ will soon be coming again to take them up to Heaven in a cloud of smoke. Pouf!'

'What? All ten million of them?' Philip asked.

'But only if they are inside of the church.'

'What if they can't make it there in time: they're ill in bed, say, or stuck in traffic?'

'Then they will be left here to face the Tribulation with the rest of us,' Hapynez said, cheerfully spooning up her pork adobo.

'But you must not worry. These people have very backwards beliefs. They are not Catholics.'

After lunch, Philip proposed taking a short walk ('to stretch my legs,' he said pointedly to Hapynez), before resuming the drive. Maribel volunteered to join him.

'You must go too, Dennis,' Hapynez said.

'They do not want me,' he replied sullenly.

'Of course they want you. Maribel is your sister,' she said in a voice that brooked no contradiction.

Hollywood was replaced by the Bible Belt when Philip and Maribel, with Dennis dragging his heels behind them, strolled past the church to face a giant billboard featuring a maimed baby caught in blazing headlights, which had themselves been doctored to resemble demonic eyes, beneath the slogan: *Abortion is a choice that kills*.

'That's disgusting,' Philip said.

'Is just doll,' Dennis replied.

A derelict wall displayed the usual hodgepodge of flyers. The University of Perpetual Help announced that it was no longer taking applicants and the Superhero bar that it was temporarily closed due to staff sickness. An estate agent offered a house for sale 'fully furnaced', and a photographer proposed to 'shoot you and your loved ones while you wait'. Philip was charmed by the advert for a 'child-friendly' school, but the notice that most intrigued him was for a clinic providing Immunisation, Computerised Eye Examination, Ear-Piercing and Circumcision.

'Is there really so much call for circumcision in this town?' he asked Maribel, who busily twirled her parasol.

'In all towns!' Dennis interjected. 'Filipinos are very healthy people. We are most circumcised country after Arabs and Jews. But is no need for clinic. Clinic is for wussies. I have it done from OJ Murro. He is *barangay* barber, top man with razor.'

'Come off it!' Philip said. 'How can you know? You were a baby.'

'I was thirteen years,' Dennis replied, affronted. 'I was becoming man. All *barangay* has been watching.'

'All the boys,' Maribel said.

'All boys, is true! This is not right place for girls. He is making me lie down on bench in front of river. He is putting this piece of wood beneath my *burat* and giving me guava leaves to chew in my mouth. Then he cuts.' He swept his hand through the air; Maribel shuddered. 'And I do not make squeal. I do not make one squeal!'

'It was funny,' Maribel said. 'You have had to wear a skirt for three weeks.'

'This was not skirt! This was cloth while wound is healing. You are girl; you know nothing!'

'You are correct,' Maribel replied, chastened. 'It was like a bandage. I am sorry.'

'Bandage, yes,' Dennis said with a grin. 'After which I am becoming man. This is not being true for everyone,' he added, staring at Philip.

'What do you mean?' Philip blushed, refusing to believe that Maribel would discuss such intimacies with her brother.

'I look when we make piss,' Dennis replied, unabashed.

'That must have been fun for you! Then perhaps you'll explain the connection between circumcision and masculinity?'

'They are silly boys,' Maribel said. 'They think that it is not possible for a girl to have babies if you still have your... I do not know this word.' She giggled.

'Foreskin,' Philip said. 'You might need it one day for your medical transcription. But surely that would be a good reason for them keeping themselves intact?'

Maribel looked at him, as if he had shattered her most treasured dream.

They returned to the café to collect Hapynez and continue their journey. Six hours later, after a brief stop at a garage, whose blazoned boast that 'We've got the magic touch' was belied by the dishevelled man, T-shirt riding over his paunch, listlessly patching a threadbare tyre in the forecourt, they arrived in Cauayan, a larger and more cosmopolitan town than Philip had imagined. The urban trappings slid away as soon as they left the centre and by the time they reached the outlying Villaflor *barangay* pigs and hens were ambling down the road as boldly as cows in India; although their safety was ensured by inertia rather than reverence. Maribel pointed out various childhood landmarks, her excitement undercut by Dennis's grunts, before falling silent when they turned a corner and pulled up outside a breeze-block bungalow with black-grilled windows set in a dusty garden, dominated by the palm tree that had loomed so large in her reminiscences. Philip gazed at the weather-worn sign on the tumbledown fence: *No Tresspissing. If you tresspiss, you will be bitten by the dog.*

'I am making this,' Dennis said proudly.

'There is no dog,' Hapynez said.

'He does not know this.'

'Everybody knows.'

Philip hung back as Maribel led the way into the house, rushing straight to her mother, a slight woman in a floral print dress who sat fanning herself to one side of the crowded room. No sooner had she spotted their arrival than she plunged into a paroxysm of weeping, flinging down her fan and beating her breast, despite a friend's attempt to wrench her hand away. The transition was so abrupt that it transcended the usual distinctions of truth and artifice, attesting to her urgent need to convey the intensity of her grief. Philip watched as she hugged her daughter and sister before falling into the arms of the son whom she had not seen for so long, tracing the contours of his face and running her fingers through his hair, as if struggling to convince herself that he was real. The strength of her emotion allowed Dennis to express his, and they clung to each other in a welter of kisses and tears.

The reunion was interrupted by a teenager, who tottered into the room on a home-made crutch and threw himself at Dennis's back. 'This is Angel Boy,' Hapynez whispered to Philip. Dennis greeted his brother with uncharacteristic warmth, tapping his cheek, rubbing his head and pressing it against his shoulder.

'He has been growing up as fast as bamboo,' Maribel said, joining in the embrace.

'He is becoming as big as me,' Dennis said, with a pride Philip suspected would have been tempered had Angel Boy's withered leg not removed any threat to his own supremacy.

While Dennis and Maribel hugged their brother, Hapynez introduced Philip to her sister. 'I regret that she is ignorant,' she said. 'She is not speaking English like me.'

'Please offer her my deepest condolences,' Philip said, as he shook Joy's hand.

'She says that she is most honoured that you have come and she is most grateful that you have brought us in your fine car, even if you have been putting too much aircon into the back.'

'I'm so sorry,' Philip said, mortified. 'You should have told me. I'll adjust it on the way back.'

'It is a matter of trivial importance. What?' Hapynez turned impatiently to Joy. 'She says also that she is most grateful for everything you have been doing for Dennis. You are most welcome in her house.'

Her mention of Dennis rather than Maribel made Philip feel like a photographer praised for his sensitive studies of mixed-race couples when his true interest lay in their contrasting skin tones. His unease grew when Joy gathered them together to see Analyn.

'Is the body in the house?' Philip asked Hapynez.

'No, she is in the garden.'

Joy led the group through a small kitchen, dominated by the precious fridge, humming loudly as if to advertise its presence, and into the back garden, which was packed with men playing cards. In the middle, a highly polished white coffin stood on trestles, with wreaths of lilies and floating candles on the lid. At the family's appearance, the players broke off their games, greeting them with varying degrees of effusiveness. To Philip's relief, he was ignored, apart from a few polite nods and bashful smiles. One man, however, lingered beside him as if waiting for an introduction.

'Is my uncle,' Dennis said. 'He is giving me money to go to Manila. See, here is this money.' He took a surprisingly thick wad of notes from his pocket and peeled off several hundred pesos for his uncle, who accepted them without demur. Despite the impropriety, Philip recognised that for Dennis it was necessary not just to pay his debts but to have the transaction witnessed. That done, he took his place alongside his mother, sister and aunt at Analyn's coffin where, after an appropriate pause, Philip joined them.

Having survived the shock of Julia's disfigurement, he had rashly assumed that death could hold no further terrors for him. Max had warned him that Analyn's corpse would be embalmed, but, while he was prepared for the waxen artificiality of her skin, he was unprepared for her resemblance to Maribel. He suppressed the urge to scream, which would have been doubly shameful in the face of the family's silence, focusing instead on incidentals, such as why there was a chicken perched on Analyn's pillow.

'Is that her pet chicken?' he whispered to Maribel.

'What?' she said. 'No. We put this there when some person is murdered because it is helping to make the punishment for the killer quicker.' Then, as if prompted by her own words, she burst into tears. With a shriek, Joy dragged her away from the coffin.

'Must she be that rough?' Philip asked Hapynez.

'Of course,' she replied. 'If someone is crying on to the corpse, it will slow down her journey into the next world.'

The family went back indoors, leaving the men to resume their games. Philip could not dismiss the feeling that they were treating the death in their midst with insufficient gravity, more like hospital visitors passing the time until a friend emerged from a coma than mourners at a wake. Uncertain whether to stay outside or return to the house, he must have conveyed his confusion to Dennis's uncle, who walked over and asked him shyly if he would like to play a hand of *sakla*.

'That's very kind, but I don't know the rules.'

'Is possible to show you.'

'I've had a long journey; I ought to go in. Maybe later?'

Back inside, Philip grappled with the sleeping arrangements, which had been exercising him ever since their arrival. Despite the nightmare of San Trinidad, he had insisted that he would be happy to stay in a hotel. Maribel, ever mindful of the proprieties, explained that her mother would be insulted if he stayed with anyone but them. He had assumed, therefore, that there would be more than the one bedroom, which he was to share with Dennis and Angel Boy, while Maribel, her mother and aunt made do with the sitting room. He felt wretched, even though Hapynez assured him that it was no hardship since they would be keeping a night-long vigil by Analyn's coffin. To make matters worse, the cramped bedroom meant that he was allotted the only mattress, while Dennis and Angel Boy were to share a sleeping mat on the floor. Angel Boy was thrilled by any chance to be close to his newly returned brother, but Dennis had other concerns. 'If you touch him, I will kill you,' he warned Philip.

'You are joking? Do you seriously think I'm the sort of man who'd hit on his girlfriend's younger brother at their sister's funeral?' he asked, staggered by a degree of cynicism rare even for Dennis.

'You are Englishman. You are in Philippines. Of course.'

Knocking tentatively at the door, Maribel summoned them into the garden to eat. 'It is *pancit cabagan*. You will not have tasted this dish in Manila,' she told Philip proudly. 'It is a most delicious speciality of Isabela province.'

'It's not the only one,' Philip said, eager to banish the memory of Dennis's suspicions.

'No, you are correct. There is also *pancit batal patong*.'

Squashed next to Hapynez on a low wooden bench, Philip watched while Joy and Maribel walked among their guests, ladling the aromatic stew on to banana leaf plates. 'I'm sure it's long-established practice and I shouldn't comment,' he said to Hapynez, 'but it strikes me as insensitive, to say the least, for the men to ignore the family all afternoon, while they sit here playing cards, and then gorge themselves on their food.'

'No, you do not understand. This is very necessary. My sister is a poor woman. She could never afford to bury her daughter alone. You see this Demos.' She pointed to a middle-aged man, with a lazy eye and a ducktail hairstyle. 'He comes to every house where there is death and he sets up these games. He collects the money in these little pots. Each evening he gives the family half of all the money in the pots. Then when there is enough, they can pay for the funeral.'

'How long does it take?'

'This depends. Sometimes one week, sometimes two.'

'The same players every day?'

'Sometimes the same, sometimes different.'

'And the priest – Father Elmo, isn't it? – has no objections?'

'Of course not. Sometimes he is playing with them.'

Noting that the gulf between East and West was never wider than when they were observing the same rites, Philip wondered whether he should offer to play, betting heavily in order to expedite the process.

'How many more days do you reckon we'll have to wait?'

'None. Demos has informed me that they have now sufficient money. The funeral will take place tomorrow.'

'That's good,' Philip replied, with a niggling sense of unease, before accepting a plate and tasting the stew: a mixture of pork, beans, eggs, vegetables and noodles, which was every bit as delicious as Maribel had claimed. Pausing to digest, he caught sight of Dennis who, sharing his enthusiasm with none of his inhibitions, was gulping it down as fast as his mother spooned it on to his plate. He felt angry on behalf of Maribel, who was too diffident to express – maybe even to feel – any grievance, that Joy should display such favouritism towards her son. It was not even a case of welcoming home the prodigal since, unlike her more worldly-wise sister, she believed him to have spent the past four years in Manila training to be a chef. Then, without warning, she began to howl, beating the ladle against her breast. While Maribel and Dennis struggled to restrain her, Philip asked Hapynez to interpret.

'She is blaming herself for Analyn's death. She is saying that God has punished her for asking her to testify against Marvin – this is her husband. She is saying that the judge will rule that there can no longer be any evidence and he will set Marvin free to come back here. She is saying that there will be no one to protect her. Now Dennis is saying that he will protect her. Now she is saying that he is a selfish, good-for-nothing boy who could not protect his sister, so how can he protect her?' Philip, his suspicions roused by a translation three times as long as the original, assumed that Hapynez was using the "critical thinking" rather than the "conversational fluency" aspect of her skills to voice her own sentiments rather than Joy's. There was no such ambiguity about Dennis's response, since he took out a large roll of notes and pressed it into his mother's hand. The gesture had a dramatic effect, eliciting a spate of kisses from Joy, a round of applause from the bystanders and a look of dismay from Maribel, which Philip sought to deflect with his brightest smile. He was anxious to reassure her and, once the guests had left, he begged her to banish all thought of wrongdoing, maintaining that Dennis's fellow dancers must have held a whip-round for him at the club.

He felt no such call to spare Dennis, tackling him about the money as soon as they were alone with Angel Boy in their room.

'I wasn't close enough to get a good look but, unless those notes were all 20 pesos, it was a hell of a bundle. So how did you come by it?'

'Is my business.'

'You mean it's your concern or one of your crooked schemes?'

'Is my business.'

'Then why were you so desperate for my loan when you already had so much cash?'

'Is my business. Now I go to sleep, yes?' Dennis asked, betraying his unease at Philip's silence. 'You are sitting on your fat *tumbong*, talking to sister, talking to aunt, when Dennis is driving all through day. Now Dennis is tiring.'

Philip watched while the two brothers lay top to toe on the sleeping mat. Angel Boy's feet smelt so rank from across the room that he dreaded to think what they must be like up close. He felt new admiration for Dennis who not only did not shrink but tickled them, to the boy's audible delight, before stroking his stunted ankle and shrivelled calf. The whispers and shrieks soon turned to snores, whose irregular rhythm alone would have been enough to keep Philip awake, even without the humidity and the moonlight streaming in through the uncurtained window. As he twisted and turned on the meagre mattress, he was further tormented by thoughts of Maribel who, although only a few yards away, might as well have been back in Manila, given the matronly guard around her.

He was woken from a nightmare, in which Maribel was squashed beside Analyn in the coffin, by frenzied barking. He turned to Dennis, his face so much younger in repose, who was clasping Angel Boy's ankles against his neck. Climbing gingerly off the mattress, he took the single step across the room and shook him by the shoulder.

'Can't you hear the dogs?' he asked, in response to the stupefied protest. 'Something's wrong.'

'What is wrong? Is hot, yes? Is not England. Here they are making noise because skin is too scratching.'

Dennis turned away, determined to snatch a few more minutes' sleep, and Philip seized the chance to be first in the shower. He made his way through the kitchen, where the women were already hard at work, and for once he was grateful that the presence of her mother and aunt prevented Maribel from greeting him with anything more than a smile before he had scrubbed the sleep from his skin. The gelid water trickling out of the hosepipe came as a shock and after drying himself on Joy's napkin-size towel, supplemented by his own dirty T-shirt, he made up for any shortcomings by dousing his chest, thighs and groin in aftershave. Fresh – and smarting – he returned to the bedroom, where Maribel brought him a dish of syrupy tofu, while the two brothers went off to the bathroom, which echoed to the sound of Angel Boy's gleeful screams.

An hour later Father Elmo, whose heartless advice to Joy still rankled with Philip, arrived to lead the cortège to the church. Dennis, his uncle and two friends lifted the coffin on to their shoulders and carried it to the road, where they were met by a crowd of friends and neighbours.

Philip walked alongside Hapynez in the procession, directly behind Maribel and her mother, and at an oblique angle to Angel Boy, who hobbled to and fro. Entering the lacklustre church, he lingered at the back of the nave, only to be ushered forward by Hapynez into the ranks of the family mourners. Promotion came at a price, since he found himself next to an arrangement of lilies with very powdery stamens. Stifling a sneeze, he concentrated on the service which, as in San Isidro, was largely in English. After the Commendation, the pallbearers carried the coffin out of the church and into the adjoining cemetery. Philip, recalling Dennis's explanation of his family name, trusted that it would hold true for Analyn, at once the victim and the scapegoat of domestic violence. He followed the cortège down a winding path to an open wall grave, which confronted them like a gaping wound. As Father Elmo said a prayer and Analyn was eased into her final resting place, Joy slumped to the ground, to be raised up by Dennis and Maribel, while Angel Boy beat his crutch against the wall.

'Do not worry about the expensive coffin,' Hapynez said to Philip, 'it is only on loan. This evening it will be returned.'

With the grave sealed, the mood of the mourners instantly lifted. Ducking behind the headstones, the women brought out plates of snacks and cold food, and the men crates of San Miguel and Sprite. Hapynez explained that it was bad luck to return home straight after a funeral and so the meal would be held here. All threat of the macabre vanished in a burst of activity, which put Philip in mind of the dead souls emerging from their tombs in Stanley Spencer's *Cookham Resurrection*. As family friend and benefactor, he found himself warmly welcomed – rather too warmly by Father Elmo, who had lined up his San Miguel bottles, downing the beer as if trying to drown his scruples. To Philip's surprise, several people asked him about Julian, whose fame had spread after Jejomar's crucifixion. He replied with a brief outline of the canonisation process, subtly embellishing his own role for an audience that might have been forgiven for supposing that he had the ear of the Pope.

After dispatching her sister to the better world in which she so fervently believed, Maribel sought out Philip, introducing him to her old friends, both male and female. With no flushed cheeks or flustered glances to indicate a childhood sweetheart, he was happy to bask in their goodwill, along with the assumption – or maybe the joke – that every Englishman was on David Beckham's guest list. His unease returned when she introduced him to her best friend, Nina, who held a toddler by the hand, carried a baby in a sling and was heavily pregnant. Seeing the tenderness with which Maribel gazed at the children, he wondered whether he had the right to suggest that on his departure, rather than remaining in Manila ready for the next foreigner to whom her brother might introduce her, she should return home, marry and start a family. Aware that he was growing mawkish, he allowed himself to be cornered by Father Elmo, who launched into a long, inebriated account of the lot of a parish priest. Just when Philip was losing patience, Maribel rushed over in a panic about Dennis, who had gathered some of his old friends for a revenge attack on their uncle.

'I am so frightened. He will be caught; he will be sent into prison. You must help him. You must promise!'

'How?' Philip asked, feeling her pain like a blade. 'I'll try; of course, I will. But you know better than anyone how headstrong he is.'

'You must take him away. Yes, we must all go at once back to Manila.'

'Don't you want to stay a few days to help your mother?'

'No. Yes. But first I must help Dennis.'

'I'll do what I can.' Searching for a plausible excuse, he made his way towards Dennis, who stood with a group of friends as if posing for a tableau entitled "Conspiracy". 'I'm sorry to break up the party, but I've just had a text from Max. The Bishop of Baguio wants to see me tomorrow morning in Manila. We must leave within the hour.'

'No, is not possible. I have business.'

'It's my business that pays for your business,' Philip said with growing conviction. 'You don't have a choice.'

Dennis's eyes blazed with a fury that was surprisingly short-lived. Philip wondered if, for all his posturing, he might be glad of a face-saving way out. 'So, what must I be saying to men?'

'You could tell them I'm preventing you committing a reckless act that will ruin your life.'

'I am not telling them this.'

'Or else that your selfish employer – so selfish, by the by, that he dropped everything he was doing to come up here with you – needs to hurry back to Manila, where he has hot water, air conditioning, curtains, pillows and all the other luxuries that red-blooded Filipinos can do without.'

'Yes, this is good. I am telling them this.'

Nine

Dear Greg,

I apologise for having to rush back here, but now that you're moving to Whitlock I'm sure you'll appreciate the shepherd and flock analogy. I apologise too for leaving you to deal with all the legal matters, but it comes so naturally to you (I mean that as a compliment). I did what I could at the funeral.

Since my return, I've been brooding on my relationship with Father. I can't help imagining what it might have been like had he not been away for the first six years of my life. Mother admitted that she hadn't even told him she was pregnant when he left, in case the strain of their parting caused her to miscarry. The first he knew of it was by letter in Singapore. It's no wonder that when he came back to find both her and Whitlock so altered, he saw me as the obvious cause. Later, when I embarked on my journey to priesthood, he took it as a personal affront. Although he always refused to elaborate on what led to his loss of faith (and it must surely have gone beyond the brutality of the prison camp), he maintained that my vocation made a mockery of everything he had undergone. So what am I to think of his bequest? Either he meant it as a joke from beyond the grave – if so, it's a very expensive one – or else it's an endorsement, however oblique, however belated, of my chosen path.

I wish you and I found it easier to talk. When we were boys, our age gap inhibited intimacy and as adults we've drifted further apart. I suppose that's inevitable when we learn from experience, and ours has been so different. You've followed the course that was laid out for you. You have a wonderful wife and three lovely daughters. And I've just heard from Isabel that in the autumn you'll be a grandfather. Many congratulations! I'm delighted for you – for us all – although I can't help feeling sad that Father won't be here to see it. Tradition and continuity were the lodestones of his life. You'll have them everywhere around you at Whitlock. I looked for them in the Church; I might even have found them had I settled in an English parish, but I came – or, as I prefer to think, was called – to a country where hope lies in change.

Therein lies the nub of my quarrel with Hugh. I'm sorry that it caused you all such distress at what was already a distressing time, but I couldn't stay silent while a man who purports to be proud of his long-standing connection with a country – a country from which, moreover, he derives a great deal of wealth – showed himself so indifferent to its people's plight. It was in one of his mines or, as he deftly pointed out, one of the mines owned by the consortium in which his family has an interest, that the massacre took place, a massacre that would have appalled me even without the personal connection.

Remember that as well as everything else, the victims were my parishioners. For hundreds of years their ancestors have dug for gold in pocket mines on the Cordilleras. Then, at the turn of the century, Hugh's grandfather and his associates built the first industrial mine. Until recently it had been content to leave well alone. After all, what match were the Ibaloi with their wooden hammers and wedges for the big boys with their heavy-duty drills? How could the few clods of earth they removed in hand-woven baskets compete with the tons transported in giant trucks? But now, furnished with spurious title deeds, the company has fenced off large tracts of land and, when the tribesmen hacked through the wire, the security guards cold-bloodedly blasted one of their tunnels, killing four men and maiming several others. I'm not saying that Hugh himself authorised the massacre, but the guards were clearly acting on orders from above.

I realise that your loyalties are divided, but why did you have to side so wholeheartedly with Hugh? After living in the country for twelve years, I do have some insight into its affairs, but you acted as though I had no right even to express an opinion. What is it that disqualifies me? Being a foreigner? Being a priest? Or simply being your little brother? A year ago your government went to war on behalf of islanders on the far side of the world (I'll say no more, except that my faith in a woman prime minister proved to be sorely misplaced); am I, on the other hand, to ignore the suffering of my own parishioners?

I'm convinced that far from being incompatible with a priest's role, political engagement stands at its heart. When you and I were boys, the mass readings were drawn entirely from the Gospels and St Paul, so it's no surprise that we felt that clergy were exclusively concerned with our souls. Since Vatican II, however, the Old Testament has been given a place. And what is its overriding theme but the freeing of an oppressed people? Indeed, liberation leads to salvation as surely as the Old Testament leads to the New.

No doubt if I were the incumbent of Gaverton, I'd see my role rather differently, and now that Father Ambrose has announced his retirement, I trust that you'll find a similarly devout and scholarly man to succeed him – although I'd like to think that he'll offer at least veiled criticism of your government's social policies. Here in Luzon, cruelty and corruption are too endemic to everyday life to allow me to confine my broadsides to the pulpit. To give you an example, let me tell you about Girlie, a young parishioner with whom I've had extensive dealings over the years and whose life has been particularly – although not uniquely – wretched. You may find it distasteful and you're at liberty to skim, but I hope you'll stick with it so that the next time you accuse me of rubbing your face in the dirt, you'll remember that while you have the chance to wash the dirt off, people here have to endure it.

Girlie first came to my notice about ten years ago, when she was a young orphan living with her aunt. To relieve their over-stretched budget, I found her a job as a maid with one of our richer families. At first all went well, but from the age of fourteen she was repeatedly raped by the son of the house. The family offered her a cash payment which, against my advice, her aunt accepted, insisting that Girlie remain with her employers. To her violator she was now fair game and when a few years later she fell pregnant, I arranged with a local convent for her confinement and the adoption of her child. This time there was no question of her returning to her job or even to the parish where she had become an object of shame. So I appealed to the Regional of our Order, who secured her a position as a household help to a banker in Manila.

I received occasional news of her from her younger sister, Tanya, who, hearing nothing for six months, grew anxious, as did I when she revealed that Girlie had left Manila and was working as a maid in Angeles City. Prostitution is as much the lifeblood of Angeles as quarrying is – or was – of Gaverton. And please forget any image you may have of dingy Soho backstreets or cryptic cards in newsagents' windows. The entire city is a shop window for its sordid trade. It's reputed to be home to around 80,000 prostitutes, although Heaven knows how they count them. From my own – admittedly limited – experience I'd say that they constitute nine out of ten of the women on the streets. Meanwhile, nine out of ten of the men come from the neighbouring Clark Air Base, enjoying a well-earned break from stemming the tide of Communism and safeguarding the American way of life. Things may look different in Whitlock and Westminster, but from where I stand the American way of life represents the greater threat. Five-year-old girls – that's FIVE in case you can't read my writing – are walking around with gonorrhoea, which I assure you they haven't picked up from Maoist rebels. Surely freedom means more than a choice between twenty-five brands of cornflakes?

The day I heard from Tanya, I wrote to Hendrik van Leyden, a friend from the Roosendaal seminary, who's been working with the women and children of Angeles – indeed, whenever I feel daunted by the scale of my task, I steel myself with thoughts of his. I sent him Girlie's address and asked him to visit her, but when he tried, he found that the building had been ransacked and boarded up by the police, and Girlie and her fellow lodgers had been evicted. Having been given a couple of leads by the neighbours, he suggested that I join him to investigate. No sooner had we fixed a date than I received the news about Father. Rescheduling the trip on my return, I took the bus to Pampanga, where the pleasure of seeing my old friend swiftly faded in the squalor of the search.

As I suspected, both the addresses that Hendrik had been given were of go-go bars. The first was called *Bloomers*, which seemed tame in a row that comprised *Caligula's Den*, *Whiplash* and *Sin City*, but Hendrik insisted that its nursery naughtiness was a deliberate ploy. The bouncer, a bald man with a strangely shaped moustache, which framed his mouth like displaced sideburns, recognised Hendrik at once. I was afraid that we'd be banned – or worse – but on the contrary, he led us straight to the manager, an elegant woman with jade drop earrings, the spitting image of your teenage pin-up, Anna Mae Wong. She greeted us fulsomely, offering us drinks, which Hendrik urged me under his breath to accept or risk losing her goodwill. It was that goodwill which made me so uneasy. I failed to understand why she should want to help a man who'd publicly expressed a desire to see her locked up, unless it were out of spite. If so, she quickly revealed her true colours when, having failed to identify Girlie's photograph, she laughed wantonly at her name. 'Girlie? Don't worry, mister, we have plenty of those,' she said, pointing to the end of the bar where dancers, who I prayed were merely dressed as schoolgirls, were stripping off their uniforms to the beery whoops of the crowd.

I intend no criticism of Hendrik – quite the reverse – but, while I realise that he needed to gain her trust, I was disturbed by their apparent complicity. Thankfully, we remained incognito at our second port of call, *The Yellow Ribbon*. The atmosphere in the packed, low-ceilinged room was as smoky and swampy as at

Bloomers, but with a harder edge. Clean-cut young men, bereft of both compassion and shame. were sitting with their – what? prizes? prey? – on their knees. Their hands greedily colonised the girls' flesh, squeezing waists as brittle as wishbones. Hendrik left me at a table while he passed round Girlie's photograph on the pretext of wanting to book her for a repeat session. Desperate for a drink, I edged towards the bar, but it was impossible to push through the men staring up at the three half-naked girls who were twirling on top of it, or to make my voice heard above the raucous cries of 'Off, off, off!'. Eventually the dancers obliged, peeling off their pants just as I succeeded in placing my order. Not knowing where to look, I gazed down at the counter, only to find that its mirrored surface offered a graphic view of their genitals.

I elbowed my way towards Hendrik, who was talking to a scrawny girl in a skimpy bikini. She immediately turned to me and asked if I wanted to go up to the prayer room. I sensed the desperation beneath the smile and, while at a loss as to why she hadn't asked Hendrik, I agreed, at which she told me that it would cost 40 pesos. My shock greatly amused Hendrik, who explained that the prayer room was a euphemism and then detailed the sexual act from which it derived. For the first time in years I wished that I were wearing a cassock. 'I'm a priest,' I managed to spit out. 'Oh,' she said calmly, 'then you will wish for a boy.'

Having run out of leads, Hendrik suggested that we visit *The Pit*, which he described as 'the last chance saloon' for both performers and clientele. Warning that it was not for the faint-hearted, he ushered me up a rickety staircase above a *sari sari* store. I found myself in a miasma of tobacco and sweat, facing a makeshift boxing ring in which two girls were pummelling one another with gloves the size of their torsos, while all around men shrieked 'Kill the bitch!', 'Murder her!' and other unspeakable commands. After a couple of minutes a fat Filipino with a badly burnt cheek (and may God forgive me for hoping that he'd suffered!) rang a bell and the two 'fighters' retreated to their corners where, instead of giving them drinks, their seconds threw pails of water over them, ensuring that their T-shirts clung to their chests, to the rapturous cheers of the spectators. The referee rang the bell again and, in a gesture I shall remember to my dying day, one of the girls kissed her crucifix before shuffling back. It wasn't enough to protect her from the savage punch that moments later her opponent landed on her nose. As blood streamed down her chin and the spectators grew frenzied, I could bear it no longer and leapt up to intervene, but Hendrik grabbed my arm and shook his head. I turned away and was violently sick. Nobody noticed, and in any case the stench was swiftly subsumed in the metallic smell of the blood and the vegetal smell of the crowd.

A few years ago the entire Philippines, with the exception of me, rejoiced when Joe Frazier and Muhammad Ali held their world title contest in Manila. But that felt like one of Granny Courtenay's tea parties compared with this. What is it that drove those young men, their mothers' pride and joy, the apples of their sweethearts' eyes, men who I've no doubt would risk their lives to save a wounded kitten, let alone a friend, to ogle two malnourished girls battering one another? Have they been so brutalised by all the blood they've seen spilt in action that they can only relax by watching it spilt in play?

Refusing to relax his hold, Hendrik steered me to the far corner of the bar where a group of girls, some looking bored, some scared and some vacant, waited for the bout to end and for the men, now at fever pitch, to point to the numbers on their chests and take them upstairs. After buying the requisite drinks, we handed round Girlie's photograph which, to my relief, one of the group recognised, having worked with her at another bar. She gave us an address and Hendrik led me there, through a web of alleyways with neon signs winking at every turn. He urged me not to raise my hopes since life in Angeles was transient and, at best, we might be directed elsewhere, but he was wrong; Girlie hadn't moved or, rather, she hadn't been able to, as her landlady volubly explained while ushering us into a minuscule alcove screened by ragged towels, where Girlie lay on a stained mat next to a guttering candle.

My one consolation was that she appeared oblivious to the suppurating sores on her forehead and arms. I crouched by her side, breathing in the fumes of the sepsis and stroking her hands. I whispered her name and she turned her face slowly towards me. Her filmy eyes were unable to focus, but she recognised my voice. 'Father?' she said. 'Yes, Girlie,' I replied, 'I've found you.' 'No,' she said with a quaver, 'it isn't me.' 'It isn't me,' she kept repeating, until she gradually fell calm. I promised to take her to the hospital, whereupon she assured me with the ghost of a smile (although it may have been the flicker of the candle) that now that I'd arrived, she could die in peace. She asked me to hear her confession, which I did, struggling to make out the words through the sobs and the gulps and the shame. No sooner had I absolved her than she exclaimed: 'Now I will die, Father.' I suggested that we said the Rosary together, but her breathing took on the unmistakable rhythm of a death rattle. I gave her the last rites and, just as she'd predicted, she died.

Having informed the police, who showed as little concern as if we were reporting a stolen camera, and an undertaker, who agreed to embalm the body overnight, we returned the next morning to transport it home. We strapped the painfully light coffin on to Hendrik's roof rack and with a lachrymose farewell from the landlady we set off. Despite our unorthodox cargo, we ran into trouble only once, when the guards at a checkpoint outside San Fernando, refusing to accept the bona fides of a pair of dirty, dishevelled and informally dressed priests, insisted on searching the coffin for arms. Three days later I conducted Girlie's simple funeral in the presence of her sisters, brother and grief-stricken aunt. I notified the family for whom she'd worked and at whose hands she'd suffered so greatly. Needless to say, they didn't send so much as a flower.

Meanwhile, my enemies are closing in. While I was in Angeles there was an arson attack on the *convento* and, had it not been for my housekeeper's quick thinking, we'd have lost everything. Of course I didn't tell Mother, but in an unguarded moment at Whitlock I let slip that we were having building work done, so if she should ask, the official line is that we're putting up an extension. Then, someone – someone rich enough to afford meat – poisoned Grump, my dog. Never can a name have been less fitting. He'd been with us for more than ten years. I find it hard to write a sermon without him lying in his customary place at – not to say, on top of – my feet; although I grant that I may be looking for an excuse.

I shan't pretend that I'm not at risk. The lifting of Martial Law may have curbed some of the military's excesses, but it's been accompanied by a steep rise in the activities of the various vigilante groups. One with a particular animus against radical clerics has even adopted the slogan: 'Be a patriot and kill a priest!' My name appears on a list of NPA sympathisers, or 'roll of honour' according to my friend and colleague, Father Benito. I'm described as Ka Julian (that's short for Kasama or Comrade), 'the Communist lapdog'. A letter sent to the Bishop (by a man who, to my certain knowledge, can neither read nor write) claims that I spend my free time in the mountains training rebels: I who had to struggle to keep up with the corps at school.

The result of all this is that I've been inspired to take a more active role in the liberation struggle. I was in two minds whether to mention it, but I need you to understand my position; although I know that your views are bound to be coloured by your government's campaign against the IRA. I make no comment on the rights and wrongs of the Irish situation, but I assure you that, in the Philippines, they're clear-cut. Moreover, I'm convinced that the axiom that today's terrorist is tomorrow's statesman will be particularly pertinent here. Don't be alarmed! I haven't started toting a machine gun, but I have forged links with an NPA unit, first conveying information and more recently giving practical help. On the night after Girlie's funeral, I was woken by a young NPA operative of my acquaintance, whose wife had been badly wounded in a shoot-out with the constabulary. He begged me to lend him my car to drive her to a well-disposed doctor in Baguio. I've received similar requests in the past and always refused, but this time, whether because of the individuals concerned or the change in my own attitude, I not only agreed but offered to drive her myself, since I was less likely to arouse suspicion.

Never have I felt more ashamed of my old jalopy than when we jounced over the unlit, potholed road. Glaiza's heart-rending groans as she rolled on the back seat, blood seeping from her ill-dressed wounds, still echo in my ears. My apprehension proved to be justified since, no sooner had we left the *poblacion* than we were stopped by a military patrol, who instructed us to step outside the vehicle and show our papers. Not only was Glaiza in no fit state to move, but she'd grown delirious and was making remarks that alarmed me. Forced to extemporise, I remembered Girlie and a previous mercy dash to Baguio. I explained that my passenger was a pregnant parishioner whom I was taking to the doctor. The guard, shining his torch on her, spotted the blood. 'She's had a miscarriage,' I said coolly, 'which is why there's no time to waste.' 'If it's urgent, why not find a doctor nearer home?' the guard asked. 'I can't,' I said, floundering. 'It's delicate. Her husband…' 'Of course,' he said, slapping me on the back, 'I understand. Your little secret.' It only dawned on me as he sent me on my way with a pumpkin-sized grin that he took us for lovers. When I returned the following day, after the doctor, a covert NPA supporter, had pronounced the operation a success and promised to hide Glaiza until she was well enough to go back to the camp, I found that rumours of my indiscretion had spread throughout the constabulary and that everyone, from its humblest officer to its sinister commander, regarded me with newfound respect.

I take no pride in celibacy. Indeed, I sometimes fear that the fact that it comes so easily to me, when so many of my fellow priests face a lifelong battle to suppress their desires, points to a deficiency in my nature. But since my visit to Angeles I've seen the discipline in a more positive light. So it's doubly ironic that on my first NPA mission my illusory liaison should have kept me safe.

There you have a fairly exhaustive account of my activities since my return and one which, with Hendrik offering to post it when he goes to Holland next week, I know I can dispatch without fear of its falling into the wrong hands. You asked me, during one of our snatched conversations at Whitlock, on what authority I based my support for the rebels, given that it runs contrary to both the traditional teaching of the Church and the direct instructions of the Pope. The answer, which as so often eluded me at the time, became clear on reflection. I follow my conscience; which is not the same as having an opinion. To listen to one's conscience is to hear the authentic voice of God.

Your loving brother,
Julian

'Over there, look! Payatas, first turning on the left.' Philip pointed to the sign, which a long line of refuse trucks made redundant.

'Why must you wish to see only dirty parts of my country?' Dennis asked, blasting his horn at an unsuspecting tricyclist. 'We go to Boracay, yes? I am best tour guide to this island: beautiful sands; beautiful girls.'

'It's not a pleasure trip,' Philip said, with a pang of sympathy for a man whose only contact with the golden beaches had been a tourist board brochure. 'I've come to interview the priest who was Father Julian's closest associate. After this, my work's done.'

'Then you go back to London?'

'Yes. Max is booking me a flight for the end of next week. If I still have to finish my report, I can do it at home.'

'And what about sister? She has been giving you sex. Many times sex.'

'She hasn't been "giving me sex",' Philip said sharply. 'We've had sex. Or rather, made love, if that isn't too innocent for you.'

Depressed by the exchange, Philip stared out at the landscape, which was equally cheerless. Tumbledown shacks, which themselves seemed to be made of refuse, lined the road to the dump. The usual Manila smog had thickened into something more toxic. Dennis pulled up at a *pagpag* stand, where two naked toddlers were paddling in an oil pool.

'Is this it?' Philip asked.

'No more cars allowed,' Dennis said. 'I go back to QC. You text me when you are over.'

Philip, who was under strict instructions from Max not to take any valuables, patted his pocket to check on his phone and stepped out of the car into an acrid stench, part industrial waste, part human decay. For a moment he was afraid that he might choke, but he caught sight of the toddlers gazing up at him and struggled to twist his grimace into a smile. Taking shallow breaths, he walked past the queue of trucks to the site entrance, where people had gathered like refugees in a transit camp, although one couple, exhausted or demoralised or both, sat listlessly on their haunches, as if waiting for the scavengers to break them down to their constituent parts.

He made his way to the barrier, where he was stopped by a guard. 'You cannot enter here, sir,' he said, as peremptorily as if he were manning the gates of the presidential palace.

'I have an appointment with Benito Bertubin of the Payatas Scavengers Association,' Philip replied.

The guard, eager to exploit to the full the authority eking away from him, made great play of examining his clipboard, before directing Philip to the office at the far end of a row of corrugated-iron huts. He walked down a path made of impacted waste at various stages of decomposition and, to judge by the roaches under his feet, degustation. He found himself at the base of a garbage mountain whose peak, a patchwork of plastic sacks, glistened like a blanket of snow in the sun.

He entered the cramped office, to be greeted by a bright-eyed young woman, who sported such an outsize crucifix that he was tempted to ask for Benito by his former title. 'Ben's expecting you,' she said, forestalling him. 'I'll give him a buzz as soon as he's finished on the phone.'

To Philip's relief she turned back to her work, attempting neither to engage him in conversation nor ply him with snacks. He took his allotted seat and affected interest in the wall charts. 'Philip Seward?' He spun round to face a small man with a shiny bald head, bulging eyes and a large scar splitting his left cheek. It looked like a knife wound, and he wondered whether it had been inflicted before he met Julian, during their association, or after his death. He could not recollect Julian mentioning it, although that proved nothing, since his overriding concern had always been for the inner man.

'Thank you so much for seeing me. I know that you're very busy.'

'And you're very persistent.'

'I'll take that as a compliment.' Benito shrugged. 'This place is quite extraordinary. I'd no idea it would be so vast!'

'Yes, the tourist board's missing a trick; they should market it to climbers. Instead of the usual challenges, they'd face typhus and tetanus and HIV.' He hesitated. 'We should go next door. We're keeping Carolyn from her work.' He led Philip into a small room whose austerity suggested that he had not thrown off all traces of the priesthood. 'Please take a seat,' he said, pointing to a rickety rattan chair. 'That was found in the refuse.'

'Really?' Philip said, resisting the impulse to scratch. 'How long has the dump been open?'

'Since 1973, although to be accurate, it's no longer a dump.'

'Really? I thought…' Philip looked blank.

'An easy mistake. But it's been reclassified as a "controlled disposal facility". Just as the squatters are now to be known as "informal settlers". The authorities maintain that it gives people back their dignity. I can think of better ways: like decent homes, decent healthcare, decent education and decent jobs; like honest government, impartial justice and fair wages.'

'Maybe the change of name's the first step?'

'Maybe.'

Philip, wary of trying Benito's patience, was keen to turn the conversation to Julian without appearing to dismiss the problems of the settlers. He was grateful for the distraction provided by the phone, only to sit in uneasy silence while Benito harangued the caller in Tagalog.

'City Hall!' Benito said, slamming down the receiver, as though that explained everything. 'Let's take a walk. I need to clear my head.'

'Sure,' Philip said, bracing himself for another blast of noxious air. They passed a line of makeshift dwellings, some of them no more than canvas sheets stretched out on poles. In one, a mother was feeding her baby from a breast as dry and dusty as the earth around her, while in another, a young girl squatted beside a recumbent old man, dipping her finger into a can of water and then into his mouth. Philip felt the tears pricking his eyes, as Benito, filled with more practical compassion, strode ahead.

'I'm not quite sure what you do here,' Philip said. 'Are you some kind of social worker?'

'Social worker; aid worker; activist; legal adviser; volunteer coordinator; anything and everything that's needed. One day – today, as it happens – I'll be fighting City Hall, who are blocking our proposals to buy land we can use to build a school and a birthing clinic. Another, I'll be liaising with one of the humanitarian agencies who are setting up craft workshops, or a group of overseas students who've come here to help. Or maybe I'll be trying to persuade our gang masters to allow fairer access to the refuse because, believe me, corruption and intimidation are as rife here as everywhere else. "Fairer access to the refuse": can you believe I said that?' He turned to Philip with his eyes blazing. 'Thirty years ago – twenty even – I could have told you exactly what I was doing. But now we've had our EDSA revolution; we've overthrown the dictator; and this is the result.' They walked past a brazier where two men and a boy were burning scrap wood to make charcoal. 'The tragedy is that when Julian and I and thousands like us fought – and I do mean, fought – for a fairer distribution of land, we never imagined that this would be the land people ended up with: that tenants forced off their farms would come to the city and find an even crueller, more unjust system in force, that children would grow up surrounded by pylons instead of palm trees, playing in fields of cardboard and plastic and broken glass.'

'Things must improve. It's just a matter of time.'

'You sound like our president telling us that there are no quick solutions. The trouble is that there seem to be no slow ones either. Let's go back inside. You've come to talk about Julian, not to listen to my moans.'

'I suspect that if he were here now, he'd be making them just as strongly.'

'There are moments – two-o'clock-in-the-morning moments – when I think he was lucky to die when he did. Look around you! Is it any wonder I left the priesthood? We're living in one of the most Catholic countries in the world – perhaps *the* most Catholic after the Vatican – but for the people of Payatas Christmas is the most miserable time of the year. And you know why?'

'Because they don't have the money to buy gifts for their children?'

'Because they don't have the money to feed them! Over the holidays the refuse collections in the city stop. No garbage: no food! Welcome to capitalism Philippine-style.'

They returned to the office where, after a brief word with Carolyn, Benito led Philip into his room.

'So what do you want to ask me about Julian? I can't see my testimony carrying much weight in Baguio, let alone Rome.'

'I'm trying to put together as full a picture as possible of the man and his work – anything that might bolster the *Positio*. You knew him better than anyone. It's clear from his letters how much he respected you.'

'You should read mine! I first met him when the oil of priesthood was fresh on my hands. We worked together for more than twelve years. We gave the Church back to the people. And, as you know, we paid the price.'

'Consolacion, his housekeeper… do you remember her?' Benito nodded. 'Credits you – though "blames" might be more accurate – for his involvement in politics.'

'Consolacion never liked me. She believed that like Our Lord Himself the best priests were white.' He laughed mirthlessly. 'That's why she was so fond of Julian. She disapproved of me for my race as much as my ideas.'

'Yet now she goes to the Philippine Independent Church.'

'Yes. I'm afraid we must have wounded her deeply.'

'We?'

'Julian, by embracing the liberating gospel of Christ. Which was all the more remarkable when you think of where he came from. He had so much to lose. I'm not talking materially, you understand, but up here.' He tapped his skull.

'He had to adjust to a new set of circumstances,' Philip said. 'At home we prefer our priests to remain above politics – like the Queen, except without the perks. Whereas, from what I gather, the Church was the only effective opposition under Marcos.'

'That's certainly what it would like you to think. And if you're talking about individual clerics – priests, nuns, even the odd bishop – it's true. But for the Church as a whole, the case is rather different. Under the leadership of Cardinal Sin – '

'I'm sorry, but the name always makes me smile.'

'He played on it. That is, he made so many puns on it, you suspected it was a double bluff. Under Sin, the Church adopted a policy of "critical collaboration", although to many of us there was too little of the first and too much of the second. True, he endorsed the EDSA revolution, but only when it became clear that if he prevaricated any longer he wouldn't just have a stain on his conscience but blood on his hands.'

'Is that why you wanted out?'

'I stayed in the Church as long as I could – far longer, perhaps, than I should have, until the gap between faith and practice grew into a chasm. I could no longer reconcile the Christ who taught that He came not to be served but to serve, with a Church that rolled up its sleeves on Holy Thursday, and the rest of the year trimmed them with lace and gold thread. I refused to be part of an institution that prayed with the poor on Sundays and preyed on them the other six days of the week. Who needs Martial Law when we have the mass?'

Philip was taken aback by the strength of Benito's anger. 'Did Julian know of your objections? Did he endorse them? If he were alive today, do you think he'd still be a priest?'

'That's not a question I can answer. His journey wasn't my journey, despite everything we shared along the way. What I can say, without hesitation, is that whether inside the Church or not, he would be fighting to bring about Christ's kingdom on earth.'

'Am I right in thinking you never saw each other again once you both left prison?'

'Yes, he went back to England and I was posted to Negros. The Bishop thought it would keep me out of trouble.' Benito smiled.

'So when Julian was given permission to return here, you made no plans to meet?'

'By then I was spending all my waking hours – and many that should have been sleeping – organising the sugar workers. Julian, too, was busy in his new parish. But we corresponded regularly. And before you ask, the letters – at least, his to me – have long disappeared.'

'So you didn't blame him for abandoning you and returning home?'

'Blame him? Why should you think that? Blame him? On the contrary, I never admired him more than during that year – a whole year, remember – we spent in prison. You can't imagine what the conditions were like. Yet of all of us – myself included – he was the only one who never complained. Indeed, I sometimes think…'

'What?'

'No matter. All right then, I sometimes think that he welcomed the privations. They gave him a chance to show how far he had escaped from his past. He was no longer Julian Tremayne or, should I say, the Honourable Julian Tremayne. He was Ka Julian, a true revolutionary.'

'He was proud of that reputation,' Philip said. 'It's impossible to say how much he left out of his letters home. But he did boast to his brother of being on a list of NPA sympathisers.'

'You're quite wrong to suggest that he abandoned us. From the moment we were arrested, he was under huge pressure to do a deal with the authorities. But he wouldn't cooperate. He refused any chance to clear his name that might incriminate others. He even refused to distance himself from the NPA.'

'Yet in the end he accepted the presidential pardon.'

'Not for his own sake, but for his mother's. She was terminally ill and desperate to see him before she died.' Philip winced, as he recalled Julian's final letter to his brother. 'Even so, he believed he'd secured cast-iron guarantees for the rest of us. After all those years he still expected the government to keep its word!'

'Is that when…?'

'Yes,' Benito replied with a lopsided grin. 'I was released and within four days I was captured – or rather, rearrested – by what was later described as an unidentified gang of vigilantes. But they were vigilantes wearing constabulary uniforms. I was used as a punch-bag and an ashtray and a urinal. I was suffocated and drowned and kicked and clubbed and burnt. Finally, I was left with this permanent souvenir.'

'Julian never spoke of it.'

'I never told him. Wounds heal, but guilt festers: I had no desire to add to his.' Benito stood up. 'I think we should stop there. I've told you all I know and you must be exhausted from taking so many notes.'

'I've one last question, then I promise I'll leave you in peace,' Philip said.

'Very well,' Benito said, resuming his seat.

'Julian wrote to his mother that he was sustained by the conviction of his innocence. But he also mentioned supplying information to the NPA and driving a wounded fighter – or at least one of their wives – to a doctor in Baguio. Consolacion admitted that he wasn't even at home on the night of the murder. Do you think he might have crossed the line?'

'That supposes I think there was a line to cross. If you know the slightest thing about Julian, you'll know that he believed it was as much a priest's job to fight for justice in this world as to promise justice in the next.'

'You mean "fight" as in work day and night for the cause?'

'I mean "fight" as in take up arms, like David and Joshua and Samson.'

'And Christ?'

'Above all, Christ: Christ who came to bring not peace but

a sword. It may not please the Bishop, who'll want him to be sanitised as well as sanctified, but Julian was first and foremost a liberator.'

'Rather than a saint?'

'That's a term I no longer recognise. It's forty years since I divided people into saints and sinners.'

'What about miracles? Or have they also been excised from your vocabulary?'

'Not exactly, but I see them as changes of consciousness, rather than of matter.'

'Yet we have sworn statements from dozens of people who witnessed Julian levitate.'

'Would you want to be the only person in the church that day to have missed out: to have been denied the sign of God's favour?'

'I wasn't there, of course, but I was in Pampanga last month for the crucifixions. I saw the prisoner, Jejomar, stepping down from the cross without a scar' – Philip flinched – 'without a mark on his hands.'

'Well, I wasn't there either, but I have attended two sessions of psychic surgery – '

'Which is what?'

'Faith healing taken to extremes. Unless I was hypnotised or hallucinating (and I'd swear on my life that I was neither), the healer opened up the patients' bodies, removed the diseased tissue, then closed up the wounds, all with a few strokes of his finger.'

'Without using any instruments?'

'None that I could see.'

'How do you explain it?'

'I don't. So-called primitive people have powers that have been lost – or not yet revealed – to the rest of us.'

'So even though you've left the Church, you haven't renounced all forms of mysticism?'

'I try to keep an open mind. Just as I do about Julian. And in my view, in spite of all the miracles and testimonies, he's more likely to have been martyred *by* the Church than *for* it.'

'I'm not sure that I follow,' Philip said, fearing that he was being drawn into a private vendetta.

'Ever since the Bishop of Baguio announced his investigation last year, I've received dozens of letters from a prisoner in Bilibid who maintains that Julian wasn't murdered by the NPA, but on the direct orders of a group of pro-Marcos clerics.'

'That's absurd!'

'No, simply far-fetched. Although no more so than the official line that he was ambushed by a gang of insurgents in the Sierra Madre mountains. For one thing, the NPA very rarely targeted foreigners and for another, unless they'd shot him on sight, they'd soon have learnt who he was and honoured him as a comrade.'

'So was this prisoner part of the plot?'

'Apparently not, but he claims to have shared a cell with one of the assassins. It was common practice when we were in Baguio for powerful men with scores to settle to bribe the guards (and even the governor) to let a prisoner out for the day to commit a murder. After all, that would give him a cast-iron alibi.'

'What's in it for the prisoner?'

'Any number of things: dropped charges; intimidated judges; cash for himself and his family; a taste of freedom; or maybe pure bloodlust.'

'Does your informant have a name?'

'Certainly. It's no anonymous tip-off.'

'Do you think it might be possible for me to meet him?'

'I doubt that the Bishop would be too keen.'

'Perhaps not, but I can't allow the opportunity to slip through my fingers. I've come this far. I need to find out the truth for myself, even if not for the *Positio*.'

'I can give you his name and address, that's no problem. Here.' Benito moved to a filing cabinet and took out a folder, copying the details as he spoke. 'The bigger problem might be getting in to see him. If the Vicar General was as reluctant as you suggest to put you in touch with me, I hardly think he's going to ease your path with the Bilibid authorities.'

'Don't worry. If bribery can get a murderer out of jail, it can surely get me in.'

'I wish you luck. Here.' He handed a scrap of paper with a name, prison and block number on it to Philip, who was struck by the copperplate script. 'Let me know if you discover anything.'

'Of course.'

Philip took his leave of Benito and made his way down to the gate, in the wake of a particularly putrid delivery. After texting Dennis to collect him, he waited beside the busy *pagpag* stall where two teenage boys, one with his teeth bared in a broad grin, the other with his teeth permanently exposed by a cleft lip, practised the ultimate form of recycling: selling scraps of chicken bone, burger patty, and pizza crust salvaged from the dustbins of McDonald's and Jollibee, shaken to dislodge the maggots, fried to kill the larvae, and swamped in tomato sauce to enhance – or conceal – the flavour. Feeling uncomfortable, he crossed the road where he was grateful for Dennis's prompt arrival.

'I have need of 10,000 pesos before six o'clock this night,' Dennis said, while Philip fastened his seat belt.

'Any special reason?' Philip asked, in no mood to humour him.

'Is for lotto. I am already knowing these numbers.'

'Don't tell me: you have a friend!'

'Yes. How are you knowing this?' Dennis sounded genuinely surprised.

'An inspired guess! Sorry but no can do.'

'Please, you must help. I have problem, big problem.'

'No, you're in a fix, a temporary bind, and you'll wriggle out of it as per usual. I've spent the morning among people with real problems, who live on rubbish: who build their homes on it, feed their families on it and, in the final obscenity, eat it. It's a reminder to the rest of us to count our blessings.'

In defiance, Dennis tuned the radio to his favourite station, raucously accompanying the rapper who told his 'one true momma' that 'I'll cut out your heart, so we'll never be apart'. Biting his lip, Philip endured the punishing journey back to the hotel.

'I won't be needing you this afternoon,' he said, when they reached the forecourt, 'but I'd like you back here at seven o'clock sharp – and I do mean *sharp* – to drive Max and me to Ray Lim's house in Forbes Park.'

'No, this is not possible! I must not be going to this house.'

'Why on earth not? Max says it's a very smart affair. I'm sure the chauffeurs will be well looked after.'

'No, you are not understanding. I must not be going there. I must be going to club.'

'Since when? Your dance or show or whatever you call it doesn't start until eleven.'

'No, I have to be early. Now we are going to Cauayan, I have to fill in for missing time. You must understand; I must not go to this house!'

'All right, there's no need to shout! If you can't, you can't. I'll text you tomorrow's schedule as soon as I know it.'

After lunch and a vigorous swim in the hotel pool, Philip returned to his room, where he planned to spend the afternoon transcribing the notes of his interview with Benito, but found himself distracted by possible plot lines for his novel. Whatever the truth of the prisoner's allegations, the theme of reactionary priests ordering the murder of a radical colleague struck him as both rich in fictional potential and a telling image for the Church's stranglehold on the country. He was so absorbed in his imaginings that he barely left sufficient time to shower and dress before taking a cab to pick up Max who, needless to say, was not ready. Rather than wait in the airless cab, he went up to the flat where, instructed to make himself at home, he flicked through the record collection, a love of vinyl being one of Max's more endearing archaisms. Among the predictable array of female singers was one that astounded him: *Imelda Papin Featuring Songs with Mrs Imelda Romualdez Marcos.*

'Is this for real?' he asked, thrusting the sleeve at Max, who at last emerged from his room, wearing a pink *barong Tagalog* and smelling strongly of lemons.

'Of course. It's an album of her husband's favourite songs, recorded while he was dying in hospital. Surely you of all people must appreciate the deluded romantic gesture?'

'Did it kill him off?' Philip asked, ignoring the jibe.

'You have no heart!' Max snatched the disc and put it tenderly back in its place. 'We can't stand here gossiping all day. We'll be late!'

He ushered Philip out of the building and into the cab, where the driver greeted them with remarkable equanimity.

'Forbes Park, please,' Philip said, edging away from Max, whose citrus tang was making him nauseous.

'Millionaires Row,' Max added smugly.

The exclusive district lived up to its name. In contrast to the teeming streets elsewhere in the city, there were no traffic jams on the elegant avenues and not a single vagrant or vendor on the grass verges. High walls and sharp railings preserved the residents' privacy, offering tantalising glimpses of chimneys, roofs and gables beneath the lush canopies of leaves. Only Ray's and Mikee's house was open to view, although the four security guards at the gate stood armed against intruders. Philip handed his invitation to one of them who, to Max's irritation, waved them through without a second glance.

'Don't I deserve a full body search? Who knows where I might be hiding a grenade?'

Deaf to his grumbles, Philip gazed down the torchlit drive to the elegant white building with its semicircular porch, Doric columns and stucco festoons across the façade. They walked through the Chinese garden, past the miniature pagoda, ornamental pond and willow tree, to the porch, where they were greeted, first by a waiter with flutes of champagne, then by their ever-ebullient host.

'Philip,' Ray said. 'I am honoured to welcome you to my humble home. Max.' He acknowledged his old friend in passing.

'It's very kind of you to invite me,' Philip said. 'I'd no idea that it would be so sumptuous.'

'The house or the guests?' Max asked tetchily.

'Both,' Philip said, surveying the huge open-plan room in which stark white sofas, stools and armchairs were set against elegant displays of antique jade, porcelain and lacquered wood. Dominating the room was a sweeping glass staircase with a steel balustrade. He wondered if the transparent design had been deliberately chosen to compensate for the secrets elsewhere in the owners' lives.

'I do not know who half of these people are,' Ray said, staring happily around the packed room.

'Are we celebrating anything particular?' Philip asked.

'My son, Brent, who is announcing his plan to run for Congress. You will see him soon. First, there is someone of much more importance for you to meet.'

'You don't mean...?' Max said.

'She is here!' Ray gestured to a small pink figure with her back to them, standing beside a white baby grand on which a pianist was playing a medley of familiar yet unidentifiable tunes.

'But how did you manage it? She goes about so little now.'

'Orlando Gozon. His wife belongs in the same health club as Mikee. He has an office next to hers in Congress. And he does business with Amel.'

'It's years since I last saw her,' Max said. 'The best years of my life. Not these, those.'

'Are we talking about who I think we are?' Philip asked.

'How should I know? I'm not a mind-reader!' Max replied, before turning back to Ray. 'I can't wait another moment. Take me over to her at once! But... but you might have to jog her memory.' An anxious look crossed his face. 'It's been so long.'

'Don't worry. Who could ever forget you, Max?'

Philip followed Ray and Max through the room with a mixture of fascination and dread. With Margot Fonteyn dead, there was only one woman who could produce this effect on Max. Repeating the phrase "blood on her hands", "blood on her hands", like a mantra, he willed himself not to be seduced by her charm or dazzled by her celebrity.

She was holding forth to a small group of admirers. Her refusal to interrupt her story gave Philip the chance to observe her at close range. Her familiar helmet of jet-black hair was in sharp contrast to the puffy cheeks on which her overemphatic make-up looked like a gesture of defiance. She wore an ankle-length pink silk dress with high pointed sleeves and a huge diamond cluster ring on her right hand, which drew attention to her chipped nails. Her shoes, which he left until last, were disappointingly plain: open-toed sandals with a plastic flower on each strap.

Having reached the denouement, she turned to the newcomers as if suddenly aware of their presence. Ray introduced Max who, with tears in his eyes, bowed to kiss her hand. Her glazed smile left Philip unsure whether she genuinely recognised him or was putting on a practised act. Her face grew animated only when he mentioned his visits to the presidential palace with Fonteyn.

'I miss her every day. We were such good friends,' Imelda said. 'She was a very great lady.'

'As are you, ma'am,' Max said.

'All my life I have had just one wish: to do what I can for my country,' she replied, as if on tape. 'That is why I am still fighting for my people when my friends are at home, playing with their grandchildren.'

Just when she seemed to be sinking into a stupor, Ray introduced Philip. She made no move to hold out her hand and he refused to ape Max by lifting it to his lips, so he gave her a guarded nod and was rewarded with a gaze straight out of Madame Tussaud's.

'Philip is a friend from England,' Ray said. 'He is writing about Father Julian, a priest – also from England – who is soon to become a saint.'

'How are you liking my country?' Imelda asked Philip, with an emphasis on the possessive.

'I'm overwhelmed by it,' he replied equivocally. 'I've never been anywhere so full of contradictions. Take today: here I am at this magnificent party, when I spent the morning on the Payatas rubbish dump.'

Philip felt a ripple of unease running through the group, but he was determined to stand his ground.

'This is the world that God gave us,' Imelda said. 'Just as we have mountains and valleys and sun and rain and land and sea, so we have rich and poor. This is something that Westerners rarely understand. In England and in America, you have many poor people but they are miserable. In the Philippines, you will see that they are always smiling.'

'They live on garbage. They bring up their children on garbage. They're constantly exposed to infection.'

'You are quite ignorant,' Imelda replied blithely. 'It's what makes them strong. As I said to the Holy Father when he came to visit me, we should think positive and see it as free immunisation. Now I need to sit down; I am an old lady. Orlando...' She turned to one of her companions, who had been hovering anxiously throughout the exchange. 'You promised me some of Mr Lim's delicious pancakes.'

'Please to come this way with me,' Ray said. 'I shall tell the waiters to bring you everything you desire.'

'She's not the only one who needs to sit down,' Philip said, as Ray led Imelda and her coterie to one of the richly appointed tables at the far end of the room.

'You should be ashamed of yourself,' Max said.

'I should? I'm not the one who robbed my country blind and was complicit – at the very least – in the deaths of thousands of innocent people.'

'Tell it to someone who gives a damn! Now we'd better get something to eat before we're slung out on our ears,' Max said. 'The buffet's outside.'

They walked through the patio doors into the back garden where a huge L-shaped table extended around two sides of a swimming pool. Philip gazed in awe at the display: the sparkling silver tureens and candlesticks; the gleaming porcelain platters; the fantail-shaped sprays of flowers; and above all, the lavishly arranged food. He strolled up from the shallow end, past melons, avocados, quiches and terrines, to dishes of cold salmon, chicken and pork, and a dauntingly large haunch of beef. Halfway along, he stopped to watch a group of chefs sweatily grilling steaks and frying the celebrated pancakes, before continuing to the deep end, where the brightly coloured salad bowls and wheels of cheese gave way to a fantasia of puddings: caramel baskets filled with crème chantilly; three-tiered chocolate towers; berry tarts piled as high as Easter bonnets.

Max walked up to him, mouth full and spirits restored. 'You must try some of this.' He held out a plate of reddish-brown meat.

'What is it?'

'Think of it as the best pussy you'll ever eat.'

'Can't you give it a rest for one evening?'

'It's true,' Max said with a smirk. '*Buto sa baboy*. Otherwise known as roast sow's vagina.'

His last shred of appetite destroyed, Philip was contemplating how to slip away when Ray came over to them.

'The lady is happy. She has encountered some old friends from the Malacañang days. She has promised to have a few words of advice in Brent's ear. But no more politics! I shall have enough of this when the campaign is starting.' He turned to Philip. 'Tell me, did the boy Dennis drive you here?'

'No, we took a cab. Why? Do you want him?' Philip asked, surprised that Ray should permit the two sides of his life to converge.

'I have lent him something which I would like back. Are you sure he is not with you?'

'Yes, of course.'

'I'm sorry; I am not doubting you. It is most inconvenient. Still, it will wait. Now, I must introduce you to my wife. She is eager to meet you again. Please do not move from this spot!'

'Not one inch,' Philip said, forcing a smile at the prospect of facing Mikee. Ray scurried away. 'He seems quite cut up about Dennis. Do you think he lent him money?'

'Not likely!' Max said. 'He's as tight as a tranny's fanny.'

'Thank you for that.' Philip frowned. 'Well, Dennis can look after himself. I'm sure he's ripped off bigger men than Ray and lived to tell the tale.'

'I wouldn't bank on it! Don't be misled by all the swish. You've heard of the butterfly that flapped its wings in Brazil and set off a tornado in Texas?'

'Yes, of course.'

'Its name is Ray.'

Philip viewed his host with newfound apprehension when he returned with Mikee, resplendent in a glittering silver cheongsam with yellow and orange tongues round the hem, as if it were on fire.

'I am sorry to be neglecting you,' Mikee said, 'but I have so many important guests.'

'I understand,' Max said, lifting her right hand and kissing it, leaving a film of grease. 'It's the social event of the season.'

'I'll second that,' Philip said, uncertain whether to kiss Mikee's hand or shake it. 'I've never seen such a gargantuan feast. You've done us proud.'

Mikee stared at him coldly. 'I must assure you that I have done nothing at all. But I thank you on behalf of my chef.' She smiled at Max and walked off, closely followed by Ray.

'How to win friends and influence people!' Max said with satisfaction.

'Why? What have I done now?'

'There's nothing worse than complimenting a hostess on her food. It's like saying she's so poor that she had to cook it herself.'

'*Dos and Don'ts in the Philippines* has a lot to answer for! No matter how hard I try, I'll never get the hang of things.'

'Don't worry, your ordeal will soon be over. A week from tomorrow you'll be on your way home.'

'You've booked the flight?'

'Oh yes. Ever so humble.' Max tugged an invisible forelock.

'Thank you,' Philip said, feeling strangely light-headed. 'No doubt it's another faux pas, but I'm calling a cab.' He took out his mobile. 'Are you coming back with me or will you hitch a ride with somebody else?'

'And forgo one moment of your scintillating company? Although I trust you'll allow the condemned man a final drink.'

No sooner had Max moved away than Philip was accosted by Amel. 'I'm sorry,' he said, 'am I interrupting?'

'Not at all. I'm texting the taxi firm to pick us up.'

'What about your driver?'

'He's busy at his second job.'

'No, I rang the manager at Mr Universe and he told me he hasn't turned up yet.'

'You know Dennis? And the club?' Philip felt the world grow both smaller and more menacing.

'I need to speak to him urgently.'

'About anything special?'

'Business,' Amel replied in a sinister echo. 'He's been doing some small jobs for Brent and me.'

'Really? He never mentioned it. But then he's not himself right now. His sister died.'

'That was three weeks ago.'

She was his sister!'

'He has another one, doesn't he?'

'So?'

'So he should take care.'

'Are you threatening him?' Philip asked, mystified by the change in Amel's manner since their lunch on Qingming.

'Not at all. Just offering him a word of advice. Which I'd be grateful if you'd pass on. Now please excuse me, I must go back to my guests. And we'll meet again on Friday, won't we, Max?'

Philip turned to find Max behind him, clasping a brimful glass of champagne.

'Don't remind me!'

'We will?' Philip asked.

'I hope so. It's Max's birthday. We're throwing him a celebration at the club.'

'Which club?'

'The Mr Universe, of course.'

'Why "of course"?' Philip asked Max, as Amel walked away. 'He talks as if he owns the place.'

'He probably does. Tucked away in some portfolio or other.'

'But Mr Universe. A male go-go… what do you call it?'

'Macho dancing.'

'Macho dancing club, that's right! It's all so tacky.'

'Believe me, "tacky" is just the tip of the Lim brothers' iceberg.'

'And they're giving you a party?'

'So it would appear.'

'Then you'll get me to the club after all. If it's not an indelicate question, how old will you be?'

'A great lady once told me – ' Philip gazed instinctively into the house. 'No, another one! This great lady once told me that a true friend was someone who remembered your birthday but forgot your age.'

'I'll be sure to put a single candle on your cake. Let's walk round to the front and wait for the car. I really don't feel comfortable among all this.' He stretched out his arms to include both the buffet and the guests.

'Not your idea of a fun evening?'

'Don't worry, it hasn't been wasted. I thought I'd understand Julian by meeting the people who were closest to him, but I've understood as much – if not more – by coming here.'

'I expect I'm being very obtuse but… what the hell do you mean?'

'What right-minded person faced with all this – the extravagance and the waste, not to mention the cruelty – wouldn't want to blow it up?'

'You are talking figuratively?'

'Am I? I used to wonder whether Julian had taken an active role in any of the NPA's campaigns and, if so, how far it would have jeopardised his faith. I feel now that his faith would have been jeopardised if he hadn't taken action.'

'I doubt that's the sort of thing that Hugh wants to hear,' Max said, his voice suddenly sombre.

'What do you mean? He sent me here to find out the truth.'

'No, he sent you here to assist the investigation.'

'And I shall do both. If the miracles are genuine – and all the evidence points that way – then it shows that God has singled Julian out. He won't be a turn-the-other-cheek saint like St Francis, but an I've-come-to-bring-a-sword saint like St Joan.'

'Well, I only hope that God is on hand to plead his cause in Rome, because he'll get short shrift from the cardinals. And, while He's at it, perhaps He'll plead mine with Hugh. If you screw this up, I'm the one he'll blame. He'll think that I haven't opened the right doors, given you the right tips, pointed you in the right direction. Sixty-nine years old, that's the answer to your question! No, who am I trying to kid? Seventy-one! My work for Hugh – however dull, however demeaning (do you think I enjoy playing nursemaid?) – is all I have left and I warn you, I won't give it up without a fight.'

Philip's phone bleeped.

'The car's outside. We should go.'

They walked back across the patio and into the house, where a crowd had gathered around a singer. Although unable to see above their heads, Philip was transfixed by the voice, which swooped up and down the scale like a pubescent boy's.

'It's her! Just like the old days. Sh-sh!' Max said to a speechless Philip. 'Isn't it wonderful? They've persuaded her to sing.'

Ten

My dear Mother,

I write straight after reading your letter. What on earth was Greg thinking? Let me put your mind at rest: I have NOT joined a gang of Communist assassins – although, to give them their due, the NPA, whom I take to be the assassins in question, are a highly professional revolutionary force. I'm touched by your concern, but please, please, I beg you not to commit such tittle-tattle to paper. I remember warning you about the vulnerability of the mail when I first came out here. The warning is even more urgent now that tensions are running so high.

That said, what's so terrible about Communists? Have you ever met one outside the pages of *The Times*? I have, and I can assure you they're not all cold-blooded commissars shooting plucky grand duchesses or brainwashed students brandishing little red books. They're decent, high-minded people who think deeply about the world and set about improving it with a zeal that would put the average priest to shame. And, before you tell me that priests should concern themselves with the next world rather than this one, may I respectfully point out that Our Lord Himself instructed his followers to feed the hungry, clothe the naked, protect the vulnerable and, here's the clincher, sell everything they had for the benefit of the poor? What's more, there are striking parallels between Christ's and Marx's social teaching. 'In so far as you did this to one of the least of these brothers of mine, you did it to me' finds echoes in 'From each according to his abilities, to each according to his needs'. And think of the first apostles who 'owned everything in common'. That's where you find the authentic note of the early Church, the true spirit of Christianity, not in papal tiaras and bishops' thrones.

I should explain what I mean by 'tensions'. Obviously, Father's funeral was neither the time nor the place to discuss parochial problems but, in the twelve years I've lived here, I can't remember a period of so much friction. If you ask whether I think that the *haciendos* have plotted with the civil and military authorities to launch a concerted attack on people's rights, my answer would have to be 'No'. If, however, you ask whether they've decided to stand shoulder to shoulder to snuff out any flicker of resistance, my answer would be 'Yes. Absolutely. Beyond a shadow of a doubt.'

Events have unfolded with a sinister synchronicity. Every *barrio* has been affected, but by far the hardest hit has been the Arriola estate. Its particular difficulties stem from the logging concession granted by President Marcos to don Bernardo's cousin back in the seventies, and the legal challenge mounted by a group of farmers to the supply road, which would have cut across their fields. The interminable case has finally exhausted don Bernardo's patience. In an effort to put pressure on the farmers, he's resorted to ever more draconian methods. First, he demanded that his *encargado* impose heavy penalties on the gleaning and foraging that provide families with a vital source of food. Then he arbitrarily revoked the traditional right of estate workers to plant their crops between his coconut palms. When they carried on regardless, he summoned the local army chief, insisting that he apply the full force of the law. Either from common decency or, as Benito would have it, an inadequate pay off, the officer refused. Quesada, the Constabulary Commander, showed no such scruples, ordering his men to shoot any 'land invader' on sight.

A week later, I stood at the altar in front of eight plain wooden coffins. The church doors were open to include the vast overspill congregation in the square, but I suspect that even those who secured a place inside caught only a fraction of my words above the shrieks and moans. None of the *haciendos* or their stooges deigned to attend although, to her credit, doña Teresa Romualdez paid her respects, standing meekly at the back, her trademark black taking on new poignancy. I neither know nor care whether the government spy, who drives down from Baguio every Sunday and sits ostentatiously taking notes during my sermons, showed his face, but if he did, he'd have been amply rewarded. Gone were the days when I exhorted the victims to turn the other cheek; now I reminded them of Christ's claim that 'I have come to bring fire to the earth, and how I wish it were blazing already!'. Moreover, I declared that we had no need to wait for Christ to return to establish His kingdom (which would merely be another form of dependency) but had it in our own hands to establish Heaven on earth.

As I led the cortège out of church, I found myself face to face with Quesada, who slowly, mockingly, doffed his cap, releasing the shoulder-length hair that he wore in defiance of official regulations and to set himself apart from his men. Flashing me a grin like a knuckleduster, he fingered the gun on his belt before raising his hand to his chest, to what at first looked like a pectoral cross, but on inspection proved to be an *anting anting* in the shape of a scimitar. Whatever its provenance, it failed to impart the necessary protection since that brief glance was the last I saw of him. Two days later he was killed, along with three soldiers in a textbook NPA ambush. While publicly and privately lamenting the loss of life, I couldn't put my hand on heart and condemn the killers. All my training has disposed me to follow Christ who, even in the turmoil of His arrest, restored the high priest's servant's ear. Lately, however, I've found alternative inspiration in the Old Testament leaders who took up arms on behalf of their downtrodden people.

As you can imagine, Quesada's death left the constabulary hell-bent on revenge. No matter that he'd treated his own men almost as brutally as he had the populace, beating them with his belt, his rifle butt and his bare fists when they failed to carry out his increasingly erratic orders (and this was a man who'd cherished ambitions to be a priest!), the honour of the company was at stake. As they combed the parish for the perpetrators, our only hope, as so often in the past, lay in the bitter rivalry between the various authorities, with the police and the regular army joining forces to prevent the constabulary from indulging in an orgy of reprisals.

I found myself in a quandary when the Constabulary Regional Commander asked me to celebrate Quesada's requiem. I'd assumed that his body would be returned to his family on Mindoro, but no one from the island came forward. To add to the confusion, when I asked to meet his widow, he turned out to have three (is there such a word as trigamist?), each of whom had been unaware of the others' existence. After much soul-searching, I informed the Commander that I would fulfil my obligation to give him a funeral blessing but I was under no such obligation to celebrate his requiem. The officer was outraged, as were the *haciendos* in whose name Quesada had been acting, along with the Mayor and Police Chief, who had no love for Quesada but a vested interest in maintaining the status quo. They appealed to the Bishop, who summoned me for a meeting. Much to my surprise, he accepted my argument that by burying Quesada in the full solemnity of the Church, we'd be tacitly endorsing his tactics. He refused to yield to the mounting pressure, and the simple service went ahead in the presence of the military top brass, the provincial elite and the three widows, who jockeyed for position beside the coffin. Quesada's baleful influence lingered to the end when, during the three volley salute on the church steps, a rifle backfired, taking out the gunner's eye.

The Bishop was bitterly attacked for backing me, with our enemies even playing the race card but, far from swaying him, their cheap jibes appear to have strengthened his resolve. He asked, in return, that I should lie low for a while and added that if I were to do anything in the future that might compromise him, I should tell him only under the seal of the confessional.

I thought that very fair, and have been happy to enjoy a time of reflection and recuperation, my own version of R & R. So here I am in my study, listening to Haydn's *Creation*, one of the records you sent me via Isabel all those years ago and which I have at last had a chance to play. Yes, the twentieth century has finally caught up with us, only eighty-three years late, bringing electricity (who knows, in another eighty-three we might have the telephone!). It's wonderful to be able to play the music of my choice – or rather, your choice, thank you – instead of depending on whatever comes crackling over the airwaves. My one regret is that Consolacion, who in another life would have been a regular concert-goer, refuses every invitation to join me, preferring to sit deferentially on a hard chair in the hall.

On which note – and a very melodious one – I shall sign off, but not before sending you every blessing for the move to the Lodge. I remember how reluctant you were to leave it at the end of the war; I pray that you and Cora will find an equally happy home there now.

Your loving son,
Julian

The Quiapo market spread out in all directions, blurring the distinction between street and mall, arcade and square. Well-stocked stalls of exotic fruit and vegetables stood beside meagre crates of carrots, leeks and turnips, which seemed to have been scratched out of dusty backyards. Fresh fish, their raw eyes gleaming accusingly from a heap of tarnished scales, lay next to strips of dried squid, redolent of rodents. Dusters, with parrot-like plumage, were jumbled with bright pink plastic bowls and coconut fibre doormats. Old men roamed through the crowd peddling cigarettes, lighters, batteries and soap, and boys with more spirit than acumen proffered matchboxes containing fighting spiders, several of which appeared to have suffocated in confinement. While other traders haggled over prices, a gnarled fortune-teller sat impassively beneath a scrawled sign setting out her services, on which there was a fifty per cent discount for senior citizens, whose futures were presumably easier to predict.

Elbowing his way through the shoppers, Philip emerged in front of the Quiapo church. A young woman, cradling a baby low in her arms, offered him a garland of wilted sampaguitas, which he politely refused, before heading for the row of herb-alists who sat, as Maribel had described, beside the railings. She had been up all night with severe menstrual cramps and, although he had begged her to see a doctor, she insisted that the most effective remedy was an infusion of *makabuhay* leaves. Despite his scepticism, he had come to buy them, partly because he could not bear to see her in such discomfort, but also out of guilt: guilt that their last full day together had been blighted by a condition which, in some indefinable way, seemed to be related to his pleasure; guilt that the very pains she was suffering relieved his fears about the split condom; guilt, above all, that he was already thinking about her in the past.

He stood in front of the least intimidating herbalist, whose stall resembled a window box, lined with plants, grasses, seeds and stones. 'Do you have any *makabuhay*?' he asked. She flashed him a suspicious look and addressed him in speech so slurred that it would have been impenetrable even in English. He passed her the paper on which Maribel had written the name. '*Makabuhay*,' he repeated. She pointed to a vine and held up three fingers of a maimed hand. 'Three hundred pesos?' Philip asked uneasily, in case the missing fourth finger were to be included in the calculation. She nodded, at which he took out his wallet and counted the notes. Just as he was giving them to her, a heavy blow from behind felled him to the ground, causing him to crack his shoulder on the edge of the stall.

His first thought was that he had been mugged, but seeing his wallet still in his hand he wondered whether a bomb had exploded, and the terrorist threat that had stalked him since the Wanted posters in the airport had finally materialised. But there was no blast, no smoke, no screams; the disturbance was centred on him. He made to rise, whereupon his arms were wrenched behind his back and his wrists handcuffed, sending a further wave of pain to his shoulder. Someone was shouting at him, but the voice was at once too high-pitched and too garbled to comprehend. He pressed his body into the ground, using the logic of dreams to escape from the nightmare, but found himself dragged to his feet and frogmarched away by two men whose faces were outside his field of vision. The crowd around him parted with ominous compliance. 'What's happening?' he cried, but any answer was drowned by the thump of his heart. He was led through the square to a white police car with the words *Manila's Finest* stencilled like a sick joke on the door. He ducked, just in time to avoid banging his head on the roof as he was bundled on to the back seat.

'What's happening?' he repeated, as he struggled to sit up straight without the use of his hands. 'There's been a terrible mistake,' he said to the officer who sat down beside him. The studied silence forced him to adopt a different approach. 'Do you know who I am?' he asked, sounding like his mother hectoring an obdurate tradesman. The officer ignored him and spoke briskly to his colleague. 'Are you arresting me? On what charge? Don't you have to read me my rights? Or don't foreigners have any rights in the Philippines?' His attempt at irony foundered on the memory of Julian. 'How do I know you're a genuine police officer?' he added, although, as he glimpsed the man's gun poking out of its holster, the alternative was too terrifying to contemplate. 'I demand to know where you're taking me!' he said. 'I'm a British citizen. You have a duty to contact the Embassy at once.'

'Be quiet,' the officer next to him said, in a voice far friendlier than his manner. 'You will have your chance to speak at the station.'

Any hope that this would mark the start of a dialogue was dashed. Philip sat back in confusion as the car, which was granted no special privileges, crawled through the streets. His senses were numbed apart from smell, which had grown more acute. He retched at the officers' body odour before realising, with disgust, that the stench stemmed from him.

Twenty minutes later – although precise calculations belonged to the world before his arrest – he was ushered out of the car and into a police station. The self-protecting haze in which he had been moving lifted, allowing him to take stock of his surroundings. A large sign above the door declared it to be *A People-Friendly Police Station*, a claim that appeared to be borne out by the docile crowd milling around the reception area. To the left a row of three metal tables was set with heavy, old-fashioned computers, at one of which an officer was eating a pot noodle. The two arresting officers conducted Philip to the front desk, where the lengthy admissions procedure was interrupted when a fresh-faced young officer dragged in two brawling women. Far from rushing to his aid, his colleagues watched in amusement as he struggled to keep them apart. Finally, the desk officer strolled over and slapped both women hard across the head, at which they abruptly fell silent, leaving the hapless neophyte to lead them to one of the tables and take their statements.

The brief reprieve from his own predicament ended when the desk officer asked Philip for his name, address and passport.

'My name is Philip Blaise Redding Seward,' he replied sonorously. 'I'm staying at the Manila Hotel. I'm a British citizen and I demand to know what this is all about.'

'Passport?'

'I don't have a passport – that is, not on me.'

'Passport?'

'I don't have a passport! I wasn't expecting to leave the country today. Won't somebody please tell me what's happening?' he asked, unable to keep his voice from cracking.

'You have been arrested for buying a plant designed to bring abortion. This is a crime punishable in the Philippines by between one month and twenty years imprisonment.'

'Twenty years?' The sentence seemed at once to stretch into infinity and to dwindle to the length of a condemned man's final walk.

'Between one month and twenty years.'

'There's been a serious misunderstanding. I went there to buy this *makabuhay* for my girlfriend's stomach cramps... menstrual pains. I wanted her to go to the chemist.'

'This is a bad plant, a very bad plant.'

'I'm a foreigner, a guest in your country. I'm a friend of the Bishop of Baguio.' The episcopal name fell flat. 'Surely I have the right to ring a lawyer? Not that I know any lawyers here. Why should I? I'm not a criminal. I need to contact the British Embassy. Will you please call them for me? This whole mess will be cleared up at once.'

'First, you must speak to my sergeant,' the desk officer said. He logged Philip's property, confiscating his watch, wallet and mobile, before asking one of the arresting officers to lock him up. As they walked through the lobby, Philip stared in dread at the pen packed with prisoners, which looked less like the holding cell in a TV detective series than the overcrowded cattle truck in a war film. A dozen or so men were leaning against the bars or squatting on the floor, since there were no chairs or benches. Many were shirtless, the symbols on their torsos a disturbing echo of the graffiti on the walls. A full clothes line hung above their heads, suggesting that several of them had been detained there for days. A couple jeered, but most watched indifferently as the officer thrust him against the whitewashed wall and, making him hold up a name card, photographed him both full face and in left and right profile.

The officer took his fingerprints and, on an impulse that appalled him even as he yielded to it, Philip smeared the inky residue down his cheeks. The officer said nothing but guided him through a door marked Exit into the bowels of the building. His relief at not being placed among the prisoners in the pen turned to panic at the recollection of Benito's scar. 'Where are you taking me?' he asked. The officer remained silent, pushing him into a small, stark room and locking the door. As his eyes adjusted to the gloom, he saw that, surprisingly for such a functional space, the walls were painted crimson, which intensified his fears of torture. He huddled on one of the two metal chairs, which along with the plain wooden desk made up the room's only furniture and gazed at its one picture, a framed heart in which Christ and the Virgin Mary were entwined like Valentine's Day lovers. The air smelt of sweat, which instead of inducing the usual repugnance felt oddly reassuring.

Time concertinaed around him, as he waited for the police to make the next move. Finally, a large officer with a sleeveful of badges entered and barely giving him a second glance, drew the remaining chair up to the desk. He opened a file and made a note, after which he turned to face Philip, whose resolve not to speak first was strengthened by his tongue sticking to the roof of his mouth.

'Good afternoon. I am Sergeant Joel Labuguen,' he said, with a show of affability. 'And you are Philip Seward?'

'Am I? I'm beginning to doubt it.'

'What?' the Sergeant asked, his expression clouding. Philip, recalling that to policemen questions of identity were purely practical, changed tack.

'I mean: how can I be sure of anything when I go out in good faith to buy a herb for my girlfriend's stomach cramps and find myself arrested for assisting an abortion?'

'The *makabuhay* vine has many uses. Some people, they use it for diarrhoea and indigestion, but these people who go to Quiapo, they buy it for one use only. This is well known.'

'Not by me. I'm a foreigner. The only thing I know about Quiapo is that the church contains the Black Nazarene icon. How can anyone buy proscribed herbs in such a sacred spot?'

'Who is to say? Perhaps they take them and then confess?' The Sergeant's laughter seemed to swill around his belly.

'In any case, my girlfriend isn't pregnant.' Philip felt a flicker of unease at the assertion. 'You can check up whenever you like.'

'Thank you, we will. What is this young person's name please?'

'Why do you say "young"? I never said she was young. She might be fifty for all you know.'

'Is this young person aged fifty?'

'No,' Philip said wretchedly. 'She is nineteen, nearly twenty.'

'You are sure about this?'

'As far as I can be sure about anything. She told me she was nineteen. She had no reason to lie.' He felt a further flicker of unease.

'It is unfortunate – even cruel – that while there is such a small difference in looks between seventeen and nineteen, there is such a big difference in law.'

'I don't understand. Are you accusing me of something else? May I please call my friend in Manila? He'll find me a lawyer. I don't know how things work here, but in England an interrogation has no validity unless you follow the correct procedures.'

'Is this an interrogation? I am sad that you think like this. I am hoping that you will see this more as a friendly head to head to clear up any misunderstanding.'

'You're the ones who've misunderstood; I'm an innocent victim!' Philip struggled to quell his indignation. 'My girlfriend's name is Maribel May Santos. I don't have her address; I've never been there. But her number is on my mobile, the one you've impounded.'

'How did you meet this young person?'

'She's the sister of my driver, Dennis Santos.'

'Very well,' the Sergeant said, sounding mollified. 'We will make our investigations and we will see what we will find. In the meanwhile, I hope you will not object to waiting here a little longer. We will do all we can do to make you feel comfortable. If you wish for anything to eat or to drink, I will instruct one of my officers to provide it. At our expense,' he added expansively.

'Just some water,' Philip said, feeling the moisture that had drained from his body trickling down his back.

'Of course. There will be nothing easier,' the Sergeant said, gathering his file and standing up.

'Before you go, may I please make a phone call? Just one call!'

'You must not concern yourself. I have taken the liberty of ringing someone on your behalf.'

'Who?' Philip asked as the Sergeant moved to the door. 'Who?' he repeated as the door slammed shut.

The silence in the room grew cavernous. What had first seemed like confusion now seemed like conspiracy. How had the police known where to find him? Had they used Maribel as a decoy? Had they threatened Dennis, who in turn threatened her? That would at least mitigate the treachery. He would lose his liberty but not his faith in human nature. On the other hand, might she have betrayed him of her own accord? Was it her revenge on him for his imminent departure? Impossible! That was not the doting, tender-hearted Maribel he knew. But how well did he actually know her? Had she led him on from the start? How many of the 'famous persons' who had refused his massage had Dennis introduced to her? What was the real reason she had never invited him back to meet her aunt?

A thought ran through him like an electric shock. What if Maribel were indeed pregnant and the charge against him were true? What if, having decided on an abortion, she had been seeking not to punish him but to involve him in the process by asking him to buy the herb? Or what if her motives were more cynical and, aware that the police would submit her to a medical examination, she had manipulated him in a bid to obtain the kind of out-of-court settlement that Leonora Veloso had obtained for Girlie? Worse still, what if the Sergeant were right and she had lied about her age in order to trap him. Sex, however consensual, with a girl under eighteen was held to be rape, leaving him with the prospect of not twenty years but a lifetime in jail. Julian had endured captivity in the knowledge of the worldwide campaign for his release. Who would organise a similar campaign for him? His parents? His brothers? Isabel and Hugh? Would they trust in his innocence or suspect him of being a paedophile? Just as he was wondering how well he knew Maribel, would they be wondering the same about him?

Philip felt like a fly caught between two panes of glass. The door opened, and after a moment of uncertainty he recognised the slight figure of the Vicar General. Reeling with relief, he asked him to sit down and apologised for his appearance. Only then did he think to ask how he had known where to find him.

'We had a call,' the Vicar General said airily.

'Yes, but who from?' Philip asked, his relief ebbing away.

'What does it matter? What matters is that you've been arrested on a very serious charge.'

'But I thought… Maribel asked me… she said that she needed the herb – vine, whatever you call it – for period pains.'

The Vicar General flinched.   'Doesn't it strike you as strange that she should ask you – a man and a foreigner – for something so intimate?'

'But we are intimate. We've been intimate for the past six weeks.'

'So I gather. That may result in an even more serious charge.'

'She's nineteen! How often do I have to say it? She's nineteen!'

'Can you be sure of that?'

'I haven't seen her birth certificate, if that's what you're asking.'

'Quite. In some of our outlying provinces, even today, the registration of births and deaths is lamentably lax. Sometimes it can be two or three years out of date.'

'What are you saying?' Philip asked, feeling the muscles in his chest contract. 'That officially she might be seventeen or even sixteen?'

'It's a possibility.'

'But you could explain things – set people straight.'

'I could, so long as the Bishop agreed,' the Vicar General replied smoothly.

'Why on earth wouldn't he?'

'At the very least he would require certain guarantees in return.'

'I swear on the Bible, on my mother's life, on everything I hold dear, that I was buying the *makabuhay* quite innocently and that Maribel is – to the best of my knowledge – over eighteen.'

'No, not those sort of guarantees. Guarantees about Father Julian.'

'Are you trying to bargain with me?'

'Let's say, to find common ground. It has been intimated to us – is that the right word? Sometimes I forget my English.'

'I won't know until I hear the rest of the sentence,' Philip said sourly.

'Of course,' the Vicar General replied with a thin smile. 'It was intimated to us that you have been exceeding your brief, contacting people with no love – indeed, quite the opposite – for the Church.'

'I take it you mean Benito Bertubin?'

'Exactly.'

'I wish I knew what you have against him. He may have left the Church, but he's still doing Christ's work.'

'Is that so?' the Vicar General asked, his eyes ablaze. 'Is it Christ's work to give the people hope that their lives can be fulfilled here on earth: hope that will inevitably turn to despair, the one sin which, as we know, will keep them from the perfect bliss of God's heavenly kingdom?'

'Do you really believe that God would be so vindictive?'

'It's not what I believe but what the Church teaches.'

'Then shouldn't the Church base its teaching and, more to the point, its practice on the truth?' Philip asked, momentarily distracted from his own plight. 'Although Benito said nothing about the Constabulary Commander's murder, he confirmed my suspicion that Julian was ready to fight – literally – for his beliefs. If the miracles are genuine, as you claim, then it must mean that God endorsed his position. And since the Church opposed it – that is opposed those who took up arms against the Marcos regime – it must also mean that He endorsed the priest against the Church.'

'That's quite impossible. A priest derives his authority wholly from the Church.'

'What if he chooses to cut out the middleman?'

'If that were so – and I don't for one moment accept that it is, either for Father Julian or anyone else – what would be the result? Anarchy! There would be no saint with the power to regenerate the community, but an empty personality cult. You say that the Church should base itself on the truth. Yes, of course, but it is the Church's role to interpret that truth, as it has done for the past two thousand years And if that means ignoring – even excising – things that would cause confusion, so be it.'

'That isn't interpretation; it's distortion.'

'I know you're a Protestant, Mr Seward, but did you discuss these views with the Olliphants before they employed you?'

'No. Although, to be honest, I didn't hold them. Coming here, seeing the Church's grip on every aspect of national life, has changed me radically.'

'And changed you into a radical?'

'I realise that I'm doing myself no favours by speaking out like this.'

'I appreciate that you're overwrought. And under the circumstances who can blame you? Plus, I see where the trouble lies. It's all down to language or, rather, terminology. When we speak of the Church, you and I, we mean two quite different things. You mean buildings and treasure and popes and power; I mean the people: the people for whom the Church is the only road to salvation.'

'What about the gospel?'

'The gospel is nothing without the Church.'

Philip was torn. While eager to hear what guarantees the Bishop would demand of him, he was determined to pin down the Vicar General. 'In which case, how far would you be willing to go to protect it?'

'As far as was necessary.'

'As far as murder?'

'That would never be necessary.' The Vicar General looked shocked.

'No? There are those who claim that Julian's death was ordered by a group of right-wing priests to whom his views were anathema.'

'We are well aware that you've made contact with a psychopath in Bilibid jail.'

'How did you…?' Philip started; to his certain knowledge the only person to whom he had mentioned it was Max.

'You keep on asking me *how*, when you should be asking yourself *why*.'

'I've told you *why* several times: to discover the truth! And, unlike the Church hierarchy, I believe that the truth is the same as the facts.'

'Then your understanding is deeply flawed. The evidence of the miracles means that Father Julian's views – and even his actions – are no longer material. What counts is his example. There is a long-standing Church tradition that on the Day of Judgement we will be made to answer not just for our actions but for the consequences of those actions after our death. So, is a saint a saint solely by virtue of… well, of his own virtues, or by virtue of the virtues he inspires in others?'

'Presumably you expect me to opt for the latter?'

'Most people have a simple faith. They have neither the time nor the training for complex – indeed, for any kind of – theological argument. They need signs, which Father Julian is already giving them. And I am sure that St Julian will give them many more. Are you still intent on taking that away?'

'Do I have any choice in the matter?'

'We all have a choice.'

'I was thinking more of my current state than the human condition.'

'There is of course an easy solution,' the Vicar General said, standing and facing the wall, where he clenched and unclenched his fists. 'Unlike some, the police have due respect for the Church. I am sure that I can persuade them to release you into my custody – not literally, of course: our humble clergy house is no match for the Manila Hotel. The charges against you will be deferred while you complete your report and then quietly dropped.'

'You have that much power?'

'Not me, no, not at all: the Church!'

'And what assurances do you have that once I'm free, I'll comply?'

'When they searched your room – '

'What?'

'Standard procedure. The officers took the precaution of removing your passport. It will be returned when you board the plane next Thursday.'

'Let me get this straight,' Philip said, anxious to assert his integrity even as he acceded to the demands and despising himself for both. 'You're asking me to lie in the report?'

'Not at all,' the Vicar General said, turning back to him. 'I had hoped that we would have understood each other by now: "to excise things which would cause confusion". Surely you see that it's the best way for everyone? For us; for the Olliphants; and above all for yourself. The Bishops Conference has strongly condemned the deplorable conditions in our jails, but so far to little effect.'

'I can't think; I think I'm going to collapse!'

'Would you like me to call for some water?'

'No, I'm fine, thank you.' Philip gulped. 'It's passed.'

'Of course we can't expect you to reach a decision at once. If you prefer, I can go now and come back on Saturday.'

'And leave me here?'

'They will no doubt move you into the holding cell.'

'That overcrowded cage at the front?'

'Exactly. I am sure that, like Father Julian, you would refuse any special treatment.'

'And if – only if – I were to agree to your proposal, how can you know that once I'm back home, I won't renege and submit a second report to Isabel and Hugh?'

The Vicar General looked hurt. 'An Englishman's word is his bond: isn't that what you say? But in case things have changed since I was in Guildford, I should remind you that although your laws on abortion may be shamefully lenient, those on child abuse – even when committed overseas – are not. We would have no trouble in proving that Miss Santos is a minor.'

'Nineteen is above the age of consent for us.'

'Nineteen? Sixteen? Fourteen? The necessary witnesses could be found.'

'Thank you,' Philip said, choked with disgust. 'I asked how far you would go to protect the Church and now I know.'

'As I said, as far as was necessary. So have you made up your mind, or would you like to talk it over with your fellow prisoners?'

'Is that meant to be a joke?'

'Not at all.'

'I accept your terms. Of course I do.'

'Of course you do. You may not thank me now, but I am confident that you will as soon as you've had a chance to think things over. I've noticed a change in you since we first met. There's definitely a new strength in your eyes, or is it your jawline? My country has been good for you.' He summoned an officer who escorted them out, past the pen, which had filled up further during the afternoon, to the reception area where, after a brief discussion, the desk officer gave Philip back both his property and his freedom. The Vicar General offered him a lift to the hotel, but he insisted on taking a cab. 'Very wise,' the Vicar General said, impervious to the snub. 'What better time to start drafting your report! You're here for another week, so I hope that once you've finished it, you'll take the chance to explore the city: the restaurants, the galleries and the malls. You'll find everything you could want: a Rolex watch or a Louis Vuitton suitcase that even the original designers would be happy to own.'

'Thank you, but I've had my fill of fakes.'

Returning to the hotel, Philip went straight to the front desk to pick up his messages. His conviction that the entire staff knew of his ordeal was confirmed by the receptionist's shudder, until he remembered that there was ink smeared across his face. With the irony that had become his fate, the only message was from the Bilibid governor's office authorising him to visit Prisoner N204P-0370 Gerron Casiscas. There was nothing from Maribel, whose continued silence, both here and on his mobile, was a sure sign of guilt. He hurried up to his room, where the tears he had held in check ever since his arrest flooded out at the sight of the clothes, books and papers strewn about the floor. He made a desultory attempt to clear up, before crawling, fully clothed, into bed and pulling the covers over his head.

The darkness failed to calm his mind. The conspiracy ranged wider than he had feared. Whatever the scope of Maribel's and Dennis's involvement, they must have colluded with Max, since no one else could have told the Vicar General of the Bilibid connection. And if Max were involved, then who else? Might the web extend as far as Whitlock? He hugged himself tighter. Had Max warned Hugh that he was looking into Julian's political activities and Hugh instructed him to use every available means to scare him off? The truth was that he could trust nobody. The one virtue of his arrest was that it freed him from any lingering remorse at leaving Maribel. Whether she were the prime mover in an elaborate subterfuge or merely a pawn, he had no desire ever to set eyes on her again. Having expected less from Dennis, he felt less wounded by his betrayal. The sensible thing would be to sack him, but with under a week before he flew home, he would keep him on, but at a distance, restoring boundaries he should never have relaxed. He would take a similar line with Max. By refusing even to mention his arrest, he would deny him the satisfaction of seeing how deeply he was hurt.

Emerging from the fug, he resolved to eat his way out of misery, ringing down for a meal of coquilles St Jacques, steak and chips, white chocolate parfait and, in a spirit of defiance, an expensive bottle of Saint Émilion. After bolting it down, he felt ugly, bloated and full of self-loathing, which he compounded by logging on to the adult channel. This time he picked an Asian film, *Banana Cream Pie*, in which, in a hotel room as bleak as his was lavish, a dazed-looking teenager was mounted orally, vaginally, anally and, after much cumbersome manoeuvring, in all three orifices at once, by a tattooed man with gold teeth, a pot-bellied man with a ponytail and a scrawny adolescent with acne. Feeling complicit in her violation, Philip switched off after ten minutes, to be left with a profound sense of shame.

He awoke the next morning with a pounding headache and a sour taste in his mouth, as though he had drunk a bottle of vinegar. Braced by a strong dose of caffeine, he embarked on his report. Sticking to the Vicar General's guidelines, he eliminated anything that might be deemed contentious. What remained was a full description of Julian's miracles, along with a history of his work in San Isidro, all of which, apart from some incidental details in the parishioners' testimonies and his own account of Jejomar's crucifixion, was well known to the investigators. After reading through the nascent hagiography he felt the futility of his visit as never before.

Apart from a workout in the hotel gym before lunch and a dip in the pool at teatime, he did not stir from his laptop all day. He received only two phone calls. The first was from Max who, making no reference to his arrest, confirmed the arrangements for the evening's party. The second was from Dennis who, with unprecedented – and unsettling – diligence, asked if he were needed for work. Curbing his surprise, Philip gave him the day off, apologising for not having informed him earlier and asking him to apologise too to Maribel for his failure to bring her the *makabuhay*. 'The traffic around Quiapo was so heavy that I was forced to give up,' he said, trusting that his pauses were as inscrutable as Dennis's grunts. 'Anyway, I expect I'll see you later. Will you be dancing at the club?'

'I am always dancing. I am star attraction. When I am not dancing, all the *baklas* are asking: "Where is Dennis?"'

'So you've solved your problem?'

'What problem is this you mean? There is no problem.'

'Your money problem: your 10,000 pesos problem! I had a hunch that it had something to do with Ray.'

'This is no problem. Ray is big friend of me. I am giving him massage. I am best masseur in Manila.'

'Fine,' Philip said wearily and put down the phone.

Although he had no wish to see Max, let alone to celebrate his birthday, Philip was determined to put up a brave front. So at 9.30 he hailed a cab to drive him to Legaspi Towers, where he found Max waiting impatiently in the forecourt. 'Many happy returns!'

'Thank you,' Max said, stepping into the car with a sly expression, which looked more than ever as if it should be set off by whiskers: not mutton-chops or sideburns, but cat's whiskers sprouting from the corners of his mouth.

After a strained ride, they pulled up outside the Mr Universe, a two-storey building in a patch of wasteland. Red, white and blue fairy lights festooned the façade and a giant plywood body-builder, whose perfectly curved biceps looked as if they had been traced with a compass, was propped up beside the door. Philip nervously surveyed the seedy display and desolate setting, while Max chatted to the hefty doorman.

'Happy birthday, Mr Max,' the doorman said. 'They're waiting for you inside.'

'Thank you, Madame.'

'He doesn't seem the sort of guy to have a female nickname,' Philip said, as they walked through the plastic-strip door.

'That's because he's a she,' Max replied.

'You're joking!'

'We call her Madame Papaya.'

'After the fruit?'

'After the tree. It's one of Nature's freaks. The male papaya bears the flowers and the female the fruit. You can turn the female into the male by cutting it. That's what she's saving up for.'

'You can't even trust the trees in this country,' Philip said, as he stood in the doorway and took in the ambience. The low ceiling was hung with paper streamers, which looked as if they had been left over from an office party. The walls and bar were painted the ox-blood of a fleapit cinema. Twenty or thirty small tables faced a raised stage, the size of the dais in his old village hall: an image he immediately tried to shrug off. The air was stale and thick with smoke.

The manager, a florid man in his forties with a shirt to match his manner, greeted Max with two hurried pecks and several waspish comments, before leading the way to an alcove where Ray and Amel were sitting. 'Your guests have arrived, sir,' he said to Amel, who stood up to welcome them, wishing Max a happy birthday and apologising for his brother's absence.

'Brent is standing for congress. We have had to put this club solely in my name.'

'Philip, my friend, you must sit here besides me,' Ray said, making room for Philip on the banquette. Philip slid into his designated place, trusting that Amel's presence would act as a restraint on Ray's roving hands.

After pouring the champagne and toasting Max, Amel excused himself for a moment, leaving Max and Ray to gossip, and Philip to watch the stage. Whatever the relevance of the club's name, it bore none to the dancers, most of whom looked as if they should still be competing on their high-school sports fields. Wearing leopard-print pouches, feathered headdresses and beaded armbands, a dozen young men were performing a tribal number. The rotating lights were, however, more animated than the dancers who, either from lack of space or the limitations of the choreography, remained rooted to the spot, gyrating their hips, rolling their bellies, sliding their hands up and down their torsos, and making no attempt whatever to engage with their audience.

'Is that all they do?' Philip asked Max.

'Patience, dear! The pants don't come off until midnight.'

'I can live with that,' Philip said. 'But I don't see any sign of Dennis.'

'Don't worry, he'll be here.'

At the end of the number the dancers jumped off the stage, resuming their gyrations beside and even on top of the tables, their pouches turning into purses in which the audience could both express their appreciation and fondle the flesh. Philip, who had abhorred every kind of audience participation since a boyhood encounter with Widow Twankey, sank back in his seat and gave thanks that the alcove was set apart. His gratitude was cut short by the arrival of a dancer, his penis poking out of his pouch like the gun in the policeman's holster. He stood by the table and stroked himself, seemingly oblivious to the two arms, one white and one brown, stretched out to squeeze his thigh. Then, lifting his right foot on to the table, he leant forward to make himself more accessible. Max and Ray took full advantage of his presence before, in an impromptu move that looked better timed than any on the stage, their hands met as they simultaneously stuffed bills into his pouch. As he drew back, Ray lowered his hand and let it rest on Philip's crotch. Philip snatched it away.

'Oh, I am so sorry. This is my mistake!'

'Big mistake!' Philip said gruffly.

'Boasting again,' Max said with a giggle.

The dancers returned to the stage, which had been reset during the break to reveal a backdrop of Manila Bay at dusk. Midnight must have passed, since they were now naked, but along with the licence came a new coyness as they kept one hand constantly clamped over their groins. The nudity had at least some bearing on a routine in which they soaped and showered themselves, and played with the giant bubbles that were blown in from the wings. Their repertoire of movements remained minimal: the same straight backs, swinging hips and rolling stomachs, with one arm after the other reaching slowly up their chests and into the air. At all times, including the fleeting crossover, they made sure to keep their genitals covered, giving the bizarre impression that these bodies for hire were as anxious to conceal their nakedness as Adam in a medieval woodcut of the Fall.

Given the lack of either erotic charge or choreographic complexity, Philip found that his only interest lay in watching Dennis, who had finally appeared. The narcissism of the performance perfectly matched that of his personality, as he caressed every inch of the well-toned flesh, which would be his sole means of survival once Philip returned home.

The number ended, and with it any artistic ambitions the show might have harboured. The dancers, half-coated in suds, dragged on chairs from the wings, which they lined up at the edge of the stage and, to a brassy soundtrack, sat down and began to masturbate. An abrupt silence was followed by a fevered clamour, as the audience cheered on their favourites, although it was impossible to tell whether they were applauding their dexterity or their physiques. Philip felt a mixture of disgust and outrage, and wondered if it would have been the same had the dancers been female, until a sudden recollection of *Banana Cream Pie* both repelled and reassured him.

'You look the way I feel,' he said to Max. 'Isn't it your thing?'

'Just a fit of the birthday blues. I'm thinking of all the nights I've spent at this club. All the boys. All the transactions. All as fleeting and as desultory as that.' He gestured to the stage where one of the boys had reached orgasm, to a smattering of applause. 'Don't worry about me. I've got a touch of the "where are they nows?", maybe married to a dash of the "what were they thens?". I'll be fine.'

Amel returned to the table, and for all his attempts to engage with the proceedings Philip was heartened by the presence of another straight man.

'Enjoying yourself?' Amel asked him.

'Well, I'm enjoying the champagne and the snacks. The floor-show's not exactly to my taste.'

'Nor mine, my friend, I can assure you. But we're here for Max. My father wants to give him a night to remember.'

'This is true,' Ray interjected.

'I'm worried about your driver,' Amel said, eyeing the stage dispassionately. 'His performance is – to put it politely – a flop.'

While several of his fellows had climaxed and resumed masturbating as if by rote, it was clear, even through his fist, that Dennis's penis was flaccid. As he tugged at himself in increasing desperation, Philip was torn between smiling at him in moral – or rather, friendly – support and looking away to spare his blushes. He was relieved of the choice when the spotlights dimmed, the music faded and a tattered tinsel curtain was drawn across the stage.

'Is that it?' Philip asked.

'Now the boys will come out for a private dance.'

'We've already had one.'

'But you haven't had Dennis. It's only right he should perform for his friend, Max, on his birthday.'

'His birthday's over now. It's 1.30 in the morning.'

'A detail! Besides, Dennis needs to do something to earn his pay. He's been a total washout so far.'

'I think he may have taken too much *shabu*.'

'I think you're right,' Amel said coldly. 'Only not for his own use. What do you say, Max?'

'So many transactions; so many meaningless transactions,' Max mumbled.

The dancers poured through the curtain, once again wearing pouches. Dennis was heading for the far side of the room when, at a nod from Amel, the manager directed him to their table. He made his way with evident reluctance.

'What kept you so long?' Amel asked. 'I told you I wanted you to give a private dance for my friend here.'

'I am best dancer in club. Many people ask for Dennis.'

'Is that so? Then what they see here will whet their appetites. Go on!'

Ignoring Philip's sympathetic smile, Dennis stood over a semi-conscious Max and ran his hands up and down his own body. Max yawned.

'You'll need to do better than that! Look at him!'

'He is half-sleeping.'

'Is it any wonder? You've bored him to death.'

'Please be kind, my boy,' Ray said.

'Well, I'm enjoying it,' Philip said.

'Dance for Max! Dance for my father! Doesn't he deserve something in return for the money you stole?'

'But is all good now. Ask Max. He is telling you. I have all this money soon.'

'Too late, my friend. Too late. And what about the *shabu*?'

With a startled look, Dennis tried to dart from the table, but Amel grabbed his wrist and held him back.

'I don't know about anyone else, but I'm shattered,' Philip said. 'I ought to make a move. Do you think Dennis could call me a cab?'

'Later,' Amel said. 'First he must dance. Dance!'

'You are having my hand,' Dennis said wretchedly.

'So I am,' Amel replied, making no attempt to release it. 'You know, Dennis, for such a big prick, your own prick is pathetically small. You couldn't even get it up before. But I've got something to help you. From one of my associates. Maybe you know him, Eric Humilde?' Dennis started to quiver. 'Yes, I thought so. He was waiting for a package from me, which never came. Why's that, do you suppose?'

'Business,' Dennis replied weakly, as he struggled to free himself from Amel's grip.

'I was telling him about your little problem: how you were finding it hard to get hard. Not much good in your line of work, is it? And he gave me a special solution, just for you.'

'No, please!'

'You might say it's the solution to all your problems. Father, take the bottle out of my pocket.'

'What is this, my boy?' Ray asked.

'Just do it, Father,' he said, addressing the dithering Ray sharply in Tagalog. Philip, meanwhile, looked around the audience, wondering whether anyone else shared his apprehension, but they were all engrossed in their private performances, conducting the transactions of which Max had finally tired. 'Now open it, carefully.' As Ray followed Amel's instructions, a puff of smoke formed at the lid and a sharp, stinging smell, like industrial bleach, wafted across the table. 'You won't need to worry about getting hard ever again,' Amel said to Dennis, as he picked up the bottle and poured it into his pouch.

Eleven

My dear Mother,

The first thing to say is that I'm in good heart. If there are any blotches on the paper, then they're sweat not tears. I'm doing my best to keep both myself and the paper dry, but when you're locked in a clammy cell twelve foot by ten with five fellow prisoners it can be hard. As you see, justice still eludes me. An Australian journalist put it to me that with all the ups and downs of the past year my life must feel like a rollercoaster. I nodded politely, while reflecting that a better analogy would be the Rotor. Do you remember taking us to it at the Festival of Britain? Greg and Agnes thought themselves too grown-up, but Cora and I relished our turn in the giant cylinder that spun ever faster, leaving us clinging to the wall, defying gravity. In here, I'm left clinging to my sense of self in a world that defies sanity. Visitors ask how I manage to survive. The answer is 'with surprising ease'. Prison life is simply everyday life turned inside out and revealed in shocking – but salutary – detail.

Of course the knowledge of my innocence helps.

In my last few letters I've reported the charges against us and the characters of my fellow accused; it's time to paint a picture of the prison itself – you may want to keep this tucked in your copy of Dante. It's a square, squat building as sturdy as a church, constructed a century ago by the Spanish to house unruly peasants and mountain bandits, mainly the Igorot (I use the colonial term not just for historical accuracy but because it denoted several different tribes: as well as the Ibaloi, there were the Bontok, the Ikalahan, the Ifugao and others). In a bitter irony, many of their descendants are locked up here today, following disputes with mining companies, logging companies, hydroelectric companies and all the other 'lowlanders' hoping to make a quick buck (the phrase is not idly chosen) by encroaching on their ancestral lands. For all I know, life in the wilds may have inured them to prison conditions, nevertheless the incarceration of such free spirits seems especially cruel.

Four blocks, each comprising six cells, accommodate the three hundred or so high-security prisoners. You don't need a maths degree to work out that however cramped Benito and I and our companions may be, ours is the honeymoon suite compared to our neighbours'. I say cells, but in fact they're more like cages since the inner walls consist of iron bars through which the men poke their heads like the dogs in Benguet market. There are no windows on the outer walls, but the bars let in light (shadows) and air (stench), along with the incessant, intolerable noise. The blocks surround a bleak stone yard through the centre of which runs an open sewer, the conduit for the entire accumulation of prison waste. Needless to say, there are no lavatories, just a plastic bucket in the corner of each cell. As you can imagine, this poses problems for one who drove Father to distraction by refusing to use the facilities in France. Of the many courtesies afforded to me by my fellow inmates, none has meant so much as their forming a human shield whenever I have to use the bucket. Propriety or prudery, it's one vestige of my nursery training I'm unable to escape.

At forty-four, I'm one of the older inmates. I've yet to discover if that's because conditions in the high-security wing militate against long-term survival, or because murder, which is what brought most of us here, is a young man's crime. The prisoners' youth is not reflected in their faces, which are lined, scarred, weathered and toothless before their time, either from brawling or malnutrition. They shave their heads to remove all trace of softness while cultivating wispy moustaches and beards. Their vaulted chests are blazoned with tattoos. In the sweltering heat, most wear nothing but a pair of stained shorts or a loincloth;

some, however, go to considerable lengths to stand out from the crowd. Three men, reputedly informers, as brazen about their activities in prison as their colleagues were in the parish, strut around in frayed trousers and *barong Tagalogs* discarded by the *haciendos*. Even more bizarre are the pair in the cell opposite, who sport the costumes of Roman centurions left over from an ancient fiesta, not caring that the tunics are ragged and the cloaks crawling with lice.

Anyone who arrives with clothes that are remotely decent soon barters them. In prison everything and everyone has a price. Some men sell their blood to hospitals, although given the prevalence of disease, including TB, I dread to think of the consequences. Others hire themselves out as assassins, the guards (and even the governor) happy to authorise their 'day release' for a cut of the fee. It may be iniquitous, but in this topsy-turvy world the punishment doesn't so much fit the crime as facilitate the next one. It's impossible to survive in here without money to pay for food. Father would have recognised the paltry daily ration of two cups of rice and three minuscule fish. Rest assured that I wouldn't be telling you any of this if Hugh and the Regional hadn't left me enough cash to order food every morning for myself and my co-accused.

Boredom is our biggest problem after diet. There are no work programmes and the men, blood rising with the heat, turn on each other at the least provocation. They mill around the yard exercising, sparring, playing basketball or *tong* (a Filipino version of rummy), all the time exchanging genial gibes; then, in a flash, the mood changes and what was a joke becomes a mortal insult. That flash is not merely figurative since knives, to which the guards turn a bribed eye, are plucked from the waistbands of shorts or the soles of shoes and brandished with murderous intent. Benito and I, who are regularly called on to intervene, have to trust to our priestly immunity.

In my own case there's a further factor in play. Over the years, as I've mentioned, I've gained a small reputation as a miracle worker, which has even featured in some of the press reports of this case – not always to my advantage, since an alibi is of limited value to a man with the alleged ability to be in two places at once. In prison, as elsewhere, this reputation is a mixed blessing. Overall, my fellow prisoners are cheered by my presence, taking the line that if God permits them to lock up someone whom He has so manifestly favoured... well, you can fill in the rest. The guards, on the other hand, feel threatened by it, resorting to taunts of the 'You saved others, why can't you save yourself?' variety (the blasphemy is theirs, not mine). I must admit that when I'm lying awake in the small hours, a cacophony of snoring in my ears and the reek of unwashed bodies in my nose, and it's all too easy to believe that I've taken the wrong path, I too am sustained by the thought that whether God were genuinely working through me or just prepared to let it seem so, He must have considered me worthy.

Despair is a constant danger. Any momentary reassurance about my own plight frees me to brood on that of others. Prisoners' rights are an alien concept here. The guards beat the inmates as a matter of course, wielding their sticks as readily as you or I might wave our arms. One guard, who I suspect was high on drugs destined for the American airbase, cudgelled a man to death for spitting on his shoes. He was fully exonerated at the inquiry, conducted by his fellow officers, which found him to have acted in self-defence. Some of the inmates have committed appalling crimes (although I incline to Benito's view that when asked for mitigating circumstances, they should reply: 'My life'); many more, however, are victims of injustice. This is exacerbated in jail, where they can spend five, ten and even twenty years on remand since there aren't enough judges or even courts to hear their cases. In my bleaker moments I fear that the same may happen to us – no, please ignore that last remark; I'd cross it out only I know it would alarm you.

Benito tells the story, which he swears is true, of a judge determined to prove his impartiality. 'I want you all to know,' he said in his opening statement, 'that the plaintiff has given me 20,000 pesos to bring in a guilty verdict and the defendant has given me 30,000 to bring in an innocent one. I'm therefore handing the defendant back 10,000 pesos to guarantee a fair trial.'

I trust that's made you smile after the gloom of the previous paragraph. Don't worry, the media spotlight (and they allow television cameras into the courtrooms here) will ensure that this is one case where bribery isn't an issue; I only wish it were equally effective in eliminating delays. So far we've made two appearances in nine months. Despite all the arguments presented by our lawyer, the judge ruled that the charge is too serious for him to grant bail. I gather from Hugh that Greg put pressure on the Foreign Office who put pressure on the Philippine government who put pressure on the judge, etc etc, to grant it at least to the two priests. Please assure him that I'm not ungrateful, but both Benito and I are resolved that we should resist any attempt to isolate us from the lay leaders, who would be far more vulnerable if left on their own.

The longer we're held in custody, the clearer it becomes that the charges against us are politically inspired. I myself have earned the undying hatred of the *haciendos* and their allies by insisting that San Isidro was not their private fiefdom. My support for the rights of the tenants and farm workers threatens the landowners' view of themselves as upstanding Christians. My refusal to celebrate a requiem for Quesada, a man whose nominal independence was belied by every meal he ate at their tables, every trip he took on their yachts and, above all, every peso he received from their slush funds, gave them the necessary pretext for action. They argue that my animus towards the man was strong enough to drive me to murder. If so, then surely the sensible plan would have been to celebrate the requiem in order to distract attention from my crime? Or do they consider me an idiot as well as a killer? By their logic any priest who denies a request to hold a service in his church would be motivated by guilt.

There's not a shred of evidence to link me or any of the accused to Quesada's death. The entire prosecution case is circumstantial. Two men claim to have seen my car at the scene of the crime. If they did – which they didn't – then I wasn't in it. A third claims to have seen me waving a rifle on the ridge from which the fatal shots were fired. His wife later told a neighbour that he was threatened with a murder charge himself if he refused to implicate me. When my lawyer tried to subpoena her, he found that she'd disappeared. So how can we place any credence in his testimony?

One of the ostensible reasons for denying me bail is that I cannot corroborate my whereabouts on the night of the murder. 'I'm a priest,' I said, 'whom do you expect to vouch for me between two and six o'clock in the morning?' Consolacion will testify on my behalf, although I had hoped to have spared her. She's a simple woman who's easily intimidated and I fear that her instinctive desire to please may assist the prosecution as much as the defence. If there's any truth in the notion of the sleep of the just (and, as I lie awake in the heart of a creaking prison, I trust that there isn't), then it's to be found in Consolacion. Someone who sleeps through Karajan's recording of Beethoven's Ninth played directly underneath her bedroom would have slept through my slipping out for a midnight rendezvous with my fellow assassins. Any halfway competent lawyer will be able to pick holes in her statement. And what if he asks her whether my bed had been slept in? During restless nights I often choose to sit up in my study or stretch out in the hammock on the porch. Were she to mention that, it'd be bound to sow seeds of doubt.

Having feared that the detention of their priest would tear the parish apart, I'm relieved to find that on the contrary, it appears to have brought it together. The crowds who gather every day at the prison gates have inevitably thinned over time, although the Daughters of St Paul maintain their round-the-clock vigil. Many of the well-wishers bring food, which we're able to distribute to the needier inmates. There are no restrictions on visitors, whether friends, reporters or even, as last week, a party of schoolgirls brought by the Sisters of the Little Flower Convent to hear Benito preach, the only requirement being to pay the guards' fee. Meanwhile, the BCCs, who are spearheading the protest campaign, plan to hold a mass rally next month to mark the first anniversary of our arrest, although it remains to be seen whether it will be licensed.

The international interest in the case seems to have taken the authorities by surprise. Rey Sison, the most methodical of the lay leaders, has kept a list of the sixteen countries that have so far sent either journalists or film crews. To have two priests on remand for murder is unusual enough even in the Philippines, especially when one of them is English and related to a man whom the *Manila Bulletin* described last week as 'a juvenile government minister' – don't tell Greg but I've kept the cutting! Messages of support pour in from around the globe. I've been reunited, at least on paper, with old friends from Ampleforth and Oxford, as well as former pupils from Liverpool with names so unfamiliar that I have to take their memories on trust. I've received sackfuls of letters from strangers, most but not all of them Catholics, offering their encouragement, their prayers and even their cash. Needless to say, some have been less friendly, written in filth that seems doubly gratuitous given the squalor of the jail. We reply to them all, including the hate mail if it comes with an address. I say 'we' because, in view of the volume, the six of us act as a team. I must be the first prisoner in history whose greatest expense is stamps. The Bishop and the Regional make regular appeals for our release, the former being so vocal in his denunciation of our confinement that he has been dubbed the Red Bishop and now travels with a bodyguard as well as a chaplain. Benito and I have received the backing, both public and private, of a gratifying number of our fellow priests. On which note, I'd rather you didn't write to Hendrik. I still respect his work, but our friendship has run its course. Should you wish to get information either to me or about me, then please contact either the Regional or the Embassy, that is when you can't ask Hugh.

I never expected to say so, but there are advantages to having such a well-connected relative. Unlike his father-in-law, who treats my political stance as if it were a deliberate attempt to embarrass him and, hence, the British government, he regards my incarceration with wry amusement, as if I were a child confined to the naughty chair. On his visits he spends as long talking to the governor as he does to me, and I suspect that he finds him more congenial company. Meanwhile, he has been using his influence behind the scenes. Two weeks ago the Regional arrived, jubilantly announcing a deal whereby all the charges against me would be dropped, in exchange for my admission that my car had been stolen and used in the crime. He claimed to have been given similar guarantees for Benito and the lay leaders, who would, however, have to stay in custody a little longer to prevent the authorities from losing face. Call me cynical, but I wouldn't have trusted those guarantees if they'd been signed by Marcos himself. Besides, while the lay leaders remain behind bars, their families are being menaced and tortured. I'll spare you the details, except to say that Felicitas Clemente, Juan's wife, was stripped naked and forced to sit for hours on a block of ice, and Regina Sison, Rey's daughter, was repeatedly raped. Despite their ordeals, they refused to betray either their men or their beliefs. As I explained to the Regional, when my parishioners were showing such fortitude, how could I do anything less?

I've every confidence that all six of us will soon be freed. The combination of international pressure and domestic protest will force even this most obdurate of governments to climb down. Until then, my greatest worry is knowing that you're worrying about me. So you see, you have to keep cheerful for my sake if not for your own. Just writing to you makes me homesick and I promise that as soon as all this is over and the Benguet Six – a name I assure you that none of us relishes – have been released, I shall accept the second, uncompromising, part of the Regional's offer and enjoy an extended holiday at Whitlock.

I miss you more than I can say.

Your loving son,
Julian

Considering the hospital's laxity in other areas, its strict visiting hours baffled Philip. The nurse who gave him news of Dennis was adamant that he would not be allowed on the ward until four, leaving him nothing to do in the meantime but rerun the events of the previous night. Caustic fumes mingled with harrowing screams as he watched Dennis fall to the ground clutching his groin, while Amel, with studied cruelty, raised his champagne glass to each of his three companions in turn. To add to the horror, no one around them stirred, both audience and dancers locked in their private performances.

Shocked and incredulous, Philip pushed past Max, knocking glasses and dishes off the table, and knelt beside Dennis. 'It's all right,' he said, cradling his head. 'You'll be fine; I promise you'll be fine. An ambulance! Somebody call an ambulance!'

The manager, finally roused, rushed over and, betraying no emotion, ordered the three nearest dancers to carry Dennis to the dressing room, before turning to his customers. 'It is nothing,' he said with a forced grin. 'The silly boy has too much heat. He has fainted. Enjoy! Please, enjoy!' The audience took him at his word, accepting the incident as if it had been part of the floorshow. Following the convoy across the stage, Philip looked back at the table, where Max sat stupefied and shaking, Ray covered his face with his fan, and Amel calmly lit a cigar.

Thrusting aside the manager who tried to bar his way, Philip entered the musty dressing room. With every surface piled high with clothes and costumes, kitbags, drink cans, food wrappers, celebrity magazines and what looked like an open maths text book, the three dancers hovered in the doorway, uncertain where to deposit Dennis, until Philip stepped forward and swept all the clutter off a narrow bench.

'Has someone rung for the ambulance?' he asked.

'No, no ambulance!' the manager said.

'What do you mean? We must get him straight to a doctor!' Philip said, only to be struck by a hazy memory of his Boy Scout training. 'Water! We need some water to wash off the acid.'

While Dennis mixed moans with entreaties, of which only the names "Hesus", "Maria" and "Diyos", were intelligible, two of the dancers filled a mop bucket with water and the third soaked a T-shirt to make a sponge. Wrapping a cloth round his fingers, Philip carefully peeled off Dennis's pouch. Dennis shrieked, only to fall silent, along with everyone else, on seeing the butcher's slab of scarred and blistered flesh.

'He is castrated,' one of the dancers said, at which Dennis shrieked louder than ever.

'Nonsense!' Philip said. 'It's just a burn.'

'Scream softly!' the manager said to Dennis, as Max appeared at the door. 'They must not hear you.'

'Oh, your beautiful cock,' Max said, aghast. 'Dennis, your beautiful cock!'

Telling two of the dancers to hold Dennis's arms and praying that his First Aid badge had been merited, Philip dabbed Dennis's skin with the wet T-shirt. With a yell, Dennis tried to kick him away and leap down, but the dancers restrained him. 'I'm sorry; I'm being as gentle as I can,' Philip said, before turning to the manager. 'He needs treatment. We must take him to hospital at once.'

'Go get Papaya,' the manager said to the third dancer. 'Fast!' Dennis's howls grew more plaintive, as Philip doused his wound.

'We should put ointment on it,' Philip said, turning back to the manager. 'Do you have a medicine chest?'

The manager shook his head.

'We have oil for the massages,' one of the dancers said.

Struck by the brutal irony, Philip wanted to echo Dennis's howls. 'Yes, it's better than nothing,' he said, as he grabbed the sticky bottle and gently rubbed the oil on to his penis, scrotum and thighs.

Papaya proved to be more resourceful than any of the men whose ranks she was eager to join, first ringing for a cab to take Dennis to hospital, then answering Philip's request for some loose-fitting clothes by fetching the lead singer's kimono.

'She will kill you,' one of the dancers said.

'She can try,' Papaya replied.

With Papaya's help, Philip raised Dennis to his feet and draped the kimono round his shoulders. 'Do you think you can walk?' he asked Dennis, who nodded, grimaced and tottered a few steps. The barman appeared at the door to inform them that the cab had arrived. 'Round the back! Round the back!' the manager shouted, only to shrink from Philip's withering gaze. With the manager and dancers watching from a distance, and Max trailing helplessly behind, Philip and Papaya dragged Dennis to the cab and laid him across the back seat.

'Perhaps it would be best if you went by yourself?' Max said, after Papaya had returned inside. 'Two Englishmen bringing in a half-naked Filipino boy with a charred crotch might cause comment.'

'Whereas one would be par for the course?' Philip asked scathingly. 'Whatever you suggest.'

'Promise you'll call me as soon as you have news.'

'Of course,' Philip said, sitting beside the unruffled driver as they set off for the nearest hospital. On arrival, they went straight to the emergency room, where the duty doctor refused to give Dennis so much as a painkiller until he was guaranteed payment. Leaving nothing to chance, he directed Philip to the accounts department, where a hare-lipped clerk took an imprint of his credit card in exchange for the requisite deposit slip, which Philip brought back to the doctor, who studied it as though it were an ECG graph before agreeing to proceed. Philip sat in the waiting room, feigning indifference to the resentful glares from people whom Dennis had displaced, until the doctor summoned him and, with Dennis sedated on the bed, proffered his diagnosis.

'The patient has deep partial thickness burns to the penis, scrotum and thighs, which will result in severe scarring. Otherwise, there should be no permanent damage.'

'Thank you so much, doctor. That's a huge relief.'

'He told me that he had spilt the acid on himself.'

'On himself?'

'On himself,' the doctor repeated, as if to set out the boundaries of his concern. 'It is rare to see such lacerations on the tip of the penis. In the normal course of events we would expect them on the base.'

'I see.'

'We will keep him here under observation for a couple of days until the wounds start to heal. We need to catheterise him to ensure that the urethra stays open and, at least initially, put him on a drip to maintain the fluid levels. There is nothing more for you to do here now. Your friend will be taken to the ward and made as comfortable as possible. I suggest that you go home and call us in the morning.'

Philip followed the doctor's advice, returning to the hotel, from where he rang Max. He reported the doctor's prognosis, but for all his insistence that Dennis's injuries were temporary Max focused on the scarring.

'How will he live? He can't dance – not just at the Mr Universe, but anywhere – if he's deformed.'

'Isn't that a bit over the top?'

'People will think he's diseased!'

'Then he'll do something else. It may turn out to be a blessing in disguise.'

'Not for Dennis: he is his cock! And what about me? How will I…? You'll sneer, but he's the only one left who can excite me. Every time he strips off, I'll think of… I'll smell that… I'll never get it up again.' Exhausted and emotional, Philip wondered if he were dreaming. 'That stupid, selfish boy! So greedy, always so greedy! I warned him never to cross the Lims, but would he listen?' Swallowing hard, Philip told Max that he needed to sleep but that he would ring him after breakfast to arrange a trip to the hospital, at which Max equivocated. 'Would you think me terribly wicked if I pass? I'll meet him the moment he comes out. I have such a phobia about hospitals. I was born in one, you see; it's traumatised me for life.'

Feeling Dennis's absence more acutely than he would ever have supposed, Philip booked a cab to take him to the hospital at three. He was anxious to avoid Maribel whom, after considerable agonising, he had rung with the news of her brother. Much to his relief, he had been diverted to voicemail, where he had left a brief message with the name of the hospital and a request that for both their sakes they should space out their visits, his at four and hers at five. By daylight the lobby looked even more chaotic than it had done the night before. A bleeding woman lay slumped in a chair, four young children playing at her feet, while a cleaner swept impassively around them. A family of Indians sat eating a pungent curry beside a giant rubber plant. A well-dressed woman brandished a fistful of forms at a bored receptionist, her clanging bracelets echoing her rage. Having called the lift, which opened with a horror-film creak, Philip made his way up to the third floor, where bed-bound patients lined the corridors as if in the aftermath of a tornado.

After a lengthy search he found Dennis's ward. Eighteen beds were packed as tightly as in a furniture showroom. Identifying Dennis's by the sheet cradle, he squeezed in next to it, narrowly missing a catheter bag full of blood-streaked urine. He laid out his offerings of a T-shirt and shorts, a toothbrush and toothpaste, two bottles of water, two Hershey bars and in a nod to convention, a bunch of grapes, on one side of the bed, and perched gingerly on the other. Flustered by a stray glance at a double amputee opposite, he fixed his gaze on Dennis.

'How are you feeling? Or is that a stupid question?'

'You are kind man,' Dennis replied, after a pause so protracted it looked set to become permanent.

'You don't have to say that,' Philip said, his eyelids pricking.

'Yes, I do not say it before. I am having to say it now.'

'Are you in a lot of pain?'

'Like fire here!' He pointed beneath the sheet cradle. 'All burnt, but still on fire.'

'It'll pass. Every day will be a little better.'

'And then what will it be?'

'Business as usual, I expect,' Philip said to his instant regret. 'The doctor told me that you'd make a complete recovery. You could even go back to the club, if you like.'

'No,' Dennis said fiercely. 'This is bad place. Never!'

'I agree. Maybe now's the time to take the plunge and set up the bakery. If you haven't raised all the cash, you could see if the bank would lend you the balance. How much have you put aside so far?'

'Nothing.'

'But I thought you'd been saving for a couple of years.'

'Is all gone.'

'I see; I'm sorry.'

'I leave this country. I make very much money abroad.'

'In Kuwait?' Philip asked, recalling the swindle that had brought him to Manila.

'No, I go round this world on boat. I am being steward in cabin with many women. They will be happy with Dennis.' The prospect appeared to revive him. 'Then I will come to England and then you will drive me.'

'It's a deal.'

'But first, you will buy me fan, yes? There is no aircon here, but this nurse, she says we can put on our own fan. So you will bring one for me?'

'Of course, but I don't think that they'll keep you here –' Philip broke off at the sight of Maribel, who walked in and threw herself on to Dennis, wetting his cheeks with her tears. He pushed her off in a gesture at once abrupt and tender, before whispering something in Tagalog.

Maribel turned to Philip, her eyes lowered. 'Hello, Mr Philip, sir,' she said, as if reverting to their first encounter. Her arrival caught Philip off guard. He strove to control his emotions, but they were changing too fast.

'I didn't think you'd be coming before five.'

'I am wishing to speak to you, if you are allowing it, sir.'

'Please don't call me sir; we're not in a shop! I can't see what purpose it'll serve, but since you're here you may as well go ahead.'

'If you please, can we be speaking outside? Then we will not be disturbing Dennis.' There could be no surer sign of Dennis's debility than his failure to respond to his name.

'As you wish. I'll be off now, Dennis. I'll call the ward in the morning and if you're still here, I'll bring you that fan,' Philip said. 'Don't worry, I won't keep Maribel more than a minute,' he added, as much for her benefit as for his.

Maribel pressed Dennis's hand and followed Philip out. Unable to find any space in the corridor, they made their way down to the lobby where, to Philip's relief, both the injured woman and the Indian family had moved on, although the bloodstains and the aroma remained.

'How are your stomach cramps?' he asked bitterly, as he swept a layer of crumbs off a chair.

'I am so sorry,' Maribel said in a diffident tone that Philip was determined to resist. 'I said "no"; I said "no" so many times.'

'But then you said "yes".'

'I am loving my brother.'

'I'm pleased to hear it,' Philip replied, remembering a time when she had professed to love him.

'No, you are not understanding. He was in trouble.'

'He's always in trouble.'

'But this was special trouble. He has been owing money when some business that is to make him rich makes him poor. So he steals money from the old man, who is the club owner's father, but this is not enough. So he steals *shabu* and the people find out.'

'What did he expect: that the drug dealers would be as lax about keeping accounts as he is himself?'

'So he asks you for money, but you do not give him this.'

'I'd already given him 3,000 pesos so that he could go home for your sister's funeral. I'm not rich; paying for his treatment here will pretty much wipe out everything I've saved during the past three months.'

'You are the most kind man.'

'So everyone keeps saying.'

'Because this is true.'

'I'm not after praise.'

'I know this is true also. But Dennis is afraid that they will be killing him, so he asks your friend Max.'

'He's not my friend.'

'No, you are right. He is a very bad man. He says that he will give Dennis this money, but only if he will help him. He tells him that there are people who wish for you to stop asking questions about the English saint.'

'What people?'

'I do not know these people. He says it is needed for them to frighten you. He gives Dennis his promise that nothing will hurt you. You are English; you have many friends.' Dennis's sudden concern for his safety seemed highly improbable, but Philip let it pass. 'Dennis tells me I must be playing my part; I must pretend... well, you know this. I do not wish to do it. I do not wish to do it so much. But I am afraid for how they will harm Dennis.'

'They've done a good enough job of that as it is.'

'I do not understand. What job is this?'

'I mean that they harmed him anyway.'

'This is not just for the money; it is a lesson. For Dennis and for all the other boys. But I am asking now if you will ever forgive me.'

'Yes, for what it's worth. In your shoes I might well have done the same. The person I can't forgive is myself.'

'What have you done?'

'I trusted. Goodbye, Maribel.' He stood up and kissed her on the forehead, the stiffness of the gesture belied by the tears in his eyes.

He returned to the hotel and rang Max with an account of Dennis's progress.

'Thank Jessica!' Max said. 'I'll call you right back. First, I promised to ring Ray. He's been worried sick.'

'Then he might have done more than sit there flicking his fan while his son mutilated Dennis.'

'Such as?' Max asked sharply.

'How about exerting some paternal pressure? Aren't the Chinese supposed to respect their elders, or do they have to be dead?'

'No one can put pressure on Amel. He's a law unto himself.'

'So I saw. And it's the law of the jungle! Are we going to let him get away with it?'

'Away with what? Didn't Dennis tell the doctor that he was the one who'd spilt the acid?'

'That's what I mean! The poor guy's terrified.'

'Just like everyone else. Including yours truly.'

'Well, I'm not!'

'So what do you intend to do? Report him to the police? Haven't you had your fill of them by now?' Max asked, unwittingly confirming Philip's suspicions. 'Besides, Amel has them all paid off. Don't suppose that drugs and macho dancers are the sum total of his business interests. Believe me, he has far bigger fish to fry.'

Max's cynicism, along with Amel's crimes and the authorities' collusion, preoccupied Philip all evening. Just as no one in the club had challenged the manager's explanation of Dennis's collapse, so no one in the wider world was prepared to stand up to Amel and his associates. Outraged by their savagery, Philip felt a renewed desire to visit Gerron Casiscas. No matter that he had already sent in his report, which was as vapid as the

THE BREATH OF NIGHT

Church authorities could have wished, he owed it to himself to unravel the final threads in the web of corruption. The Vicar General might well have informants within the prison, but short of arranging to eliminate him as his fellow clerics had Julian – a conjecture that Philip was increasingly disposed to take as a fact – there was nothing he could do. Even so, he realised that he should not venture into the prison alone. Having no idea whether Gerron spoke any English, he rang the one Tagalog speaker he could trust and, to his delight, Benito agreed to accompany him the next day.

'That's fine by me. But do you have authorisation?'

At eleven the next morning Philip met Benito as planned outside New Bilibid Prison. Although built in the 1930s, the white crenellated towers showed a strong Iberian influence, as if justice had remained equated with colonial power for decades after the Spanish were expelled. Philip glanced at Benito to see whether it brought back memories of his own incarceration, but his face gave nothing away. For himself, he felt a new sense of purpose, as though, by entering its walls, he were not only back on the path from which the Vicar General had deflected him, but in some indefinable way both reaching closer to Julian, who had spent a year in just such a jail, and making amends for the blandness of his report.

A guard escorted them to the reception area, where another guard, mopping his brow after every sentence, inspected their passes. Philip handed him the email from the governor's office and Benito an envelope, which he pocketed unopened. After stamping the visitors' wrists, he sent them to a third guard, who conducted a cursory body search and an equally brief examination of the bag of cigarettes, chocolates and fizzy drinks that

Philip had brought for Gerron. He then ushered them down a long corridor lined with a Soviet-style mural of rural life and through a vast yard in which several prisoners were playing basketball. Greeting their shouts and whistles with a friendly wave, Philip felt a twinge of unease at the thought that he was trapped among some of the most dangerous men in the Philippines with only token protection.

Even that was withdrawn when the guard led them to one of the squat concrete blocks around the yard and, after summoning a trusty to unlock the gate, walked away.

'Where's he going?' Philip asked Benito.

'Who knows? The guards never enter the blocks. The prisoners run them themselves through their elected mayors.'

'You mean gang leaders?'

'Exactly. Perfect training for the outside world.'

'But will we be safe?'

'In my experience we're far safer in the hands of the prisoners than the guards,' Benito said grimly. 'We represent their most precious commodity: hope.'

As he gazed at the toothless grins and tattooed biceps of the prisoners who came out to watch them, Philip trusted that Benito was right. 'Hello, I'm Philip. Good to meet you,' he said, affecting a carefree smile. 'No one's speaking,' he whispered to Benito.

'No, as I told you, visitors are precious. Only the host has the right to say if his visitor can be shared.'

In an offer of assistance that brooked no refusal, the trusty grabbed Philip's bag of gifts and led him into the block. Praying that the stamps on his arm would withstand the sweat, he made his way down a corridor, which was even dimmer than the alcove at the Mr Universe, the brightest light coming from the flicker of a television at the far end. Through an open cell door, he glimpsed two men stirring a pot on a paraffin stove, its cloying smell mingling with the faecal stench from a slop bucket. The trusty steered the visitors into a cramped cell containing four bunk beds, lit by a small, heavily barred window. With a commanding gesture he instructed them to sit on the two lower bunks, placed the untouched bag of gifts at Philip's feet and went out.

'What now?'

'We wait. This is how it must be. Remember, it is you who have asked to see him.'

Five minutes later the trusty returned with two prisoners, one thickset and bald, sporting an elaborate tattoo of Christ flanked by a pair of green mambas, as if paradise had been lost and regained on a single torso, and the other pustular and scrawny, with crudely inked signatures on every visible inch of skin and several disappearing ominously under his shorts, turning him into a human plaster cast.

Philip stood up to greet them, banging his head on the upper bunk and prompting the scrawny prisoner to laugh wildly until his companion kicked him in the shin.

'You Philip?' he asked.

'That's right.'

'Me Gerron.'

'Pleased to meet you,' Philip said, shaking his calloused palm. 'And you are?' He smiled at the scrawny prisoner.

'He JJ,' Gerron said. 'He no use. He no speak English. He no speak Filipino.'

'This is my friend – '

'Ricardo,' Benito interposed so fast that Philip wondered if the name were a random choice or held a deeper significance.

'He'll translate, if it's easier for you to speak Tagalog.'

'Easy, yes. Thanking you.'

Philip handed Gerron the bag of gifts, which he scrupulously appraised, finding new notes of appreciation for each cigarette packet and chocolate bar.

'He says that he will be sharing them with his friends in the cell.'

'What about JJ here?'

'I doubt it. It's obvious he's his janitor.'

'Janitor?'

'Prison slang for slave.'

Gerron had registered the term. 'Janitor yes. Me very good to him. Me making money for him. You wish name, yes? Me good price.'

'Is he suggesting what I think he is?' Philip asked Benito.

'Yes,' Benito said, after a brief clarification. 'The normal price is five hundred pesos per tattoo. But for us, he'll do it for two.'

'See, names,' Gerron said, spinning JJ around to reveal the signatures on his back, thighs and calves. 'See, names.' He pulled down JJ's shorts to display his inky buttocks. 'See, names.'

'Enough, thank you,' Philip said, putting up his hand. 'What's the appeal?' he asked Benito. 'Is it the only way left to them to make their mark? It's forbidden to write on walls but permissible on flesh?'

'Names, see. Good price for English.'

'Does the price vary according to length or size or position? Is a buttock cheaper than an elbow or a thigh?'

'Do you really want me to ask?' Benito said.

'No, I want you to ask about Julian.'

'Julian, here?' Gerron said, tracing a line across JJ's cheek.

'No, Father Julian. You wrote to Benito Bertubin that you had evidence of a murder plot against him.' He turned to Benito. 'Translate please.'

Gerron's response was to ignore the question and offer them snacks. Asking Benito to refuse on his behalf, Philip wondered whether Gerron were dragging out the meeting to gain status from his visitors or playing for time because he had nothing to say. At last he sent JJ away and, in a halting exchange, which Benito both conducted and translated, recalled events from twenty years before. He had been sharing a cell in Nueva Ecija jail with one Alvin Japos, who had boasted how he had been recruited by a group of high-ranking priests to kill an English missionary, whom they accused of betraying the Church. When the priests failed either to pay him his fee or to have the charges against him dropped, Alvin had joined an NPA unit active in the jail and later, during a mass breakout, fled to one of their mountain training camps in the Sierra Madre.

Despite his own recent experience of clerical intrigue, Philip recognised that the evidence Gerron presented was thin. 'So the last time he saw him was in this provincial prison in the early nineties?' he asked Benito, who put the question to Gerron.

'No. He claims that he met him three years ago, shortly before he was arrested and sent here. He – Alvin that is, not Gerron – grows onions outside Bongabon, a small town in the east of Nueva Ecija. Presumably, his knowledge of the territory was why the priests chose him for the job. Not – ' he added in an undertone – 'that I believe for one moment they did.'

'But he said that this guy Alvin was a member of the NPA.'

'NPA, yes!' Gerron interjected.

'So how can he be growing onions?' Philip asked, directing his question to a space midway between Benito and Gerron.

'That part's credible enough,' Benito replied. 'You can be a farmer and a member of the NPA, or a doctor and a member of the NPA, or even a priest and a member of the NPA.' He smiled. 'They do not sit around in their uniforms all day, like firemen waiting to put out a fire.'

'But isn't it dangerous? If the government is determined to track them down. The first things I saw at the airport were the Wanted posters for NPA terrorists.'

'These are the leaders and of course it is dangerous for them. But, for the rest, it is quite different. They grow crops in the lowlands alongside the regular farmers, who know when not to ask questions. In some places they even mix with the military, who are willing to turn a blind eye provided peace is maintained.'

'And when it's not?'

'Then the rebels retreat to their camps high in the mountains, which are hard to reach even by foot.'

'It doesn't make sense.'

'Maybe not to a European. Now, do you wish to ask him anything else? I think that he has told us all he knows.'

Having established that he had no more precise address for Alvin than the name of the town, Philip and Benito took their leave of Gerron, who led them out into the compound where several prisoners were sunning themselves. JJ was sitting a few yards apart and, as they waited for the trusty to unlock the gate, Gerron called him over and casually pulled down his lower lip.

'Look!' he said to Philip, pointing at the six blue letters bathed in spit beside a row of broken and decaying teeth. 'My name. Is secret. Look!'

After quitting the prison Philip and Benito headed for the bus that would take them back to the city centre.

'I hope you found what you were looking for,' Benito said.

'Nothing short of a signed confession from the guilty priests could have done that. But it was good to hear his story. It would be even better to hear it at first hand.'

'From Alvin Japos?' Benito asked. Philip nodded. 'To what end?'

'To discover the truth, which is a pretty elusive commodity around here. I've been hovering on the fringes of this conspiracy for too long. It's time to reach the heart.'

'What if it has no heart? Just more and more skins, like one of Japos's onions.'

'It's still worth a try. Do you know how far Bongabon is from here?'

'Not offhand, why? You're not seriously thinking of going there?'

'Why not?'

'And how do you propose to find Japos? There are hundreds of onion growers in the region. It's the onion capital of the Philippines! And if, by some remote chance – '

'Some miracle?'

'You do find him, how will you gain his trust? That is, even supposing you're able to communicate. Or do you have someone else to go there with you to translate?'

'Don't you want to know what the Church is capable of?'

'I was a priest for thirty years; I know what the Church is capable of! I also know what the army is capable of and the NPA is capable of. And, for that matter, what the landscape is capable of. We're talking of very rough and inhospitable terrain.'

'Then why did the Bishop allow Julian to go on retreat there? Given the terrorist activity, it's the perfect place to commit a murder and escape scot-free. But you're right,' he said, afraid that Benito would come up with further objections. 'It's impractical and pointless. I only have three more days in Manila. I should lounge by the pool and work on my tan.'

After thanking Benito for his help, Philip returned to the hotel, where he asked the receptionist to make arrangements for his immediate departure to Bongabon. As he went up to his room to prepare, he had a strong premonition that however slim his chances might be of meeting Alvin, he would nevertheless learn something of consequence about Julian.

'You've been here too long,' he said, as he stared at himself in the mirror. 'Time to go home for a shot of English rationalism.'

The receptionist rang to tell him that there was a four o'clock bus from the Victory terminal in Cubao to Cabanatuan City, from where it was a thirty minute jeepney ride to Bongabon. The only hotels in the district were in Cabanatuan although, she added primly, they were not necessarily ones that she would recommend. With no time to lose, Philip asked her to book him a room at whichever was the most central. Explaining that he would return to Manila on Tuesday, he appealed for her discretion should anyone enquire about his whereabouts, to be met with an affronted: 'We never give out personal information on any of our guests, sir'. Duly admonished, he took a cab to Cubao and, in what he saw as a propitious sign, boarded the bus just as it was about to pull out. He occupied the three-hour journey by working on the preface to his novel, in which his protagonist, Philip (to be renamed in a later draft), was sent out to the Philippines. Arriving in Cabanatuan, he drove through the twilit streets to the La Panilla Hotel which, for all the receptionist's qualms, turned out to be clean, comfortable and fully air-conditioned. After a quick shower and a modest dinner, he fell exhausted into bed.

The downpour the next morning was so heavy that he feared the road to Bongabon would be impassable, but the manageress, as helpful as she was attractive, not only assured him that it would remain open but escorted him to the jeepney. For once he was grateful for the crush of passengers, whose composure heartened him as they drove through a landscape both mountainous and submerged. Alighting in the town square, he sheltered under the awning of a pawnshop, while three tricycles, oblivious to the rain, vied for his custom. Selecting the most sturdy, he instructed the driver to take him to the Town Hall. His words meeting nothing but a grizzled smile, he tried "City Hall", "Municipal Headquarters", "Mayor's Office" and "Town Council" in quick succession, all to no avail. He was about to give up when, in desperation, he threw out "Tax", at which the smile broadened and the driver set off, juddering over ruts and puddles, to deposit Philip outside a long green building, fronted by a row of palms so badly buckled by the storm that they seemed to be clinging to each other for support.

Shaking himself like a dog, he made his way inside, where he spoke to three officials whose grasp of English seemed to stop at the recognition of that word, before coming to a bespectacled young man, who identified himself, felicitously, as Noah.

'How am I best able to help you, sir?' he asked.

'I'm trying to contact someone who lives in your municipality: Alvin Japos.'

'Why, if I may ask this question, are you wishing to contact this person?'

'I was at university with his sister. We became great friends and then lost touch. You know how it is.' Noah, who looked as though he could recite the addresses, including postcodes, of every one of his friends, did not reply. 'She often mentioned her brother. He grows onions. They were very close.'

'And the sister of this onion grower has been going to university in England?' Noah asked incredulously.

'She was a post-graduate. On a special scholarship – I think it was from the UN. She was very bright.'

Making no reply, Noah typed a sentence into his computer. A moment later he looked up with such a furrowed brow that Philip was afraid there might be a special administrative code for suspected members of the NPA.

'Why are you wishing to see this man?'

'I told you, he's my friend's brother.'

'It cannot be the same person. This man is fifty-seven years. He has his children and grandchildren living in the same house with him.'

'Maybe she made a mistake?' Philip said, floundering. 'Do Filipinos easily confuse the English for "uncle" and "brother"?'

'Not the ones who are given special scholarships from the UN,' Noah replied coldly.

'Then the mistake must be mine. Now I think of it, I'm sure she said "uncle". Why did I say "brother"? Must be because I have two brothers of my own. If you'll give me his address, I can go and see.'

Noah's reluctance to comply was compounded by Philip's inability to produce his passport. In the nick of time he thought to show him a crumpled letter from the Bishop of Baguio, adding that it was proof not just of his identity but of his good faith. Noah studied the letter, even holding it up to the light as if inspecting a watermark, before declaring that he would consult his superiors and give Philip an answer the next morning.

'But that's no use! I have to go back to Manila tomorrow. Besides, surely his address is on the electoral roll? It's in the public domain, if only I knew where to look.'

'Very well,' Noah said, relenting. 'If you wish to come back after lunchtime, I will try to find out for you then.'

'That's really kind. Thank you. But how about I wait in the corridor? It's far too wet to walk around town. Then, if you have your answer sooner, I'll be on hand.'

The presence of a bedraggled Englishman, beaming broadly at everyone who passed, concentrated the bureaucratic mind and an hour later Noah came out to say that he had not only been authorised to give Philip the address but told to take him there in person.

'That's very kind,' Philip said, weighing his antipathy to the man against the expediency of his offer, 'but there's really no need. I can get a cab.'

'This is not Manila.'

'Then a tricycle. I don't want to put you to any trouble.'

'It is not trouble; this is what I have been told.'

'Well, so long as you're sure.'

To his surprise, Noah led him to a small motorcycle and, neither putting on a helmet nor offering one to his passenger, told Philip to sit behind him before setting off. Philip felt as if he had stepped into a late Turner landscape, as the familiar shapes of buildings and trees and fields and mountains all dissolved in a shimmering haze. To his relief, Noah kept on course, even when the unpaved road turned into a sea of mud. All at once he screeched to a halt.

'Now you must go on alone.'

'What?' Philip asked. 'You can't be serious!'

'The bike will not proceed any more. It is too dangerous. You must go on your feet.'

'But where is it? I've no idea where we are.'

'The farm is only a few hundred metres up this road,' Noah said with a gesture that disappeared into the mist.

'And how will I get back? I'll be trapped.'

'This man whom you wish to see so much, he will bring you.'

'What if I've made a mistake?'

'Then you have made a mistake.'

Without another word, Noah laboriously turned his bike

round and headed back into town, leaving Philip feeling more alone than at any time since his arrival in the Philippines. Shocked by Noah's negligence, he wondered whether he had taken against something he said or simply harboured a blanket hatred of the English. He sniffed and shuddered, uncertain how much of the moisture in his eyes and nose came from himself and how much from the atmosphere. Trying not to picture all the half-drowned reptiles and rodents that might be swept along the tide and up his trouser legs, he took several squelchy steps forwards. Suddenly, he collided with something that he took first for a gatepost and then for a scarecrow, until it pointed a rifle at his neck.

'Don't shoot,' he screamed, 'I'm English!'

Two more figures emerged from the mist, one carrying a rifle and the other, who was a head taller than his companions, unarmed. Refusing to believe that he was the victim of a second ambush or that the Vicar General's writ would extend so far, Philip assumed that he must be imagining them – the monsoon equivalent of a desert mirage – but the cold steel on his carotid artery felt all too real.

'Who are you?' he shouted, as the tall figure moved to within a foot of him and removed the scarf that muffled his face. Reason disappeared as Philip stared at the man who had haunted his imagination for so long.

'No, it isn't possible,' he said, tumbling backwards. 'Not you!'

Twelve

Dear Greg,

I'm sorry for the delay in replying, but your letter reached me by a roundabout route. I've left Sariaya and am staying in a small hut in the Sierra Madre, a mountain range in the north-east of the province. It's vast and spectacular and sparsely populated and pure. The hermit in me has come into its own. It's the perfect place to reflect and pray and try to sort out all the clutter and confusion in my head. Nanny P would have talked of blowing away the cobwebs, but that's far too gentle an image for the despair that's gripped me ever since my return to the Philippines. I can think of nowhere more conducive to clarity of thought than here – and not just on account of its beauty. There's a reason that Moses and Elijah and Jesus all went up into the mountains to see the face of God.

I trust that by the time you read this your fears will have been allayed and Mother be fully recovered. Isn't a heart murmur a common effect of ageing? Something to do with thickening valves? Granted I'm no expert, but to my ears the phrase itself sounds reassuring. After all, it's not a heart shriek or a heart roar. I'm touched to know that she's asked for me and in the past I'd have done everything I could to oblige, but I think you'll agree that I've earned the right to be sceptical. My diagnosis – and, I repeat, I'm no expert – is that with Father dead and nurses now looking after Cora, she has too much time on her hands. She has forgotten how to express her own needs – that's if she ever knew – and her only recourse is to be ill.

I shall write to her, reaffirming my promise to attend her eightieth next March and explaining that I won't be able to make it before then. I think we should leave it at that, don't you? You're my brother and I love you, but I find it hard to forgive the subterfuge by which you lured me back last time. Without your claim that Mother was at death's door and I must return at once to have any hope of seeing her, I should never have done a deal with the Philippine government. Besides, I'd have been more convinced by your talk of a dramatic recovery if I'd seen the slightest indication that she had been ill. I suppose I should be grateful for your bid to secure my release. But at what a cost! I accepted a pardon, Greg. A pardon is not an acquittal. A pardon comes courtesy of the President; it's a token of his clemency, not my innocence. Besides which, it offers no protection to those who don't have British passports, let alone brothers in high places. Benito, thank the Lord, is safe. The Bishop gave him leave to go to Negros; but of the four lay leaders only Rey Sison has resumed a normal life. Julius Morales, together with his wife and three children, were killed in a blaze, which was officially blamed on a stray firecracker; Rodel Jimenez had both his tongue and his testicles cut off by a group of vigilantes (presumably to stop him either spreading or spawning rebellion); Juan Clemente was hacked to death by Quesada's twelve-year-old son, who was then arrested by members of his father's old unit, from whom he escaped on the way to jail. Despite an extensive search he has yet to be found.

I trust that putting inverted commas around escaped would be superfluous.

My return has not been painless. When the Aquino government finally restored my visa and the Regional agreed to take me back, his one stipulation was that I shouldn't expect to be reinstated in San Isidro. Hard as that was, I was bound to obey. Besides, the parish has long since had a new priest, Father Marlon Davidas, the son of the Arriola *encargado*, so it's safe to assume that normal service, and services, have been resumed: the fiesta is back in the hands of the *haciendos*, whose daughters will once again dress the *santos*, while they dispense largesse to a deferential crowd. The Regional placed no bar, however, on my visiting the parish and I took the first opportunity to go up there. Wherever I went, I was greeted with such warmth, such a mixture of tears and smiles, that only someone who knew the people as well as I did could detect the hidden resentment: the ubiquitous, unspoken accusation that I'd abandoned them in order to save my own skin. 'How is your mother, Father?' Felicitas Clemente asked, when I called on her to offer my condolences. 'She's very well,' I said, 'remarkable, really, for a woman of seventy-eight.' She looked at me through glazed eyes. 'That's good,' she replied. 'Juan was fifty-five.'

I owe you an apology. In the past I accused you of wilfully ignoring the iniquities of the Marcos government; I've seen for myself how hard it is to obtain a true picture of a country from the outside. During my two years at St Columba's, when I sat in the common room poring over every newspaper report from the Philippines, I was swept up on a tide of false optimism. It was as though I, along with people all over the world – not to mention the Filipinos themselves – had invested so much faith in regime change that we refused to acknowledge how little had been achieved. I was barely off the plane – in fact, talking to the taxi driver on the way from the airport – before I learnt how the elation of the EDSA revolution had evaporated. True, we have a new president: a shy, bespectacled woman whose very humility promises hope, but the same powers are lined up behind her. American soldiers strut through the streets; American advisers occupy the ministries; American dollars fill the banks. When Secretary of State Schultz came to Manila two years ago to offer aid, he had a Cory Aquino doll pinned to his lapel. Could he have made their relationship any clearer?

Aquino has not disappointed her US masters. Despite a huge balance of payments deficit, she has promised to honour all Marcos's overseas contracts, quite literally putting returns to foreign investors before food for the poor. Her much vaunted election pledge to break up the great estates and redistribute the land to the tenant farmers has been undermined by a rigged assessment process. Meanwhile, such land as has been transferred has plunged its new owners into even worse debt, since its value has increased, making them liable to capital gains tax, which they can't afford to pay. So what do they do? Sell it back to the old owners at a discount. And who has been a major beneficiary of this chicanery? You've guessed it! One C. Aquino, whose family owns some of the country's largest estates.

Just as the *haciendos* have held on to their land, so the politicians have held on to their jobs. The most notorious Marcos ministers have been removed, but by and large the faces in both the Senate and the House of Representatives remain identical. The army has been granted immunity for all its crimes during the State of Emergency – and, believe me, they were legion. At the same time church leaders, trade unionists and human rights workers still regularly disappear. Am I alone in seeing a parallel with post-war Germany, where the US and its allies kept hundreds of former Nazis in power in order to counter the Soviet threat? I can't help wondering if, here too, a new generation of activists will rise up to fight the corruption. If so, will they carry the country with them, or will their protest degenerate, as in Germany, into random, self-defeating violence?

So, there you have a taste of the many questions that preoccupy me as I sit, both literally and figuratively, above the fray. The Bishop has given me indefinite leave and since I've forged fewer bonds in the nine months I've been in Sariaya than I did in my first nine days in San Isidro, I feel no guilt at abandoning my flock. I trust that by the next time I write I'll have found at least some of the answers. Meanwhile, should you need to contact me, please do so care of the Society's house in Manila. I'll be sure to keep them informed of my whereabouts.

With every blessing to you and Alice,

Your loving brother,
Julian

Colours so vivid and images so sharp flooded his vision that Philip felt as if he had had a bandage removed after surgery, rather than a hood pulled off after the long climb to the camp. The mountains were carpeted in more varied shades of green than he had seen even in a Rousseau jungle. Two giant butterflies fluttered past: one an iridescent blue with yellow and white speckles; the other striped red and purple and bordered in black, like a stained-glass window. Overhead, two birds with crimson breasts and turquoise tails soared high, either courting or fighting. The view was so resplendent that for a moment he forgot that his ankles had been lashed by creepers and scratched by thorns, his arms and legs devoured by mosquitoes, his shoulders wrenched by unceremonious hands, and his feet reduced to bloody and suppurating blisters by the six-day hike.

Eight bamboo and cogon-grass huts were dotted about the clearing, the kind of ramshackle structures he had passed on the road to Cauayan with a there-but-for-the-grace-of-God sigh (he did not want to think of God for the moment). Felix and Jayson, his abductors, led him to the one that had been assigned to him. It stood a short distance from the others, and its heavy lock and musty smell suggested it had served a similar purpose before. Inside, he was able to make out a blanket and pillow, a pitcher of water with a palm-leaf cover (a token of concern that he wished had extended to a mat for the roach-infested floor), a coconut-shell cup, and a rusty slop bucket, which set the seal on his privations. The two men went out, locking the door and plunging the room into darkness, which was slowly lifted by light filtering through the cracks in the bamboo. He took it as a sign of hope, until a ray fell on a red-and-black beetle with inch-long feelers crawling towards his foot.

The following morning Felix and Jayson introduced him to the remaining seven members of the platoon: Dante, Lester, Juriz, Rommel, Irene, Allen and Nina. "Platoon" was an odd word to apply to a group who, deprived of their guns, would resemble a commune of ageing hippies, but Philip's perilous position forced him to take them at their own estimate. All appeared friendly, apart from Nina, who stood out as much on account of her permanent scowl as of the colour of her skin. Later in the day he learnt from Irene that Nina's mother had been a prostitute in Olongapo City, working in a street that catered exclusively for black servicemen. Doubly stigmatised by having a mixed-race child, she had pimped her between the ages of five and fifteen, when Nina had escaped to join the NPA, who taught her to read and write and channel her hatred. 'There are very many girls like this,' Irene said, her flat tones at odds with her blazing eyes. 'The daughters of American fathers who must survive by sleeping with American sons.'

Philip remained perplexed by Julian's disappearance. Having been hooded throughout the gruelling journey (a precaution which, given the vastness of the terrain and the inaccessibility of the trail, seemed more symbolic than real), he had been sensitive to every sound: leaves rustling; birds singing; insects humming; frogs croaking; cicadas chirping; monkeys howling; not to mention the murmurs and hisses that were all the more menacing for being mysterious. On the first day there had been three voices and sets of footsteps and then, without warning, one had vanished, and neither Felix nor Jayson, whom he knew simply as the softly-spoken and the heavy-handed man, would say where he had gone.

While discussion of Julian remained off-limits, the group gradually opened up to Philip, so much so that he wondered whether, despite the lock on his door, he might be their first hostage. After two days they allowed him to sit outside his hut, and after two more they unbound his hands and feet, enabling him to roam freely around the camp. That freedom, however, was severely restricted. The walls might be wider and the ceilings higher, but he felt as much a prisoner as Gerron in Bilibid or Julian in Baguio. The tortuous path through the trees, the treacherous bogs and briars, the poisonous frogs and snakes were as effective constraints as the toughest iron bars. Acutely aware that his life was in his captors' hands, he set about winning them over, treading a fine line between curiosity and ingratiation as he familiarised himself with their daily routines: the cooking which, for all their talk of equality, was left to the two women; the care of the chickens and goats, whose meagre yield had been declared counter-revolutionary; the long ideological debates which, either as a point of principle or else to exclude him, were conducted in Tagalog.

Despite their apparent friendliness, none of his captors ever approached him unarmed. Indeed, for a camp lacking so many basic facilities, it was remarkably well stocked with weapons. The morning after his arrival he had woken to the sound of gunfire which, with his heart pounding as loudly as the shots, he had taken for an attempt to rescue him until Irene, in her first display of goodwill, had come to explain that they were trying out a new batch of rifles that Felix and Jayson had brought back.

'Where do they get them?' Philip asked. Irene cast him a suspicious glance, which she quickly relaxed, showing either that she trusted him or, more ominously, that it made no difference since he would not live to tell the tale.

'They are coming from the local military.'

'You mean you steal them from their bases?'

'No, we buy them with cash.'

'Now I'm really confused!'

'But it is easy! The government is not paying the soldiers enough wages for them to live. So they sell us their weapons – like this M16 gun.' She held out the rifle for him to inspect the way his mother might have held out a freshly baked cake. 'For 20,000 pesos. They tell their chief that it was lost and buy a new one for 8,000 pesos. Then they can keep the difference.'

'But surely the officers must be wise to it?'

'Of course. They are the ones who are selling us the ammunition. Five pesos a round. They send – how do you say? – a middleman, with a military escorting.'

'So they sell you the bullets that you'll be firing at them?'

'They are making the judgement that we will not be firing at them. Or, if we do, that they have more bullets than we do.'

'It's insanity.'

'Of course. This is capitalism. This is what we are fighting against.'

For all his aversion to their methods, Philip felt considerable sympathy for the group's green agenda and would have felt even more had it not led directly to his present plight. The NPA was spearheading the resistance to the Laiban Dam, a massive engineering project, which entailed diverting two rivers, destroying eight villages and displacing thousands of tribespeople, in order to build a reservoir to relieve the water shortage in Manila. The project had met with widespread opposition, and the government sent in the army both to intimidate the protesters and to protect the site. Alongside it came a host of US advisers to safeguard the international investment. Noah, a local activist, had taken Philip for just such a man. Under the guise of consulting his superiors, he had alerted Felix who, suspecting that Philip's arrival marked the start of a covert offensive, had both arranged for his abduction and instructed the platoon to move their command centre back up to the mountains.

Philip, convinced that even the most inept American adviser would have devised a more successful cover story, had the dubious consolation of knowing that he was the victim of mistaken identity. Whereas her comrades were full of chagrin at the confusion, Nina clearly regarded it as his own fault. 'You are lucky to be still living,' she said. 'In my mind we should have executed you on the spot. Now we must bring you here and go with all the cost of feeding you.' The Philip who was acting in the film version of his kidnap – the one that Hollywood would be hiring him both to write and star in on his release – retorted boldly that he would be happy to indemnify them for any expense, although he doubted that the squid flakes, dried sea cucumbers and rice they had served him for the past three days would amount to more than a few pesos; but the Philip who was in her custody, disorientated, panic-stricken and struggling to gain the confidence of his captors without revealing his hand, said only that he trusted the problem would be quickly resolved.

That prospect came sooner than expected when, later that afternoon, two weeks after his capture and eight days since his arrival in the camp, Felix walked into the glade where Philip was busy writing and told him, with a regret that sounded genuine, he would once again have to be blindfolded and bound.

'Please, no!' Philip said, eyeing the vegetation for somewhere to hide. 'I promise that I'll speak up for you. I'll issue a statement saying that I joined the NPA of my own accord.'

'Why is this?'

'I can help with liaison and translation work. Don't kill me, please!'

'No one wishes to kill you,' Felix said, looking both hurt and bewildered. 'But we are having this meeting to talk over your fate – no, this is the wrong word, I mean your future. This is not just a matter for us to decide on our own. We have representative members of the four other platoons in our company who are coming here for this talk. It is safer – safer for you – if you see no more than you need.'

The meeting took place in the central clearing. Philip, who was permitted to observe (a concession that struck him as hollow, given that he was wearing a hood and they were talking Tagalog), sat at the back, trying to gauge the mood from the timbre of the voices. After a lengthy discussion – around two hours, to judge by the chill in the air and the tingling in his legs – the meeting seemed to break up. Shortly afterwards Irene approached, removed his hood and ropes, and offered him a scoop of water. When he had finished, she squatted beside him and described the proceedings.

'There are many different views. There are always many different views, so you must not worry. Some say that it is our mistake that we have captured you, and so we must take you back to the lowlands and set you free.'

'That sounds fair.'

'But it is not possible. We do not have the people or the time. On top of that, it would not be safe. Since you have been disappearing the army has been sent to look for you.'

'Really?' Philip asked, trying not to betray his excitement.

'Many of our comrades have had to escape into the mountains. Your capture gives the government the reason it is needing to massacre us all, while the world will look on and clap.'

'So what about the other views?' Philip asked in growing alarm.

'Some say that we should take you into the forest and let you find your way down by yourself.'

'But how?' Philip asked, now more afraid of liberty than of confinement. 'It took us six days to climb up here! We had to wade across a river! And take paths that seemed to open and close around us like something in a horror film. And how would I survive the nights? You might as well shoot me now and be done with it!'

'It is true that there were some who thought that this would be the best solution.'

'You mean they want to kill me?'

'They are in a minority.'

'How big a minority?'

'We are a democratic organisation. Whether it is a one or it is many, it is the majority that decides.'

'And what has it decided this time?'

'That we are to keep you here and to demand a ransom.'

'A ransom? How much?'

'Five million.'

'That much?'

'Pesos.'

'Of course.' Philip adjusted the price tag with a mixture of disappointment and relief.

'It has not been your intention, but you have brought us many difficulties. You have made us use up our small resources; we have given the enemy a clear view of where we are. It is only right that someone must pay.'

'But who? My parents don't have much money. And the British government has a strict policy of never dealing with foreign terror – freedom fighters.'

'The demand is being made to the people who sent you here. You have shown their names in a letter in Bongabon.'

'Yes, of course,' Philip said, berating himself for having left it with Noah.

'According to one of our comrades, they are rich. Much of their money comes from gold stolen from the Filipino people.'

'Which comrade was that? It must be Julian! I didn't know he was here!'

'I cannot discuss this with you.'

'But I know that he's one of you; I saw him with Felix and Jayson when they captured me. Unless your legends of wood-land spirits are true.' Irene laughed. 'No, I thought not. So why won't he meet me? I've followed him halfway across the world. The least he can do is speak to me.'

'He is a busy man. He is on the political section of the General Staff. He has responsibility for strategic planning, as well as rev-olutionary education and training.'

'Revolutionary training? Julian? Father Julian?'

'He is Ka Julian now,' Irene said severely.

'You'd think he'd want to see me, if only out of curiosity. We have a family connection. I was engaged to his niece.'

'His niece?'

'I mean his great-niece. I'm so muddled. And miserable and frightened. I try to bluff it out, but to tell you the truth I'm ter-rified. We're sitting here chatting like two friends. Not that we aren't friends. But you're the one holding the gun.'

'Do not give it another thought. It is just a precaution.'

'Which means that one day it may be used. Even that threat would be bearable if only Julian would acknowledge that I exist.'

'I understand. I promise nothing, but I will speak to him. He is now in a camp in Bicol province.'

'So he didn't come here this afternoon?'

'It is a great distance away, but I will send a message to him. Until then you must be brave and not be unhappy. I am sure that when the people have received our demands they will waste no time in paying them. Soon you will again be free.'

Irene's confidence proved to be misplaced. Ever since they had untied his hands, Philip had notched the days of his captivity on the mossy trunk of a giant laurel, at first as a straightforward record, but latterly as if it held the key to his survival. As the weeks went by with relentless monotony, he devised complex strategies to ensure that he was calculating correctly, equally afraid of missing a day as of including it twice. Boredom appeared to be as much a part of his captors' lives as his own. Confined to the camp by the pebble-like rain, with nothing but a shortwave radio and some mildewed, broken-backed volumes of political theory to divert them, they passed the time smoking, drinking and playing cards, as mindlessly as the masses they were seeking to liberate. Philip, at least, was able to work on his novel, sitting for hours on end in the doorway of his hut, filling reams of NPA graph paper. While the rest of the platoon viewed his writing with genial indifference, Nina was as hostile as she was to any manifestation of an inner life.

'This is paper for military purposes. Rommel has no right to be giving it to you. When this book is finished it will belong to the NPA.'

'No way!' Philip said, his authorial assurance emboldening him. 'Although, if you are lucky, I may give you a share of my royalties.'

'You English are sick. You care for nothing but money. You even call it after your kings and queens.'

Unlike his fellow writers, whom he envisaged taking regular breaks to make coffee, read the papers and ring friends, Philip found his only diversion was to visit the goats. Watching them tethered in their pen, he felt a rush of sympathy, which he knew to be little more than self-pity. That was confirmed by his readiness to eat the goat-and-torron-root stew, which was served up to celebrate Dante's and Allen's successful mission to 'disable' an illegal wood-processing plant in Rizal. The platoon was in higher spirits than at any time since his arrival, bolstered by a copious intake of *tuba*, a bitter but intoxicating drink brewed from coconut sap. Philip knew better than to shatter the mood with an awkward – possibly dangerous – question; nevertheless he longed to know whether anyone had been hurt in the blast, concerned as much for the manager and security guards as for the workers: men with no knowledge of the history and function of the forest but who, when faced with the need to feed their families, would readily have turned the most venerable tree into plywood.

His scruples, numbed by the *tuba*, were destroyed when Rommel handed him the strongest spliff he had ever smoked. He felt a surge of love for his captors, whom he was sure that he now saw in their true light: not the ruthless killers of government propaganda but selfless eco-warriors. Their overriding concern was to preserve the bounty of nature which, with rare generosity, they were willing to share with him.

He awoke in the early hours, to find himself lying alone by the ashes of the fire, caught in the primordial gaze of a gecko. Staggering to his feet, he dragged himself to his hut which, while neither warm nor cosy, at least offered a measure of protection against the dark. The next morning he detected a greater reserve in the platoon's treatment of him. He wondered whether he had offended them while he was stoned by singing the 'Star-Spangled Banner' or uttering some other blasphemy. Finally, he plucked up courage to ask Irene, trusting that she, if anyone, would forgive him. After assuring him of his innocence, she explained that they had just heard news that Hugh Olliphant had rejected their ransom demands.

'Surely he's still willing to negotiate?' Philip asked.

'But he is not willing to pay any cash. He says that for this to happen, he will be putting at risk all the managers in his mines in the Cordilleras.'

'Can't you find a formula that allows him to deny it publicly but pay it just the same? Or is that against your principles?'

'We have only one principle: to make the revolution.'

Philip wondered how much Max had told Hugh about the tenor of his investigations. Even in his current paranoia – compounded by the effects of last night's dope – he refused to believe that either man had had a hand in his kidnap. Nevertheless, it was clear that having filed his report he was expendable. 'What happens if Hugh sticks to his guns... I mean digs in his heels?' he said swiftly.

'I am sure he will be seeing sense soon.'

'But what if he won't? Do you have a plan B? It's all very well for Allen and Dante; they've been away for two weeks. But I can feel the rest of you growing edgy.'

'You must not worry about us. We are soldiers. We are used to this waiting. And I am sure that in England there will be many people who will pay for having you back.'

'Of course! They'll be queuing round the block at the Philippine Embassy!' Philip said, feeling a failure even as a hostage.

'Why must you have come here?' Irene asked sadly.

'I've told you before; I was sent to assist, to monitor, to galvanise (I no longer know myself) the official investigation into Julian's sainthood.'

'No, I am not speaking of why you have come to the Philippines, but why you have come to the Sierra Madre. Why must you have put your trust in Alvin Japos?'

'I'd had my own clash with the Church and I was looking for any evidence, however slight, that Julian might have had one too. I realise now that I wasn't thinking straight.'

'You can never believe any words that this man is saying.'

'Who, Japos?'

'Yes. You must remember that he is a criminal. We have used him only in actions in which criminals must be used.'

'Such as?' he asked, but she did not choose to elaborate. 'So why should he concoct such an elaborate story?'

'He is a small man. Such men wish to make themselves bigger. And who knows? There may have been a plot like this, but it has not worked out.'

'To think that a casual remark should have led to all this!'

'I am sorry for you. You must be finding the life here hard. And now there is bad news to add to the pain.'

'There's one compensation, I suppose; the writing's going great guns,' Philip said, ruing another inopportune image. 'Coming here has given an unexpected boost to my novel. I've had so much time on my hands that I might even finish it before I return home.'

'Then you will have to send us a book and we will read it in turns.'

'I can hardly put "somewhere in the Sierra Madre" on the package.'

'This is true,' Irene said, walking away. 'Then you must tell us the story, so that we can read it in our heads.'

After more than four months in the camp and nearly five hundred pages of his novel, Philip gave up the daily tally of his captivity. He could no longer listen to Irene and her comrades extolling the spirit of the forest without feeling as brutish as one of the prisoners who had tattooed their names on JJ's skin. Besides, it felt increasingly irrelevant. The notches, now well into three figures, were no longer his primary timescale. Although he woke up every morning in the mountains, he spent the rest of the day in Manila, San Isidro, Pampanga or Cauayan, with Maribel, Max and Dennis; his imagination had become more real to him than his life. His captors remarked incredulously on his good humour, but it was no act. 'The healing power of art', which had hitherto struck him as an empty phrase, coined by people with neither the talent nor the discipline to be doctors, had taken on new meaning. Not the dirt or the lice or the rain or the cold or the unchanging diet or the primitive sanitation could dampen his enthusiasm for his work. Suspecting that confinement had freed his creativity, he even worried that a precipitate ransom or rescue might stifle his inspiration. He wondered whether his obsession, bordering on mania, were the mark of a true artist, or whether he had absorbed the fanaticism of the platoon.

So it was with mixed feelings that he greeted Rommel's announcement that Julian, who had been in Bicol throughout his detention, was coming to the camp on official business. After months of longing for just such a visit, Philip felt threatened. The Julian whom he had read about, talked about and written about had attained such near-mythic status that he was convinced the man himself must be a disappointment. To calm his nerves, he left his hut on the morning of Julian's arrival, slipping into a secluded clearing where he sheltered beneath his favourite tree, its huge trunk crowned by an umbrella-like canopy of leaves, with a sheet of moss hanging from one of its lower boughs. He was perched on its buttress of roots, studying the mosaic of foliage, when he was roused by a discreet but emphatic cough.

'I trust that I'm not disturbing you.'

'Hardly!' Philip replied with an unexpected burst of resentment. 'You're the reason I'm here.'

'Not at my behest, I assure you. Shall we be very English and shake hands?'

'Of course.' As he stood to face Julian, Philip was struck by a series of anomalies. He walked with a stick (which looked to have been freshly stripped from a laurel branch), but his grip was firm. His shoulders were stooped, but his spine was straight and his stomach taut. His pewter hair was thick, but his skin was blotchy with unshaven patches on his cheeks and chin. A milky film covered his eyes.

'Julian Tremayne, I presume.'

'That sounds rehearsed.'

'Only since yesterday, when they told me you were finally coming. I thought I'd got as close to you as I ever would when I visited your tomb.'

'Ah, there you have the advantage of me.'

'That's not the way it looks from where I'm standing. *Requiescat in Pace*, according to the inscription.'

'I apologise if you're here under false pretences.'

'That doesn't begin to describe it.'

'I'm a little confused as to why you're here at all. My comrades informed me that you were sent out by my niece and her husband. Do you work for Hugh?'

'I was engaged to their daughter.'

'Really?' Julian smiled shyly. 'I christened her, if it's the same one, when I was last in England.'

'She had no sister.'

'Then it is. How idiotic of me! I forget her name.'

'Julia. She was named after you.'

'Oh, yes.' He looked wretched. 'That must be why I've forgotten. But you speak as if the engagement's over.'

'She died.'

'No. How terrible! I'm so sorry. But how? She was young. She can't have been – '

'Twenty-three.'

'I'm so sorry.'

'And I should also tell you that her brother, Greg, died at the same time. There was a car crash.'

'Poor Isabel! My poor dear Isabel! She so longed for children. I can't begin... Are there any other boys?'

'No.'

'This is one time when I feel truly dead. When there's nothing I can say or do to comfort her: when I can't even write.'

'Believe me, you've brought her more comfort than a thousand letters of condolence. The only thing that she lives for now is to see you canonised. The one way she can leave her mark. A kind of sanctity by association.'

'That's sad.'

'Under the circumstances I'd have to agree. She was so frustrated with the pace of the episcopal investigation that she sent me out here to speed things up.'

'She hasn't changed. Even as a girl she was always bubbling with enthusiasm for her latest cause.'

'But at least then they had some value: animal welfare and the like.'

'She discussed them with you?'

'I read your letters. I'm sorry; I thought you were dead.'

'An easy mistake.'

'I would never have presumed if I'd known the truth.'

'Do you mind if we walk a little? My back tends to seize up if I stand still for too long.'

'Not at all. Just a second.' Philip rubbed his arms and legs with the crushed leaves that Irene had given him. 'Once bitten...'

'Akapulko leaves. I'm impressed. You're becoming a true man of the forest.'

'The mosquitoes don't think so. They make a beeline for me – if that's not a contradiction in terms.'

'Me too! My friends used to claim it was poetic justice. Nature's revenge on Caucasians. Ready?'

'Sure. Is there anywhere special you want to go?'

'Everywhere is special up here. Shall we say "wherever the spirit moves us"?'

Philip watched anxiously as Julian strode off through a clump of ferns and down a path lined with bracken, fungus and pine needles. 'Are you sure you can manage? It's fairly rough underfoot.'

'Don't worry, I've been down far rougher paths than this. And not just figuratively.'

Philip felt impelled to keep pace with the older man, while maintaining a steady flow of conversation. 'Did you have any idea that the Bishop of Baguio had launched an investigation into your' – He struggled to articulate the phrase ' – "heroic virtue"?'

'Certainly,' Julian replied. 'I follow the news on the radio and in the papers far more assiduously than I ever did in San Isidro.'

'So how do you feel about the prospect of becoming a saint?'

'I can honestly say it has no meaning for me at all. I may not be dead, but the priest they're investigating is.'

'It may not mean anything to you, but it means a great deal to the people who believe in you: who've based their faith on an illusion.'

'Mightn't an illusion lead them towards a deeper truth? I remember when I was at the seminary in Holland and, without (it should be said) official sanction, we each chose a handful of the ten thousand or so saints and tried to assess their authenticity. One of mine was St Margaret, who escaped from the belly of a dragon by making the sign of the cross. Yet she was a great favourite in San Isidro. Must we dispatch her into some kind of spiritual lumber room, or can we acknowledge that as a focus of devotion she can be a force for good?'

'You amaze me! You sound exactly like the Vicar General of Baguio.'

'I don't know him, I'm afraid. He's new since my day.'

'He professes a kind of Christian utilitarianism: the greatest good is what promotes the greatest belief in the greatest number.'

'I think you'd find that where we part company is in the application of that belief.'

'True! I haven't read any letters he wrote thirty or forty years ago – and I may be doing him an injustice – but I doubt that there'd be page after page about the need to live according to the gospel.'

'I'm relieved; I was afraid there'd be interminable accounts of domestic trivia.'

'You're missing the point! For the past twenty years – more – you've been living a lie.'

'Have I?' Julian came to a halt on a narrow ridge overlooking a vast coniferous slope, dotted with waterlogged gullies. 'Don't forget that Father Julian Tremayne isn't living at all. I went to immense efforts – there's "heroic", if you like – to kill him off. I make no claims of any sort on his behalf. But, if you're speaking of the claims that others make for him, remember that there were those who credited him with miraculous powers during his lifetime.'

'What about you?' Philip asked, perturbed by Julian's switch to the third person.

'As a priest, I always believed that I was an instrument of the Divine Will, irrespective of my own merits. Perhaps God will choose to work through me again? Perhaps the Blessed – even Saint – Julian will keep alive the memory of Father Julian and his lifelong quest for justice which will in turn inspire others to take up the cause?'

'That may already have started. There's an Ibaloi tribesman who swears that he woke one night to see you standing over him, holding up two rifles in the shape of a cross.' Julian burst out laughing. 'Why's that funny?'

'I'm sorry. Did he say where he saw me?'

'Not that I recall. I've only read the official report.'

'If you check the dates, I think you'll find it was the night of a raid on the Lamtang gold mine. As we were driving away, we passed a drunk sprawled in the middle of the road. I jumped out of the truck to move him. He must have seen and recognised me in the glare of the headlights. Now that truly is a miracle!'

'Have you taken part in a lot of raids?' Philip asked tentatively.

'I've obeyed whatever orders I've been given. That's something that has never changed. When I was ordained, I was taught that the essence of priesthood is to offer up one's life unconditionally. The same holds true for a revolutionary.'

'The commitment may be the same, but everything else – doctrine, practice, let alone the end result – couldn't be more different.'

'Not at all. It took me many years, but I finally came to realise that the gun is as much an instrument of salvation as the chalice.'

Philip wondered whether spending so long undercover had affected Julian's brain. 'So are you saying that you became a revolutionary because you lost your faith?'

'No, I've never lost my faith – at least not in the way you imply. But I've lost my faith in the power of faith. I no longer believe that all I have to do is to ask and God will answer, even if it's only to tell me that I'm not worthy of His help. I believe that He has already given us all the answers: in Christ, of course, but also in Moses.'

'You mean in the Ten Commandments?'

'No, in the Exodus. The hero who set his people free.'

'But what if people don't want to be free? What if bitter experience has left them wary of change? Better the devil you know and all that!'

'Didn't the Jews turn against Moses? Remember how they attacked him: "Was it for lack of graves in Egypt that you had to lead us out to die in the desert?" The paradox is that like all great revolutionaries (and I choose my words with care), Moses had to impose his own will on the people in order that they could express theirs.'

'And you're suggesting that the same applies to you?'

'No, not at all.' Julian sounded offended. 'I'm saying the same applies to the movement of which I'm a part.'

'A movement which, unless I've got it wrong, is implacably secular. In the four months I've been held captive, I've not once heard God mentioned, except in a curse.'

'I'd be surprised if you had. I'm here not as a priest but as a fighter. My comrades don't see my presence as legitimising theirs. If anything, they feel it's the other way round. But my priesthood – my former priesthood – informs everything I do.'

'Including murder?'

'In certain circumstances.' Julian paused. 'I understand – and respect – your objections to bloodshed, but as a Christian I've always believed in the "just war". I was born during one and I've no doubt that I will die during another, the only difference being that the first took place on a world stage and the second is locked within national borders. Our enemies can smear us with terms such as "terrorists", but the truth is that we're fighters for justice and freedom: in other words, soldiers for Christ.'

'I feel as if the rug has been pulled out from under me. I came here suspecting that you'd been the victim of a murder plot and instead find that you're the one brandishing the gun.'

'If it's any consolation, I haven't fired a shot in years. I'm going blind, which makes me a liability.'

Philip was suddenly aware of Julian's proximity to the edge of the ridge. In quick succession he imagined the harrowing scream as he stumbled and fell, the guilty verdict of the kangaroo court and the volley of shots as he himself was condemned to summary execution. 'Don't you think you should stand a bit further back?' he asked.

'Don't worry. I can make out shapes, just not details.'

'So long as you're sure,' Philip said doubtfully. 'I don't want to open old wounds, but I have to ask about Quesada. Were you in any way involved in his death?'

'No. I've no reason to lie to you. I've made it clear that I have no qualms – although I may have regrets – about taking all necessary steps to advance the revolution. But while I supported the NPA's aims and gave them whatever help and information I could, I didn't take part in any of their actions until I joined them in 1989.'

'Can you remind me of the chronology? You came back to the Philippines in the autumn of 1988; you were posted to a new parish in Quezon province; then, six months later, you faked your own death and defected to the NPA?'

'I prefer "enlisted".'

'But why? I don't mean why enlist, but why then? Marcos had been deposed. Shouldn't you have given the new government a chance?'

'I did. They'd been in power for three years.'

'Three years, really! I don't wish to sound facetious, but really!'

'It's easy to mock, but we'd waited so long. I returned from England to find that not a single soldier had been brought to trial for his actions under Martial Law. Aquino governed in the interests of her own class – at times even her own family! When 10,000 farmers marched down Mendiola Street, demanding that she implement her promised land reforms, she sent in the army to disperse them. Thirteen were killed and hundreds were injured. Her predecessor would have been proud.'

'So you joined the NPA out of disillusion?'

'No, not at all. Is that what it sounds like? It's my fault for trying to simplify. The truth is that there was no single reason. On one level I was hitting fifty and taking stock of my life. On another I'd spent two years in England, which had convinced me – if I'd needed any convincing – that it was no longer my home. My brother's party was in power and avarice was in the ascendant. My one thought was to come back and play a part in the new Philippines. I'd hoped to return to San Isidro, but after representations from the *haciendos* the Bishop sent me instead to Sariaya, an urban parish in Quezon, where I found it hard to settle. So I came up here on retreat, to pray and to meditate, but also to visit Rommel Clemente, the son of... well, of course, you know. Although it was a military camp, I felt utterly at peace with him and his friends. Even their arguments seemed more reasonable and sincere than the ones I was used to in the Church. They were ready to fight – and die – for their beliefs (no, that's too abstract!): for the people, the very people whom Christ taught us to put first, but whom the Church, with its gelded gospel and bloodless chalice, had so often failed. Rommel asked me – not for the first time – why I didn't throw in my lot with them.'

'But you were a priest!'

'I wouldn't have been the only one. You'd be amazed at how many of my fellow clerics were involved in the struggle: in the CNL, in the BCCs, in the *Chi Rho*, in the *Kabataang Makabayan*.

The difference was that I was a public figure. So although I was tempted by his offer, I felt bound to refuse, not on my own account but for the many thousands of people who'd given me their love and support, especially during my year in prison. If I'd abandoned the Church and proclaimed my faith in the revolution, they'd have felt betrayed. They wouldn't have seen the logic, only the scandal. They'd no doubt have felt, like you, that I was guilty of Quesada's murder, and added deceit and hypocrisy to my list of crimes. Then, by an extraordinary stroke of luck, on the day I was due to return to the parish, news came from a nearby camp that an American hostage had been shot trying to escape.'

'That's what you call luck?' Philip asked, feeling vulnerable.

'Very well then, providence.'

'No! I was pointing out that a man had died.'

'He was a former marine turned mercenary, attached to one of the most ruthless right-wing death squads in the Philippines. Trust me, he was a legitimate target. And in a further stroke of luck – or what you will – he was exactly my height and build. I can't remember who it was that first suggested I take on... what? Not his identity, not even his body, but rather his bones. But as soon as the scheme was mooted, I knew that it solved everything. We hid the corpse in the forest, where it was stripped clean by an army of carrion beetles and flesh flies. Then we put my ring on its finger, hung my crucifix round its neck and left the skeleton in a ditch to be discovered.'

'Didn't the authorities think to do a DNA test or to check dental records?'

'We're talking 1989. DNA tests were in their infancy, even in the West. The regional police chief had no wish to waste valuable resources on a case which, to his mind, was closed.'

'But what about the mysterious light and the heavenly music, so vividly described by the foresters and the police? Not to mention the odour of sanctity? Or are we to we conclude that it emanated from the mercenary?'

'That's always a chance, but I don't suppose that I – that is, the mercenary – was the only decomposing matter in the vicinity. It's quite possible that the build-up of methane produced will-o'-the-wisp. And that a nearby acacia or sampaguita bush gave off the fragrance. The music is more puzzling, but our Filipino policemen have always had a weakness for a good story, especially one they dream up themselves.'

'So that was all it took for you to vanish?'

'Yes. For the first time in my life, I was truly free.'

'But invisible.'

'*And* invisible!'

'What about your family? Didn't you think about the effect on them?' Philip asked, picturing his own family waiting desperately for news.

'You said you'd read my letters; so you must realise that we weren't that close.'

'Was there no one you were sorry to leave?'

'Oh yes, my former parishioners. I'd grown very attached to them over the years. I've had the occasional piece of news via Rommel, but it's no longer safe for him to contact his mother.'

'I saw Felicitas when I was in San Isidro. If I'd known, I could have passed on a message.' Philip laughed. 'I saw several of your other old friends. As well as your housekeeper.'

'Consolacion?' Julian asked eagerly. 'Is she still alive? I've asked Rommel time and again but he can never tell me anything. Is she really alive?'

'Well, I know that such distinctions are blurred around here – '

'Touché!' Julian said with a smile.

'But in March she was in fine fettle.'

'I always said she'd live to be a hundred. She can't be far off it now. How wonderful! Did she mention me at all?'

'Lots,' Philip said, reluctant to add to the toll of shattered illusions. 'That was the point of my meeting her. She told me that the years she'd spent with you were the happiest of her life.'

'Really?' Julian asked, his eyes welling with tears.

'Scout's honour. How about Benito Bertubin? Didn't you ever want to get back in touch with him? Or maybe you have and he was being discreet?'

'No, I haven't seen him in twenty-five years. I expect you've spoken to him too. How is he? The same as ever?'

'Well, I didn't know him twenty-five years ago.'

'No, of course not.'

'He's doing remarkable work for the families who live on the Payatas rubbish dump.'

'I don't doubt it. He's a remarkable man. But it's everything we swore we'd never do. It's dusting the rubble after an earthquake; it's wiping the blood off the walls after a raid.'

'And it's giving the dispossessed back their dignity,' Philip said, feeling as strong an urge to hurt Julian for belittling Benito as he had done to spare him the truth about Consolacion. 'Every day he sits at his desk and does battle with the bureaucrats. You may denounce it as collusion with a corrupt and oppressive system, but it's a collusion that brings clean water and flush toilets and schools and birthing clinics. Isn't that more valuable: isn't that more Christian: isn't that more truly revolutionary than hiding out in the mountains with a tiny group of fanatics blowing up saw mills and buses and mobile phone masts, along with the occasional person?'

'Revolutions are made by tiny groups of fanatics, as you call them. Look at Christ! He changed the world with just twelve disciples.'

'Yes, but as far as I recall, he didn't stockpile weapons illegally obtained from the occupying Roman army, or pay for them with money extorted from Galilean farmers.'

'Meaning what? That I'm as big a fraud now as I was as a priest? That I'm a fool for ever supposing I could do any good?'

'Not at all,' Philip said, disturbed by Julian's anguish. 'Besides, unlike the rest of us, you'll have a chance to do good long after your death.'

'Which one?'

'Both. Once the *Positio* is approved and they make you a saint.'

'In which case I'll be a still bigger fraud. When the faithful gather at my tomb, the bones they're venerating won't even be mine.'

'Isn't that the case for half the saints in Christendom?'

'Then at least I'll be in good company,' Julian replied with the hint of a smile. 'We'd better go back. The others will be wondering what's happened to us. They might suspect me of spiriting you away.' Philip felt a fleeting hope that Julian would free him from the trap into which he had, however unwittingly, drawn him, but he knew that it was vain. As Julian himself had explained, the one thing that linked the priest and the revolutionary was obedience.

'I'm sorry I couldn't get here sooner,' Julian said. 'But I'm training young men and women to dedicate their lives to the cause; I have to lead by example.'

'I understand.'

'I'll do all that I can to speed up your release. Unfortunately, I wasn't consulted on the ransom. From what little I know of my nephew-in-law, he's not the sort of man to respond to threats, particularly financial ones. I'll speak to the Central Committee and try to persuade them to compromise. The trouble is, with numbers dwindling, they're frightened of doing anything that makes themselves look weak.'

'Thank you, I appreciate it.' Philip walked on, his eyes no longer fixed on the undergrowth. 'Maybe it's what they call Stockholm Syndrome, but I've been surprisingly happy here. After years of drifting, I know who I am and what I'm good at – at least what I think I'm good at.'

'Which is what?'

'Writing. Fiction – or sort of.' He blushed. 'I can't pretend that there wouldn't have been easier ways to find out; the sight of Nina with a loaded rifle isn't the most encouraging start to the day. But perhaps that's what it took to concentrate my mind. Just as you saw the death of the mercenary as some kind of portent, so I do my kidnap. That said, I'm counting on you to win over your comrades. I'm ready to go home.'

Afterword

Philip Seward died on 11 October 2012, during a bungled attempt by the Philippine Army to rescue him from the NPA terrorist unit that was holding him hostage. While in captivity, he wrote a long account of a visit to the Philippines, undertaken at the behest of my wife, Isabel, and myself. In view of his decision to use actual names, readers – especially those who followed the extensive reports of his kidnap during the spring and summer of 2012 – might suppose the entire account to be equally factual. They would be gravely mistaken. Had he lived to prepare the book for publication, Philip would no doubt have renamed all the characters (and not just his protagonist, as he proposes on the coach to Cabanatuan), thereby accentuating their fictional nature. His tragic death has, however, destroyed that opportunity, along with so many others. I must therefore emphasise that *The Breath of Night* is a work of the imagination which, while rooted in real-life events, deviates ever more widely from them, ending up in the realm of pure fantasy.

After Philip's death, the Philippine authorities returned the manuscript to his parents with a diligence that belies the bureaucratic ineptitude that figures so prominently within its pages. In an accompanying note, Philip expressed his hope of interpolating Julian Tremayne's twelve extant letters into his narrative, one at the head of each chapter, although whether for the sake of authenticity or contrast remains unclear. The Sewards who, understandably, wished to honour their son, sought my wife's permission to publish the letters, of which she is the sole copyright holder, and my own permission to publish a book that contained such defamatory material. My wife, despite her horror at the depiction of her revered uncle as a Marxist murderer, showed typical generosity in acceding to the request of the bereaved parents. I followed suit, in return for this right of reply.

I flatter myself that my shoulders are broad enough to withstand the scurrilous portrayal of 'Hugh Olliphant', which is shot through with the rancour that Philip had harboured for me ever since my unguarded admission, ten years earlier, that I disapproved of his relationship with my daughter. From the first, I detected a weakness in his character, which subsequent events have borne out. In deference to my wife, who is by nature disposed to see the good in people, I dispatched him to the Philippines where, besides drawing a generous salary, he contrived with my former agent to run up astronomical bills. Far from thanking me, he repaid me with this gross libel.

To my relief, he is more magnanimous to my wife, who showed him nothing but kindness, although even then he cannot resist a note of ridicule. He describes her 'elegantly sipping tea beneath the El Greco', as if she were a languid Edwardian hostess rather than the hard-working owner of a busy estate. Moreover, he resorts as so often to phrase-making. We do not possess an El Greco. Family portraits aside, the highlights of our collection are some eighteenth-century watercolours, five Atkinson Grimshaws and a 'school of Tintoretto'. Despite his career in the art world having ended in ignominy, Philip regarded himself as an expert on aesthetics, as can be seen in his contempt for my Filipino treasures. But whatever his right to question my taste, he had none to question my probity. Every item was acquired and exported legitimately. All the relevant documentation has been entrusted to the British Museum, to which the collection will ultimately pass. I take particular issue with the denigration of Ray Lim, who has done so much to enhance the reputation of the National Museum and who has acted for me only as an unpaid adviser. That said, Philip finds vice and venality wherever he looks in the Philippines. I am tempted to echo his long-suffering chauffeur when he asks: 'Why must you wish to see only dirty parts of my country?'

By far the most serious of the novel's calumnies is its portrait of Julian Tremayne. Nina Subrabas, the only one of the terrorists to have been taken alive, has recounted how Philip wrote day and night, to the wonderment of the unit. They even held a meeting to discuss the propriety of providing him with the means to work on something of which the Party might disapprove. Yet, with the exception of some over-elaborate descriptions of meals (no doubt to compensate for his meagre and unpalatable rations), the book shows remarkably little sign of having been written in confinement. It is my contention, nonetheless, that Philip was far more influenced by his ordeal than he was prepared to allow. Although we will never know what changes he would have made had he lived, I share the view of other early readers that *The Breath of Night* is complete as it stands. So it is no coincidence that its very last page alludes to the Stockholm Syndrome. Philip mentions that his captors excluded him from their ideological debates, yet the book is infused with radical and, above all, anticlerical sentiment, which he must surely have imbibed from them.

Meanwhile, unaware that both his parents and I had offered to pay the ransom, only to be thwarted, first by the reluctance of the British and Philippine governments to negotiate with terrorists, and then by the increasingly confused demands of the terrorists themselves, he grew convinced that the cash would not be forthcoming. Political indoctrination combined with personal anxiety to plunge him into the paranoia (his own word), which informed his characterisation of Julian Tremayne in the final chapter.

No one would deny that, in common with many priests during the Marcos era, Julian had left-wing sympathies. But to accuse him of faking his own death and becoming a rebel leader is a monstrous slur on a man who is no longer able to defend himself. Nina Subrabas has affirmed that there was no Englishman, let alone a priest, in any known NPA unit. There has never been the slightest doubt that the remains unearthed by the foresters in the Sierra Madre were those of Julian Tremayne. There is no record of any missing mercenary, and it is inconceivable that the US Embassy would have abandoned its responsibility for a fellow citizen, let alone a former marine, whatever his crimes. Nevertheless, with Julian's body having been exhumed for the gathering of relics, my wife and her sisters have written to the Roman Curia, stating their readiness to take part in any DNA tests that might be required.

Finally, for those readers concerned with fact rather than fantasy, I am proud to report that in August this year the Congregation for the Causes of Saints found evidence that the Servant of God, Julian Tremayne, had practised both the cardinal and heroic virtues, and that the miracles of healing in the cases of Benigna Vaollota and Jericho Ilaban took place through his intercession. It therefore proposed his beatification to the Pope who, having commended the matter to God, conducted the Solemn Beatification in St Peter's Basilica on 3 December 2012, a ceremony my wife and I had the honour to attend.

The final phase of the canonisation process is now under way and, with God's grace, the Philippines will have its new saint.

Hugh Olliphant
Whitlock Hall,
County Durham
18 January 2013

Acknowledgements

I am indebted to many people in both England and the Philippines for their assistance with my research, among them Father John Ball, Edward Christopher Baguio, Chicoy Enerio, Rod Hall, Father Bernard Lynch, Garnet Montano, Father Anthony Meredith and Mark Woodruff.

Rupert Christiansen, Emmanuel Cooper, Andrew Gordon, Liz Jensen and James Kent gave me invaluable advice on early drafts of the novel, as did Hilary Sage and Ilsa Yardley on the final text.

I consulted various books in the course of writing, among the most insightful and informative were:
Dead Season by Alan Berlow
Passion and Power by Shay Cullen
The Philippines by T. M. Burley
Revolutionary Struggle in the Philippines by Leonard Davis
Leaving the Priesthood by Emmanuel R. Fernandez
America's Boy by James Hamilton Patterson
Growing Up in a Philippine Barrio by F. Landa Jocano
Everyday Politics in the Philippines by Benedict J Tria Kerkvliet
Priests on Trial by Alfred W McCoy
The History of the Philippines by Kathleen Nadeau
Revolution From The Heart by Niall O'Brien
Seeds of Injustice by Niall O'Brien
Culture Shock by Alfredo Roces and Grace Roces
The Philippines by David Joel Steinberg
Promised Lands by Paul Vallely
Sentenced to Death by Earl K. Wilkinson with Alan C. Atkins
Trial of the Century by Earl K. Wilkinson
Marcos Against the Church by Robert L. Youngblood